Gifted

Children

by Christine Morgan

Published by:

Sabledrake Enterprises
PO Box 30751
Seattle, WA 98113
http://www.sabledrake.com
sabledrake@sabledrake.com

*To my mother, Laurie Atkins,
who always encouraged us to live up to our potential*

Prologue

Saturday, April 12

The dragon rose from its cave in a coil of smoky-blue, the scales along its sinuous neck rippling like fog on the water. Its hungry golden eyes swept the deep forest before settling on the bold challenger standing before it.

Sir Lora the Fearless adjusted her silvery helm, raised her shield to protect her face from the dragon's fiery breath, and brandished her magic sword. At her side, her fierce but loyal wolf-companion bared his teeth at the monstrous wyrm.

"Knightsbane!" Sir Lora cried. "Behold your doom! I am come to slay you!"

Steam chuffed from its nostrils as the dragon chuckled. It swayed like a snake, trying to hypnotize her into immobility.

"No more shall you feed on the people of this kingdom and steal their treasures! I will chop you into dragon-burgers!"

She lunged and slashed with her sword, striking a blow against the dragon's treetrunk of a foreleg. The impact jarred the weapon from her hand. Before she could pick it up, the wolf snatched it up in his jaws and bounded in a gleeful tail-wagging circle.

"Drop it!" Sir Lora commanded.

The wolf hunkered low to the ground, forepaws extended and haunches waggling. His ears canted forward. He grinned.

"I said drop it." She grabbed at the sword, but the wolf scampered out of her way just enough to taunt her.

"Ruff, darn it!" Lora yanked off her helmet, freeing her long dark hair.

"How can we kill the great dragon if you won't let me have my sword? The whole kingdom is depending on us, you know. Now, give it. Give it here."

The dog let the stick fall from his mouth, but by then the fantasy was broken. Gone was brave Sir Lora, champion of the land, in her shining armor. Instead, she was regular old Lora Blake again. Only nine, not champion of anything except for the fourth-grade spelling bee.

"You're six years old," Lora said. "That's forty-two in dog years. So why do you have to act like such a little kid?"

Ruff barked, picked up the stick again, and dropped it closer to her feet. He hopped side to side and hunkered down again, eyes never leaving her.

Lora sighed. "Okay, okay." She hurled the stick across the clearing that used to be the barren rocky plain descending from the dragon's cave but was now just a bare patch in the woods.

With a yip of joy, Ruff was off. Lora shook her head and unhooked her plastic armor. Underneath, she wore jeans and a bright red sweatshirt over a tee shirt, but the warmth of the day encouraged her to take the sweatshirt off and tie the sleeves around her neck so that it hung like a cape.

Ruff came back, cavorting, teasing, trying to make her chase him. With Sir Lora's heroic quest shot, she gave in.

They played with the stick until even Ruff was exhausted and the stick itself was seriously gnawed, slobbery, and bedraggled.

"Yuck," Lora said, scrubbing her hands on her jeans. "Dog spit, Ruff, gross."

He lolled his tongue at her, trailing runners of saliva, apparently not sharing her opinion.

"Come on, let's go exploring."

She found a new branch. It was too big for Ruff to steal and get up to dickens. Using it as a walking stick, she turned away from the clearing and the big gnarled tree that a little imagination could turn into a dragon looming from a cave formed by two boulders tilted together.

In her mind, she became Frodo Baggins, except as a girl.

"You can be my faithful friend Samwise," she said to Ruff. "And we're going to Mordor, so look out for Ringwraiths."

They moved into the cool green shadows, rich with the scent of redwood and sea spray. Here and there, a few trees and flowering bushes were starting to show their spring colors amid the backdrop of evergreen. The sky was puffed with white clouds like lambs roaming a sapphire meadow.

It was the sort of rare spring day, her stepdad joked, that made the county tourism board and the college rush out and shoot photos for postcards, to prove to people that it didn't rain all the time in this part of the state.

The rain would be back, Lora knew. It was only April. They could count on a few more weeks of wet-and-grey before Trinity Bay's short-lived summer season began in earnest.

Rain or no, Lora loved it here. The Arizona desert where she used to live had been beautiful in its own stark way, but most of the time everybody stayed out of the sun, going from one air-conditioned place to another in equally air-conditioned cars.

Whenever she thought about her old home, a knot tightened in her stomach. She was glad to be here, glad to be with her mother again . . . she loved Grandpa and her stepdad and her new baby brothers . . . but it was horrible that her real father had died that way.

Trying to put those sad, scary thoughts out of her mind, she concentrated on her progress through the forest. Frodo and Sam, setting out on the loneliest leg of their journey.

To further the illusion, she took the birthstone ring off her pinkie finger and strung it on a piece of cord. She slipped the loop over her head so that the ring dangled against her chest.

"One Ring to rule them all," she said to Ruff. "Are you still looking out for Nazgul?"

He was, but so far there were only birds and chipmunks.

"When the twins get bigger, they can play with us. They can be Merry and Pippin, maybe."

The prospect cheered her, until she realized that by the time the twins were old enough to be interesting, she would have advanced well toward being a boring grown-up. Jenny Forrester, her nearest neighbor, was only twelve and already cared more about music and clothes than about having fun.

"I wish they'd made Seacliff a place for *regular* kids," she said, looking in the direction of the mansion that had recently reopened as some sort of hospital or institution.

Lora silently repeated the words to herself – *autistic, catatonic, brain-damaged.* Her mom had explained them to her last year, when the sale had been finalized.

Autistic, catatonic, brain-damaged. They all meant pretty much the same thing, at least in her mind. If the Seacliff kids couldn't talk, go to school, or play, it didn't much matter what fancy names the doctors used.

The redwood trunks soared to towering heights around her. The ground was springy with untold ages of needles compressed into an earthen bed. The foliage overhead was so densely interlocked that it prevented any other plants from surviving at ground level and only allowed a little sunlight to pierce the gloom.

Kind of spooky . . .

A furtive little chill crept up and down the back of Lora's neck, the kind of chill she got when reading a ghost story. Like Mom's new book. While Lora hadn't read it – Mom said she was too young – Lora knew it was about a girl who'd been killed and then come back as a ghost.

It was nothing like Mom's other books, which were kind of embarrassing, really. When Lora had been a little kid, she'd thought that it was neat to have a series of storybooks named after herself and her dog. Mom sometimes got shocked letters now from people – ladies, mostly – who had read the *Lora and Ruff* books to their kids and then thought that *Mourning Glory* would be okay for them, too.

Lora wished that she was old enough to read the new one. She didn't see why she shouldn't be allowed to. Didn't she read all of *The Lord of the Rings?* All of the Harry Potter books?

She could take it. She wasn't a baby.

And she liked being scared. Sort of.

She turned in a slow circle to look around. She wouldn't have been surprised to see a pallid form float out from between the trees, arms outstretched, fingers curled and beckoning . . .

Ruff barked.

Lora, carried away by her fantasy, uttered a surprised little squeal and whirled, sure that she *was* going to see a ghost. Goosebumps ran up her arms all the way to the sleeves of her white *Pokémon* tee shirt.

But there was nothing but Ruff, standing with his ears perked forward.

"What's the matter, Ruff?"

He barked again, then began prancing and bobbing his head like he was begging for playful attention.

"Go away, dog!" a boy's voice shouted. It came from within a deep split in the base of a dead tree.

Ruff, not normally cowed by yelling, turned tail and bolted to Lora's side. There, he crouched, trembling and whining, all of his playfulness gone.

"Hey!" Lora said, stalking forward. "You didn't have to be mean to him, whoever you are!"

"Leave me alone!"

A strong and sudden wave of resentment went through her. She almost told the kid fine, if he wanted to be like that, she'd go. The urge was overpowering. She turned to leave.

But, as she looked back, her gaze found that opening in the redwood again. The lumpy sides of it widened in an inverted V, and she thought again of the whimsy that had been leading her through the forest in the first place.

Instead of stomping away, she giggled. The urge to leave dissipated with the sound of her merriment.

"Oops, Ruff . . . this isn't Mordor, this is near Tom Bombadil's house. And that's Old Man Willow! So one of our hobbit friends must be trapped inside."

A head poked out of the tree. It belonged to a boy with tangled light brown hair, suspicious hazel eyes, and a scratched, smudged, dirty face.

"What are you talking about?" he asked.

"*The Lord of the Rings.*"

"What's that?"

"What's that? Only the best books and movies *ever!* I've seen the movies ten times each, and read the books three times. What are you doing in there?"

"What does it look like?"

"It looks like you're hiding."

"Well, duh."

"You don't need to be so mean," she said. "We didn't do anything to you."

"You sicced your dog on me."

"I did not. He just wanted to play. His name's Ruff."

"So?"

"So . . . mine's Lora. What's yours?"

He studied her for almost a whole minute, his face a sullen scowl. "Chris," he finally said.

"Why don't you come out of there?" Lora asked.

Chris emerged from the tree. He was twig-thin and bony, a little taller than Lora. His tee shirt had a fierce dinosaur on the front. His jeans and shoes were scuffed and muddy. She saw a white plastic band on his wrist that looked like a cheap watch.

"Do you go to my school? I haven't ever seen you before. Are you new?"

"Quit staring at me," Chris snapped.

Lora turned away so fast her head felt dizzy. "Sor-*ry!*"

"Are you gonna tattle on me? If you tell anyone I was out here, I'll get in trouble."

"I won't tell."

"Swear?"

"Sure."

"Then do it. Say it."

"I swear I won't tell!" She risked an impatient glance at him even though she didn't really want to. "Okay?"

"Okay," he said.

Lora smiled. "Wanna play?"

"Play what?" Chris regarded her with one raised, skeptical eyebrow.

Before she could choose one of her many, many suggestions, Ruff uttered a low warning growl. His fur bristling, he took a few stalking, stiff-legged steps away from them.

"Ruff?"

"Shh!" Chris warned, a strange, desperate look in his eyes.

Critch-crump – heavy footsteps on pine needles.

Crack! – a breaking branch.

Low voices, muttering . . . drawing closer.

"I got to get out of here!" With a horrible hunted expression, Chris started running.

Lora gaped after him.

"Over there!" a woman called. "I see him through the trees. There he goes!"

The *critch-crump*ing sped up, veered in the direction that Chris was fleeing. Lora sensed that Ruff was about to bark again an instant before he did it, and jerked on his collar. All that came out was a muffled 'wrf.' He gave her a stinging look of reproach.

"Hush!" she hissed.

The pursuers flashed past a gap between tree trunks. Lora caught a glimpse of a tall man in brown pants and a plaid hunters' shirt, and a blonde woman in dark grey pants and a black jacket. They were so intent on Chris that they never glanced her way, though she stood right in the open with her sweatshirt hanging down her back red as a bullfighter's cape.

As soon as they were out of sight, Lora succumbed to the fear she'd caught from Chris. Ruff, too, seemed to understand that this was no time for games, and fell in beside her as she hurried away from the spot.

She went as fast as she could while trying not to make much noise, somehow sure that if those grown-ups found out she'd seen them, she'd be in big trouble.

"Leave me alone!" Chris' voice floated through the woods. He sounded like he'd gotten pretty far, but not far enough.

Lora shivered at his anguished tone. She berated herself for cowardice – bold Sir Lora would have dashed to the rescue! – but only quickened her pace.

Ruff whimpered and surged ahead. She stumbled at the sudden tug, fell to her knees, and skinned them both on an exposed root. She lost her grip on Ruff's collar.

"Ruff, stay!" she whispered urgently.

But with her grasp on his collar gone, Ruff didn't even pretend to obey. He streaked ahead into the shadows.

She could hear the grown-ups again, doubling back, getting closer.

They'd heard her, she just knew it. They'd heard her and they'd find her and who knew what would happen to her?

Lora scrambled back to her feet. Her jeans were torn, both knees skinned and sizzling with pain. She hobbled after Ruff and came to a place where one of the old redwood giants had fallen.

The massive trunk was almost as high as she was tall, its spongy surface riddled with insect-tunnels and sprouting with a layer of new growth. Lora ran to the larger end and found that the tree hadn't broken off but uprooted. The exposed roots, clotted with earth and stringy weeds, looked like clutching fingers at the end of a skeletal arm.

The space they enclosed made a shallow cave. She crouched there despite the fact that she shared the space with beetles, spiders, and other crawly things that would normally have sent her scurrying.

As the grown-ups came even closer, Lora's heart sank in dismay. They were bound to find her, and then what? Then what?

"– sloppy," the woman said.

"But we have him now. No harm done."

"*This* time."

She could see them now, quite clearly through the screen of roots. The woman, tall and strong-looking, had blond hair pulled back in a ponytail. She wore a headband of dull metal that gleamed in a semicircle across her forehead from temple to temple. The man was old, not Grampa-Travis old but with more grey than brown in his hair. His face was tanned, weathered, and lined. He had a big pale scar, and his eyes were like chips of stone poking out of the earth, jagged and sharp. Like the woman, he wore a metal headband.

He was carrying Chris . . . and Chris was either sleeping, knocked out, or . . .

Lora's mind quailed away from that last *or.*

They passed by only a few feet from her hiding place and kept going.

When she could neither see nor hear them anymore, Lora slowly blew out the breath she'd been holding.

She slid down until she was sitting on the soft soil with her back against one of the larger roots, and only then noticed that her face was wet from tears.

*　*　*

Monday,

May 9

1

Roger Brockman glanced out of the raindrop-pearled oval window into a grey dimness that deepened as the plane sank through layers of clouds.

He was aware of the woman across the aisle eyeing him sidelong. He could feel her keen curiosity and interest, and hoped she wouldn't act on them.

The flight attendant came by on a final toss of the cabin, collecting cups and wrappers. "We've begun our descent, sir," he said to Roger. "Please put up your tray table."

"Of course." Roger latched it into place. He looked out again, but there was still little to see, and resumed reading.

The woman cleared her throat in a timid yet expectant manner.

Roger turned a page.

"Pardon me . . ." she said. "I'm sorry, I've been trying not to bother you, but here we are about to land and if I didn't say something I'd never forgive myself. You're an actor, aren't you?"

He sighed, thinking, *here we go again!* "Um, no, I'm not."

"*Aren't* you Jeff Goldblum?" she pressed.

"I'm a doctor. A scientist," he said.

She nodded. "Sure, in the movies. Except for *Silverado,* when you were a gambler."

"I'm a real scientist. Not an actor. Never have been."

"You look exactly like Jeff Goldblum," the woman said, frowning in a way that turned her plain face into something that belonged on a cathedral gargoyle. "Are you sure you're not him?"

"Pretty sure."

"After all, it would be a surprise, Jeff Goldblum, here of all places. Unless you were making a movie. They filmed *The Lost World* in this area, but you'd know that, wouldn't you?"

As it happened, Roger did know that, but he just smiled. The smile felt false and strained.

Tall and lanky, with a head of unruly black hair, he supposed he must bear a faint resemblance to the actor, because it was a rare month that he wasn't asked that very question.

On the one hand, when he got up at a podium to lecture, the unconscious association with all those movies lent him an additional air of credibility.

On the other hand, people sometimes believed he'd actually encountered dinosaurs or aliens . . . or worse, wanted to talk about *Earth Girls Are Easy.*

"I don't suppose I could have your autograph anyway?" the woman asked.

"I only sign copies of my book," Roger said. "*Unlocking the Brain's Creative Potential.*"

That frown was back, and uglier than ever. "I've never heard of it."

"I'm not surprised," he muttered.

The publisher had insisted on something catchy-sounding to appeal to the common reader, but the common reader was usually lost after the introduction. Those who would grasp the concepts and technical jargon – his fellow scientists – were too put off by the smarmy self-help title to pick it up in the first place. The worst of both worlds.

The woman glowered at him for several more seconds, then huffed. "You shouldn't go around claiming to be someone you're not." Then, pointedly, she immersed herself once more in the summer blockbuster issue of some celebrity gossip rag.

Roger sank his forehead into his hand and clawed at his temples.

Someday, just once in his life, he'd like to actually meet his Hollywood look-alike, stand them side by side, and show the world that the resemblance truly was not that strong.

At least in a town the size of Trinity Bay, he shouldn't have to deal with these situations very often.

The plane emerged from the low-lying cloud cover into an afternoon of grey light that paradoxically made everything seem gloomy while at the same time bringing vivid rainwashed color to the surroundings.

And this is summer, Roger thought. *Could have fooled me.*

To the west, he had a brief view of the slate-colored sea blending into the misty horizon. To the east were the foothills of the mountains. Below and straight ahead was the tiny Arcata-Eureka airport.

The plane touched down and rolled to a stop. Roger unhooked his seatbelt to retrieve his briefcase and laptop computer from the overhead compartment. Through the window, he could see airline personnel trundling a wheeled staircase out to meet the plane.

There weren't many passengers, and he was fifth to emerge into the damp, chilly air. He zipped up his quilted nylon jacket and descended the steps, searching the meager crowd that waited inside the glass doors of the terminal.

None of them looked familiar, which was only reasonable since he'd never met Dr. McGuire in person. He knew her only through months of correspondence, e-mails, computer chats, and conference calls.

All of which had led him to formulate a mental image promptly proved wrong.

"Dr. Brockman? I'm Gwynne McGuire."

He had been about to pass the woman, certain that she could not be the one he was supposed to be meeting. But her low, cool voice stopped him in his tracks.

Roger had been expecting, though shame on him and he should have known better, the typical bookish female scientist: drab of dress, bunned of hair, eyeglassed, plain. His astonishment and appreciation must have been blatant as he sized her up. Any less self control, and his tongue might have unrolled like that of a cartoon character.

I'd like to see Jeff Goldblum do that, he thought.

Gwynne McGuire did not seem to notice his drooling. "It's a pleasure to finally meet you face to face, and a privilege to be working with you."

Roger set down his briefcase and clasped her proffered hand. Everything about her seemed remote, cool, and controlled . . . but he thought he detected an undercurrent of intensity. "May I say the same?"

Her grip was light but strong, businesslike. She was a petite, willowy woman from whom the force of her intellect seemed to glow as if she were made from clear crystal filled with radiant liquid.

Out of deference to the weather, she wore indigo knit slacks and a striped sweater in several shades of blue. The outfit brought out her blue-grey eyes and set off a loose fall of pale apricot hair. She had a white coat draped over one arm.

A fine gold chain around her graceful neck supported a pendant, a gold disk half-edged in a crescent of platinum, suggesting the moon.

Underneath it all, Roger was sure, lurked a hot-tempered and passionate woman. The trouble would be chipping through all the ice.

"The items you shipped ahead arrived yesterday," Gwynne said. "Do you have checked bags?"

"Two," he replied. "Clothing, personal effects." Scanning the sparsely-populated terminal, he added, "I doubt there'll be much of a crowd at the baggage carousel."

She indicated a conveyer belt along one wall. "That is the baggage carousel."

As if on cue, a light began flashing in warning and then the belt started moving. Moments later, suitcases and duffel bags pushed their way through a doorway blocked by overlapping strips of black rubber.

Laden with his belongings, Roger followed Gwynne to a maroon Saturn sedan. The dreary rain pattered coldly down his collar while he stowed his suitcases in the trunk.

He settled into the passenger seat and closed the door. "It was ninety degrees and eighty-five percent humidity when I left Atlanta," he observed.

"The fickle climate does take some getting used to." She started the car. "Last week could have passed for a proper springtime, and now it's as if the calendar was turned ahead to November."

"I'm eager to see the institute."

"No, no," she corrected. "The *school*. Or the *house*. Never an institute, facility, center, or hospital. Dr. Lundquist is very clear on that point."

Roger raised his eyebrows. "I see."

"He is dedicated to making the environment as comfortable as possible for our —"

"Students?" he guessed. "Not patients, clients, or inmates?"

"Exactly. Most of these children have spent their entire lives in an institutional setting, some of them under abominable conditions. His wish is that they feel at home during their stay with us. Even if our work proves unsuccessful, we will at least have given them that."

"Of course. What is it like working with Dr. Lundquist in person? I've only met him at a few seminars, though my work has been inspired by and based on his for almost twenty years."

"His standards are exceptionally high," she said, with the air of someone who probably drove herself harder than any external authority could ever do. "As you know, the implications of his theories, the *applications* of his theories, are tremendously innovative and exciting. But unlike many in this field, his decades of experience haven't worn away his compassion. He thinks of the children as his own family, caring more about their welfare than his own."

"With his history, that's understandable," Roger said, keeping his tone professional and neutral.

Gwynne took a right turn, merging onto Highway 101 northbound. "In terms of his interactions with the staff, he is at once reserved and charming, and while there is a touch of condescension in him, it's all but impossible to take offense. He is, for example, the only one who can call me 'my lamb' and get away with it."

Roger studied her as she piloted the car through the increasing downpour, trying to imagine anyone calling her 'my lamb.' He knew he'd never have the guts.

As she drove, she filled him in on the progress at Seacliff. A few of the specially-chosen children had already arrived, and in a matter of weeks there would be eighteen 'students' living in the house. Several of the staff would also be live-ins, the two of them and Dr. Lundquist included.

"The site is perfect," she went on. "I still have trouble believing it came together so effortlessly. It is exactly what we need. We lucked into a wonderful opportunity."

There was no emotion other than pride and exultation in her statement. It struck him a little odd, given the circumstances. Luck? It had been the suicide of Gwynne's own sister three years before that had led to her discovery of Seacliff.

The house, built by a lumber baron in the late 1800's and left empty in the wake of the death of the man who had been planning to turn it into a resort, was situated on a bluff overlooking Trinity Bay. After a complicated series of legal back-and-forthing involving various peoples' wills and competency hearings, it had eventually been put on the market.

Seacliff was, according to Gwynne McGuire, just the sort of thing that she and Dr. Lundquist had been looking for. It was the perfect setting to start a 'school' where chronic, severely impaired children could enjoy a quality of life free of dismal hospitals and institutions.

And where, just possibly, some progress could be made in treating or even curing their disabilities.

The negotiations, funding, remodeling, and other details had taken over two years to complete, but now their shared dream was about to become a reality. Roger regretted having missed out on the initial hands-on stages. His other work had by necessity kept him on the other side of the country. Now, he was finally here, and the plans of a lifetime were about to see fruit.

"I can't tell you how much I'm looking forward to pursuing such valid, meaningful, important work," he said. "Let alone in the company of such highly esteemed colleagues."

He and Gwynne shared a smile, a smile of accomplishment and anticipation. They'd been through so much together already, just in organizing this. It was a relief to Roger to find that, her demeanor notwithstanding, they did not look to be starting off on a sour note.

The Trinity Bay exit appeared out of the rain. Gwynne took it, turning onto an underpass that carried them beneath the freeway. Trees closed thickly around the road, seeming to loom and overhang all the more ominously with their boughs weighed down by rain.

"Trinity Bay is very small and fairly isolated, but not so insular as many other small towns," Gwynne said. "There are a few college students that commute to HSU. The sawmill is still in operation, owned jointly by the employees. Summer brings a fair amount of tourism to the region. Motor homes as far as the eye can see."

They crested a mild rise and descended into the town proper. Trinity Bay was nestled between two rising points of land. A protuberance to the north looked like a single massive boulder half-buried in the earth – Agate Head, if Roger remembered the map correctly. A number of smaller rocky islands clustered around the Head's base, and the sea churned in whitecaps among them. To the south, the land rose in a dramatic sweep to a wooded bluff, where Seacliff perched.

Roger didn't look at the big house except for that brief glimpse, wanting to take in the rest of the town first. "So this is it?"

"This is the Square, or the Plaza," Gwynne said, following a series of one-way streets around a grassy park. "Bookshop, deli, pharmacy, bar, salon, arcade, boutique, preschool, post office, the municipal building, produce shop, bath shop, the Leland building, eatery, bank, and movie theater . . . and that's essentially it for downtown."

"They shouldn't be allowed to name bath shops 'Scents and Sensibility.'"

"If that bothers you, then you'd better hope you never need to take a car in for repairs."

He didn't ask. "And the movie theater's boarded up."

"Yes."

"So, what do people do for fun?"

"Drive somewhere else. There's talk of a multiplex and bowling alley going in at North Valley, but the tone of the *Trinity Bay Gazette* seems to be that they'll believe it when they see it. All of the more commercial businesses are out there – grocery store, fast food, motels, et cetera." She pointed to the north side of town. "Over that way is the medical center and Silver Grove, a nursing home and eldercare facility. One of my brother's projects."

"Is he going to be working with us in any capacity?"

"Kel?" Her laugh, though pretty, was derisive. "Kel represents the entirety of Trinity Bay's social services. He spends his time running back and forth as a geriatric case manager, a school counselor, a hypnotherapist, and all-purpose wailing wall for this little corner of what he calls paradise. He lacks the focus and self-discipline to be a part of our team."

Roger elected not to pursue the topic further. He knew a little something about family troubles and rivalries.

They left the business district – such as it was – behind and cruised residential streets. Most of the houses were in good repair with neatly-kept yards. The few people braving the rainy outdoors tended to be pale as a result of not seeing the sun for much of the year.

The road curved toward the shore, where an upscale-looking restaurant named Jordano's offered views of the bay, and boats bobbed at a small marina. From there, the road began a gentle climb up the sloped side of the bluff.

"Just like in the pictures you sent me," Roger said as he finally took his first up-close look at Seacliff.

It deserved the title of 'mansion,' sitting on the top of the cliff like a lord surveying his realm. The central section soared to three stories high and was topped with a dome of blue and green stained glass. Angling back from the center were two long wings.

A wrought-iron fence stretched from the ends of the wings to enclose a garden. Beyond the fence, a mowed meadow of a lawn sprawled toward the woods. Roger knew that the perimeter security fence had only been added within the last year, but a very successful effort had been made to match it to the house's style, so it seemed as if it had been there for the past century.

Gwynne parked in front of a stable that had been converted to a garage. "Welcome to Seacliff, Dr. Brockman."

"It's magnificent."

"Wait until you see the inside."

"I'm ready for a tour whenever you are."

"Don't you want to rest from your flight?"

"Later. Seeing the place in the flesh . . . it's a surefire cure for jet lag."

She smiled. "Then let's go look around."

He left his bags in the car and followed her across the wide crushed-gravel driveway to the covered entryway. Window-flanked double doors, beneath an arched half-circle of stained glass, led into a foyer done in mahogany, crisp black and white tile, and creamy gold drapes.

Twin staircases, sweeping curves of polished wood with carpet runners down their middles, rose to the second floor mezzanine. Between them was an ornate brass-cage elevator.

Straight ahead, a wood-paneled hallway with two doors on either side ended in another set of double doors. These ones were of clear but thick glass, too thick to be easily broken. Beyond them, the light shifted and shimmered turquoise.

"It's called the atrium," Gwynne said.

Roger walked down the hall to look in. The octagonal room was floored in pale green and white marble tiles, soaring to the stained-glass dome he'd seen from outside. Railed hallways ringed the room at the second and third floor levels.

In the center was a sunken pool roughly half Olympic size, surrounded by deck furniture. A row of curtained changing booths lined one wall, and French doors led out into the terraced gardens.

"All the comforts of home," he said.

"Not quite. We removed the wet bar."

"Now there's a shame. I could use a drink."

"We can take care of that in the library."

She led him to one of the doors on the east side of the hallway. The windowless two-story room was floor to ceiling with bookshelves. A walkway, accessible by a spiral staircase, ran around the room at the halfway point. The carpet was a rich dark brown, the chairs upholstered in fine leather. A small but serviceable bar took up one corner.

"Very nice!" Roger said, gazing at the books.

"Dr. Lundquist's personal collection. The conference room is across the hall, and above that is his private study." She smiled as she mixed them each a drink. "Complete with secret passage over here to the library. The door is up there behind one of the bookshelves."

"Well, it wouldn't be right, a place like this, without at least one secret passage."

Gwynne sat down, crossing her slim legs in an elegant motion. She seemed amused, but secretively so. "But of course!"

"And the east and west wings?"

"The east wing, which was once primarily the servants' quarters, is devoted to the students. On the first floor are the kitchen, dining room, laundry, janitorial closets, and so on. The second and third floors have been broken up into classrooms, observed play areas, and bedrooms."

"Leaving the west wing for staff?"

"Yes. Offices, labs, a smaller kitchen and dining area, private apartments for those of us who'll be living in, break rooms for the others. We have a fully-equipped operating room that would be the envy of hospitals ten times the size of the Trinity Bay Medical Center."

"And our . . . off-site personnel?" he asked.

She inclined her head. "In place, established in the community. With a few likely prospects already located and identified."

"Incredible. What you've done here . . . I can't help but feel ashamed for not arriving sooner to help out."

"Not at all. I enjoyed the challenge. How are things at CFHM, by the way?" She pronounced the initials C-F-H-M as everyone in the field did – *cuffem,* what a gruff cop might command his partner. They stood for Center For the Human Mind.

He sipped his drink. "Interesting . . . in general, they're still decades behind us in terms of accomplishments, but they did have a few novel approaches."

"That you didn't hesitate to incorporate into your own theories, of course."

"Oh, naturally. And if they work, I'll take full credit."

"No mercy in this field."

"None."

"I'm looking forward to this, Dr. Brockman. I anticipate a highly successful project."

"As do I. But please, call me Roger. We got well enough acquainted to use first names in cyberspace, so we needn't backslide to formality now that we'll be working together more closely than ever."

"True. Roger."

"Gwynne."

They clinked glasses.

"To Seacliff," he said.

"To Seacliff."

*   *   *

2

Brooding in the dark was a sign of an unhealthy mind.

Benjamin Lundquist knew that, but it didn't stop him from doing it anyway.

In the dark, he couldn't see the faces on the framed photograph he held. Not that he needed to see them. They were engraved on the walls of his heart like epitaphs.

The tattered, faded, sepia-toned photograph didn't do them justice. A stranger would have been hard-pressed to say whether the figures shown were male or female, or of what age.

It had been seventy years since that moment in time was captured on film, and while the decades had withered his body, they had not dimmed his memory or blunted the keenness of his mind.

Anton had been seven, Gerda only four, on the day their mother coaxed them to sit together on the sofa for that one last picture. She'd been sobbing as she took it, but her hands had held the camera straight.

Somehow, by some trick of the light, they looked alert and sweet and dear and *normal*. They looked like bright, happy children. Gerda's face was angelic rather than slack and dull; the fierce grimace that presaged another of Anton's sudden violent outbursts looked more like an impish grin.

The picture was a lie, but it was all he had to remember them by and he clung to it. He had been a boy then, his life as respected doctor Benjamin Lundquist a far-future fiction as yet undreamed, his purpose unknown, unsuspected.

All he had known on that long-ago day was how bitterly his mother had wept when she surrendered her two youngest chicks to people who claimed they'd be better off in some other place. Who had promised to take care of Anton and little Gerda. When all they were really doing was putting them out of the way.

Someplace where their mother didn't need to work herself to the bone trying to care for them, someplace where their father wouldn't have to see the defective children his drunken loins had produced. Someplace where they wouldn't be the shame, and the talk, of the neighbors.

Benjamin ran his thumb over the smooth glass that protected the photograph. He had failed Anton and Gerda, believed in the lies even after he'd seen the wretched place for himself, seen the care and treatment his brother and sister were receiving.

No more. He would do better. It was too late for Anton and Gerda, but he could still atone for his failure to help them. And for his subsequent failures with his wife and son.

It had taken him a lifetime of preparations, but he was finally ready.

The children here would be cared for, yes, cared for lovingly and with compassion . . . but he would do more. They would be uplifted, made well, made *better.* No more cruelty, no more neglect. Instead, a chance to reach for the potential that circumstance had denied them.

It was his vow, which he renewed every day.

He reached for the lamp on the table beside his chair, finding it by memory in the darkness and switching it on. Its mild yellow light spread like melting butter.

Now he could see the photograph in its heavy, tarnished silver frame. He set it on the table beside the one of Elizabeth and William that had been taken only a week before the accident, and picked up his watch.

One minute until the hour . . .

Someone rapped softly on the door. "Dr. Lundquist? It's seven o'clock."

"Come in, Aiden. You're forty-five seconds early."

The door to his study opened to admit an elfin girl, with hair of utterly neutral beige-blond and a face of forgettable, nondescript prettiness. She was eighteen, but could have easily passed for three or four years younger.

Her timid grey eyes could never meet anyone's for long, flitting like moths for a quick brushing glance and then away again.

But, he thought, *considering where she was when I met her, she's made remarkable progress. The poor, dear thing.*

Her lips moved soundlessly. Benjamin was perplexed until she smiled – fast, flickering, gone – and said, "*Now* it's seven o'clock."

He checked his watch; she'd been counting off the seconds. "So it is."

"You asked me to let you know."

"Yes, thank you. Has Dr. Brockman arrived?"

"An hour ago. Dr. McGuire gave him the tour, and now I think he's getting ready for dinner." Again with the flickering smile, like lightning viewed from many miles distant. "He looks just like Jeff Goldblum."

Benjamin recalled his previous meetings with Roger Brockman, at various conferences over the years. "Now that you mention it, he does. Well. The core of our staff finally assembled under one roof. I've been looking forward to this. Will you be joining us for dinner?"

She shrugged and twisted the toe of her shoe into the carpet.

"Please, my pet. And extend the invitation to Mr. Sorenson as well."

Aiden quailed visibly at the prospect and Benjamin sighed.

"I'm sure he doesn't bite, Aiden."

"No, sir, of course not," she whispered, staring down at her folded hands.

Benjamin rose carefully from his chair. No particular aches or sufferings plagued him, but he was always well-aware of the general decrease in function of his aging body. His cane, a length of stout black wood topped with a silver knob, was within easy arm's reach.

"I do want you to join us, Aiden."

"But . . . it's just for the staff, isn't it?"

"Why, I consider you a valued part of the staff. My Girl Friday, as it were. Every good leader knows that the strength of any organization lies not with the laborers but with the administration. You and Mrs. Willis keep Seacliff running smoothly."

Distant-lightning smile. "Thank you, Dr. Lundquist, but really, I'd rather not." She slipped wraithlike out and away before he could pursue the issue.

He sighed again. Tremendous progress in the past five years, but still . . .

Not for the first time, he wondered if he was doing the right thing by continuing to allow her to remain so isolated from the world. The accident that had taken her mother's life had left Aiden deeply traumatized, and losing her father not so many years later had struck her a serious setback just as she'd been beginning to show some signs of improvement.

He wanted no harm to come to her, but sooner or later he would have to examine his decision, and see where the line was between not rushing her, and hampering her recovery.

In the meanwhile, he had a staff dinner to attend.

* * *

3

Roger followed Gwynne McGuire into what had once been the Cliffwood family's breakfast room, designed for informal meals away from the cavernous opulence of the main dining room.

Not that the main dining room was all that opulent anymore, following the remodeling to make it more suitable for Seacliff's new status as a school.

He was pleased to see that they hadn't done the same to the breakfast room. At the far end of the west wing, it boasted a bay window that truly deserved the name, showing as it did the bay and the ocean beyond in panoramic beauty.

Light golden wood paneling rose halfway before yielding the walls to wallpaper in a muted green pattern. The ceiling was inset with plaster reliefs of arboreal scenes. The effect of the room was one of light and airiness, though the sky outside was drab and leaden.

Several people were already seated at the long table. Gwynne introduced them, allowing him to put faces to names that he'd already known from the detailed profiles he'd read.

Laverne Willis was Seacliff's chief administrator, a handsome mocha-skinned woman about Roger's age, stylishly dressed. She handled herself with a calculated reserve, as if emotion, like money, was something to be parceled out in measured amounts.

Counseling supervisor Adam Raleigh had the thinning brown hair and myopic inquisitive expression of the classic academic, but Roger knew he was a talented artist and musician, a computer programmer of some skill, and a first-rate auto mechanic as well. A modern-day Renaissance-man range of interests.

Michael Lee, R.N., was their nursing supervisor. A well-built man of Chinese descent, he was highly animated, energetic, and outgoing. He was also a Southern California health nut, and before dinner was even on the table, he was regaling them with the reasons why they should all go vegan.

Brian Sorenson, the computer expert, fit every preconceived image of his type. Thin, mumbling of speech, and indifferent to fashion, he could probably expound at length on the relative merits of every *Star Trek* captain and name the best websites to find nude images of Lucy Lawless and Gillian Anderson.

As Gwynne was also introducing the nursing assistants and counselors not currently on duty attending the students, the clack of a cane on the hallway's parquet floor brought a sudden respectful hush to the room.

Roger hadn't seen Dr. Benjamin Lundquist in person for a few years, but the man remained as impressive a figure as ever.

His piercingly direct green eyes commanded the attention of everyone present. The stiffness of his gait and posture gave him an almost military bearing, making it seem like the cane was more a prop in the dramatic than physical sense. The steel-grey suit was unusually but strikingly combined with a black silk shirt, the only touch of color being a burgundy handkerchief in his breast pocket.

He paused in the doorway, resting his cane between his feet and folding both hands over the silver knob. There was something eerily falcon-like in the pose, or perhaps it was in the intensity of his gaze.

Despite the close-cropped hair of blindingly pure white and the deep lines that marked his skin, he appeared far younger than his eighty-plus years. The vitality of his genius seemed to shine from him like a beacon.

Lundquist smiled, and in that instant his entire demeanor changed from that of a stern admiral to that of a doting grandfather. It was a convincing illusion, one that even Roger almost believed.

"At last, we are all together," he said, looking from one of them to the next. "Thank you for bringing your skills to work on behalf of making this dream into reality."

"Thank you for inspiring us, Dr. Lundquist," Roger said. "I'm sure I don't just speak for myself when I say what a privilege it is to be here."

That sentiment was echoed by the others, and brought a wider, more genuine smile to Lundquist's face. He made his way to the head of the table and took his seat.

Three members of the household staff appeared as if they had been waiting in the wings for their cue. They began serving the meal with the prompt unobtrusive speed associated with manor servants, calling up images of European lords and ladies, country estates, English squires.

And come to think of it, Roger felt that there was a good deal of the European lord or English squire about Lundquist. It didn't come across in his lectures, it certainly didn't come across in his articles, but it was unmistakably there.

Roger even thought he heard a trace of an accent, though that might have been his own mind putting a filtering veneer over Lundquist's words.

"We are embarked on a splendid journey, my friends," Lundquist said, raising a glass of wine. "Welcome aboard."

*   *   *

Wednesday,

August 6

1

Elliot Shaw shuffled papers and folders on the surface of his desk, pretending to read but not seeing any of the words.

He was supposed to be reviewing the files for a Friday morning staff meeting at the hospital, but he could not concentrate.

Hope, dread, and shame churned inside of him, making a sickening mix of emotion. Today was the day that his life would change forever. His life, and more importantly, David's.

He had taken over as the Trinity Bay Medical Center's chief of staff a year and a half ago, replacing Arthur Kensington, and was still referred to as 'the new doctor.' It wasn't so bad now, but he had the sneaking feeling that he would be 'the new doctor' in five years, even ten.

Doc Kensington was still something of a legend at the TBMC. Elliot had never met the man personally, but had heard so many stories about him that it was impossible not to feel as if he knew him. The nurses had lived in fear of him, and he had been notorious for bullying administrators.

Some said that the only reason Kensington's patients recovered so swiftly and suffered illnesses so infrequently was because they were frantic to escape or avoid him. The local farmer's market had always done a booming business in apple sales, in hopes of keeping that doctor away.

Even the tyrant's death had been noteworthy. A practicer of every vice he'd advised his patients to forsake – smoking, drinking, meat three meals a day, an abhorrance and avoidance of exercise – Kensington had dropped dead in his office one day, victim of a massive heart attack.

Elliot had personally witnessed the aftermath, which hadn't been without some beneficial repercussions. The patient Kensington had been with at the time, Tom Harmon, subsequently went off cigarettes cold-turkey, took up jogging, lost forty pounds, and sold his bar in favor of buying a fishing boat.

Nothing like a good scare to encourage a change of habits, and there weren't many scares more effective than having one's own doctor go down like a felled tree, mid-lecture.

Elliot snapped himself out of his half-daydreaming state and looked at the clock. Quarter to ten in the morning.

Almost ten. Almost time.

The television's drone couldn't drown out the sounds from the den. Nor could the wind-stirred rustle of the leaves of the tree outside his window. Not to Elliot's ears. If he turned on the stereo and thundered his favorite classical pieces until the house rattled, he'd still be able to hear David.

The low, cycling moans made it seem like the boy's every movement was agony. His glottal animalistic grunts were interspersed with the loud suck-ing-rattling gasp of air harshly drawn in through clenched teeth. Every now and then there would be a gabble of senseless, wordless syllables.

A new noise joined in, a blunted heavy banging. Elliot got up and went down the short hall, stepping over the gate, into the den.

The only pieces of furniture were a low couch and a scattering of pil-lows. The television and VCR were bolted to high shelves. The carpeting was indoor-outdoor, thick and durable. Toys suitable for an infant or toddler were strewn around a Playskool plastic toybox with rounded edges and a wide base to prevent it from tipping over.

The walls were coated with a sprayed-on foam-based paint, not padding but making them at least a little softer than bare plasterboard or paneling might have been. Posters of animals, landscapes, and cartoon characters brought color to the room.

David was on his back in the corner, drumming his heels against the wall. His arms flapped as if he were trying to swim or fly.

"Hi there, big guy," Elliot said. "Video's over, huh?"

He moved to correct the source of David's displeasure, pressing the re-wind button.

The seven-year-old did not react to his father's presence or his words. He just kept slamming his feet into the wall, so hard that the jolts shook his entire body.

While the cassette was rewinding, Elliot sat on the floor beside his son and talked to him in a calm and soothing tone.

It hurt his heart to see so much of Sharon in David's features. He had her curly caramel-colored hair and deep brown eyes. If his face hadn't been at once slack and contorted, he might have been an adorable child. He was clad only in diapers, rubber pants, and an oversized soft cotton tee shirt.

David's eyes swept the room in great looping circles, never focusing on anything for more than a few seconds, passing over his father as though Elliot were just another one of the room's furnishings. He subsided to muttering, growling vocalizations separated by more of his convulsive slurpings-in of breath.

The doorbell rang.

Time.

"It's going to be all right," he promised. "It's going to be better. You'll see. Oh, David . . . Davey . . . Daddy loves you."

He got up and pushed 'play.' While the animated films couldn't capture David's attention, he seemed more *here,* less likely to lash out physically, when in the company of Disney's characters and songs.

Elliot stepped over the gate again and headed for the front of the spacious brick house that had been part of the package deal he got for taking over for Arthur Kensington. At one point, years ago before the TBMC was built, the house had doubled as Kensington's office as well. There was still a vaguely 'waiting room' aura to the living room.

The silhouette of a man was visible through the sheer curtains on the tall narrow window. Elliot opened the door.

"Hello, Adam."

"Good morning, Elliot. Ready for the big day?"

Behind Adam Raleigh, parked at the curb at the base of the sloping lawn and partly hidden by a hydrangea bush, waited a green van. The sight of it renewed Elliot's inner mix of hope-dread-shame. He could see another man in the driver's seat.

"Who's that?"

"Stan, one of the attendants. Ready?" he repeated.

Elliot ran a hand fitfully through his hair. "I . . . how could I be ready for this? I feel like I'm failing him. Failing him for the second time. I don't know if I can go through with it."

Adam nodded in understanding. "I know. But this is what's best for David, Elliot. And for you." He waved to the driver and came in, closing the door behind him.

"David is the one we should be thinking about," Elliot insisted. "Not me."

"What's best for him is what's best for you."

"Taking him away from home . . ."

"Giving him a chance at the help he needs."

"Yes . . . I know. You don't have to convince me. It's just . . . it's so hard. I don't know what I'll do without him."

Adam laughed. "You make it sound like we're carting him off to Siberia! Seacliff is just up the hill. You can see it from your own front porch. You're welcome to visit whenever you want. Not only that, you're part of the staff. When you come up on-call, for whatever reason, you'll be able to spend time with David."

"Turning him over to strangers . . . it's like I'm abandoning him."

"You're giving him what he needs. You've done so much for him . . . don't think I don't appreciate what you've sacrificed! I do. I know what it's like."

"It's not a sacrifice —"

"It's repayment."

Elliot froze, and looked at Adam. "Why do you say that?"

"I've been through the same thing. When my wife died, I blamed myself for things that were beyond my control. I felt like I'd failed in my duties as a husband. I quit my job, I gave up my friends, I did nothing but take care of Joey – our son. He was born with Down's Syndrome. I thought that if I sent him away, it would be for my own selfish reasons. But keeping him at home was just as selfish. I did it for me, to try and relieve my own guilt, to try and make it up to him, but not for him. For me."

"It's not the same —"

"Isn't it?"

"What happened to Sharon was my fault. I knew it was dangerous for her and for the baby. I let my promise to her get in the way of my professional knowledge."

"You can't change what happened, Elliot. It's done. That's the hardest part to accept, believe me. But you can't go on punishing yourself and David."

"I'm not punishing him. I'd never punish him."

"Which is why it's best for him to come to Seacliff."

Elliot exhaled in a sigh. "I know it's best. I know I can't deny him what he needs, deny him a chance of improvement."

"And it's not a betrayal, a failure, an abandonment. You're not putting him out of the way so you don't have to think about him or be bothered. You're helping him."

He bowed his head and stood in silence, listening to David moan and babble in the other room.

Would he still hear that when David was at Seacliff? When he had started going back to work, he'd paused sometimes in the middle of an examination or procedure, certain that he was hearing David. Mistaking the groans of patients or the distant chatter of a radio for the voice of his son.

Seacliff . . . or home? Which was the more selfish course? Which was more of a giving in to guilt? Which was more of a punishment, and a punishment for whom?

What choice did he have? He couldn't afford to retire and stay home full time, and every caregiver he'd hired hadn't been able to last more than a few months before quitting, too unnerved to stay on no matter how professional their credentials.

Elliot made himself take a deep breath. If Lundquist could help David, he could not let his own feelings of guilt and shame stand in the way. Adam was right. David was the important one here. David's welfare had to come before anything else.

"I'm sorry," he finally said. "You're right. This is best for David and I've known it all along. I just have trouble admitting it to myself."

Adam nodded. "I understand. I really do."

"And Lundquist can help him. There will be improvement." He heard the pleading in his own voice and knew he was trying to convince himself as well as seek reassurance from Adam Raleigh.

"That's the plan." Evidently sensing that the matter was settled, Adam smiled. "Let's take him to see the place, what do you say?"

"I packed some of his things. Clothes, toys, his favorite videos. He'll be able to watch them, won't he?"

"Absolutely."

"All right. It's time. Let's do it before I lose my nerve."

*   *   *

2

"Here are the records on the Shaw boy," Gwynne McGuire said.

Benjamin Lundquist took the sheaf of papers and skimmed over them. "The poor child. The poor family! We live in an age of such tragedies."

"Yes." She sat down opposite him. "I propose beginning with a –"

"The mother was so determined to undergo natural childbirth," Benjamin mused, reading the history. "So much so that she was willing to put her own life and that of the child at risk rather than submit to medications."

"If the scan shows –"

"And the father, who handled the delivery, did not overrule her when complications arose. He chose to abide by his wife's convictions against his better judgment." He blew a slow whistle through pursed lips. "And then to have her die in the throes of labor, undertake emergency surgery to save the baby, and find that it had been half-strangled by the umbilicus so that severe brain damage resulted . . . my God, his guilt must be tremendous."

"The MRI in his records seems to indicate –"

"That poor, poor man! He has gone above and beyond. The boy is seven, barely able to feed himself, incontinent, with motor control equivalent to that of a child less than one year of age, compounded by the involuntary muscular spasms . . . he's been keeping this child at home for seven years rather than submit him to be institutionalized."

"Admirable," Gwynne said. "If I may –"

"There comes a point at which the admirable becomes the absurd. The life they must have led! Look at this! He has tried his very best to expose the child to a variety of stimuli, taking him out to the park, to the beach, to movies . . . can you imagine what that must have been like for him? The cruelty to which they must have been exposed . . . ranging from innocent and well-meaning advice to deliberate scorn and taunting . . ."

"I believe we can make progress with this case, Doctor Lundquist." Amazing! She'd gotten an entire sentence out that time.

"Yes, yes . . ." Benjamin held up a photograph of David Shaw. "He has such potential, my dear Doctor McGuire. They all have such potential."

She settled back in her chair, knowing what was coming. She had heard it all before, but there was no stopping Lundquist once he got to sermonizing on his favorite topic.

Benjamin rose from his seat and walked stiffly to the wall, which was made of two-way glass. From the other side, it was a mirror, preventing anyone from seeing into the conference room. From in here, it was a tinted window looking out into the atrium, where the pool rippled silvery-turquoise.

"It is never too early, or too late, to start living up to one's potential," he said. "That is the one thing that saddens me most about this world. How few people reach the heights they could attain. We feel so limited, so restricted, by what others see as success. A high-paying job, a good education, wealth and all of its trappings, social standing . . . these are the measures of success, and they are meaningless."

Gwynne quirked her lips, unable to keep from thinking what a fine attitude that was for someone who had attained each of those measures. *Would he be so quick to dismiss them as meaningless,* she wondered, *if he lacked them himself?*

"When all that really matters," he went on, "is to be happy. To be content. On whatever level that might mean to the individual. Not bound by what someone else tells us we must have to make us happy, but by what balm eases our own souls."

She nodded, knowing that while he wouldn't see the movement, he'd sense her silent agreement.

He planted both hands on the head of his cane and sighed heavily. "I've spent many years railing against God, society, government, whatever force you please, for the miseries of my life. And then came a day when I realized that everything I so hated was not caused by fate and circumstance, but by me. How I responded to what the world offered was all in my own control."

"We have all benefited from your teachings," she said. "Your work has paved the way for revolutionary new theories and developments. And this . . . Seacliff . . . is the most noble project of them all."

"I only hope that we are able to help those most in need. The children,

Gwynne, these poor children whose lives stretch out before them as bleak and empty places of torment . . . when they could be so much more!"

"I know. We will succeed, Dr. Lundquist. The children will live up to their full potential, I am sure of it."

He smiled faintly. "You have such surety of will, my lamb. Do you never doubt yourself?"

"Very rarely."

"How proud your parents must be, to have a daughter that burns with such brilliant fire."

She breathed a soft laugh. "I like to think of myself as proof, Doctor . . . proof of your theory that with effort and determination, we can all reach great heights. I had the same benefits of genetics and upbringing as my brother and sister, but made myself something more."

"Which is why it seemed odd to me that you, with such a promising career and countless and lucrative offers from hospitals and research facilities the world over, chose to come to work with me. Not that I am trying to get rid of you. Far from it! I'm merely surprised."

"Are you?" Gwynne shook her head in amazement. "A chance to work with Benjamin Lundquist, one of the greatest minds, the greatest geniuses, of our time? I'd have to be a lunatic or an idiot to turn down that opportunity. Your theories challenge me to think along paths I'd never considered. As for the money, it's never been a concern to me. Which isn't to say that you're not paying me enough, of course, only that yes, some of the other offers named higher figures. But it didn't matter. I love my work, Dr. Lundquist. The accomplishment, not the paycheck."

"Well," he said, nodding. "I am quite pleased to hear it."

"And now, if we could continue reviewing the Shaw case? They'll be arriving any moment and I'd like to discuss my ideas with you before we see the boy."

"Carry on, my lamb. Carry on."

*   *   *

3

Elliot Shaw had seen the interior of Seacliff before, when he'd been interviewed for the job of on-call physician. It seemed different now that he was seeing it as his son's new home.

Different, but not bad.

"East wing," Dr. Roger Brockman announced. "It's been entirely remodeled to accommodate the needs of the students while still maintaining much of the feel of the original construction."

Adam Raleigh had accompanied the attendant, Stan Montgomery, to get David settled in his room. Elliot had wanted to go, but they felt that it would be better for David to get used to the idea of other people helping care for him.

"How many other children are here so far?" he asked as they moved from the dining room into the enormous kitchen.

He noted that the door was sealed with an electronic lock, opening by key card . . . and that the key card had a whorled, oval depression in it that fitted the pad of Roger's thumb exactly.

"David's the tenth. Once he's settled, we'll be ready to start going over the files with you, so you'll be familiar with their case and medical histories."

"Strict security," he said, indicating the card.

"I know it seems extreme for only a kitchen," Roger chuckled, "but we certainly don't want to take any chances. Which reminds me, I need to get you a key of your own." He pulled a small black device that looked like a miniature cross between a cellular phone and a walkie-talkie from his pocket.

"Brian? We need to issue a key card. I'll transmit you the print now."

Elliot raised his eyebrows as Roger flipped the device over, slid open a panel on the back, and revealed a glass screen.

"Okay, stick your thumb there . . ."

"You're kidding."

"High-tech toys, got to love them."

He pressed his thumb to the screen and watched as a luminescent green line ran from top to bottom, then right to left. "Cute."

"Isn't it, though?" Roger closed the screen, pushed some buttons, and spoke into the phone again. "Here you go, Brian. We'll be down to pick it up in about half an hour."

"So no one can use the key but me?" Elliot asked.

"That's right." He winked. "The card even picks up the temperature and electrical activity in your skin, so it won't work if someone were to, say, steal it and chop off your thumb."

"Good God! Why do you even need all of this?"

"Oh, we don't, really. It just gets to be a habit for those of us who've done some work for top-secret research companies or government agencies. And there are a few things here we need to keep protected. The labs have some pretty delicate and valuable equipment. Dr. Lundquist's not worried about anyone stealing our secrets, though. His work is meant to benefit everyone, not to be stingily guarded for profit."

"Then where is the funding coming from?"

"Mainly Dr. Lundquist himself. He's built up a considerable personal fortune during his lifetime, partly from inheritance, partly from his work, and then of course there was the settlement."

"Settlement?" Elliot frowned.

Roger's voice dropped to just above a whisper, not in the manner of one imparting a juicy secret, but in the manner of one maintaining a level of discretion. "He had a younger brother and sister who were committed to an institution. This was back when 'therapy' consisted of icewater baths, lobotomies, and so on. Terrible conditions. Patients left in restraints and straitjackets for weeks at a time. Shock treatments in their most primitive state of development. A lot of the patients died. The institution was shut down in the fifties and the families launched a massive lawsuit."

"It certainly explains his dedication," Elliot said. "He's made it his life's work, helping children, so that no other families have to go through what his did."

"I might even go so far as to say it's an obsession, especially after his fanatic devotion to his work cost him his wife and son. I think that plays a part in how intent he's become on Seacliff. If what we're doing here is successful, the Seacliff model could become an industry standard of care." He clapped a friendly hand on Elliot's shoulder. "Now, shall we go see how David's liking his new room?"

They went up to the second floor. The hallway was long but not oppressively so, with high vaulted ceilings and a floor covered in textured linoleum nearly indistinguishable from hardwood. The doors were not the originals, each having a wire-reinforced window in the middle.

David's room was the first one down from an open space that served as a combination staff area and lounge. It was on the north side of the east wing, with a view of Trinity Bay.

"If you look carefully," Adam said as Eliot and Roger came in, "you can see your house from here."

Adam sat on a cushiony block of a sofa that looked like a four-foot-long Three Musketeers bar. David was hitching himself around in the bed mumbling to himself in what sounded like a low and thoughtful tone, interrupted now and then with short sharp barking cries.

"There's my guy," Elliot said, going in with a sense of relief and approval.

The walls were a warm lemony yellow with white wainscoting and trim. A four-foot-high runner of quilted chocolate-brown cloth circumnavigated the room and managed not to look like padding. The floor was carpeted in attractive golden-brown with an abstract woven pattern of deep brown, yellow, and white.

The bed was built to rest flat on the ground, and its sides rose in foam-wrapped rails. It had yellow sheets and a white bedspread, and David's favorite stuffed animal was already perched on the pillow. The television was, like the one at home, bolted high and out of reach . . . and beside the glassy eye of a surveillance camera.

"We have cameras covering each room," Roger explained when Elliot pointed it out. "The bedroom doors operate by conventional locks and the stairway doors are, as you saw, secured by the electronic version. That's to make sure none of the kids go wandering. There are two bathrooms, one for the boys and one for the girls, with shower stalls and tubs —"

"David doesn't wander, and he can't go to the bathroom on his own."

"Yet," Adam said with such surety that the nape of Elliot's neck prickled with hope.

"Yet," Roger seconded. "I can't promise you anything, Dr. Shaw, but I share Adam's confidence that we'll be able to, in time, bring David to that level of functioning at least."

"How?" he begged, finally asking the question he hadn't dared ask before, not in all the months he'd been preparing himself for this day. "I've read some of Dr. Lundquist's articles, and none of them are clear on the exact process. I have to know what you'll be doing here. Not just as a concerned father, but if I'm going to be working with you to take care of the medical needs of these children, I will have to know everything."

"I couldn't agree more," Roger said. "And I will make sure you're fully up to speed on our entire program. Legal mumbo-jumbo and all."

"Legal . . . so the treatments *are* experimental?"

"It's not nearly as extreme as it sounds," Adam said reassuringly. "We're mainly working with alternate forms of therapy, focusing on creativity as a way to stimulate unused areas of the brain."

Roger nodded. "With those areas then taking over some of the functions of the damaged areas. It's all a matter of forging new neural pathways, encouraging other sections to pick up the slack, as it were."

"And that's what you have in mind for David?" More than the nape of his neck was prickling now; goosebumps of excitement were breaking out all over him. "To . . . to have other sections of his brain compensate for the damage?"

"That's the plan," Adam said.

"But he's too old, isn't he? I've read studies, children denied stimulation as babies –"

"The box orphans?" Roger cut in, shaking his head with a sighing scowl. "This isn't the same thing. We've all heard how the younger a child is, the more versatile the brain. A baby suffering an injury to the speech center, for instance, can still learn to talk by re-routing the pathways. Or how it's easier to learn a foreign language the younger you are. The older the child, the less flexible the brain . . . but David's only seven."

Elliot looked down at David, who had fallen into his usual fitful, restless sleep. Every few seconds, he twitched, or grimaced, or grunted.

"If you can do this . . ." he whispered. "I . . . I don't know how I could ever repay you."

"That's not what we're here for, Dr. Shaw," Roger said. "We just want the same thing you want. To see David, and others like him, have the opportunity to live up to their potential. That's Dr. Lundquist's philosophy . . . no, it's more than a philosophy. It's . . ."

"Practically a sacred vow," Adam finished. "His *raison d'etre*. I've known him for over fifteen years, and the only thing that makes him truly happy is being able to give a child a second chance at happiness. You should see how happy he is with Aiden's improvement . . ."

"Did he use these treatments on her, on his daughter?"

"She's not his daughter. More like a . . . ward, I suppose you could say. And it wasn't quite the same, since her condition was the result of a psychological trauma, but he did use a variation of his theories in developing her treatment regimen."

"And it helped her," Elliot probed, searching for hope, searching for encouragement.

"She's not the outgoing girl she was before her parents died," Adam admitted, "but she's come a long way back. I know that she'll continue to improve, and I think most of her lingering difficulties are as much a matter of habit as anything else."

Elliot thought it over, rubbing his hand along the padded rail of David's bed. "I want him to be happy. To lead a fulfilling and meaningful life. Do you really think it's possible?"

Roger squeezed his shoulder. "We wouldn't be here if we didn't."

"That's right," Adam said.

"I'll do anything to help him," Elliot said. "Anything at all."

"Of course . . . you're a father." Roger glanced down at his pager. "Your key card is ready. Come on down to Brian's office with me, and then I'll show you around the labs."

*   *   *

Friday,

September 12

1

Jenny Forrester studied herself in the mirror and decided that the lipstick was too much. Even her dad would notice that vivid a shade of pink.

She wiped it off on a tissue and went with gloss instead, slicking it on until her full lips were nice and shiny.

Satisfied, she opened the drawer in her dressing table and swept the cosmetics inside in an untidy jumble. She shoved the latest copy of *Stunner* in too, and covered it all up with a stack of old comic books on the extreme off-chance that Dad went snooping.

He wouldn't, of course, but it never hurt to be prepared. Which was why, as Jenny readied herself for her big Friday night on the town, the first weekend of the new school year, she checked to be sure that the stuff hidden in her purse was still there.

Yep. Couple of condoms in foil wrappers. Along with a half a pack of cigarettes and a lighter. And tampons.

Not that she had any use for any of it. She was twelve. Hadn't gotten her period yet – any day now, she was sure of it, any day now! She had never let a boy get his hands on her boobies, let alone do more. And anyway, smoking was for losers.

But the looks on her friends' faces when they saw the stuff she carried in her purse proclaimed that she, Jenny Forrester, was the coolest of the cool.

"Daaa-aad!" she bugled. "Going out!"

"No, Peanut, I'm home."

"*I'm* going out," she clarified, putting on an artfully tattered denim jacket to help hide her too-tight, too-low-cut blouse. Since she'd been the first girl in her grade to get them, she figured it was her job . . . her duty! . . . to show them off.

She sashayed down the hall, practicing swinging her hips, but quit it as she reached the living room where her dad was stretched out on the couch with their dog Bingo.

Charlie Forrester was a lanky scarecrow of a man, swimming in his clothes and looking like a strong wind would blow him away like a raggedy kite. He had always been gangly, but in the past three years, he had passed the boundary between thin and scrawny.

He left off watching Daffy Duck cartoons to glance at Jenny. No change came over his gaunt Ichabod Crane face, so she figured she had succeeded in making herself look surface-innocent. Though sometimes she wondered if Dad would even notice if she paraded through the house as tarted-up as one of the hookers they said hung out in Oldtown Eureka.

"Where'll you be?" he asked.

"The arcade, where else?"

"Back when?"

"Midnight."

Was that a flicker of disapproval? No . . . he just nodded and reached out one bony, callused hand to scratch Bingo's head. "Have fun, Peanut."

"Can I have ten dollars?"

"My wallet's by the phone."

"Thanks, Dad!"

She could hardly wait to be sixteen so he'd let her have the car. Disdaining her bike, she went down the woods path shortcut that led to town all the way from the Zane place – or was it the Blake place now? Theresa Zane had kept her maiden name, but given Chief Blake's name to the twins and to Lora . . . but it was still Travis Zane's house . . .

At any rate, the path started up there and led to town, past the Forrester abode with its Victorian garden and examples of Dad's woodcarving.

Jenny knew the route well enough to follow it in a pitch black rainstorm, which this wasn't. The evening was pearly with low-hanging mist wreathing a crescent moon.

She sang all her favorite Flirty Boys songs to keep herself company, and paused a few times to try out some of the hottest new dance moves she'd seen on MTV. She flung her hair around in wild abandon, imagining herself on a concert stage dancing with Joey Mack, the dreamiest of the Flirty Boys.

The Square tonight was as close as Trinity Bay ever got to hopping. Most of the shops were closed for the night, but the door to Nate's was propped open and rock music rolled out. It had to compete with the folksy stuff being performed live by a street band at the center of the Square. Periodically, both types were swallowed up by a rousing cheer from the ball field behind the Municipal Building, where the flag football teams from Tom's Market and The Sports Den were indulging their customary rivalry.

And last but not least, Galaxy West. The sign was bright pulsing neon, the G made to look like a stylized version of Saturn. The outside walls were a mural of stars, planets, and comets on a field of dark blue. The windows jittered and flashed with light.

Jenny passed Red's Salon, wondering if it was time to take another stab at getting Dad's permission to have her ears double-pierced. Her attempt last fall had been met with a "gee, Peanut, let me think about that," and then he'd never mentioned it again.

"Jenny!" Kaylee Neeman hailed, waving from the patch of sidewalk out front of Galaxy West. The neon turned her glittering braces into an incandescent mouthful of red fire.

Kaylee, short, blond, chubby-cheeked, bouncy, and dressed almost as saucily as Jenny herself, was standing with Eva Mittleschut. Eva wore plain black pants and a black long-sleeved blouse buttoned all the way up. Her hair, likewise black, hung straight to her shoulders from a ruler-perfect central part.

"Donny Peterson is here," Kaylee reported as Jenny joined them. "And Brett James!"

"And Rocky," Eva added, crinkling her eyes in the way she showed displeasure. "He asked about you."

"Oh, ick . . ." Jenny threw a pleading look at Kaylee. "Can't you call off your brother?"

"He thinks you're cute."

"He's a total jerkoid."

"*Tell* me about it!" Kaylee groaned. "It's 'cause he's the only boy in the family. Our dad acts like he's all special and everything."

"Your dad is weird," Jenny said.

"So's yours," Eva pointed out.

"In a different way!"

"He and Mom were fighting about it again," Kaylee said. "He wants her to have another baby, can you imagine?"

Eva tilted her head. "Isn't she too old?"

"Yeah," Jenny said. "Your sister Traci's the same age as my brother Jerry, so that makes her twenty. How old is your mom?"

Kaylee did some math on her fingers. "Thirty-seven."

"Only thirty-seven?" Jenny gasped. "She looks . . . wow, lots older than that!"

"After eight babies, you'd look old too," Eva said. "Not to mention irresponsible. Overpopulation is destroying our Earth. MY parents limited their family to one child."

"*Your* father isn't convinced his DNA's so magnificent that everyone should want a Neeman baby," Jenny snorted.

"Jenny!" Kaylee tried to look indignant and ruined it by laughing.

"Lisa Garrick told me that your jerkoid brother told her that she should go all the way with him because your father told him that Neeman sperm is better than anyone else's!"

"I am not going to stand out here all night talking about *sperm!*" Kaylee announced. "That's just sick, sick, sick, Jennifer Forrester."

"Okay, okay, sorry!" Snickering, she followed Kaylee into the light-wild, noisy chaos of Galaxy West.

The space theme was continued within, the walls like alien moonscapes and the roof a solid black dome pocked with tiny twinkling light bulbs. Neon tubes encircled the base of the dome, glowing eerily steady in the flashing screens of video games.

The electronic din was one step short of horrific — lasers, gunfire, screeching tires, grunts, screams, explosions, roaring monsters, and recorded voices exhorting the players to try again. Tokens jangled out of the change machines. Kids called to each other, exclaimed in excitement, cursed in frustration, shouted their conversations in an effort to be heard. Weaving through like a single thread in a tapestry, top-forty music issued from speakers embedded in the ceiling.

Jenny spotted Rocky Neeman right away, hunched over a game of Death Mutant while a couple of his co-jerkoids cheered him on.

The worst thing about Rocky was that he *was* actually kind of cute. Rocky was fourteen, with thick wavy hair as blond as Kaylee's — as blond as all the Neemans' — and a tall, broad-shouldered build.

Cute, he may have been, but that didn't change the fact that he was an insufferable snot.

Galaxy West was crammed with kids every Friday and Saturday night, but tonight was special. Tonight was the first weekend of the new school year, a time to see and be seen.

Every table was full. The air was thick with the scents of pizza-by-the-slice, popcorn, and hot dogs. The floor was sticky with spilled soda and melted ice cream.

Jenny and her friends were the youngest ones present, but they did their best to pass for full-fledged teenagers. It didn't work very well in Kaylee's case, as she still had no notable progress in the boob department despite her plumpness. Eva was also flat as a board, but she was the tallest of their trio and her broody-Goth-artsy image made her seem older than her years.

They bought sodas and cruised through the crowd, chattering brightly – Jen and Kaylee did, anyway; Eva was lost in thought, probably musing about overpopulation. Jenny let her jacket hang open, and basked in the appraising looks she got from the boys.

Seeing and being seen, that was what it was all about. Proving that, while maybe they still went to the baby-grades, they were high-schoolers at heart.

That was the worst thing about Trinity Bay. The elementary building housed grades K through 8, while the high-school was the same plot of land. They shared a gymnasium, athletic field, and even cafeteria. But junior-high-age people like Jenny and her friends still had to go to the baby school.

Trés uncool.

"Hi, Jenny. Guess who just set the new high score on Death Mutant?" Rocky Neeman swaggered up to her, his entourage in tow.

Jenny beamed a saccharine-false smile at Neil Scribner, a hopeless dork caught in Rocky's orbit like a pasty-faced asteroid. "Congratulations, Neil!"

Eva, Kaylee, and Kirby Underwood started laughing. A tentative smile tugged at the corner of Neil's mouth, but it faded almost at once when he realized they were teasing him.

"Ha-ha, very funny," Rocky said. "I did. Broke eighty thousand points. Want a soda?"

She held up her cup and shook it so the ice sloshed. "Got one."

"Ooh, shot *down!*" Kirby crowed.

Rocky's face darkened. "Shut up, Kirby! Who cares, who wants to hang out with little girls anyway? They have to be home by nine for bedtime."

"I don't have to be home until midnight," Jenny said archly.

"And we're not little girls!" Kaylee glared at her brother. "We're more mature than you'll ever be. You don't see us wasting our time on stupid games."

"Only because you're no good at them," Rocky fired back.

"We could be if we wanted to."

"Go ahead, then!" He thrust a fistful of tokens at her. "Let's see you try."

"We're busy," Kaylee said as if he was the dumbest thing that ever lived.

"Yeah, Barbie's Dream House won't play with itself," Kirby chuckled.

"That's one thing it doesn't have in common with you, then," Eva said. Before any of the boys could respond, before it had even sunk in, she nudged Jenny. "I see a table."

Neil got it then, and yodeled freaky laughter that always made him sound like the village idiot instead of one of the school brains.

"Fine, go on!" Rocky yelled after them. "Bunch of babies!"

"If we're such babies, why are you always staring at me?" Jenny shot back over her shoulder as she followed Eva.

Whatever he replied was lost as they moved too far away, leaving Rocky in the noisy depths of the arcade. A group of bigger kids was leaving a table, not bothering to pick up after themselves.

Eva slid in like a lean black snake and claimed the spot before someone else could beat her to it. "Slobs," she announced, flicking at a pizza-smeared paper plate.

"Not going to start in on how bad those are for the environment?" Jenny said, half-teasing, as she and Kaylee stuffed trash into the can – in keeping with the Galaxy West theme, it was made to resemble a vaguely R2D2-esque robot.

Eva gave her a world-weary look. "At least they're not polystyrene."

"Look, there's Donny Peterson," Kaylee squealed in Jenny's ear.

"Look, there's Rachel Carter with him though," Jenny said.

"Rachel Carter!" Kaylee sniffed, fluffing her bouncy curls. "My sister Diane says Rachel's the biggest tramp in the eleventh grade."

Jenny glanced at Donny, who was dark and sultry, then past him to Brett James, a senior and total hunk.

"Why are boys our age so feeble?" she said. "It's so not fair!"

Kaylee sighed as Donny put an arm around Rachel's waist, low so he could tuck his fingers into the back pocket of her tight pants. "What are we doing? These guys are four, five years older than us . . . they're never going to give us a second look. Or even a first look! Not when they have Rachel look-at-my-big-ones Carter to drool over."

"Don't be lame," Jenny said. "We may be young, but we've got what it takes."

"We . . ." Eva trailed off, looking toward the door. "Isn't that Eric Raney?"

"Eric Raney?!" Kaylee and Jenny chorused, whirling in their chairs.

"Subtle," Eva muttered.

"It *is* him." Jenny pressed a hand to her chest as if to calm the pounding therein. "Eric Raney, *here?*"

He had paused just inside the door as if evaluating whether to come all the way in or not, poised like a panther full of hidden lazy strength. Like Eva, he was dressed primarily in black. Black jeans, black athletic shoes, black shirt unbuttoned and with the sleeves rolled to the elbows, plain white tee shirt beneath.

His hair was ink-black and short, with a tuft of it that fell down over his left eye . . . the exact style, if not color, of Flirty Boy Joey Mack's hair. He had sharply defined features and hooded eyes that implied they had seen the darker underside of the universe.

Jenny's heart did a giddy little flip-flop.

"He should have a motorcycle," Kaylee said.

"Why, is it in the 'bad boy' handbook?" Eva said.

"Shh," Jenny hissed. "He's coming in!"

Eric started through the crowd, greeting no one and being greeted by no one, but Jenny saw several people observing him out of the corners of their eyes. The guys with a sort of speculative challenge, wondering if they could take him. The girls with the same sort of drawn-to-danger compulsion that filled Jenny herself.

He'd only moved to Trinity Bay a few months ago, last May, shortly before the end of the school year. Not long enough to give anyone a chance to get to know him, but plenty long enough to get them all speculating.

The arrival of a new kid was always an event. Especially when the new kid was someone like Eric. Hardly anybody ever talked to him but everyone talked *about* him.

For starters, he lived with his mom in a shabby house on the beach south of Seacliff – probably the only ugly stretch of coast on the Pacific. When the tide was in, it was a swampy salty morass. When the tide was out, it was a stagnant mud flat.

Mrs. Raney, who hardly any of them had ever seen, worked a couple of late-night and weekend jobs. Opinions were equally divided as to whether she was a stripper or a cocktail waitress, and most kids thought she was probably also an alcoholic. There was no Mr. Raney in the picture.

Eric himself was sixteen and, depending on who you listened to, a junkie, a biker, a drug dealer, gay, on parole, or any combination thereof. But people also said he was smart, that he'd come in as the new kid in school and promptly aced all his tests.

Either way, Eric didn't seem to care what people said about him. That was part of what made him so cool. In the cafeteria, which was where Jenny had first seen him last spring, he always ate in solitude and studied his schoolmates with an intensity that bordered on bizarre.

Tuesday, Jenny and her friends had been having lunch when Eric sat down by himself at the next table over. They'd been able to feel his gaze upon them like a tangible sensation. Kaylee had fluffed and fluttered and pretended she wasn't aware of him.

But Jenny had turned and met his stare boldly. She'd never been close enough to him before to notice the color of his eyes, and saw they were the unusual copper-brown of brand-new pennies.

She'd been able to sustain the eye contact for two seconds before totally losing her nerve. It felt like he could look straight into her brain and learn things about her that she didn't know about herself.

Now here he was again, headed for the snack bar. Plenty of girls were carrying on in what to Jenny was the most blatantly transparent fashion, giggling overloud, and so on.

Eric ordered a Dr. Pepper. Jenny and her friends continued watching in silent fascination, until he turned from the counter with his soda and saw them. They quickly started talking about nothing, as if they had been all along.

Under Kaylee's babbling about some new Orlando Bloom movie at the Bayshore Mall, Eva spoke without moving her lips, as skillfully as a ventriloquist. "He's coming over here!"

Jenny risked a glance and he was, Eric Raney, coming toward their table! And he was looking right at her!

An effervescent little squeal rose up inside her like a bubble in a bottle of pop and she locked her jaw against it.

He stopped right at the end of their table, sipped more Dr. Pepper, let the straw slide from between his lips. "Hey," he said to Jenny, with an upward nod of his head.

"Hey," she said, just as casual.

And he left. Walked away, back into the crowded arcade and out the door. Gone into the night.

"Jenny!" Kaylee shrieked breathlessly. "Omigod, Jenny, he *talked* to you!"

Eva was gaping at her. So were many other girls, older girls, bona-fide babes like Rachel Carter, all gaping at her, Jenny Forrester, with surprise and envy.

The urge to squeal was nearly overpowering but she fought it down again. "Yeah."

"He *talked* to you! Eric Raney!" In her ebullience, Kaylee knocked over her cup.

The resultant river of Coke drenched Eva's leg, necessitating a sudden flight for the bathroom by all three of them. The moment the door wheezed shut behind them and Jenny ascertained there were no feet in the stalls, she finally loosed the squeal.

"He talked to me, did you hear him, he said 'hey,' he was looking right at me!" She couldn't keep her cool, hopping and clapping her hands like a hyper four-year-old, but Eric Raney! Talking to *her!*

Eva sopped the worst of the spill up with paper towels and satisfied herself that the rest wouldn't show up on black anyway. "So what's the deal?"

"I don't know!" Jenny caught sight of her reflection, all shiny-starry eyes in the mirror. "I mean, he was looking at us the other day and I didn't look away, maybe he liked that. Maybe he likes . . . *me.*"

"Do you think he's going to ask you out?" Kaylee seemed about to faint at the very thought.

Jenny felt a little like fainting herself. "I don't know."

"I hope Rocky saw. That'll teach him, calling us babies. Eric Raney wouldn't be interested in babies. Jenny, this is so great!"

"He could be trouble," Eva said.

"Don't be jealous," Kaylee ordered. Her eyes widened. "Jen! Maybe he wanted you to follow him."

"Shit!" Jenny yelped, grabbing her purse off the counter. "Maybe he did!"

She bolted out of the restroom with Eva and Kaylee close on her heels. All at once the interior of Galaxy West seemed five times as big and more crowded than a super-sale. She struggled to get through, more sure with every step that Eric was out there waiting for her, getting impatient, deciding she wasn't worth it, leaving . . .

"No!" She exploded out the front door and into the street before she could stop herself.

The football game had just ended and the Square was filling with people, streaming every which way, over to the Trinity Bar and Grill for a milkshake, up the street to the all-night donut shop, across to Nate's for a beer.

Jenny turned frantically left and right and all around, and saw no sign of Eric Raney. A crushing wave of dejection pressed down on her, so hard she was sure she must be leaving deep footprints in the sidewalk.

"Where's the fire?" someone asked.

She spun with hope blazing all through her veins, but it was only Toby Edwards.

"Toby!"

"What?"

"It's you."

"Last I checked."

"Where is he?" Kaylee demanded.

"I don't see him," Jenny said, anguished.

"Wasn't he waiting for you?" Eva asked.

"Who?" Toby said.

Kaylee grabbed Toby by the shoulders. He was a year younger than them but a grade ahead, and as short as she was. "Did you see Eric Raney come out of the arcade?"

"Sure, he said hi to me."

"What?" Jenny grabbed Toby away from Kaylee. "He said hi to you?"

"Yeah, why wouldn't he?" Toby plucked her wrists off of his shoulders. "Ease off, huh?"

"*You* know Eric Raney?" Eva said.

Toby rolled his eyes at her dubious tone. "Of course I do. Nice guy. Pretty smart. I saw him in the library just the other day. He was reading about – "

"Who cares what he was reading about?" Kaylee cut in. "Did he ask you about Jenny?"

"No, why?"

"Well, was he waiting for me out here?"

"No."

"Tell us what happened," Eva said.

"I was at the ball game, told my folks I was going to get either an ice cream cone or go up to the donut shop and then meet them at Dad's store. I was trying to decide when Eric came out. We said hi, how's it, fine. He kept going toward the bus stop. I'd just made up my mind for a buttermilk bar when Jenny came busting out the door and almost ran me over."

Jenny slumped onto the bench in front of Red's Salon. "He left?"

"What's the big deal about Eric Raney?" Toby asked.

"You're Mister Smarty, skipped two grades, you figure it out," Eva said.

"Ohhh!" Toby bobbed his head in comprehension. He broke into a chant. "Jenny likes Eric! Jenny likes Eric!"

"For your information, *Eric* likes *Jenny*," Kaylee said loftily.

"Really?" His face creased in puzzlement. "Even though she's Rocky's girlfriend?"

Jenny shot off the bench as if propelled by a spring. "Rocky's what? Are you crazy?"

"That's what I heard!" Toby said, backing off. "Though maybe Eric just didn't know."

"What gave you the idea I'm Rocky's . . . Rocky's . . ." she gagged on the word and finally hocked it out. "Girlfriend?"

"Rocky did. He told everyone."

Kaylee's mouth dropped open. "No way!"

Toby's nod was emphatic bordering on licentious. "Yes, he did. It was in P.E. last year. We were playing basketball and you girls were doing laps and Jeff Garrick said something about . . . well . . ." He faltered and blinked at their chests, particularly Jenny's.

She snatched her jacket closed. "And what did Rocky say? Tell me exactly."

And Toby, being Toby, could do just that thanks to the flawless memory that made him the envy of every kid in school.

"He said, *Yeah, Jenny Forrester may only be a kid but she doesn't stuff her bra,* and Jeff asks, *Yeah, so how do you know?* and Rocky says, *Because these hands don't lie —*" here Toby paused to waggle his fingers lewdly and Jenny almost smacked him. "And Cody Devons tells him he's full of it, and Rocky says that he is not, that you've let him go almost all the way —"

Jenny screeched in outrage. "That lying scumbucket! I have not! I wouldn't let him touch me if he was the last boy on earth!"

"I'm just telling you what he said," Toby cried, backing off still further.

"What else?" Eva prompted.

"A bunch of stuff . . . like about how ever since her mom went to the hospital her dad can't control her and she runs wild and *she* was chasing after *him,*" Toby said in a rush.

He was speaking to Eva instead of Jenny, maybe because Eva looked a tad less likely to kill the messenger. Jenny certainly felt like killing someone, but if she was making a list the first person on there would definitely be one Reginald "Rocky" Neeman. With maybe Jeff Garrick as a runner-up.

"That is all *so* not true!" she spat, tears of fury and shame burning her eyes. "What a . . . what a . . ." Words failed her.

"Asshole," Eva supplied.

"Yes!" Jenny spun toward the front door of the arcade and raised her voice to its most hectoring shout. "You're an asshole, Rocky Neeman!"

Several kids were standing on the sidewalk, and most of them laughed. But it was a mean-spirited laugh directed more at her than at Rocky, and she just knew that he'd spread his dumb lie to everyone in school and now they all thought she was mad because he was dumping her or something.

"I'll show him," she grumbled. "He'll be sorry."

"What are you going to do?" Kaylee leaned forward, avid at the prospect of some sort of revenge being dished out on her brother.

"I don't know yet."

"Jenny . . ." Toby began. "Look, hey, I'm . . . I didn't mean . . ."

"That's okay, Toby, it's not your fault."

"You . . . uh . . . want to come up the street with me and get a donut? My treat."

"No." She looked at Eva and Kaylee, and sighed. "I'm going home."

"Don't go!" Kaylee protested. "Maybe all the stupid boys believe Rocky's crap, but we know better!"

"I'm going home," Jenny repeated. She zipped up her jacket, burrowed her chin down into the collar, and crossed the street into the grassy Square.

So that's what people thought about her. Wild girl, out of control. Desperate enough to go after Rocky, for pete's sake. And that stuff about her mother . . . that was a low blow.

Her breath hitched once as she passed Agate River Books and Coffee, Mr. Edwards' shop. Inside, a single light was on over the coffee bar, and she could see Toby's parents sitting side by side on the stools.

They looked nothing like her own parents, being black and old and everything, but she could still remember how it used to be at her house when both Mom and Dad were there. Never mushy, but there had always been an absent-minded comfortable warm affection between them.

Thinking about Mom only made Jenny nudge even closer to crying. She tried to put it out of her mind as she hurried onto the woods path leading home. It wasn't easy, because now that she'd started she couldn't help wondering what her mother was doing right this minute.

Did they still strap her down?

Dad said no, he said they were even considering moving her to something called a 'less-restrictive environment.' They didn't have to keep her in the rubber room anymore, if they even still used rubber rooms.

A single tear trickled down her face, startling her. She stopped inside the shelter of the woods and scrubbed angrily at her eyes with her sleeves.

"Hey."

Jenny drew in a whistling breath and almost jumped clear out of her skin.

Eric Raney was leaning against a tree, one foot propped up behind him, his dark hair a tumble over his pale forehead. He was cleaning his fingernails with a small pocketknife. "S'up?"

"Uh . . . eh . . . Eric?" she stammered.

"Yeah."

"Um . . . hi."

"Hi. S'matter?"

"Nothing!"

"You got eyeliner and stuff . . ." he flapped a hand in the general direction of her eyes.

Jenny clapped her hands over her face and felt the smeary residue of eyeshadow, mascara, and eyeliner. Mortified, she pawed at it but realized she was only making it worse.

"Here." He fished in his back pocket and came up with a tissue.

She was so astounded that she couldn't even move when he came right up to her – Eric Raney only a foot from her! – and started wiping away the makeup.

Eric Raney touching her! Eva and Kaylee would never believe it!

And then without warning, she burst into tears all over again.

"Hey," he said, an expression of concern rather than a greeting this time. "Jenny . . ."

Eric Raney knew her name!

She sobbed all the harder.

He handed her the tissue and she cried into it, more humiliated than ever. Crying, and she was probably leaking snot, too! Of all the times for the dam to break!

"I miss my mom," she hiccupped through her weeping. "I want her to come home!"

"Yeah?"

"It's just not the same anymore, with her in the hospital and Jerry at college. I love Dad, but even when he's there he's not all there."

"That's rough."

"And half the time he doesn't even notice I'm around. No matter what I do, he never pays attention. Mom would never let me go out dressed like this."

"S'okay, Jenny. You don't have to worry about it any more."

She looked up at him, into copper-colored eyes that were dark as blood in the forest night. "Really?"

"Really. Promise."

Something happened then, something that Jenny couldn't understand. It was as if a towering wave rushed against the shore of her mind, and carried her away into a cold black sea.

*   *   *

Saturday,

September 13

1

"Dawn, it's time to go."

The words, spoken in an icy tone, trickled into Dawn Jessec's consciousness. She raised her head from her hands and looked blankly at the woman standing in front of her for several seconds, before recognition came.

"Mom . . . no, I can't, I can't leave him."

"The doctors say there's nothing you can do by sitting here and being in their way." Eleanor Jessec's voice remained cold and without compassion as she held out Dawn's purse.

"He needs me. He's my baby and he needs me." Dawn pushed the purse out of the way, because it blocked her view of her son.

She could barely see him anyway, covered as he was with tubes and wires. She had no idea what all the machines were for, only understanding that they were keeping Richie alive.

Which meant they were already doing much better than his own mother, who'd nearly let him die.

A sob tore its way up her throat. She rose from the hard plastic chair and moved to the edge of the crib.

"Dawn —" Eleanor said.

"I can't leave him, don't you understand?"

"You should have thought of that a week ago!"

"El," Peter Jessec said, taking his wife's arm. "That's not going to help."

"Well, maybe it needs to be said!"

"What? What needs to be said?" Dawn dashed tears from her eyes and turned to face her parents. "That it's my fault?"

"Nobody's saying that —" Peter began, but Eleanor cut him off.

"If the shoe fits."

Dawn gaped at her. "Mom . . . how can you be so awful? I didn't mean for him to get hurt!"

"You didn't mean to get pregnant, you didn't mean to have that no-good son of a bitch walk out on you, you didn't mean to drop out of school . . . a lot of things happen that you claim not to mean, Dawn Elaine!"

"I hate you!" she screamed. "Get out of here, go away, I hate you!"

Eleanor raised a hand to slap her, but Peter moved between them. "Everybody's upset," he said. "Let's just calm down and not be doing this!"

"Don't you take her side this time, Peter Jessec!" Eleanor's eyes flashed sparks. "You always take her side, and look what it's gotten us. A spoiled junkie dropout whore of a daughter, and a grandson who'd be better off dead!"

"Get out!" Dawn screamed again, at the top of her lungs.

A nurse pushed through the crowd of curious people that were gathering in the hall, all of them drawn by the shouting. Elsewhere in the hospital wing, children and babies began to cry. They were disturbing everyone in the place . . . everyone except Richie. Because even with all that was going on, Dawn couldn't help seeing how he kept lying there, not moving, not responding.

Her mother was ranting at the nurse now, who had his hands full trying to deal with the outpourings of venom. Her father was doing his best to help. Dawn ignored them all and returned to the crib.

She reached in, careful not to touch any of the tubes and wires, and ran her finger along his little arm. Her heart twisted at the touch of his smooth skin. It was pink now, not blue-grey like it had been when she'd pulled him out of the wading pool.

The memory stabbed her as viciously as ever, undulled by the passage of a week.

It hadn't even been that much. An afternoon with some of her friends. One afternoon. Not even a whole day. One afternoon away from the dreary reality in which Bobby Arliss had jumped in his piece-of-shit pickup and roared out of Joshua Flats two days after she'd told him she was pregnant. One afternoon away from the trailer that captured the desert heat and turned the interior into an oven even with fans spinning in every open window.

Only that . . . and when she'd come home, happy and excited and feeling like her old self for the first time in months, she'd found Mrs. Modesto asleep on the couch, the back door ajar, and Richie gone.

Hands were on her arm. She looked around and saw the nurse.

"Miss Jessec, visiting hours are done. You can come back tomorrow at ten."

Coming from him, it didn't sting the way it did coming from her mother. Dawn nodded, mute, glancing over her shoulder. Her parents had already left, and the crowd in the hall had dispersed.

"You'll call me if . . . if . . ."

"Right away," he promised. "Don't worry. We're taking good care of him."

Dawn could hear her mother's voice adding something to the effect that at least *they* were, but she shoved it out of her thoughts and mustered up a weak smile for the nurse. "Thank you."

She left the room, already aching to see her baby again. He had been in the pediatric I.C.U. for six days, only moved to a private room today, and she'd spent several hours sitting in that chair, watching him, silently pleading with him to wake up, to move, to open his eyes and be glad to see her. To forgive her.

The long vigil made itself apparent to her as she walked down the hall. Her legs and back were stiff, her stomach a growling cavern. She had no appetite, it seeming so wrong to want to eat, sleep, and do other things when Richie could only sleep the deep dead sleep of his coma.

Her parents were nowhere in sight, and Dawn wasn't surprised. Things had been getting better, Richie's sweet-natured charm endearing him even to Eleanor, but now . . .

Unable to bring herself to leave, unable to face the empty trailer where all of Richie's second-hand toys would be waiting, Dawn headed for the elevator.

"Excuse me, Dawn Jessec?"

The woman who'd addressed her was short and slender, but carried herself confident as a queen. Although she wasn't wearing a white coat to give it away, Dawn instinctively knew that she was a doctor.

"Yeah?" she asked nervously.

Here it came . . . they hadn't told her much about Richie's condition that she could understand, but this would be it, this strawberry-blonde who looked like she'd never made a mistake in her life was about to break the news that Dawn had been most dreading to hear.

"I'm Dr. McGuire," the woman said. "I'd like to talk with you, if you have a few moments. Could I buy you a cup of coffee?"

"It's about Richie, isn't it? If he's going to die, just tell me, don't try and break it to me gently." She got the words out without breaking into tears, but it was close.

"It is about Richie, but not what you're thinking. Please. Let's go to the cafeteria and talk."

Dawn followed her uncertainly. "I haven't seen you before."

"I don't work at this hospital. One of the neurologists contacted me, and I flew down this morning from Eureka to consult on Richie's case."

The elevator arrived, and squashed into that small moving box with a bunch of other people Dawn managed to keep her questions to herself. When they were in the cafeteria, each with a cup of the terrible tar-water that passed for coffee, and Dawn with a sandwich so old and stale it might have come over on the *Mayflower*, Dr. McGuire handed her a photograph.

Dawn stared blankly at it. "Nice house."

It was, indeed, a nice house. In fact, it was a gorgeous house, set against a backdrop of trees so green they made Dawn's eyes ache. There was precious little green in Joshua Flats, a wide spot in the road between Mojave and the foothills of the Tehachapis.

"It's called Seacliff," Dr. McGuire said. "It has recently been turned into a school and a home for children like your son."

"What? Like Richie? I don't get it."

"Children suffering from a very specific form of brain damage, the result of oxygen deprivation. As is found in cases of suffocation, strangulation, or drowning."

Dawn listened, trying hard to understand as Dr. McGuire told her about Benjamin Lundquist and his theory of alternate-pathway stimulation, and how she believed it could be put to use to help Richie recover from the accident.

"But I could never afford a place like that," she whispered. "I don't have insurance or anything."

"Seacliff isn't about profit. It's about helping children. Dr. Lundquist feels very strongly about it. For people in your situation, the last thing you need on top of all your other worries is the burden of expensive care."

"You mean it's free?"

"Yes."

Dawn frowned in suspicion. "Did my mother put you up to this? Oh, that's just the sort of thing she'd like, for me to send Richie to the other end of the state where none of us would have to think about him. Just yesterday she was telling me that I was probably *glad* about all this, so that I wouldn't have to take care of him anymore."

Dr. McGuire raised her slim hands. "Miss Jessec, I assure you, I have not spoken to your parents. Only to your son's doctors, and now to you."

"I can't forget about him."

"I'm certainly not asking you to. He is your son, your child. It's only natural that you would want what is best for him. Seacliff may be able to help him, and give him a chance that he won't otherwise have."

"But he needs me. I'm his mother. He knows I'm there, I'm sure he does! If I sent him away, he'd think I didn't love him anymore and he'd die!"

"I won't tell you that I know what you're going through, because I can't. I have never had children, and can only imagine how terrible this must be for you. I've seen many parents in the same situation, torn by conflicting emotions." She sipped her coffee, grimaced, and pushed it away. "Would you consider moving to Trinity Bay?"

Dawn laughed bleakly. "Me? Move? I've lived here all my life!"

"Forgive me for being blunt, but it doesn't seem like you'd be giving up that much."

"I . . ." She was about to argue, then paused. "You're . . . you're right. My mom can't stand me, my dad's no help, I'm not in school . . . I mean, things couldn't get much worse. If Richie really could be in a place like this, where he'd have everything he needs . . . if I could find a job . . ."

For a moment, the tantalizing possibility danced in front of her. A fresh new start in a fresh new place. But then it came crashing down around her like a sculpture of glass.

"I can't," she said.

"Why not? You are over eighteen, even if just barely –"

"And broke. I'm sorry, Dr. McGuire, but how could I do it? I have maybe all of fifty bucks in the bank, and that's not enough for a month's rent here in Hell's Armpit. I don't have a car, and plane tickets –"

"Suppose all of that was taken care of? Your ticket, six months' rent, and a stipend to last you until you've found work and gotten on your feet? What would you say then?"

"I'd say what's the catch?" Dawn replied. "You're offering to do all this for Richie and me, but why? What do you guys get out of it?"

"As I said, Dr. Lundquist is very devoted to helping children like Richie. He understands that a good therapeutic model includes involving the family whenever possible. For many of our students, for varying reasons, it isn't possible. But when we can, we try to be accommodating."

"Yeah?" Dawn said, unconvinced.

Dr. McGuire's cool blue eyes searched Dawn's face, and then she allowed herself a small, wry smile. "And, to be honest, what we get out of it, besides the sense of accomplishment, is to take all the credit for working miracles. We get articles published in psychiatric and medical journals. We get invited to lecture at universities all around the world – I was flown first-class to

Vienna three years ago as the guest of a conference, for example. Compared to that . . ." She spread her hands and shrugged.

"Compared to that, footing my bills for a few months is peanuts," Dawn finished.

"Exactly."

Dawn picked up the photograph again. Trees and water, that *green* so rich that she felt as if she could sink her fingers through the glossy surface and feel it, plush as a mink's pelt.

"No matter what my mom says, I'm not an idiot. I'll do it. I'll do whatever you say."

"I'm glad to hear it. Now, there are arrangements to be made, forms that you'll need to sign to effect Richie's transfer, and we'll want to be sure he's medically cleared to be moved. It should take three or four days. That should give you plenty of time to pack and take care of any business and goodbyes."

"I don't have much of either, or much to pack," Dawn said.

"This is the phone and room number at the hotel where I'm staying," Dr. McGuire said, giving her a slip of paper. "Feel free to contact me with any questions."

"I should give you my number too, then."

"That's all right, I already got it from the hospital's records."

"Oh . . ." That left Dawn feeling nonplussed, but she didn't let it bother her for long. She was already trying to think how she'd broach this with her parents, how they'd react.

As if Dr. McGuire was reading her mind, she said, "Remember, this is your decision. Not your parents'. You are old enough and responsible enough to make it."

"Mom isn't going to see it that way," Dawn said.

"This may sound cold, Miss Jessec, but if your mother is so concerned about the welfare of yourself and Richie, she could have shown it by being more supportive."

It was the same thing Dawn had been hearing from her friends just a week ago, that if her mom was so sure what was good for Richie, why had she kicked Dawn out of the house, refused to give her any money, refused to baby-sit so Dawn could go to school or get a job? But hearing it from an adult, from a doctor, convinced her.

"Now it's up to you to do what needs to be done," Dr. McGuire went on. "For yourself, and for Richie."

Dawn was suddenly and horribly sure that this would be the point at which she woke up, the whole conversation having turned out to be a dream. But Dr. McGuire excused herself and left the table, and Dawn was still there.

She finished her tasteless sandwich and the foul, room-temperature coffee and she was *still* there, still with the photograph of the house and the note with the phone number to prove it.

*   *   *

2

"Looks like an ear infection," Dr. Elliot Shaw said.

Helen Carlyle, who had the soft white hair and sweet face of a cookie-baking grandmother and the disconcertingly taut figure of an aerobics instructor, nodded sagely. "That's what I suspected, but it's good to be sure."

"Antibiotics will take care of it in a few days, and she should be fine." Elliot smiled down at the girl. "You'll be just fine, Mindy."

The child in the bed didn't respond, but her gaze was fixed intently on Elliot's and he didn't doubt that she could hear him. Whether she fully understood or not was another matter, but she was clearly paying attention. She had one arm wrapped tightly around a stuffed giraffe in an eye-watering shade of pink, and the other hand rubbed fitfully at her ear.

"Of course she will." Helen Carlyle smoothed Mindy's hair. "You stay put, and I'll be right back with your medicine. Then it'll be time to get up and dressed, so we can go down to lunch and the playroom."

At the word 'playroom,' an unmistakable brightness came into the child's eyes.

"She seems to be doing well," Elliot murmured as he followed the older woman out of the bedroom.

"Yes, she is. A few weeks ago, she didn't seem to notice or care when anyone came into the room, but now I know she recognizes me. Such a little darling, too. I have a granddaughter about that age."

"Does your family live nearby?"

"Oh, heavens no, they're all in Florida. Which isn't the way things are supposed to be, now, is it? When someone gets to my age, they should be thinking about nice warm retirement communities. And here I am in Trinity Bay."

Her age . . . Elliot knew that she was healthier and more fit than he was. And had far better legs. Tina-Turner-class legs.

"From what I've seen, Florida's loss is Seacliff's gain. The children are lucky to have you."

"I'm lucky to be here. I was a trauma nurse for years, and while it was never boring, there was never much of a long-term connection with the patients. I like this much better. Though I'd be happy to give it up if there were no more little ones who needed us. It's so sad, especially in cases like Mindy's."

"I know what you mean." He did, having read the histories.

Unlike most of the other children at Seacliff, Mindy's condition wasn't the result of an accident. Her father, not wanting the responsibilities of marriage or children, had attempted to suffocate her before her first birthday and pass off her death as SIDS. A neighbor's intervention had saved Mindy's life but hadn't been in time to prevent the damage to her brain.

She'd spent two years in a state-run care home before being accepted into the Seacliff program, and was showing improvement already. After six months, she seemed to be aware of her surroundings, more alert, and have better motor control.

Elliot had no reason to be anything less than impressed by Lundquist's team. The attendants were unfailingly dedicated and devoted to their charges, with none of the apathy and indifference that so frequently affected those who worked with chronic populations.

Then again, they were paid exceedingly well and had a very nice working environment. Plus, as Mindy proved, they were seeing results instead of the same plodding cycle of bad to worse to bad again. Those factors kept them on the job, kept them motivated and optimistic. That, in turn, had a beneficial effect on the children by keeping burnout and turnover low.

He jotted down the prescription amount and dosage, and gave it to Helen. "Would you like me to call it in to a pharmacy?"

"I'm sure our little in-house one can handle it. Thank you, Dr. Shaw." She glanced at it. "And there won't be any problem taking it with her cerebregens?"

"Her what?"

Helen's expression went suddenly guarded, then turned into a placid mask. "With her vitamins. She's on a nutritional supplement."

"There shouldn't be any adverse interactions with vitamins," he said slowly, watching her. "Is she on anything else?"

"There's nothing in the chart."

"No, nothing that I saw."

"I'll run this over to the pharmacy right away." She smiled at him, though Elliot thought it seemed forced, and hurried down the hall.

He stayed where he was, frowning skeptically, then turned and went back to Mindy's room. It was decorated in the same style as David's, but in cream and soft pink with violet and blue accents.

She stirred as he came in, and he went over to say hello. "It's only me, Mindy. Helen will be back in a minute to take you to lunch. I need to check something in your chart."

The chart was in a high rack beside the door. Elliot paged through it, and found the reference to Mindy's daily vitamins. But nothing about any other sort of medication. Nothing mentioning . . . what had the word been?

Cerebregens.

He'd never heard the term before, but it sounded like it had to have something to do with the brain.

At the back of the chart was a form that Elliot recognized, a release like the one he'd signed before admitting David to Seacliff. But as he scanned it, he realized that it wasn't identical. There was an extra paragraph, authorizing the use of "any and all treatments deemed appropriate by the practice team, up to and including newly-developed measures."

Newly-developed.

Experimental?

His frown deepened. The signatures on the release were those of a court-appointed legal guardian – Mindy's parents having been arrested and sentenced – and a judge, as well as two notarized witnesses and Dr. Lundquist himself.

Surely Dr. Lundquist wouldn't advocate the use of untried drug treatments! It was one thing to implement new therapy strategies, but it was something else entirely to fiddle around with the brain chemistry of children!

Elliot had known several doctors in the course of his career whose motto had been "don't hesitate, medicate," opting for drugs as the treatment of first resort. Take care of the symptoms, never mind the underlying cause, whether dealing with physical or mental ailments. He thought of them as quick-fix artists, and in his mind Lundquist just did not fit the breed.

There was one way to find out for sure.

He replaced Mindy's chart and went down the hall to the nurses' station. "Stan?"

"Morning, Dr. Shaw. How's our girl?"

"She's doing fine. It's an ear infection, and we'll get it cleared up in no time. Do you know where Dr. Lundquist is?"

"Dining room. He likes to take meals with the students on the weekends."

"Thanks, I'll see if I can find him there."

"David's ready to go down, if you want to take him with you."

"Good idea."

His son was in bed, but his grumblings and mutterings were at low tide, and he was dressed in a simple pair of cotton pants and a pullover. Unlike Mindy, David gave no sign of knowing he was no longer alone in the room.

"Hey, Davey."

Before going to him, Elliot gave in to a suspicious urge and took down David's chart. Upon seeing that the release was the same one he remembered signing and that nothing was other than he expected, he put it back, feeling ashamed of himself for even thinking what he'd been thinking.

He picked David up from the large crib, and for the first time David did something more than be slack dead weight or struggle. For the first time, he seemed to be making an effort to support himself and hold on, by hooking an arm clumsily around Elliot's neck.

"That's my boy!" Elliot encouraged, hugging David close.

Carrying his son, he passed Stan with a nod and took the elevator to the first floor. There were a dozen students at Seacliff now, including David, and most of them were already in the spacious dining room. Some could sit upright unaided, some needed special seats, but all were clean and well-groomed.

Dr. Lundquist was seated at the head of the table like a proud patriarch. He rose, beaming, as Elliot and David came in.

"Elliot, David, hello! Joining us?"

"I was hoping to talk to you."

"Certainly. But we pulled you away from home on a Saturday, the least we can do is repay the trouble with some lunch." He gestured to a chair, and reached toward the various carafes on the table. "Coffee? Milk? Apple juice?"

Elliot helped one of the staff secure David in one of the modified high chairs, and sat down. "Juice, please."

"I saw Helen. She tells me you've had a look at little Mindy. I do appreciate it."

"No need . . . it's what you pay me for. And I'm happy to help. But about Mindy . . ."

"Ah, here she comes now."

Helen Carlyle brought the girl in, and with the household assembled, breakfast began. Elliot had been at Seacliff mealtimes on occasion before, and was always impressed.

The staff had come, he'd been told, from Dr. McGuire's parents' home in Connecticut when the senior McGuires had closed up Greybridge to take a lengthy world cruise as a retirement present to themselves. They went about their duties with an efficient and nearly invisible skill.

The on-duty attendants gave the children whatever degree of help was needed, from feeding them each bite to simply keeping an eye on the higher-functioning ones. Nothing about the meal was an ordeal, and everyone seemed to accept the varying behavioral peculiarities of the children as a matter of course.

Elliot put his questions to the back of his mind for the time being and concentrated on David. While David made no effort to feed himself, neither did he resist or spit out what Elliot fed him.

"He's doing very well," Lundquist remarked as the staff began to clear the plates away. "The first couple of weeks may have been difficult as he acclimated to the change of environment, but he's already begun to respond to the program."

"If you have a few minutes, I would like to ask you something."

"Shall we go to my office? We'll be having a new student arrive soon, and I'd like to go over the file with you. Dear Gwynne, our Dr. McGuire, is away making the arrangements even now."

Elliot gave David over to Stan Montgomery's care, and accompanied Dr. Lundquist to his private, windowless office in the central section of the house. Along the way, Lundquist continued.

"He'll be the youngest of our children, being less than a year old. And his injury is the most recent. Apparently, he clambered into a neighbor's back-yard wading pool only a week ago, and was underwater for several minutes. Gwynne has faxed me copies of the hospital's records and I'd just like you to take a look at them and give me your opinion as to how soon he could be medically cleared to move."

"All right." Elliot took the papers but didn't immediately look at them. "First, about Mindy."

"Oh, yes. Antibiotics."

"Yes. Which hopefully won't react adversely with her cerebregens." He said it in a deliberate and clipped tone.

Lundquist sighed. "I sense annoyance on your part, my friend."

"Dr. Brockman led me to believe that I was fully conversant with every aspect of the care and treatment these children are receiving. If Mindy is on something that isn't reflected in the chart, I need to know about it. I don't like being kept in the dark, especially when it could have an impact on the health of my patients."

"You're cross, and rightfully so. If it is any consolation, I had been meaning to discuss the cerebregen compound with you anyway."

"I also noticed the release in her chart authorizes you to perform any treatments, tested or untested. What is going on here? What are you doing to these kids?"

"Good heavens, Dr. Shaw, please. My main concern is, and has always been, the best interests of the children. Yes, we obtained agreement to be free to pursue alternate options in some of their cases, but only because of my sincere desire to help them. We are hardly performing unethical deeds willy-nilly, using them as lab animals."

"Then what exactly are you doing?"

"Trying to help. Too often, the FDA and other bodies of officiality delay and delay on approving things that are known to be safe. Much of it is petty bureaucracy, part of it is a fear of litigation, and very little of it has to do with what's best for those most concerned. Our students here come to us from a position of utter hopelessness. Not one of them would otherwise have a chance of leading anything approximating a normal life. Their parents, and in Mindy's case, the courts, agreed that a developmental procedure or medication that might help is better than nothing at all."

Elliot could see his point, albeit grudgingly. "Why wasn't I told before?"

"Precisely because of this very reaction," Lundquist said in a way that succeeded in making Elliot feel three inches tall. "It was my hope that you would come to recognize us for what we are and what we're trying to do, rather than suffer the knee-jerk distrust of so many scientific professionals who should clearly know better."

"But experimental medicine –"

Lundquist sat back and steepled his fingers in front of him. "I'd hardly call it that, after a lifetime's work in perfecting it. But even if I did, you must realize that every breakthrough has to start somewhere. And without a breakthrough, these children will never have an appreciable quality of life. Their young and shining potentials will be otherwise snuffed out, dooming them to institutionalization."

"What, exactly, is it?" Elliot demanded.

"The cerebregen compound? A synthesized and improved version of one of the body's own natural healing agents. Its aim, of course, is to aid in the regeneration of damaged brain tissue."

"A regenerative agent? And it's effective?"

"I could show you PET scans of Mindy's brain, taken before and after we began the treatment. You'd see for yourself the indications of activity in previously dead or dormant areas. This soon, the changes are slight, but they are there. We've all noted the corresponding improvements in her condition."

"My God." Elliot slumped against the back of the chair. "That's . . . that's . . ."

"I share your wonder. Although I have been working on this for more than thirty years, it still awes me to witness the results."

"Then the therapy strategies are ineffective?"

"Hardly! They are necessary. Beneficial on their own, yes, but when used in conjunction with the cerebregens, the effectiveness is dramatically increased. I'd even go so far as to say that a near-full recovery might not be beyond the realms of possibility for many of our children."

"Are all of the students on them?"

"No. Not all of the parents or guardians would consent, and we would never proceed without their full and cognizant permission. It is my hope that they will change their minds once we've compiled enough data to reflect the success we've attained."

"What about David?"

"I fully believe he could greatly benefit from the cerebregens, and it had been my eventual plan to broach the subject with you."

Elliot stared at Benjamin Lundquist, his mind jostling with conflicting thoughts. "I'd have to consider it very carefully. I will also want the full records for the children, and all the information about this compound that you have."

"Fair enough. I shall instruct young Mr. Sorenson to give you password access to the restricted files when he comes in this afternoon, but I shall first require you to sign an agreement of confidentiality and non-disclosure."

"I understand."

"I'm pleased to see that you're able to overcome that knee-jerk distrust. Dr. Shaw. Do pardon my reticence. I've been denounced and decried a few times too often for my tastes." He stood.

Elliot echoed the movement. "I like to make up my own mind, Dr. Lundquist. Once I've had a chance to read the records and research, I'll let you know."

Lundquist smiled confidently. "It will be a privilege to have you on the team, dear fellow. I'll look forward to discussing the matter further."

He offered his hand, and Elliot automatically shook it.

*   *   *

3

Charlie Forrester woke on the couch. He slept there more than in the bed these days, that queen-size expanse too big and too full of memories.

He yawned and stretched, dislodging the blanket that had already almost fallen off him. It slid the rest of the way to the floor. He had a dim recollection of waking cold in the night and dragging it over himself.

The television was on, the volume low so that the cartoon mayhem was robbed of its elemental vitality. Saturday morning cartoons.

Saturday morning.

The clock, a wood-burl piece he'd made himself, chimed the half-hour and he saw that it was only technically Saturday morning for another thirty minutes. He'd slept until almost noon, more than fourteen hours.

Some nights it was like that, other nights he couldn't get a wink. He preferred the oversleeping, because then he didn't have to think. Didn't have to remember.

He got up, joints popping in protest, and shuffled down the hall to the bathroom. He splashed water on his face, raked his unkempt hair and beard with his skinny fingers, and brushed his teeth.

Shower?

Why bother? It was Saturday. He'd be sure to take one tomorrow, before his weekly drive out to Blue Lake to visit Sandy.

Jenny's door was closed. He tapped on it as he passed by on his way to the kitchen.

"Peanut?"

No answer, which didn't surprise him. She would have been up and out long since, not wanting to waste a moment of the precious weekend.

Half a toasted whole wheat bagel and the last of the orange juice sufficed for breakfast. He refilled Bingo's food and water dishes, which brought the mutt capering around instantly.

The blinking red light on the answering machine caught his attention. He kept the ringer turned down, since most of the time he was either asleep or out in his workroom anyway, and if it was important he could get back to people when he was in the right frame of mind. Besides, it kept him from being driven buggy by Jenny's friends calling a dozen times a day.

The messages were probably for her, but he pushed the button anyway.

"You have . . . three . . . new messages," the robotic voice informed him.

"Hi, Jenny, it's Kaylee. Diane says if we're not ready by ten-thirty, she's going to the mall without us. You better be on your way!"

"Ten-eighteen A.M.," the machine said. "Next message."

"Jen-ny, it's me again, where *are* you?"

"Ten-twenty-five A.M. Next message."

"Diane is leaving *right now!*" Pause. "You're not still mad about last night, are you? Call me!"

"Ten-thirty-two A.M. No more messages."

Charlie grunted to himself and erased the tape. "Jenny? Peanut?" he called, raising his voice.

Still nothing but silence, except for Bingo slurping water and the windchime clang of his license against the rim of the dish.

He went back down the hall and stopped at Jenny's door, which was pasted over with Flirty Boys posters and magazine clippings. He knocked.

"Peanut?"

Bingo had padded after him and now cocked his head quizzically.

Charlie hesitated. He and Sandy had always agreed that they wouldn't go poking their noses in the kids' rooms, because kids were people too and had just as much right to privacy as anyone else.

But it was weird she hadn't shown up at Kaylee's house. Jenny never missed a trip to the mall, and hadn't she just been saying something the other day about a new game or album or something that she wanted to pick up?

Maybe she'd gotten there right after.

He went back to the kitchen, searched out the Neemans' number, and dialed.

"Hello, Neeman residence, Chelsea Neeman speaking," a child piped.

"Is Jenny there? Jenny Forrester, Kaylee's friend? This is her dad."

"Kaylee went to the mall."

In the background, a woman asked, "Who is it, Chel-Chel?"

Charlie stood there feeling like an idiot on the other end of the line as Chelsea told her mother who was calling. Then Barb Neeman came on.

"Charlie?"

"Yeah."

"You're looking for Jenny?"

"Yeah . . . she and Kaylee went to the mall?"

"No, Jenny never showed up, so Kaylee and Diane left without her. Kaylee said Jenny was upset last night, but she wouldn't tell me why. Did she talk to you?"

"I haven't seen her," Charlie admitted. "Fell asleep before she got home, and she was gone when I got up."

"If she and Kaylee had a fight, then Jenny's probably just sulking. I'm sure it'll blow over."

"Sorry to bother you."

"Oh, it's no bother, Charlie. When Kaylee gets back, I'll see what I can do to smooth things out."

"Thanks, Barb." He hung up and looked at the phone.

Probably just sulking.

He went back down the hall again and tried the knob. The door opened readily enough, or at least for a few inches before it was stopped by a mound of clothes.

Charlie wormed his head and shoulders through the crack and surveyed a bedroom that looked like a hurricane had blasted through it. There were clothes all over the place, and Beanie Babies, and CD cases, and magazines, and general mounds of *stuff*. The bed was a tangled twist of sheets and blankets, empty.

No Jenny. Not here.

Sulking?

He checked the bathroom, forgetting that he'd just been in there to brush and wash not twenty minutes before. No Jenny there, either.

Jerry's room, full of everything he couldn't fit in his dorm room on campus, was tidier than it had ever been while he still lived at home, and was undisturbed. The master bedroom wasn't anything out of *Good Housekeeping* either, and Jenny hadn't chosen it as a sulky-spot.

The more he thought about it as he wandered his way through the house and out to his workshop, the less sulking in private seemed like Jenny. When she was mad or upset, everybody knew about it.

He stood in the yard midway between the workshop and the house, while

Bingo stuck his head out the doggy door as if wondering what was the matter with the silly human.

Jenny wouldn't stand Kaylee up without a word. Especially not if it meant missing a trip to the mall.

So where was she, then?

A brown car stopped at the foot of the driveway. Charlie was only peripherally aware of it at first, but it gradually seeped into his consciousness that it was one of the Trinity Bay P.D. cruisers.

As he realized that and turned more fully toward it, the driver's side door opened and police chief Damon Blake got out. His smile was dazzling against his chocolate-brown skin, but it didn't reassure Charlie at all.

"Is it Jenny?" he asked before Damon even reached the edge of the driveway.

"What about Jenny? I was passing by and saw you standing here, and wondered what was up."

"Oh . . ." Charlie understood. It was just past twelve now, and Damon Blake made a habit most days of going home for his lunch hour. He half-smiled, relieved. "I thought you had some bad news about Jenny."

"Nosir, why?" Damon's expression shifted to one of concern. "Something wrong?"

"Well . . . she's not here. I don't know where she is."

"You mean Jenny's missing? For how long?"

Charlie shook his head. "Not missing . . . she's just not here."

"Why don't we go inside for a minute and clear this up?"

In the kitchen, Charlie told Damon Blake about Kaylee Neeman's calls, his conversation with Barb, and how he didn't think it was like Jenny to go off and sulk.

"She's never been one for suffering in silence, that's true," Damon agreed. "When did you see her?"

"Last night, around seven I guess."

"So you didn't see her come in?"

"I was asleep. Didn't wake up until almost noon." His brows knit dubiously. "Do you think she didn't even come home?"

"That's what I'd like to know. Where else might she have gone?"

"A friend's house?" Charlie suggested. "But when she stays over, she usually calls, and the only messages were from Kaylee."

"Mind if I borrow your phone? I'd like to do a little asking around."

The tendril of fear was back, creeping along Charlie's spine. "But . . . you don't think anything happened to her?"

"Who else does she chum with?"

"Um . . . I don't know, really, she doesn't bring her friends over that much. There was one, kind of pale looking, black hair, Wednesday Addams –"

"The Mittleschut girl. Let's start there."

Jenny wasn't at the Mittleschut house, but Eva confirmed that Jenny had indeed been upset the night before. She'd left Galaxy West around eight, stating she was going home.

He tried the Edwardses next and got the same story from Toby, with an addendum from Malachi Edwards that he and Ruth had seen Jenny passing their shop just a little bit later, on the route she would have taken from the arcade toward the path that led home.

"But she never made it?" Charlie asked, starting to get more worried now.

Damon smacked his thigh. "I bet she's next door, with Theresa and the kids. Should have thought of that right off."

But she wasn't there, either, and after hanging up the phone Damon Blake turned to Charlie with concern in his coffee-dark eyes.

"Charlie, even though it hasn't been twenty-four hours yet, maybe you'd better consider filing a report."

* * *

4

By three o'clock that Saturday afternoon, the effective network of small-town communication had spread the word from one end of Trinity Bay to the other.

Damon Blake's concern had given way to a deep unease. Something in his gut – cop instinct – told him that this wasn't anything as simple as a case of an upset child trying to give everyone a good scare and get plenty of attention by hiding out.

He had dozens of witnesses who had seen Jenny leaving the Square right around the time the football game finished up. And no one who had seen her since. What with Charlie's unlikely inheritance – a convoluted affair that went back to Charlie's institutionalized wife's childhood friendship with April Cliffwood – the Forresters had become wealthy, and even more well-known in town than they had ever been before.

The question was, where was Jenny now?

"And I thought my room was a pit when I was a teenager," Scott James said, coming into Damon's glassed-in office at the back of the police station bullpen.

Trinity Bay P.D.'s second-in-command was the only member of the Nordic-looking James clan to have topped out well under five-foot-ten. He made up for it with a muscular build that would have been impressive on any man.

"What have you got for me, Scott?"

"I went through the whole mess, couldn't find the clothes that her friends said she was wearing, her jacket, or her purse. It doesn't look like she got home at all."

"Ideas?"

"Well, she could have gotten lost," Scott said, but his expression stated that he didn't buy it any more than Damon did. "But Damon, Jenny Forrester's been using that path all her life, could probably do it blindfolded."

"My thoughts exactly. So we've got to figure that she either didn't go home on purpose, or . . ." He couldn't bring himself to voice the rest.

"Or someone nabbed her," Scott finished.

"It's a possibility," Damon said. "One I sure as hell don't like to think about, but it is. Even in Trinity Bay."

"She could have taken off on her own," Scott said. "Going on impulse. Jerry's not the only one in the family with a dramatic streak."

Damon nodded. "I'll see if I can get in touch with the driver on last night's Green Line route."

"Speaking of Jerry, has anyone tried him?"

"Haven't been able to get hold of him yet." Damon grinned humorlessly. "Every time I call the dorm, I get some fool who thinks I'm playing a joke. I may just have to mosey on down there and look into it personally."

"So what's my next move?"

"Have Chet Underwood bring his dogs, and see what you can turn up in the woods. I've got Kel McGuire talking with the kids to make sure we haven't missed anything. I'm going to make a few more calls."

"On my way." Scott headed out.

Damon called Green Line, and got the name of the driver who'd handled the Trinity Bay route the previous night. The man had no recollection of a girl of Jenny's description, and said that no one had even gotten on the bus at that stop.

Next, Damon called Theresa at the Forrester house where she was staying with Charlie, and asked her to check if Jenny's bike was there. It was, leaning against the wall of the workshop where it almost always stayed; Jenny claimed riding a bike was for little kids, not nearly-teenagers, and was 'uncool.'

No bus, no bike. And taxis were out, because Trinity Bay was not New York City.

Damon tapped his pen on the desk, pattering out complex rhythms without being aware of them.

Jenny. He knew her pretty well, as she lived just down the hill, played with Lora, and babysat the twins every now and then. He doubted she would have tried hitching a ride; she was too worldly-wise for that, even for a small-town kid.

The bell over the door jingled with a merry sound incongruous to a day that was shaping up right grim. The bell had been installed by one of his predecessors, and Damon had never bothered to have it taken down despite Scott's aggrieved insistence that it made the police station sound like an old-timey general store.

Sometimes, Damon had found, being viewed as a hick cop was an advantage, especially when he really wasn't.

Tom Harmon came in, shaking off water like a rangy greyhound brought in from the storm. "Afternoon, Chief Blake."

"Tom," Damon acknowledged, taking a moment to marvel at the changes that had come over the bartender in the past year. "How's the boat?"

"That's what I came to see you about. But first, something going on? Half the town's staking out the Bar and Grill, looks like."

"We've got a missing kid."

"Aww, no." Tom grimaced. "Which one?"

"Charlie Forrester's girl."

"Anything I can do to help?"

"Right now we're doing all we can, but thanks. What brings you in, Tom?"

"Nothing that can't wait, not when you've got something a whole lot more important to do. Unless you maybe have a form I could fill out, for stolen property?"

Damon opened a drawer and rooted for the appropriate piece of paperwork. "Sure. What's going on?"

"I drove up to Crescent City yesterday for a boat show, and when I came back, I found someone stole my dinghy."

"Off of the *Harmony?*"

"That's right. Lines weren't worn through. Untied, and coiled up nice and neat."

"That's downright peculiar, Tom." In times of stress as well as in times of good humor, Damon often found himself taking on a drawl more befitting a gunslinger sheriff of the Old West. It earned him a lot of flack, but helped him collect his mind.

"Don't I know it! But I'm still counting myself lucky, because whoever did it could have made off with the whole boat!" He accepted the form. "Mind if I sit down and fill this out?"

"Have a seat." Damon waved at Scott's unoccupied desk. "Just shove the clutter out of the way, and mind you don't get buried in pictures of Dani Kensington."

Tom chuckled. "Can't fault the boy's taste, now, can we? I'm glad to see Dani getting serious about someone. Nothing pleased me more than being able to sell her the bar. Have you seen it? She's really fixing the place up, too."

"I have. A fine job."

So fine, in fact, that Damon could almost forget that Dani Kensington had once tried to blow his head off with an antique shotgun in that very bar.

*　　*　　*

5

"Mr. Neeman," Kel McGuire said with all the patience he could muster, "I'd like to talk to Rocky, please. Just to Rocky."

John Neeman, who looked like a provincial and ponderous corn-fed farmboy, leaned forward in his chair so fast that it squawked on the linoleum. His words fired out of him as if expelled from a rapid-fire staple gun.

"Rocky's never been in trouble a day in his life. I'm well aware of our legal rights in this matter. I know people. I have a lawyer."

"John, please," Barb Neeman said, but with no real strength.

Rocky curled his lip in a sneer. "I didn't do anything."

"No one is saying you did. I'm just talking to anyone who saw Jenny last night, to try and figure out what happened."

"Isn't it obvious?" John Neeman said. "That girl is wild, out of control. Father can't set limits, and with the mother in the lockdown ward, the girl can get away with anything." He scowled with such bitterness that Kel was taken aback.

"Did you see Jenny last night?" Kel said, speaking solely to Rocky.

"You don't have to answer, Rock. You have rights." John looked defiantly at Kel. "He has rights."

"Did you talk to her?"

"Yeah, so what if I did?"

"This has gone far enough," the senior Neeman declared. "You can't put my son through the third degree like this. We'll sue you for every nickel you have. Don't think I don't know how. I've sued people before. Plenty of them."

"I'm not here accusing your son of anything. Let's focus on the important thing here, which is that a girl seems to be missing." Kel's patience frayed a little more.

"The important thing is that you're badgering my son and I won't have it!"

"I understand."

"Good."

"Now, Rocky, I've heard Jenny was upset last night. Any idea why she might have been?"

"Because she's a brat, a baby, and a tease," Rocky said. "Everybody knows it. I was trying to be nice, but she had to go and make fun of me."

"That won't be tolerated, McGuire," John Neeman said. "People making fun of my son . . ."

"What happened?" Kel asked Rocky, ignoring the father.

"I asked her if I could buy her a soda but she already had one." He sat back and crossed his arms as if that was all that needed be said.

"What have you been telling the guys in P.E. class about her?" Kel asked.

"*Objection!*" John Neeman roared, slamming his fist on the table. His wife jumped and uttered a little scream, and four of the daughters still living at home peeked in from the living room.

"We're not in court, Mr. Neeman."

"We will be if you keep this up! What are you insinuating? And who does this girl think she is, snubbing my Rocky? She should be flattered! Rocky could date any girl he wanted! If she didn't have money —" He broke off, his face florid.

"I think you've answered all my questions for now," Kel said. "Sorry to trouble you."

"What's that supposed to mean?" John demanded.

"My home, office, and cell phone numbers are on this card if you think of anything else." He nodded to Mrs. Neeman, who looked stricken and embarrassed, and went out to his car.

Just before he started the engine, he heard someone calling him. "Mr. McGuire? Mr. McGuire!"

He saw eighteen-year-old Sarah Neeman running toward his car. He rolled down the window, letting in the rain.

She leaned in and spoke quietly but urgently. "Dad told Rocky that he should date Jenny Forrester, because when she turns eighteen she gets her share of the trust fund from the Cliffwood estate and everything, you know?"

Kel nodded.

"Dad's always trying to hit it big. Lawsuits, the lottery, get-rich-quick books, you name it. He hates Charlie Forrester, says it's not fair that *he* works so hard and Mr. Forrester doesn't do anything, and then the Cliffwood fortune lands in his lap."

"It must really annoy him that Charlie Forrester turned right around and gave most of the money away."

Sarah bobbed her head, wide-eyed. "Oh, sure! Giving those big settlements to Dani Kensington, and the Haverley kids . . . I think Dad wishes one of *us* had gotten hurt or killed so he could have collected on it! I don't know if it means anything, but I just wanted to tell you what Dad said about Rocky and Jenny."

She backed away from the car and Kel rolled up his window again.

"Paranoia, grandiosity, and a gold-digger to boot," he said aloud into the rain-drumming hush. "Very nice."

He drove back toward town, the beginnings of a headache throbbing in his temples. By the time he had gone through downtown Trinity Bay and headed onto Vista Beach Drive, it had firmly entrenched itself.

Vista Beach Drive was one of the more inaptly-named streets he'd ever encountered. The beach was not part of the 'vista,' and the 'drive' was a badly potholed stretch of asphalt that turned into a jouncy bed of gravel a half mile from the Raney residence.

His cellular phone buzzed and he tucked it in the cradle of chin and shoulder, getting an immediate crick in his neck to go with the headache but not daring proceed without both hands on the wheel. No wonder most places wanted to make this illegal.

"Mr. McGuire? This is Diane Neeman, you were just at our house?"

She was whispering, and he had the sudden image of the sixteen-year-old hunched with her hand cupped over the phone.

"This is nuts . . . I don't know if I should be telling you . . . it's probably nothing . . . but my father –"

He hit a pothole roughly the size of an open grave and the phone clattered into the foot well on the passenger side. Kel braked and leaned over to retrieve it.

"Diane? Are you still there?"

"Don't you believe me?"

"I didn't hear you. I dropped the phone. What about your father?"

"He didn't get home last night until almost two in the morning," she said in a breathless flood. "And I know it's stupid, but I . . . I had to tell someone."

"Diane –"

"Can't talk now!" she hissed, and then in a louder, phony voice, laughed and said, "Okay, Vickie. Okay! Later! See ya! Bye!"

Click.

Kel put the phone back and sat in the idling car for a moment, rubbing his chin and thinking. When he came to plenty of troubling conclusions but no satisfactory ones, he put the car in gear and continued down Vista Beach Drive.

*　　*　　*

6

"Oh, hell," Chet Underwood said, staring at the ground.

Scott James hurried up to him, fast as he could without slipping in the mud. One misstep here, and he'd be going headlong down the sharply slanted embankment that plunged from the side of the bluff down to the proverbial jagged rocks below.

"Find her?"

Even as he asked it, he knew it couldn't be the case, because the dogs were picking their way down the steep slope, barking as if shouting their progress reports to each other.

As he reached Chet's side, Scott looked down and saw it right away.

A track. A single footprint.

It was the first distinguishable one they'd found. The rain had been coming down steadily all afternoon, erasing what little would show up on the sodden bed of leaves and needles and wiping out most of the scent-trail too. Underwood's dogs had spent the past hour casting around determinedly but with little to show for it.

But here was a track, protected from the elements by virtue of being in the shelter of a leaning tree. Runnels of muddy water flowed to either side of it, but it had been spared just long enough.

The track was not from a child's shoe. It was too big, too deep. A man's print.

"Ground's soft here but not that soft," Chet said. "The way it's pressed down . . . either a real heavyweight or he was carrying something."

"Oh, hell," Scott said, echoing Underwood's words because he shared the sentiment. "Headed which way?"

"Down toward the beach, is my guess. But someone'd have to be nuts to try that slope carrying a twelve-year-old, especially in this weather."

"It wasn't raining hard last night. An agile person could have done it. But if not, where would be the best place to look for . . . anything that might have washed up?" Scott mentally cringed at the prospect of finding a waterlogged, battered body.

"Over at the marina breakwater, most likely."

"You got your plaster kit in your truck?"

"Like American Express, I don't leave home without it." Chet turned and hollered back to his son. "Kirby! Bring the kit!"

"Great. Get me a cast of this before it erodes, thanks."

Chet beamed, delighted that his Sasquatch hobby was proving so unexpectedly useful. He spent his vacations backpacking into the wilderness, armed with cameras, tranquilizer darts, and of course his plaster kit for making casts of alleged Bigfoot-prints. Never mind that the whole thing had been repeatedly debunked and declared a hoax. Chet refused to believe it.

Well, everyone had to have a hobby . . .

Scott radioed Officer Avery Scribner, who was heading the search party that had fanned out from the head of the trail to move systematically into the woods. He relayed to Avery what they had found, and what his and Chet's conjectures were.

"Jesus Christ," Avery said. "Who's going to tell Charlie?"

"I want to have something more than one footprint to go on before we tell him anything," Scott said. "Same goes for your uncle."

Though Avery didn't say anything, Scott could feel the other man's embarrassment coming over the radio. His uncle, Lan Scribner seemed to think that having one blood relative on the town's police force and another as the mayor gave him an inside scoop and first dibs on what few newsworthy events happened in Trinity Bay. The fact that Avery also got a little loose-lipped when he'd had one too many at Nate's didn't help.

"No problem, Scott. Not one word. Scout's honor."

"We could be on the wrong trail here, in fact I hope we are. But meanwhile, I'm headed for the marina."

He hooked the radio back on his belt and started down the embankment.

*   *   *

7

Without taking his eyes from the screen, Brian Sorenson reached into the bag of Cheetos resting atop the printer. Plastic crinkled, but instead of encountering any cheesy lengths of snack food, all he found were a few nuggets and crumbs.

"Damn."

He looked into the bag, licking specks from the ends of his orange-tinted fingers, but the visual only confirmed what he'd already found by touch.

Empty.

His stomach rumbled. He wiped his fingertips on his pants, and drained the last of a stale Coke from the can.

The digital clock set into the bottom corner of his monitor informed him that he'd been working nonstop for four hours. His last break had been when he'd gone down to the staff lounge for the Coke after reprogramming Dr. Shaw's key card to access the restricted files.

Deciding to finish the program first, Brian ignored his complaining belly and hunched over the keyboard, rattling out the last several strokes.

His chair was wheeled and the carpet in his office was covered wall-to-wall in plastic mats, enabling him to give one hard push and roll across to the other computer workstation that took up the rest of the office. This machine was his spare from home, as evidenced by the *Dork Tower* screensaver. Every few seconds, the image changed to display another panel he'd scanned from his collection of the comic books.

He logged on briefly while his work computer was processing the new program, sent some messages confirming that he'd be at a role-playing chat later that night, and switched everything off with a great sigh of relief.

To think, they paid him for this!

With everything done, he was finally ready to pay attention to his hunger. And his need to pee.

His office was on the second floor of Seacliff, at the inside near corner of the west wing. The view wasn't the greatest, since it mostly showed the back wall of the atrium and the east wing, but it didn't matter to Brian because the high side of his computer desk blocked most of it anyway.

Nor did he much care that the room was paneled in wood, except that it meant he'd needed to use gum-tack instead of thumbtacks to put up the posters of Jeri Ryan, Sarah Michelle Gellar, and his other dream girls.

Dr. Lundquist and Dr. McGuire had been very clear that they didn't care how he decorated the office, or what his personal dress code was, within reason – meaning no Starfleet uniform or furry hobbit feet. Fair enough. Brian could live with that.

He went into the hall. The west wing was quiet, most of the rest of the staff being at work in their own offices or over in the east wing tending to the students.

The bathroom was groaningly opulent, with an outer sitting room complete with rose-pink couch and multiple mirrors above a long marble counter pocked with four sinks. And this was just on the floor where the offices were. Upstairs, where the live-in staff slept, each suite consisted of bedroom, parlor, and bath. His first glimpse of them had made Brian wish he'd given more thought to the offer, instead of electing to stay in his cramped Birdwood Lane apartment.

One order of business taken care of, Brian poked his nose into the lounge. The coffee pot was half-full, and he knew from experience that the fridge would be well-stocked with the various staff members' favorite brands of juice, soda, and mineral water.

His own cubby was in need of replenishing; the Cheetos had been the last of his cache except for one lonely packet of microwave popcorn and a snack-size ring-tab can of peaches.

No good. He was hungry for real food, something hot and substantial. He headed for the center of the house, where the brass elevator that looked like it should be jerky and rattly instead descended with silent smoothness.

The small staff kitchen, less than a third the size of the industrial one in the east wing, was in what had once been Seacliff's conservatory. No effort had been made in here at least to keep to the old-fashioned style. Everything was gloss-black, pearly white, and gleaming chrome.

Aiden Ferguson was busy at the stove, stirring something that smelled like clam chowder. Brian hesitated, not wanting to startle her. He was trying to think of the best way to alert her to his presence when she turned to get the pepper shaker, saw him, and gasped. The shaker hit the floor and bounced.

"It's only me, sorry," Brian said.

Her eyes skittered quickly to his face and away. "I was making soup for everyone," she said, making it sound like an apology.

"It smells great." He tried to exude harmlessness, but he was inept around girls at the best of times, and she was even more shy than he was. Which, had anyone told him in advance, he would have sworn was impossible.

She bent and snatched up the pepper shaker, then used a damp paper towel to blot the spilled flecks from the tile.

Realizing she wasn't going to say anything, Brian attempted to continue the conversation. "Can I help?"

"Oh, that's okay, I've got it, really."

"I think there's some French bread in the pantry," he suggested. "I could slice that while you finish the soup."

"Um . . . okay." She stared into the pot as intently as a medium looking for the future in a teacup.

"So, how do you like Trinity Bay?" he asked as he got the bread and a knife from the block on the counter.

"It's very pretty here."

"I grew up here," he said. "My dad works at the mill, my mom teaches fourth grade, my sister works at the donut shop, and my uncle's a mechanic."

She nodded to show she'd heard, but didn't volunteer anything in return.

The silence was awful. To his surprise, Brian found himself filling it by talking freely about the first things that popped into his head. Why he'd chosen a career in computers, for instance. The shows he watched, almost obsessively.

And she seemed interested, or gave the impression of it out of politeness, which was a lot better than the eye-rolling scorn he was accustomed to encountering. Talking about his real interests – gaming, comics, and *Star Trek* – was usually a sure-fire way of assuring that a girl would never want to be around him again.

She even responded. "I watch that show sometimes."

Brian couldn't believe his ears. "Really? Which one? *TNG, DS9, Voyager, Enterprise –*"

Aiden drew in on herself like a turtle, and he could have kicked himself.

"Sorry," he said. "I don't meet many people in real life who like the things I do."

"Real life?" she ventured tremulously.

"Yeah . . . in person, instead of online. I've been to a couple conventions, though. That's one problem with Trinity Bay. It's so far away from everything. The nearest good game store is in Eureka, even. There's a game club on campus every Friday night, but I've been trying to get a group together here in town."

"What kind of game? Like *Monopoly?*"

"No, role-playing games. Like *Dungeons and Dragons.*"

A glimmer of recognition lit her pale grey eyes, and Brian hurried onward before recognition could turn to the old familiar wariness.

"I know what you're thinking and it's not like that. All the stuff about people going nuts, running around in the sewers, killing themselves, stuff like that. It's crap. We're not that way. My dad sure thought so, though. He was convinced I was going to end up a suicidal devil-worshipper. Put me in counseling over it. But it's just not true. Gamers have a *lower* suicide rate than the rest of our age groups, are better adjusted. It's all problem-solving, isn't it?"

She blew him out of the water. "My father used to play those games."

"No way. Your *father?* You're kidding me!"

"He did," she said, once more sounding like she was apologizing. "Three or four of his friends would come over every weekend and play for hours. They had books, and tons of dice, and little painted figures."

"Did you ever play?"

"I was too young." Her head bowed, letting her hair fall forward like a beige curtain. "Then he . . . he died."

"Wow, but he was a gamer!" Brian grimaced when he realized how he'd sounded. "Oops. I mean, sorry. But hey, if I do get this game started . . . you want to play too?"

"Me?"

"Sure, why not?"

"I don't know how."

"It's easy. The rulebooks might look complicated at first, but once you get going, it's a snap. I've even got this idea for a cliffhanger adventure, you know, like Indiana Jones?"

He shut up as he realized she was retreating into her shell. Her breathing had quickened into near-frantic puffs and her hands were working convulsively at each other. She looked like she was about to have a full-blown panic attack.

"Sorry," he said again. "I get carried away."

Gradually, as he continued not saying anything and busied himself with the bread, her breathing returned to normal. He'd known plenty of shy people, even was one, but this . . . this was extreme. For a minute there he thought she was going to faint or run or something.

Her posture changed suddenly to one of alertness. Brian followed her gaze, out the kitchen window and across the garden. It was starting to get dark, the cloud-heavy sky taking on a peculiar dying glow.

The wide grassy space at the back of the house was too big to be called a lawn, but not wild-grown enough to be a meadow. At the far edge, near the bone-and-ash spot where a large rosebush had once been burned, a group of men had just emerged from the woods.

Even at this distance, in their rain slickers, Brian recognized one of them. It was impossible not to, the way that one lurched grimly along.

"Oh, man, Lucas Gordon," he groaned. Sensing Aiden's inquisitive look, he elaborated. "School bully when I was growing up."

She looked out the window again, her fine brow furrowing. "Was he an athlete?"

Brian laughed ruefully. "You'd think, wouldn't you? Me being king of the geeks and all. But no. See the way he limps? He fell, did something to his spine when he was a kid. Had to wear a back brace, leg braces. He's supposed to use crutches but sometimes he just won't. He was always trying to beat the snot out of us scrawnier kids, and we weren't supposed to hit back."

"Did you?"

"What, hit back?"

"Yes."

"Once . . . but I was provoked. I took one of my starship models for show-and-tell, and he hit it off my desk with his crutch. Smashed it. So I called him a —" Brian faltered, not quite capable of saying 'dickhead' in front of Aiden. "I called him a name, and he took a swing at me. I hit him in the gut. Not even a very good hit. But it knocked him down and he had to get five stitches in his scalp."

"Did you get in trouble?"

He nodded emphatically. "Oh, yeah. The teacher, my mom, Lucas' folks, they all had their turns yelling at me. But my dad and uncle couldn't have been happier. I'd been in a fight. Mixed message city."

She gazed out the window again, as the group of men split up, some heading back into the woods, others starting across the meadow toward the house. "But what are they doing, what do they want?" she asked nervously.

"Good question. Let's go find out."

*   *   *

8

Lucas saw Brian Sorenson approaching, and the familiar anger bubbled up inside him.

His legs felt like chunks of meat with long slivers of glass replacing the bones. His backache was a corset of ice and fire no matter how tightly he cinched the brace. He was soaked, tired, hungry, and generally pissed at the world.

Still, he kept plodding doggedly, determined to keep up with Bruce Garrick and the others as Avery Scribner led the rest of the searchers back into the woods. He would show them. Despite the wet, muddy, treacherous ground, he would show them he could hang in there. And that he could do it without the hated crutches.

But it would have to be Brian Sorenson coming to meet them. Smug, smartass Brian Sorenson. It had been over ten years since Brian had socked him, but the memory rankled more with each passing day.

He'd been glad when he'd finally gotten someone to take a swing at him instead of holding off on account of him being a gimp. But the way the script was written in Lucas' mind had called for him to then rise up and whale the living hell out of the other guy, *proving* once and for all that he was as able as anybody.

It did *not* call for him to go down after one punch! One lame sissy-ass punch! Not to the tune of five stitches, a ride in the ambulance, and an overnight in the hospital because his hysterical father was convinced he had a skull fracture.

Bruce Garrick stopped and hailed Brian. Lucas trudged five more paces to show he wasn't so tired he'd grab at the first chance to rest like the other guys. He halted with his knees locked so they wouldn't dump him to the ground.

Lucas glowered, deliberately not looking at Brian while Bruce explained about the missing girl. But the strength and sharpness of his glower faded as he began to get the creepy feeling of being watched.

Brian wasn't paying any attention to him. Why would he? Brian was a success now. Brian didn't live with his parents anymore. Lucas would have to put up with his Chihuahua-nervous dad until the day he died . . . or, preferably, the day *Dad* died. Brian had turned his nerdy computer obsession into a sweet job at Seacliff, while Lucas was still working at the pet shop, and he didn't even like animals.

No, Brian could ignore Lucas with impunity.

But *someone* wasn't ignoring him, not now.

Oh, he'd always been able to know when they were watching him, talking about him, laughing behind their hands, mocking him. He didn't have to catch them to know when it was happening. He could feel it.

Just as he felt it now. Someone was watching him.

As casually as he could, he looked toward Seacliff. Its many windows shimmered with the rain that rippled down their panes, making it impossible for him to tell if anyone was standing there.

Concealed but watching. Snide and hateful. Watching.

A girl was on the back terrace in a light blue hooded raincoat, but though she was looking in their direction, it wasn't her stare that he sensed.

Wait . . .

He was sure he saw movement at one of the windows after all. A dark shape, on the second floor of the west wing. Standing in a way that even suggested, to Lucas' eyes, someone holding a pair of binoculars.

That, he knew, was the source of his unease.

Even when Brian returned to the house and Bruce suggested they head down the south slope toward the deeper woods, Lucas could feel that phantom stare upon him.

Refusing to give any indication that the creepy observer was getting to him, he slogged around to follow Bruce. But at the edge of the woods, he nonchalantly found a reason to look back.

The shape was gone.

*   *   *

9

Vista Beach Drive forked at the Raney mailbox. The left turn vanished into a stand of woods that would have been gloomy and forbidding even in full sunlight. To the right was the Raney driveway, two muddy ruts descending into a squelchy mess.

Kel McGuire patted his car on the dashboard, apologizing in advance, and turned right. He passed the mailbox and went down the gentle hill into the squelch, his tires churning the mud with gruesome splattering noises.

If not for the telephone poles, which also supported the power lines, he would have wondered if anyone but him had been along this way in the past century.

The house was huddled at the edge of the treeline, separated from the shore by a stretch of marshy land densely green with reeds. Whoever had been fool enough to buy this plot hadn't bothered throwing good money after bad by building a nice home here on the dismal beach.

The structure was either unpainted or had been so long between coats that it didn't matter anymore. The iron chimney of a woodstove poked through roof.

The battered pickup truck was the brightest thing visible, being of an unhealthy yellow where it wasn't blotched with old primer paint. A wooden camper cap that looked as if it might have come west with Lewis and Clark sagged dispiritedly on the back.

Kel parked where he hoped the ground was fairly firm, so that his car wouldn't sink into the earth. He picked his way through the yard by stepping from one clump of coarse marsh grass to the next.

The boards of the porch were uneven and ill-met, and bowed down spongily when he stepped on them. He knocked on the front door with care, afraid his fist would go right through the soft wood.

No one answered. He spied a doorbell screwed to the frame, and pressed it. A dolorous bong sounded from inside the house.

"Just a minute, just a minute," a woman called, her voice groggy and annoyed.

She opened the door and squinted at Kel. Within, the room was curtained and dark, so he couldn't see more than a few feet.

"Mrs. Raney?"

"Yes, I'm Marge Raney."

She was wrapped in a bathrobe. Mahogany hair stood out around her head in sleep-corkscrews. Her face was puffy and her eyes bleary.

Belatedly, Kel recalled hearing that she worked the night shift. "I'm sorry to wake you, Mrs. Raney. I'm Kel McGuire. We spoke on the phone when you enrolled Eric in school."

"I remember." She covered a yawn and shuffled backward, pulling the door wider. "Come in, Mr. McGuire, and call me Marge. Coffee?"

"No, thank you. I was hoping to talk to Eric."

That woke her up and dropped a visor of guardedness over her eyes. "Did something happen at school? No, isn't it Saturday? I can never tell what day it is during my work week."

"Eric's not in any trouble," Kel assured her. He told her the situation, stressing that he wasn't singling out her son.

"Oh, my God," Marge murmured. "You don't think she might have . . . hurt herself, do you? I mean, you hear about teenagers . . . but you said she's only twelve."

"I don't know what happened. That's what we're trying to find out."

"Eric's not here, or else he would have answered when you knocked. He was still sleeping when I got in this morning."

"Did you see him last night?"

"He came in around nine, just as I was getting ready to leave for work."

Now that his eyes had adjusted to the dimness, Kel realized that the interior was considerably better-kept than the exterior. The furniture was inexpensive but of decent quality, and except for some clutter, the house was very clean. He also realized that despite her disheveled, just-wakened state, Marge Raney was a very nice-looking woman.

Two doors and a postage-stamp kitchen opened off the living room. One was half-open, presumably leading to her bedroom. Marge went to the other, rapped, waited, and cracked it enough to peek inside.

She shook her head, combing her hair with her fingers. "Nope. Gone. Is the truck here?"

"A yellow one? Yes, it's out front."

"Then he's around someplace. He might have walked into town."

Kel thought of the long, muddy drive he'd had getting here, and his dubiousness must have showed on his face because Marge laughed.

"There's a path, or so he says, that leads along the beach and around the bluff. I wouldn't try it myself, but he's twenty years younger than me and a lot more fit."

She didn't look all that unfit herself, and in the clinging satiny robe she was in fact was very nicely shaped, but this would hardly be the time to comment on it.

Averting his gaze from a hint of cleavage, he asked, "A path?"

"If you could call it that, climbing over the rocks. It's a miracle he hasn't broken his neck out there. Are you sure about that coffee? I have to jump-start my system with a jolt or I'm never going to make it through my shift."

"Well, all right, I wouldn't mind a cup," he said, rising to help. "Again, I'm sorry to have woken you early."

She waved him down. "I'm sorry I couldn't be more help. I can get by on a couple hours less sleep. You've got a missing girl to worry about."

Moments later, the rich scent of hazelnut-flavored coffee filled the small house. As Kel accepted the cup she offered, footsteps creaked the boards of the porch.

Eric Raney came in with narrowed eyes that narrowed further as he found them sitting in the shadows drinking coffee. He flipped a switch and the overhead light came on, dusty yellow.

"Mom?"

"Hello, Eric. Do you know Mr. McGuire?"

He nodded, and jerked his head to toss an unruly lock of hair out of his face. "Yeah."

Kel set down his cup. "Hi, Eric. Have you been to town?"

"Why, am I not allowed?"

"Eric," his mother said warningly.

"If you had," Kel said, "you might know why I'm here. That's all."

"I was at the library," Eric said, staring at Kel as if challenging him to make something of it, a guy like him being at the library on a Saturday afternoon. "What did you think I've been doing?"

Kel stifled a sigh, knowing that they were off on the wrong foot but that there probably wasn't a right foot where this boy was concerned. "Maybe you heard that Jenny Forrester is missing. I've just been trying to talk to everyone who saw her last night. Some of her friends say you were at the arcade."

"For a little while, yeah, so?"

"Did you talk to her?"

"Jeez!" Eric rolled his eyes. "I said 'hey,' she said 'hey,' and that was it. That a crime or something?"

"Eric, Mr. McGuire's just trying to help." She threw Kel a look of appeal. "When we lived in Redding, there was a policeman that always gave Eric and his friends a hard time —"

"Mom, come on, you don't need to tell him that. The cop didn't like our music and the way we dressed, that's all."

"I'm just interested in finding out what Jenny did last night," Kel said earnestly. "So that was all you said to her? You didn't see her after that?"

"I left. Stopped by the donut place. Ate a maple bar. Walked home. You want to search my room?"

"That's not necessary." Kel stood and held out another of his business cards. "Thank you for your help. If you think of anything else, you can reach me —"

Eric snorted and turned away without taking the card. He stalked into his room and raked the door shut with a resounding bang that shuddered the house.

"God, I'm sorry," Marge said in a low voice. "He's a good boy, but . . ."

"It's understandable. A lot of kids that age feel persecuted. All us meddling old people, don't you know."

She smiled wryly. "Don't I! Some days all I have to do is ask him how school went and he thinks I'm accusing him of cutting class."

"If you'd like, I do some family counseling."

"I can imagine what he'd say to that! No, really, he is a good boy. He gets excellent grades, he helps out around the house without a word of complaint, he puts up with my crazy schedule. I wish he had a few more friends, but that will happen eventually. It's only times like this that bring out that side of him."

"Not to pry, but what about his father?"

"We're divorced. Seven years ago." Her gaze met his, and he knew he wasn't imagining things. "Why do you ask?"

"Curiosity."

"Oh? Just what were you curious about?"

"Whether or not you'd like to have lunch with me sometime?"

"I think I might like that very much. I'm off on Wednesday. Anyplace except where I work. I'd like to have someone waiting on me for a change."

Kel grinned, liking her forthrightness. "How about the Trinity Bar and Grill? It's on the Square. We could meet at one o'clock."

Marge glanced down at herself and chuckled. "I'd always heard that psychologists became psychologists because they needed one. You ask me out when I'm looking like this, I can certainly believe it!"

"I don't think you're giving yourself enough credit. Thank you for the coffee, and I'll see you on Wednesday."

"I'm looking forward to it."

She walked him to the door – all of five steps from the couch – and waved as he retraced his route to his car. It hadn't sunk in the mud, and the rain was finally letting up.

Just as he was about to start down the long rutted driveway, Kel happened to glimpse Eric in his rearview mirror. The boy was holding aside the curtain of his bedroom window, watching the departing car.

But instead of the scowl Kel would have expected to see, he could have sworn that Eric was smiling.

*　*　*

Sunday,

September 14

1

Lora Blake couldn't sleep.

She knelt on the windowseat in her bedroom, nose pressed to the glass, breath fogging a cloud around her mouth.

Only darkness looked back in at her. She couldn't see anything.

Well, no, that wasn't true. She could see the same things she always saw from this window. The front yard, the driveway, the path leading to the Forresters' house, and the woods.

But she couldn't see anyone in the woods, least of all the person she hoped to see. She didn't see Jenny Forrester coming up the path to tell everyone that she was okay.

Lora felt sick to her stomach. She left the windowseat and paced around in her slippers.

She'd been eavesdropping and knew that most people figured Jenny was off pouting, wanting to make everyone feel bad for making *her* feel bad. But even someone as stubborn as Jenny would have given up and come home by now.

It's something worse. Something lots worse. I just know it.

And this wasn't pretend. Jenny, a real person, was honest-to-God missing.

What should I do about it, though?

She'd promised herself last spring that she wouldn't tell anyone about what had happened in the woods. About Chris, and the bad grown-ups.

But what if the bad grown-ups are still out there? What if they'd kidnapped Jenny too?

She could just see how it would have been with Chris . . .

Her mind's eye conjured up a plain panel van. Not speeding, not doing anything that might attract attention. The stony-eyed man behind the wheel, the blonde woman in the passenger seat. Chris in the back.

Pulling over at a rest stop or one of the fast-food restaurants out at the North Valley shopping center. Chris seeing a chance and taking it, escaping. Heading for the woods.

When the grown-ups found him missing, they would have played it cool. Driven someplace secluded where their van wouldn't be noticed. Tracked him into the woods.

Tracked him how? The springy needle-layered forest floor wouldn't leave much in the way of footprints.

Maybe with special gear. Those headbands, those dull metal headbands, could have been some sort of high-tech surveillance gadgets. And Chris could have had a transmitter stuck to his clothes. Lora knew all about that sort of thing because Damon's friend Scott, another police officer, was always reading magazines about the latest hardware and watching all the spy shows. He was the only grown-up she knew who liked all of the *Spy Kids* movies.

So, sure, there could have been infrared or homing devices or anything in those weird metal headbands.

And the same thing could have happened to Jenny! Bad people could have tracked her down and carried her away in a van.

Her brain sent up a tentative alternative. *Or, maybe . . . maybe I only imagined all that stuff in the woods.*

Lora stared at herself in the mirror over her dresser.

"I didn't," she whispered.

But . . . could she have? Everyone always said what a vivid imagination she had. A little earlier that same day, while pretending to be Sir Lora the Fearless, she almost actually *saw* the dragon, smelled the sootiness of its cave.

It was one thing to be imaginative. Mom was all in favor of that, proud of it even. But sometimes it got away from her. Like the time she saw Bigfoot. Or the time she mistook a seal for a mermaid. Both of those times had turned out to be nothing, though she'd been so sure!

"It was real," she insisted to her reflection. "Why would I make up something like that?"

Unless . . . unless I'm crazy.

Again.

Lora watched her mirror image shake her head. "No . . . I wasn't ever crazy. Mr. McGuire's a counselor, that's all. Mom said so. He was just helping me cope with stuff. Dad dying like that and everything. Lots of people need help coping. He said I didn't need to come see him anymore, once the nightmares and crying stopped."

But maybe there had been more to it than grief. Maybe there really was something wrong with her, and Mr. McGuire just hadn't seen it. Ever since, she'd been worried that something would happen again, except this time they'd have to send her away to Blue Lake.

Like Jenny's mother. In a straitjacket and everything.

Shuddering at the prospect, Lora curled her hands into fists and met her own mirrored gaze with determination.

"I did *not* imagine it," she said. "Chris was real, I know he was! And something happened to Jenny too. She didn't just run away."

Lora was sure of that because Damon was sure of that. She'd heard him and Mom and Scott and Grandpa Travis talking about it last night when they thought she was asleep. Damon joked sometimes that their house might as well be the police station annex, and Mom and Grandpa honorary deputies.

None of them believed that Jenny was a runaway. They thought Jenny got grabbed by some creep. They had a footprint, and Mr. Harmon's boat was gone, and Scott said that whoever got her probably tied her up and put her in the boat and rowed away.

In her mind's eye, she saw the stony-eyed man pull a rowboat up on a stretch of beach, and unload Jenny into the same van in which she'd envisioned Chris being held captive. Jenny, all scared, with a big grey patch of duct tape over her mouth.

What do kidnappers do, anyway? Hold her for ransom? Jenny's family is sort of rich, in a way. But there would be demands, notes, things like that.

Sell her to the Gypsies? Did people still do that?

Devil worshippers? Sex molesters?

Lora realized she was scaring herself almost to tears imagining one horrible hideous fate for Jenny after another. That wasn't going to do any good.

I have to do something.

But she couldn't tell anyone or they'd think she was making it up.

Unless I had some sort of proof.

If I could find something in the woods that would show Chris had really been there . . . then they'd believe me!

Except that she wasn't supposed to go anywhere by herself until the grownups figured out what was going on. She hadn't been allowed to play in the woods all day today, and had to stay inside even though it wasn't raining anymore.

Sir Lora the Fearless wouldn't stay inside like a chicken. Sir Lora the Fearless would go out even in the middle of the night and look for clues. Even if it meant getting in trouble.

Even if it means getting kidnapped?

Lora suppressed a tremor. She wasn't going to get kidnapped. Jenny had been walking home and had no idea there was danger. Poor Chris had probably been doing the same thing. But she, she would be ready! She'd be prepared! If she saw a kidnapper, she'd . . .

Well, she'd run like lightning, for starters. Which might not be very brave, but it was prudent. And she'd fight. Kick, slap, even bite. And scream.

All she'd have to do would be to go out there and find something, and then maybe she could tell Mom and Damon and have them believe her.

"What, now?" she asked herself in a strained whisper. "Now, in the dark?"

Her resolve faltered as she looked at night's onyx face pressing against the windowglass. But if not now, then when? She was supposed to go to school tomorrow, and Mom would pick her up, and she'd never have a chance except by sneaking out at night.

And she might never be able to work herself up to this pitch again. It had to be now or she'd talk herself out of it.

She thought of how proud everyone would be when she solved this mystery, and that settled it. Pulling off her nightgown, Lora started getting dressed.

* * *

2

"Look at how he stares at you. Like a savage animal. He'd kill you if he could judge."

Jenny Forrester surfaced with those words in her ears, spoken in a woman's husky voice with a trace of a German accent.

If he could judge?

Who?

Judge what?

She fought to make sense of it but her head felt fuzzy as the scooped-out shell of a Halloween pumpkin two weeks into November.

"He probably would," a man said in reply. "The little shit."

Other sensations gradually made themselves known to Jenny.

Cold. Dampness. Thirst.

An ache that encompassed her from head to toe, as if she was wearing a thin nylon bodysuit of dull pain. Sharper points of soreness on the back of one hand, the crook of her elbow, the small of her back.

She was lying flat on what felt like a hard mattress. Bands of firm pressure held her wrists, her ankles.

Strapped down?

She tried opening her eyes. The lids were sticky, gummed together, and peeled apart from one another like envelope flaps.

Bright light speared into them.

Jenny groaned as she quickly shut them again. Blazing white-orange sunspots filled the red darkness of her vision.

Footsteps approached her, from either side. Fingers pinched her wrist, holding, and she understood someone was taking her pulse.

"She's awake."

"Good." That was a second woman, not husky-voiced, not accented.

Hospital?

What had happened to her?

The last thing she remembered . . . what was the last thing she remembered?

Walking home . . . and someone . . . someone . . .

Eric!

Meeting Eric Raney in the woods! He'd talked to her, and then . . . something had happened.

What?

Jenny tried her eyes again, squinting. The first thing she saw was the light fixture hanging over her, suspended from the ceiling on a long chain. It had a conical white metal shade that directed the light straight down at her.

But instead of acoustical hospital-tiles, the ceiling was dark, rough, uneven. Shadowy. Strange.

She focused on the people standing over her. There were three, two women and a man, and she didn't recognize any of them. A worm of worry burrowed into her as she realized that while one of the women, the one just now releasing her wrist, was wearing a lab coat, the others weren't in any sort of doctor's or nurse's garb.

Those metal things on their heads . . . what's that all about?

A rusty wheeze emerged from her mouth as she tried to ask them where she was. Her dry lips split in thin stinging painful lines. She ran out her tongue to wet them but it was raspy and coarse as sandpaper.

"Water," the woman in the lab coat ordered.

The man moved away, and Jenny heard a faucet running.

The other woman did something, and the back of Jenny's bed rose with a mechanical hum. Her head gave a swimming-sickly thump as she was elevated into a semi-sitting position, and for a second she thought she was going to throw up. When it passed, she looked down at herself.

A hospital bed, for sure. It had chrome rails along the sides, to which her arms were bound with canvas straps. An I.V. needle was taped to the back of her hand, and a cotton ball was taped to the inside of her elbow. She knew what that meant. They'd drawn blood.

There was a plastic wristband thing around her wrist, too. Instead of her name, it had a sort of code. KG-F1196.

But instead of one of those silly gowns that tied up the back, she was wearing her same clothes that she'd put on to go to the arcade. Her jacket was gone, and her blouse was open to reveal discs – electrodes? – stuck above and below her bra. The wires from them were twisted together into one cable, which snaked into a machine sitting beside the bed.

The man came back with a disposable cup that had a bendy straw poking out of it. Though she was starting to get seriously freaked out here, Jenny closed her lips around it and slurped. It was cool and had the familiar taste of Trinity Bay tapwater.

She drank until the straw gurgled and sucked air at the bottom of the cup, then sank her head against the pillow with a gusty sigh. Just that small effort had worn her out.

"Where am I?" she asked. It came out hoarse, weak. She sounded terrible. "Am I hurt?"

"Do you want to begin now?" the accented woman said to the one in the lab coat.

"Not yet. Let her rest. We should be sure she's healthy first."

"Where am I?" Jenny asked, louder.

The man glanced at her as if she wasn't a girl at all but a talking parrot or something. He fiddled with the I.V. bag hanging on a tall metal rack.

Fear bubbled up in Jenny. This wasn't right. This wasn't how doctors were supposed to act.

"Sedate her," the lab-coat woman told the man.

"No!"

But her protest went ignored. The man brought a syringe and inserted it into a juncture of the I.V. line. Jenny stared in horror as the fluid flowed into the tube.

It moved inexorably toward, and then into, her body. Into her veins. She fancied she could even feel it, a strange cold alien tide.

"Hey! Let me go! Who are you? Where am I? What's going on?"

"How is she?" a new voice, a man's, asked.

"So far, so good," the lab-coat woman responded. "We triple-checked the blood and spinal fluid as you requested."

"And?"

"And there's no error. Our sniffer was right. All the indicators are there, even without the pre-existing condition."

"Well, that is interesting, isn't it? But not entirely unexpected. We knew that the enzyme existed even in normal subjects, in low levels."

Jenny tried to turn and see the newcomer, but all at once drowsiness dropped over her like a billowing sheet. While she could still hear them talking, it seemed very far away and unimportant.

Drugged. Doped up. Getting woozier by the second.

Mustering all of her energy, she tugged at the straps. But her arms only moved listlessly, barely more than a twitch.

Her head lolled. Her eyes were still open, but a dreamlike film was creeping in around the edges so she couldn't be sure if what she was seeing was real. It *couldn't* be real . . . because the room she was in didn't look like a room at all.

It looked like a cave.

*   *   *

3

The beam of Lora's flashlight bobbed across the tree trunks and cast a glow in the shape of a bunny's head. It had been the prize in a kid-size meal from Pizza X-Press. Dorky, but at least the batteries worked.

She'd managed to slip out without even waking Ruff, who'd been sprawled in front of the hearth to bask in the dying heat of the fireplace. Only her mother's cat Jack, his eyes twinkling like emeralds from the back of Grandpa Travis' chair, took note of her stealthy exit.

Now she was deep in the woods, the redwoods clustering around her.

Her first effort to muster a Sir Lora fantasy failed miserably. All she could think of were evil Ents, or Shelob's lair, or the black and deadly mines of Moria.

Everything looked so different in the dark! And sounded different too . . . strange noises seemed to come from all around.

What if I get lost?

That was dumb. She'd been playing in these woods practically every day for three years.

But never at night . . .

It didn't matter. She still knew where she was, where she was going.

Resolute, Lora pressed on. The beam swung down and up, illuminating the ground at her feet so she didn't trip, then spearing ahead.

Just when she was starting to think she really was lost, she spied the fallen log, the roots of which had provided her hiding place.

After that, it was no problem to find the old split trunk where she'd first seen Chris. She shined the light into the hollow interior, and when nothing jumped out at her, ducked her head and went inside.

The old fire had eaten away a chimney up the trunk. Lora was able to stand upright in the middle. There was barely enough room to move around inside.

As she turned around, the bunny-face of light fell squarely on a small plastic dinosaur. She picked it up and brushed it off. Allosaurus, maybe a T. Rex. Reddish-orange with darker markings.

She clutched it tight, this proof that she hadn't imagined the whole thing.

A further search turned up no more clues, so Lora emerged from the dead tree and looked around, thinking hard.

Dinosaur in one hand, flashlight in the other, Lora headed in the direction the grown-ups in the metal headbands had come from.

The sea-scent in the air intensified. She could hear the churning of the surf. The treeline ended, and Lora was at the edge of the bluff.

Enough moonlight penetrated the clouds to show her the water below, rushing in to beat itself against the rocks. Gouts of foam sprayed up with each wave, then fell away to reveal boulders glistening black.

Lora automatically looked to her right, but she couldn't see the spot from here. The spot where Angela Cliffwood had dived to her death. It had been pointed out to her by her classmates last year, just as it would be pointed out to each successive generation of Trinity Bay kids.

That part of the shore, a gravelly stretch of sand hemmed in by rocks, had been where the high-schoolers gathered for bonfires and beach parties. They didn't use it any more, not since that night.

But she couldn't see the beach from here. If the ghost of Angela Cliffwood was wandering the bluff in her nightgown, she did so without an audience.

Lora looked down, scowling.

The grown-ups had come from this way, had gone this way with Chris when they'd left. She was sure of it. But there wasn't a road or even a trail.

Could they have gone by boat?

She picked her way closer to the edge, then stopped. A path led down the bluff. Parts of the boulders had been cut away, sometimes into crude stairs.

A secret path! Hidden, unless you knew exactly where to look!

She put the toy dinosaur in her pocket and started down. Every time she needed a handhold, one was conveniently presented, making her more certain that someone had made this path on purpose.

Down and down, and to anyone watching it would have looked incredible, miraculous, that she could proceed with such ease and surefootedness. Her rubber-soled shoes found good traction on the ocean-slicked rocks.

The path continued into a crevice in a massive slab that had been split in two by the forces of earth, water, and time. The sheer sides, veined with minerals, rose above Lora like castle walls.

She emerged onto a ledge, where the cliff dropped away, not straight down but undercut so deeply that she couldn't see without leaning way out — which she was not about to do. A chuckling, booming noise came with each surge of the sea, as the waves were forced into the undercut.

Pressing close to the side opposite the drop, Lora inched her way along. She sighed in relief when the ledge broadened to a more comfortable width.

Ahead, she saw two uneven ridges of rock, rising from the water like teeth in the jaw of a gigantic crocodile. The current whirled and frothed against their outsides, but in the wedge-shaped expanse sheltered by the ridges, the water was smooth and calm.

The ledge that Lora was on ran along the inner edge of the crescent-shaped inlet, and vanished into the mouth of a sea cave.

Lora's eyes widened. A secret path, *and* a secret cave! Her teacher, Mrs. Sorenson, told them just last week about how Jacob Cliffwood had been suspected of being a smuggler.

This would have been perfect. A captain could bring a small ship through that ridge of rocks, into this hidden inlet.

And then all the stuff he'd smuggled – furs, amber, and jewels! – could have been brought in unseen by anyone in town.

"Wow," Lora breathed, thoughts of treasure overflowing her imagination. Then more sober thoughts presented themselves. The very hideout that would have been ideal for smugglers might also work for kidnappers.

She knew she should go back right now and get Damon.

That would be the smart, safe thing to do.

But the siren call of the secret cave was too strong.

*　　*　　*

4

Jenny Forrester was drifting off into a soft foggy bed of sleep, against her will but impossible to resist, when a muted but persistent beeping intruded itself on her consciousness.

Her first thought was that she was dreaming all this weirdness, that she was listening to Jerry's alarm which he'd forgotten to turn off . . .

"We have a visitor," one of the men said.

Jenny swiveled her heavy head on the pillow. She saw the man seated at a bank of monitors lit with scenes in the bluish-grey black and white. She couldn't make out any details.

"It's the Blake girl," the woman in the lab coat said. "What's she doing?"

"My guess," said the other man, who had also donned a lab coat, "is that she's snuck out to look for her friend."

"I'll go bring her in." The other woman picked up what to Jenny's befuddled eyes looked incredulously like a gun.

"Wait," the woman in the lab coat ordered. "Can we risk it? This one, they'll eventually have to conclude that she ran away or hooked a ride with bad luck. If *two* go missing . . ."

Jenny tried to protest, indignantly. Run away? Get in a car with a stranger? She would do no such thing!

"We can use her," the man in the lab coat said, his tone one of decision and authority. "Judge, Inge, go get her. I have an idea."

Alarm shot through Jenny, but it wasn't enough to break her free of the lethargy that was seeping into her bones. She watched helplessly as the man

– it was a *name*, Judge – and the woman with the gun nodded, rising.

The woman was an arctic-eyed Valkyrie, hair yanked back in a severe ponytail. She fiddled with the side of her metal headband and a transparent red visor slid down from it.

Judge waited only long enough to accept a second gun, which Jenny now guessed was a tranquilizer pistol, from the man in the lab coat. Then he followed Inge.

"Use her? What are you planning?" the woman in the lab coat asked with a worried frown.

"It seems that young Miss Blake is about to have an accident," he said, examining his fingernails.

On the console, which had an array of devices that would have intimidated the pilot of a jumbo jet, a red light flashed.

"He's active again!" the woman said. "But we're shielded, so who –?"

The man didn't waste words answering. He crossed the room in swift strides, and Jenny's head followed him as if there were magnets in her eyes.

On the far side of the room . . . the cave . . . whatever it was . . . was a row of large partitions. A dozen or so. Cells, almost, fronted with thick sheets of glass or plastic instead of bars. Doors like airlocks. Most of them dark, only three lit.

And on the inside . . .

It was like a museum, like a zoo . . . exhibits set up to look like bedrooms . . . habitats . . . habitats for . . . for kids?

Jenny tried to shake the grogginess away, but the sight still made no sense.

The man stalked to one of the enclosures, his face a fierce mask of anger. "What do you think you're doing?"

He was addressing a skinny little boy huddled beside a desk. The boy's posture was fearful, but his glare was defiant. His slight body shook with either emotion or strain.

"You know you can't affect us, so what are you trying to do?" The man swiped a key-card through a slot and punched in a series of numbers.

Smoky whitish gas hissed from vents positioned all around the inside of the boy's enclosure.

The boy struggled to hold his breath but eventually, had to suck in the gas. He tottered against the desk, knocking over a herd of toy dinosaurs, and collapsed.

"He's being very difficult lately." The man looked impassively at the small, crumpled form. "If he didn't have such intriguing . . . potential, I'd be tempted to have him destroyed."

* * *

5

As Lora advanced, her sense of adventure was overlaid with creeping dread.

She stopped, aware of the rapid thumping of her pulse and the quickness of her breath.

Dark. Sinister.

She didn't want to go there.

She could hardly bear to look at the cave.

It was as if the very essence of evil was pulsing from the opening. No mere sea cave, but the lair of some terrible beast that would put her most vivid imaginings of dragons to shame.

Don't be silly, she thought sternly to herself. *It's only a cave. No monsters, no devils.*

She tried to take another step but her feet were rooted solidly to the rocks.

Who was she fooling? This wasn't a story or movie in which the brave little kid outfoxed the villain and saved the day! This was real life! In real life, kids got in trouble all the time! They got hurt! They got killed!

But Jenny . . . Chris . . .

But nothing! Even thinking about moving another inch toward that cave turned Lora's blood to water and her bones to jelly.

Icy fingers of terror slipped along the back of her neck, trailed down her spine.

With a helpless cry, Lora spun and fled.

She was suddenly positive that the monster was coming after her, snorting in fury. It would overtake her, bear her down screaming onto the wet rocks, drag her back to the cave and eat her there in the dark.

Yes . . . she could almost hear it . . . the clatter and pound of its pursuit! Talons or claws scraping and clicking on stone. Any second she'd smell its cold, reeking, demonic breath.

Fear surged up so great that she almost jumped off the cliff rather than be caught and eaten. But then she was off the ledge and going through the crevice.

She kept on going as fast as she could, up the hidden path with the wind of her fast passage whistling in her ears, hair flaring behind her like a dark curtain, eyes so staring and huge that they took up half of her face.

Only when she reached the top of the bluff did she make herself stop and look back.

The path was empty.

*   *   *

Monday,

September 15

1

Tom Harmon woke with a leisurely stretch and his usual morning thought about how great it was to feel so damn good.

He got out of bed and launched into his daily routine of calisthenics. Jumping jacks, toe-touches, sit-ups, push-ups. When he was done, he paused to take a quick inventory.

Lungs: a little raspy but much clearer than they'd been back when he would spend the first half of the day fighting a deep, phlegmy smoker's cough.

Heart: thumping along briskly but not walloping the way it would have done a year ago.

Bones and joints: nary an ache or pain, nary a crackle or creak to speak of.

He was in better shape now, at pushing-sixty, than he'd ever been in his life. He'd also, surprisingly, found that he liked the mornings.

Most of his life spent as a night person, running a bar, sleeping until noon . . .

Ah, well, it was what Uncle Nate had always said . . . everyone eventually becomes that which they can't stand.

He pulled on a sweatsuit, laced up his running shoes, and prepared for his jog. Two miles down the beach and back, by the end of which he'd be more than ready for a breakfast of grapefruit, bran flakes, and a single boiled egg.

The *Harmony,* the one true love he'd discovered so late in life, bobbed serenely in her slip. Tom was the only one to live full-time aboard his boat, and had the marina to himself as he headed along the dock.

The world was quiet and secretive, blanketed in muffling fog. It'd likely be a fair day later. Maybe he'd take the *Harmony* up the coast a ways, now that the tourist season was past. Pretty country up north toward Orick . . .

At the end of the marina's walkway, a series of wide flat stones stepped down to the beach. Tom descended and jogged north along the wet sand, toward the park around the footbridge that spanned the Agate River.

He hadn't gotten more than thirty yards when he heard the cawing of gulls, and glanced over to see a flock of them hopping in their ungainly way around a lump by the waterline. He veered that way, expecting to find a sea lion or otter washed up on shore.

The gulls scattered as he approached, but only to retreat to a safe distance and regard him with beady petulant eyes.

When he was a dozen feet away, he realized it wasn't a sea lion at all. Adrenaline dumped into his system and his heart gave a great lurch.

His first thought was that it was Jenny Forrester, but as he ran to the child crumpled on the beach he knew he was wrong. Jenny was big for her age and getting shapely, and this body was far smaller. Further, the tangle of sand-speckled hair was black, while Jenny's was a lighter honey-brown.

Tom fell to his knees and tore a few strands of kelp from the little girl. She was lying on her side, curled into a comma-shape with one arm flung behind her. He gingerly turned her onto her back and pushed her hair out of her face.

He froze, recognizing her.

Lora Blake.

*   *   *

2

Damon Blake rolled over and drew his wife into his arms. "Mornin, ma'am," he drawled, slipping his hands under the long flannel shirt she wore.

"Why, Sheriff, isn't that a mite impertinent of you?" she teased.

"It may be at that," he said.

Theresa pressed her lips to his bare shoulder. "Not that I mind."

Chuckling, he pulled her atop him and bunched her shirt around her waist, caressing her back, hips, and buttocks while they kissed. She moved against him, her midnight hair tickling the sides of his face.

Just as she was fumbling for the drawstring of his pajama pants, a baby began to cry down the hall. He was joined only seconds later by his brother, and then both of them were wailing to raise the roof.

"Well, damn," Theresa sighed.

"Your dad'll get them." Damon unbuttoned her shirt, cupping her breasts.

"No, he won't, not upstairs." She arched into him, her dark eyes half-lidded with frustrated longing.

"They can cry at each other for twenty minutes," he said.

"Like either of us could stay in the mood with that ruckus going on."

"I can." He moved her hand to prove it.

"I reckon so," she said, gripping him firmly through the cloth. "But you're a pig of a man interested in nothing but your own selfish desires."

"You say that like it's a bad thing."

"Tell you what, cowboy . . . I'll change them and feed them and take them downstairs while you shower and shave, and then maybe Dad and Lora can watch them for a few minutes."

"Sounds like a deal."

She leaned down and kissed him again. "Back in a bit."

Damon propped himself up on one elbow to watch as Theresa changed into faded denims and one of his old uniform shirts. "You are one lovely lady, ma'am. I don't think I tell you that often enough."

Theresa smiled and tipped him a wink. "And you are too handsome, Damon Blake. Look at you, lying there, knowing how well those yellow pajamas contrast with your skin . . . you know I want to come back over there and jump on you."

"Jump away," he invited.

One of the boys attained new heights of howling. And from downstairs, Ruff began to bark for his morning trip outside.

"I would, but duty calls." She let herself into the hall. "Lora? School day, and Ruff needs to go out!"

Travis Zane's voice drifted up. "I was about to think you'd run off and left me with all the grandkids, honey!"

"You're not getting rid of me that easily, Dad," Theresa called back.

Damon grinned. He heard her go into the twins' room, the pitch of their cries instantly changing to more strident demands for food and attention.

He went into the master bathroom and showered. As he smeared shaving cream onto his chin, a car door chunked closed outside. Damon wiped a clear spot in the steam-clouded window and looked out.

When Damon saw Scott James hurrying toward the house, he experienced a sinking feeling in his gut.

Goddamn. Someone must have found Jenny Forrester and the news could only be the worst. Too bad to relay on the phone.

He washed the lather off his face and threw on a bathrobe, reaching the upstairs hall just as Scott knocked.

"Lora, come on, I mean it," Theresa was saying to Lora's closed door. She turned and saw Damon. "What is it?"

"It's Scott."

"Oh, no!" Theresa reached for the knob. "Lora, I'm not . . . Lora?"

Damon went downstairs, waving his father-in-law down as Travis was about to heave himself out of his chair. On the floor in front of him, a quilt bordered by pillows had been laid out, and the twins were scootching around burbling contentedly at each other.

He opened the door. Scott looked up at him, his face ashen.

"Damon . . ." Scott swallowed and swiped a hand across his mouth. "Jesus, Damon, I don't know how to tell you . . ."

Theresa leaned over the railing. "Dad, Damon, is Lora down there?"

"Haven't seen her," Travis replied.

Damon saw Scott's eyes go bleak, and his sinking feeling turned into a plummet.

"It's Jenny, isn't it?" Damon asked, ashamed to hear himself sound almost hopeful for that bad news. Anything but the alternative that was already worming its way into his gut.

"No," Scott said. "It's Lora. Tom Harmon found her on the beach, not thirty minutes ago."

"What do you mean, found her on the beach?" Theresa's voice rose. "Lora's here! Isn't she? She's . . . she's got to be here!"

"Is she dead?" Damon asked, clenching his fists until the knuckles stood out pale against his skin.

"Not my Lora," Theresa moaned.

"She's alive," Scott said, looking at the floor. "But she's unconscious. Been in the water, we don't know how long."

Damon exhaled, but it did nothing to relieve the tension coiling in him. Travis had risen from his chair but stood holding onto the back of it as if he feared his legs might fail him. Theresa was coming down the stairs one disbelieving step at a time. Even the twins had ceased their babbling and were watching the adults solemnly.

"What happened?" Theresa asked, with at least the pretense of calm.

"Tom found her about halfway between the marina and the park. She was breathing, so he carried her to a pay phone. The ambulance took her to the hospital, and I came straight here."

"What happened to *Lora?*" Theresa had reached Damon by then, and when he put his arm around her shoulders she was quivering like a taut wire. "Was she . . . was she . . ."

"She was fully dressed except for one shoe, no marks on her that I could see. The docs will have to say for sure."

"Fully dressed?" Travis said.

"Oh, God." Theresa raised haunted eyes to Damon. "She went out. That's what she did. She decided to go search for Jenny."

Damon nodded. "Give me three seconds to get clothes on, and we'll go to the hospital. Travis, can you –?"

"Don't worry about us." Travis looked down at the babies, then back at Damon. "We'll be fine."

He took the stairs two at a time, grabbed the first clothes that came to hand, donned them, and raced back down. Theresa had her jacket and her purse and was waiting by the door.

"Are you okay to drive or do you need a lift?" Scott asked.

"I can handle it." Damon and Theresa got into the other cruiser while Scott returned to his. With lights but not sirens, they backed out of the driveway and started down the road as fast as the misty conditions would allow.

"She wasn't in her room," Theresa said. "I opened the door and she wasn't there. I didn't feel a thing, Damon. That's not how it's supposed to be. In the books, the mother always can sense it when something's wrong with one of her children, when something's wrong in the house. And I didn't feel anything!"

"It's all right. Tom found her, and she's going to be fine."

"We don't know that."

"We have to believe it. She's alive." He took a hand off the wheel long enough to grip hers firmly. "That's what matters."

They drew startled looks as the two cruisers sped by with lights revolving and flashing. Minutes later, they were in the parking lot beside the tiny emergency room of Trinity Bay Medical Center.

*   *   *

3

Elliot Shaw took a deep breath and let it out slowly as he paused on the other side of the door. Through its oval glass window, he could see Damon Blake and Theresa Zane sitting exactly where they'd been sitting for the past two hours.

He knew them, had been their family doctor since taking over for Kensington. He knew Lora, too . . . bright, lively, imaginative Lora. Always such a brave little patient, even when she'd gashed her leg "fighting the Uruk-Hais" and needed a dozen stitches.

Now he had to do one of the hardest things he'd ever faced.

"Theresa? Damon?"

They got up at once, and he saw everything in their expressions he'd known he would see.

There were several other people gathered at a discreet distance, Tom Harmon among them, all straining their ears to listen.

"How's Lora?" Theresa Zane asked.

"I'm afraid she's in a coma," Elliot said. He didn't believe in dragging out the suspense, when they were already prepared to hear the worst.

Damon Blake winced as if he'd been struck. "How bad is it?"

"It's too soon to tell. She was under water for a long time. The cold temperature slowed her metabolism, which is good because it kept her alive, but she was also hypothermic. We don't know how long she was deprived of oxygen."

"You're talking about brain damage," Theresa said.

"We have to be prepared for that possibility."

She didn't burst into tears or collapse, she remained upright and looking at him, but something about her changed, something about her shattered. On the inside, where it couldn't be seen. "Can I see her?"

"I'll take you in."

If not for the fact that Lora had been intubated to help her breathe, she could have been sleeping. Her skin no longer had a blue-tinged pallor, and a considerate nurse had rinsed the sand and combed the tangles from her hair so that it spread over the pillow in black waves.

"Lora . . ." Theresa whispered, and then tried again louder. "Lora? Honey?"

Elliot checked the EEG monitor, relieved to note that, on some level at least, Lora was aware of her mother's voice. "She can't respond, but she knows you're here. That's a good sign."

Theresa stroked Lora's cheek. "I'm here, honey. I'm here and we're doing everything we can to help."

Damon drew Elliot aside as Theresa continued to talk quietly to Lora. "Was she in a struggle?"

He shook his head. "A couple of minor scrapes and bruises, mostly on her hands, that could have come from climbing over rocks. But there's no indication of assault, or molestation."

"She went out looking for Jenny Forrester," Damon said. "Snuck out. She must have been out by the bluff below Seacliff."

"If she fell from the bluff, she's a very lucky girl not to have more serious injuries," Elliot said. "Though I know it's hard to believe there's anything lucky about this."

"What can we do for her?"

"Right now, we're monitoring her blood gases, keeping an eye on her electrolytes. We'll want her to stay here, be closely observed, for several days. After that, it depends on how she's doing."

Damon looked intently, searchingly, at Elliot. "How *might* she be doing?"

"It's hard to say . . ." he hedged, but Damon's eyes hardened and Elliot sighed. "At the very least, her memory will probably be impaired. The hippocampus suffers most of the brunt of the effects of hypoxia, and that is where our spatial navigation systems are stored. It's also in charge of making sense of sensations."

Theresa had been listening to his summary, stricken. "How soon will we know?"

"I wish I could say for sure. We don't have all the equipment here to perform the more advanced tests. She needs an MRI, and a PET scan."

"I know what MRI is," Damon said. "Magnetic resonance imagery. But what's a PET?"

"Positron emission tomography," Elliot explained. "It uses radioisotopes to measure activity, while an MRI can show us images of the physical structure."

"So she'd need to be taken, where, Eureka? Blue Lake?" Theresa brushed Lora's hand against the side of her face.

"We might talk to Dr. Lundquist's people at Seacliff," Elliot said. "They specialize in exactly this kind of case, and I know they have the equipment. Let me give Lundquist a call in a day or two, and see what he has to say."

"Your boy's been up there for a month now, hasn't he?" Damon asked. "How's he doing?"

"He's doing very well. They started him on a . . . a new medication regime recently. He's showing some improvement already. I wouldn't go so far as to say they're miracle workers, but they're good. Very, very good."

"We'll do whatever needs to be done for Lora," Theresa said. "Just tell us what you want us to do."

"For now, the important thing is to keep your hopes up, think positive. Talk to her, read to her, that might help."

"Can we stay with her?" Theresa asked.

"One at a time. We'll be moving her up to a private room, and I'll have a rollaway cot brought in."

A discreet tap on the door heralded the entrance of Mary Christiansen, the nursing supervisor. Her expression softened as she glanced at Lora, then became businesslike.

"Chief Blake? Officer James is here, asking to speak with you." She set a plastic bag on the chair nearest the door. "Lora's clothes are in here, and her little toy."

Theresa nodded her thanks.

Damon leaned over to kiss her. "I'll go see what Scott wants, and be back soon."

"If you need anything," Elliot said, "just let us know. We're all here for you, and Lora."

"Thank you, Dr. Shaw," Theresa said. "Right now, I'd just like to sit with her a while, if that's okay."

He smiled sympathetically, knowing all too well what she was going through. He'd lived it himself for the past seven years. But they'd both be feeling better soon. He had faith in that. Dr. Lundquist would help both of their children.

Elliot picked up Lora's chart, and went to his office to make a call.

*   *   *

4

Toby Edwards shuffled into the auditorium along with the rest of his class. Having been skipped ahead just at the age when development became crucial, he was stuck in the middle of a crowd of kids way bigger than him. Especially the girls, who were outgrowing their male classmates in more ways than one, and all right at eye level.

An air of apprehension hung over the room rather than the usual gassing and horseplay. The students simply filed in and took their seats.

Toby hitched himself up to peer over someone's head and saw the principal, Officer Scribner – older brother of the dimwit Neil – and the school counselor, Mr. McGuire, on the stage.

The principal, Mr. Lemke, was a round little man with the pinched, nervous eyes of a rabbit. He approached the podium and gripped it, blinking out at the audience of grades three-to-twelve.

Toby knew what was coming. There probably wasn't a person in Trinity Bay who didn't.

Principal Lemke cleared his throat and consulted his notes. "Welcome, students, to the first assembly of the school year," he began in a quavery voice that was often imitated in the lunchroom. "We can all look forward to –"

Kel McGuire stepped up and murmured to Principal Lemke, who flushed and looked again at his notes. Turning an even darker shade, nearly plum now, he stuffed them back in his pocket and pulled out another sheaf.

"As many of you already know, we have a very serious matter at hand," he said. "Jennifer Forrester, has been missing since Friday night. I'm sorry to tell you that while search parties have been making their best effort, there hasn't been much progress. We're forced to face the prospect that Jenny might not simply be lost, but that something might have happened to her. I've asked Officer Avery Scribner to join us today and talk to you about what you can do to keep yourselves safe and help the police in their efforts."

With hugely evident relief, Principal Lemke turned over the podium to the tall, gangly policeman. Toby listened absently, his flawless memory storing it all away for later review, while around him his classmates either sat in attentive silence, or boredom, or scoffed in undertones to each other that they didn't need the stranger-danger talk.

Toby bristled at the way some of them mentioned Jenny, as if they really thought she'd hitched a ride or run off with some guy. He liked Jenny, not just because she was the prettiest girl in the eighth grade

But who could tell what a girl might do? They seemed not only a different sex but a different species altogether. He couldn't understand half the things they did and eighty percent of the things they said.

He'd asked his father about it once and Malachi Edwards had just chuckled and told him he may as well get used to it. At that, Toby's mother Ruth had swatted Mal on the rear with a kitchen mitt, and they'd all shared a good laugh.

But different as they were, *alien* as they were, Toby still couldn't believe that Jenny would do something stupid.

Officer Scribner finished with a plea for anyone who noticed anything odd to talk to parents, a teacher, or the police. Then he turned things over to Mr. McGuire.

Several girls started paying more attention now. Plenty of them had crushes on him, even to the point of making up problems so they could get appointments. Half the boys thought he was gay, and all the girls were wasting their time.

Girls. Just plain bizarre.

"I'm afraid I have some unpleasant news," Kel McGuire said. "Lora Blake went out last night, apparently taking it on herself to look for Jenny. We believe she fell from the bluff below Seacliff, and she is now in the hospital."

Astonished gasps greeted this. Lora, like Jenny, was especially visible because of her family connections – daughter of a local celebrity, stepdaughter of the chief of police. Toby knew a little that the rest of the kids didn't, about how Lora's biological father had died. Been murdered, even. That was why she'd come to live with her mother.

Mr. McGuire answered what questions he could and deflected the more decidedly ghoulish ones – had she landed on her head, was she blue when Mr. Harmon found her on the beach, had she discovered any clues about Jenny, like bones or anything?

"While our thoughts are with Lora and her family, as well as with Jenny and hers, we have to make certain this isn't repeated," Mr. McGuire continued. "It's admirable to want to help, but the best way to do that is by doing what Officer Scribner said. Do not put yourselves at risk."

That pretty much ended the assembly, and the students crowded back out to mill around before next bell. Toby had a free period, at least until the school clubs schedule got organized.

He broke away from the hallway gossip, threading his way through clusters of kids until he got to the double doors leading out onto the quad. A cement walkway, covered out of deference to Trinity Bay's long months of rain, branched off in many directions.

Toby headed for the library. He waved to Mr. Price as he came in, and made for his favorite corner. Someone else was already there.

Toby recognized Eric Raney by the black bad-boy jacket draped over the back of a chair, even before Eric raised his head.

"Hey," he said, pitched quietly.

"Hi, Eric." Toby unslung his backpack and set it on the floor. "Were you at the assembly?"

"No. Had a library pass." He flicked the slip of pink paper stuck in his spiral-bound notebook. The cover was shiny silver, with the black logo of a metal band floating eerily in a 3-D effect. The same logo, a horned bull's head inside a pentagram, was visible below the sleeve of Eric's T-shirt, inked onto his arm in a crude makeshift Bic-pen tattoo.

Toby, whose taste in music began with classical and ended with his dad's Motown oldies, had no clue who the Lords of Haarkon were. He wanted to ask if Eric really liked them, or if it was calculated as part of the image.

The older boy looked like he should be hanging around at a bar where patrons had to show a switchblade just to get in the door. Not parked in a patch of pearl-grey rainlight beside a window, bent over books with titles like *The Complete Anatomy of the Brain* and *Paranorm: a Rational Discourse on Psychic Powers.*

"Wow," Toby said, picking up a heavy one called *Case Studies on ESP.* "Whatcha working on?"

"Term paper."

"Already?"

Eric hoisted one shoulder in an indifferent shrug. "Might as well. Nothing better to do."

"I thought I was early! On what, on psychics? That's all fake, isn't it?" Eric shrugged again. "Maybe, maybe not. Some of these studies were done at major universities. Duke, Columbia, Stanford."

"Gee —" Toby wished he hadn't said *gee,* feeling more like he was eight years old again and still into Theresa Zane's *Lora and Ruff* books. "You believe in this stuff?"

Eric's unsettling copper-colored eyes fixed on him. "You gonna tell everyone I'm a nut?"

"No way!"

"So what was the assembly? Usual bullshit?"

"Nuh-unh, it was about Jenny."

"Oh, hey, yeah." Eric closed his notebook. "They find her?"

"Nope."

"That McGuire guy came to my house." Eric's voice took on a sullen and dangerous tone. "All because I said hi to her."

"He came to my house too," Toby said. "It's not like he had it in for you personally or anything."

"Yeah?"

"Yeah, honest."

Eric's tone mellowed. "Well, s'okay then."

"He just wants to find Jenny." Toby glanced out the window, a sudden wistful melancholy coming over him. "I miss her . . . hope she's okay. She used to study with me sometimes."

"Yeah?"

"It was after her mom got put in the hospital, before she started hanging around with Kaylee and Eva so much, trying to be more grown-up. I think she didn't want to go home."

"So maybe she ran away," Eric suggested. "Haven't you ever felt like it's all too much, be better off if you just up and split?"

"No."

"Lucky you."

"But Jenny wouldn't." Staring across at the chair that had habitually been Jenny's, the chair over which Eric now had his jacket, Toby heard himself voicing his worst fear. "I think they're right. I think someone got her. So what if she's only twelve . . . she didn't look it, and the papers are full of crazy people who don't care about that."

Eric nodded. "Bet you're right. I bet that's just what happened. Someone got her, and wherever she is, the worst is still to come."

*   *   *

Tuesday,

September 16

1

Her father had insisted on having equal time at Lora's bedside, and so it was with a mix of reluctance, relief, and guilt that Theresa went home with Damon after lunch.

The babies were fussy and fretful, picking up on their parents' distress. When they sat on the couch, Theresa with Mark and Damon with Travis, they automatically sat so as to leave a space in the middle for Lora, and the awareness that she wasn't going to fill it sent Theresa perilously close to renewed tears.

Ruff whined at Lora's door and kept butting his head into their knees, gazing up with hopeful doggy eyes. Jack, the orange-striped tabby cat, was more skittish and ill-tempered than Theresa had seen him in years, ever since the incident with the ghosts.

"It's going to be all right," Damon said, with no trace of his customary cowboy drawl. "You heard Dr. Shaw. They'll be able to help her. And if they can't, we'll find some others who can. Whatever it takes, Theresa."

"I know . . . but it still feels like there should be more! How could it have happened, Damon? How could I not know?"

"Don't." He slid closer, freeing one arm from Travis though that left the squirmy boy free to try his best to fall off the couch. Damon put it around Theresa. "It's not your fault. No one's fault."

Ruff rested his chin on Theresa's leg and chuffed, either trying to comfort or sharing the blame. Mark closed one chubby fist around the dog's ear, a deed that would normally send Ruff scurrying for cover. But he endured it like penance.

"I should call my mother," Theresa said. She looked at the phone and made absolutely no movement toward it.

Damon pursed his lips. "You sure?"

"No. God, no. I mean, yes. I am sure, sure that I don't want to call her. What if she insists on coming down? What if she has George drive her, and bring his whole family? I can't take that, Damon, I swear I can't."

"Then don't. We can manage fine without her." He spoke firmly, having no desire to be confronted with his mother-in-law. Just twice, once at the wedding and again when the boys were born, had been more than enough.

"If I don't tell her, she'll never let up." Theresa sank her forehead onto the top of Mark's fuzzy curls. "It doesn't matter that she never has a thing to do with Lora."

"Theresa, stop." He plucked the twins from their laps and set them on the pillow-ringed blanket that served as their playpen. "Your mother's the last thing you should be worrying about."

She sagged into his arms and laid her head against his chest. "Lora . . . my poor Lora!"

The tears came again, more than she thought she could possibly hold. Yesterday had been the same, between bouts of trying to put on a brave face for the doctors and their neighbors. Crying her eyes out in the hospital restroom, locking herself in the car and sobbing until she felt drained to the core . . . yet like a fabulously bountiful bitter spring, the tears kept coming back.

It was the worst feeling Theresa had ever known. The loss and fear formed an ache at once sharp and deep, a pit down the center of her lined with razor-edged barbs. The guilt was a weight, pressing her inexorably down into that pit.

Hope eluded her like a flickering minnow in a vast, desolate sea. When she caught it briefly in her tremulous hands, it was a slim and sorry hope indeed.

Brain damage! The words slammed in Theresa's mind like vault doors. It was the worst fate she could conceive of, except perhaps death itself. Or maybe even worse than that. In death, Lora would be gone, but whole. Their memories of her would be of Lora, the essential Lora in all her wonder and delight. To think of a Lora diminished and dulled, that essential *she* forever snuffed out or altered . . . that was unbearable.

Theresa held Damon and let the storm rage until it was blown out. The twins, alarmed by her outburst, were shocked into a solemn silence.

When she could finally sit up and wipe her face and manage a fragile smile for her husband and sons, Theresa felt a little bit better. Not much, still miles from 'all right' and she'd probably never reach that point again, but better.

"I can call her if you'd rather."

"No . . . she'll think I'm a weakling hiding behind you." Theresa slid onto the floor, onto the blanket, and pulled the boys to her. They patted at her cheeks and hair, gabbling in their baby-speak.

The doorbell rang, and Damon rose. "Probably Scott with the latest."

"You should go to work," Theresa said. "Find Jenny. We at least know where Lora is, how she's doing. Poor Charlie . . ."

"Scott's got everything well in hand," Damon said. "I'm here if he needs me, but you and our family come first."

It wasn't Scott James but Kel McGuire, shaking drops from an umbrella.

Jack, who had up until now been aloofly ignoring everyone, hopped down from the mantle and made a beeline for Kel. Standing on his hind legs, the cat stretched up and up to bat at Kel's hand.

"He always remembers me," Kel said. "Just can't wait to shed on me and make me sneeze, can you, Jack?"

"You're probably his favorite person," Theresa said. She saw him take her in at a glance, red-puffed eyes and all, and knew that she was transparent to him. Then again, given the circumstances, one didn't need to be a psychologist to know the state she was in.

"I was just at the Forrester place and thought I'd swing by, see how you were doing," Kel said as he bent over to kiss Theresa's cheek, then sat. Resigned, he let Jack spring into his lap, where the cat began kneading his leg.

"Holding on," Theresa said, which was a lie and of course Kel knew it; she was flying apart like a sand castle in a windstorm, and would soon collapse in on herself in a shapeless heap. "How's Charlie?"

"Holding on." He said it in the same tone, and Theresa smiled wanly. "I don't think he's told Sandy yet. Jerry wants to get a leave from classes and come stay with him, but Charlie told him no, said he needed to stay at school and do his best."

"I hate to think of Charlie there alone," Theresa murmured. "But I just can't . . ."

"You've got other things to worry about," Kel said. "Ruth Edwards has gotten half the ladies in town organized in shifts to go out there and cook and clean and look after Charlie. Just say the word, you know, and they'll do all they can for you, too."

Theresa nodded her thanks. "I'm okay . . . as far as that goes, I'm okay. The hardest part is not being able to do anything. I was just telling Damon he should get back to work. To *do* something. To find Jenny . . . and that might help Lora too. If we could go in there and say, 'we found her, honey,' maybe that'd help her come back to us."

"We just don't have much to go on," Damon reminded her with a sigh. "Just the plaster cast Chet Underwood got of that footprint. I had Scott send it off to a forensics lab in San Fran, but until they get back to us with what kind of shoe we're looking for, we've got no place to start."

"Actually," Kel said dubiously, "there is one thing that Scott thought I should mention to you. Happened Saturday as I was leaving the Neeman place –"

Damon groaned. "He going to sue you now?"

"I wouldn't be surprised. You'd have thought I was bullying the kid into confessing multiple murder. But as I was driving off, one of the girls called me on my cell phone. Diane, it was."

"The speed demon," Damon said. "I pulled her over on 101 a while back. She had her mother's old minivan up to 90, Lord knows how."

"According to Diane, her father was out on Friday night until almost two in the morning. She said it was probably nothing, but felt like she should tell someone. It's been on my mind ever since."

"I should just deputize the man," Damon said to Theresa.

"Friday's John Neeman's bowling night," Kel said. "He's on a team with Gus Sorenson and a few other guys – their team name is, unsurprisingly, 'Strike It Rich.' But their league usually wraps up no later than eight, with the post-game beer-and-brag usually done by nine."

"So what are you thinking? That John Neeman, on his way home from the bowling alley, sees Jenny Forrester alone and all the old resentments just come seething up?"

"One of the other daughters, Sarah, chased my car halfway down the driveway –"

"I've warned you about those high-school girls."

Kel regarded him sourly. "To tell me that her father still holds a big grudge about the Cliffwood estate."

"I can't see John Neeman kidnapping anyone," mused Damon. "He makes such a stink anytime he thinks he sees someone's rights being violated –"

"But that's not it," Kel cut in. "If he thinks *his* rights are being violated, he'll move heaven and earth. If it's something profitable, that is, if there's someone he can sue. I doubt he gives a damn for anyone else."

"Nice attitude," Theresa said.

"He has a wife and seven daughters," Kel said, "and treats them like part of the furniture at best, or millstones 'round his neck at worst. The one boy,

Rocky, is as far as his father's concerned, the pinnacle of human evolution. It's easy to see where some anger could build up on behalf of the girls."

"He's a varmint," Damon summed up, laying heavy on the accent. "What you'd get if'n a sneaky coyote and a drunk skunk shared a rassle in the hayloft."

*　*　*

2

Dawn Jessec was convinced she was dreaming, and would have given anything not to wake up.

This couldn't be real, just couldn't. That she, Dawn Jessec, who had never been further from home than a trip to San Diego, was clear at the other end of the state not just for a vacation but to live there . . . who would have thought?

The amazement, her first-ever plane ride, and the eye-popping change of scenery had been enough to take her mind off of Richie for the first time since finding him in the Mercers' wading pool. He wasn't out of her thoughts *completely,* but she knew he was in the best possible hands and therefore she was able to let herself relax. Finally relax.

They'd flown up last evening, and what a difference an hour and a half made when it was by air! Dawn had a new role model and idol in Dr. Gwynne McGuire, whose steadfast determination to do what was best for Richie no matter what his grandparents thought, had held Dawn up when she otherwise would have crumbled in her resolve.

Now Richie was at Seacliff, which was every bit as gorgeous as it had looked in the pictures. His room was twice the size of her trailer's living room, and much nicer. The Seacliff people had set up equipment and arranged for nursing care above and beyond what even the hospital had been able to provide.

Everyone here so wonderful to her that she kept waiting for it all to come crashing down. For them to mention a fee schedule that would reduce her to slavery, and she'd spend the rest of her life working off the bills in the kitchen and laundry room.

But that hadn't happened. Instead, everything that Dr. McGuire had promised was coming true. She felt like a princess, a dizzied Cinderella whose fairy godmother had appeared not in a sparkle of light but in a pristine white lab coat.

She had a new checkbook in her purse, full of fresh checks to an account with a balance of five thousand dollars – the number alone had nearly made her choke on her ginger ale when Dr. McGuire gave it to her on the plane. She had a suitcase full of new clothes and sweaters.

And she had an appointment to look at an apartment.

Birdwood Lane was the name of the complex, on Cadmoore Street. It was two-storied, shaped like a capital L enclosing a central garden/courtyard with a small playground and a few picnic tables ringing a barbecue on a post. A covered carport lined the outside of the L. With its wooden siding and dark shingles, the building seemed to nestle right up against a row of towering redwoods like it had grown there.

Dawn had walked down the hill from Seacliff, marveling all the way at the rich green beauty of her surroundings and barely noticing the chill to which her desert-bred body was not at all accustomed.

She rapped on the door to 1-A, the manager's apartment. A woman opened it, making a swift grab to snare the collar of the ugliest dog –

It wasn't a dog, and Dawn's eyebrows shot to her hairline. It was a pig, a black potbellied pig with a ribbon-trimmed collar and . . . earrings? She'd heard the expression 'pearls before swine' once and had no idea what it meant, but was pretty sure it didn't refer to earrings. Pierced ones, no less.

"Carlotta! You stay, girl!" a woman admonished the pig, as Carlotta snuffled toward Dawn, making low inquisitive grunting noises.

Whatever she'd been preparing herself to say evaporated, and Dawn just gawked helplessly from the pig to the owner and back again.

She was a short and wide-hipped woman with a puff of grey hair like a cloud fallen to earth. Her face was round and cheery, and her hazel eyes sparkled merrily at Dawn.

"No one told you about Carlotta?"

"Uh . . . no . . ."

"You must be the new girl. Dawn, was it? Dr. McGuire called to tell me you'd be by. Would you like to come in for a coffee or soft drink, or see the apartment first?"

"Whichever," Dawn said, still looking at Carlotta with some apprehension.

"Don't let her scare you. She's a big one, my Lottie, but she's all heart. A hundred and twenty-five pounds of heart, and a snout that just loves to give kisses. Hold out your hand."

With extreme dubiousness, Dawn did. Carlotta's moist quivering nose squelched into her palm, whiskers tickling.

"Looks like she likes you! Come on in, honey. I'm Francie Howe." She nearly pulled Dawn inside, and Dawn's sense of unreality tripled.

Every available surface was given over to pigs. Paintings, knick-knacks, stuffed animals . . . everywhere Dawn looked, she saw pigs. Mostly pink ones with cartoony smiles. A few celebrities were among them: Porky and Petunia Pig, Disney's versions of the *Three Little Pigs, Babe,* Wilbur from *Charlotte's Web.*

And photos, a whole wall of photos showing a progression of Francies going back to a yellowed old snapshot of a grade school girl proudly holding a piglet.

"You must really like pigs," Dawn said, feeling inane.

"The love of my life, yes indeed," said Francie, and bent over to make kissy noises at Carlotta. "Smarter and more loyal than dogs, cleaner than cats. You'll never find a better pet than a pig!"

"Oh."

"Do you have pets?"

"No . . . my mother had parakeets for a while, but she got rid of them. Too noisy."

"Because we do allow pets. A lot of places don't, but as someone whose life has been touched for the better by animals myself, who am I to tell someone that they can't have a pet? When were you planning to move in?"

"Don't I need to interview?"

"What's there to interview? You look like a good reliable girl, not the sort to make any trouble. I've got two available. 2-C is a one bedroom, and 2-J on the end is a studio. I'll show you them both, and you can decide."

"Did Dr. McGuire tell you much about me?" Dawn asked hesitantly.

"You mean your baby? Oh, yes. So you'd probably want the bigger one, for when he's ready to come home. Doesn't matter to me that you're not married, if that's what you were wondering. I've never been, and personally don't see much use to it." She plucked a ring of keys down from a pegboard in the shape of — what else? — a smiling pig.

Carlotta wanted to come along, and had to be gently but firmly admonished by Francie to stay. She trotted off to a large wicker basket lined with fleece instead.

Apartment 2-C was on the second floor. The drapes to 2-B next door were open enough to give Dawn a fleeting glimpse of a table covered with papers, a mobile of the solar system hanging from the overhead lighting fixture, a fleet of spaceship models on fishing line apparently attacking the outer planets, and a life-sized cardboard stand-up of Xena, the famed warrior princess.

Francie sifted through her keys and unlocked 2-C, then stepped back with a flourish to allow Dawn to precede her.

"The ad says 'furnished,' but I'm afraid it's not as fancy as that makes it sound," she apologized. "There's a double bed, a couch, a kitchen table, a couple of chairs, a dresser, and a coffee table. Some dishes, pots and pans, silverware. Nothing matches, though."

Dawn stepped inside. The living room had burnt-orange carpet and wood paneling, and the couch along one wall was navy blue plaid, but it was clean and mildew-free. The country-blue kitchen opened right off the living room, and a short hall connected to the single bedroom and bath.

She toured the place, poking into the old fridge and drawers, sliding back the salmon-colored shower curtain, pulling back the plain white bedroom curtains to take in the view of the redwoods. Finally, she turned to Francie Howe with a smile.

"It's great!"

Francie beamed. "You want it?"

From the front door, she could see Seacliff. "Yes, please!"

"Then let's go back down and sign the papers, and you can move right in."

*   *   *

3

Music. The Flirty Boys . . .

Meant to be Together. Joey Mack singing. Singing to her. Looking at her like she was the only one in the whole world that mattered. Telling her by the true love shining from his eyes that she was the one for him. In all the interviews, he said he was just waiting for the right girl. Now he'd found her.

So they danced, close-danced like he did with that girl from their videos only this time he was really meaning it, wasn't putting on a show for the cameras. They danced as the music rocked all around them . . .

The click of a latch woke Jenny at once. She didn't even get a second of drowsy just-wakedness to trick herself into believing she was safe back home and about to hear her dad calling her for breakfast, or Bingo scratching to be let out. She knew where she was.

The latch had been the small portal in the front wall of her enclosure locking shut. On the clear shelf jutting from the inside was a plastic tray, and she saw the back of a woman moving away from the door. Brown hair, lab coat. One of those metal gadgets with the wires and tiny flashing lights girding her head.

Jenny smelled soup and toast. Lunch was served. Feeding time at the zoo.

That's just what it was. A zoo for kids.

And now they had a new exhibit. *Adolescentus MTV us,* the common American teenager – well, almost-teenager; her thirteenth birthday was still a few months away.

She sat up in the narrow bed and pushed back the blankets. The only light in her enclosure came from a single bulb sealed in a cage, but it was enough to show her the surroundings that had become boringly familiar to her over the past however-many days.

In the cave, no windows gave clues as to the passage of day and night. And because they kept sedating her at weird times, she couldn't keep track of the people on the outside and come up with an idea of how many shifts had gone by.

Her head felt strange. It had to have something to do with what they were giving her. The drugs, whatever they were. She never smoked, didn't drink even on a dare, and despite what everyone in town seemed to think, her dad wasn't always stoned or noshing on freaky fungi. And here she was, being drugged by total strangers.

For what? She wasn't sure she even wanted to know. Not that they'd tell her anyway. As far as those people were concerned, she was a lab rat.

One of four. There was the boy she'd seen before, the skinny kid called Chris. And herself. And two others.

She wished she could see them from her cell, but the clear wall only let her look out into the cave with its ranks of computers and medical equipment. She could only remember what she'd seen as they carried her into her prison.

Hers was on the end. The next one over housed a dark-haired boy of about four. When she'd seen him, he had been rocking ceaselessly so that his back banged against the headboard, thumb in his mouth. His eyes were dark and haunted, eyes that had known more pain and misery than anyone should ever have to know.

The little boy and Chris, Jenny was pretty sure, wore plastic wristbands just like hers. Except that the plastic wasn't exactly plastic. It was tough, unbreakable. Even when she tore at it with her teeth, she couldn't get it off.

She hadn't been able to see much of the fourth kid. Only that the bed looked like an over-large crib with a weird lid on it, and the form under the sheets was curled in the fetal position.

The brown-haired woman had moved on, pushing a wheeled stainless steel cart in front of her. The headband with its lowered red visor concealed most of her face.

Jenny got up. She still had her own clothes, which she determinedly wore though her captors had also provided several changes of sweatsuits in uninspired shades of grey or blue. Her stomach rumbled expectantly.

The tray on the shelf held a bowl of soup and two pieces of toast, as well as a carton of milk, a cup of grape juice, and applesauce. The dishes were all disposable, with nothing she could use to hurt herself or anyone else.

The first time they'd fed her, she'd tried to refuse. For all the good that had done. They'd just threatened to send in the merciless Judge and Inge to strap her to her bed and feed her by glucose drip.

She took the tray to the desk. Everything was bolted in place except for the chair and the drawers. She was trapped, and if what had happened to Chris was any example, they didn't take kindly to disobedience.

What *had* happened to Chris? She'd been mulling it over whenever her head was clear enough to allow her to think, and couldn't figure it out. They'd gassed him, knocked him out, but why? What had he been doing? Had it been something to do with Lora?

Jenny finished her meal, even the applesauce that she despised. When she had dumped the dishes in the trash and put the tray back on the shelf, she knew there was no putting it off any longer.

She had to pee.

This was the part she hated most of this entire ordeal. They could have built a little stall in here, would that have been so hard? Instead, there was just a toilet right there in the corner. Like in a jail cell. Not even a curtain around it! She had to drop her pants and go right there in full view of anybody in the cave.

She peed as fast as she could. A real bathroom with a shower, was that so much to ask? She wanted a shower. Not a sink and a pile of towels. No thanks, no way, *nyet, nein.* She was totally not about to stand there sponging herself off in front of everyone. She'd rather stink.

Though she might have to break down and wash her hair soon. It was stringy and gross, and she'd ponytailed it because she couldn't stand having it flop all oily and lank in her face anymore.

Movement in the mirror made Jenny whirl around. Three people were approaching her cell. One of them was the brown-haired woman, the other two were Judge and Inge.

Jenny backed up until her butt was pressed against the cool unyielding wall. The door opened, and the three of them came in. Judge was carrying what looked like a folding table, and Inge had a box.

"I ate!" Jenny said, stabbing her finger at the empty tray. "I ate it all, every speck. I swear!"

"Calm down," said the woman. "I want to talk to you."

Warily, Jenny didn't budge from the wall. "Nobody talks to lab rats."

"On the contrary, you're a very special young lady, and I'd like to find out some more about you. My name's Anne."

Jenny didn't answer, and watched as Judge and Inge set up the table next to the bed. Anne took the desk chair and swung it around so that she could sit facing the bed, and beckoned to Jenny.

"Come on over here and have a seat."

Jenny didn't doubt that Judge or Inge would paralyze her with a karate chop if she tried anything. So she sidled over and perched where she'd been directed.

Inge opened the box, which looked like a steel briefcase, and set it in front of Anne. With the lid in the way, Jenny couldn't see what was inside.

Anne unbuckled the strap that held her metal headband and visor in place, and removed it. She shook out her hair and smiled at Jenny. "That's better . . . always a relief to get that thing off. Now, shall we begin?"

"I'm not saying anything until someone tells me what's going on!" Jenny demanded. "I want to go home. You people kidnapped me and shot me up with drugs, and I don't even know why."

"I'm afraid you can't go home yet, Jenny. You have a medical condition that needs to be treated."

"I'm not sick! I'm hardly ever sick."

"I know. But there's something very different about you, something that could be dangerous if we can't find out more about it. I know it seems scary, and might feel like we're the bad guys, but we're only trying to help you."

"I don't want any help. I want to see my dad."

"That's not possible right now."

Jenny wanted to kick over the table and bust out of there. She wanted to scream and cry and throw a major fit. She wanted to punch someone in the eye and flip the rest of them off and tell them where to stick it. But she knew that any of those courses would only get her in worse trouble, so she stayed put as Anne rummaged in the box.

"We'll start with a few tests," Anne said.

Judge and Inge took up spots on either side of Anne, their faces emotionless and impassive, their postures alert. They weren't armed, but each of them had capped hypodermics hooked to their belts, ready to jab her if she acted up.

"What kind of tests? What's wrong with me?"

Anne's voice was reassuring, but her words certainly weren't. "Don't worry. We just need to find out what's different about your brain."

*   *   *

Wednesday,

September 17

1

Roger Brockman couldn't help comparing the Trinity Bay Medical Center to the massive and sprawling hospital complex with which the Center For the Human Mind was associated.

Not that there was much comparison. The entire TBMC could have fit inside the building that had only housed Atlanta National's surgical wing. Still, it was clean and not shabby, and in most cases would be perfectly suitable for the needs of the community.

In most cases.

Not this one.

But on another level, there was something about this hospital that was superior to others where he'd worked. A sense of community that had been missing in the clinical, impersonal, almost military atmosphere of CFHM.

Trinity Bay was different. These people knew each other, lived side by side, shared happiness and tragedy. When there was trouble, they banded together.

Roger paused halfway between the front doors and the desk to get his sudden surge of emotion under control. He was here as a doctor, after all, and doctors, even ones with an interest in art as well as science, were supposed to retain a level of professional decorum.

He passed beneath a ceiling mural that had been done by Trinity Bay High's Class of 1980. It depicted the town as it had appeared in the year of its official founding, as rendered by those graduating in its centennial. Roger was fairly sure that the reality had been a lot harsher and less sanitary than the scenes shown on the ceiling above him.

He approached the main desk and addressed the receptionist. "Good morning. I'm Roger Brockman, from Seacliff. I spoke to Dr. Shaw —"

"Yes, Dr. Brockman. He left instructions that you were to go right up to his office. Third floor." She pointed, as if he needed help seeing the large sign above the elevators.

"Thank you." He proceeded that way.

"Pardon me . . . Doctor?"

Roger turned and found himself faced with a striking woman with cream-copper skin and rich black hair. He smiled and held out a hand. "Miss Zane . . . or do you prefer Mrs. Blake?"

"Theresa."

"I'm pleased to finally meet you, though I am certainly sorry about the circumstances. How is your daughter?"

"There hadn't been a change as of an hour ago." She held up a canvas tote bag. "I went home to get some of her favorite books and toys. My husband is with her."

"Shall we go up together and have a look?" He offered to take the bag, but she demurred.

They were stopped frequently by well-wishers who offered what words of comfort they could. Not that there were many, Roger knew. But it was to their credit that they tried, for finding something, anything, to say to the parent of a seriously injured child was never easy.

"I read *Mourning Glory*," Roger said. "Very scary. Imagine my surprise when I realized I'd be living in the very same town as the author, let alone in the very same building where so much tragedy struck!"

The doors slid open, and Roger followed Theresa to a room at the end of the hall. It was one of the few in the hospital that did not have a view of the beach, a kind thought on someone's part.

Roger had met Damon Blake on a couple of previous occasions, usually when the chief of police was in uniform and on duty.

Today was not the case. He had on a pair of grey Dockers, an old N.Y.P.D. sweatshirt that bore the paint and wood-stain marks of many a home improvement project, and Nikes that had seen better days.

They exchanged greetings, and Roger went to the foot of Lora's bed. A quick scan of the medical equipment and an even quicker skimming of her chart told him what he already knew.

"I haven't fully discussed the case with Dr. Shaw yet, but I imagine you'd like to know my preliminary opinion right now."

Theresa slipped her hand into Damon's. "Go ahead."

"As it stands, I'd expect Lora to have a fifty-fifty chance of a moderate recovery."

"What do you mean by moderate?" Damon asked.

"That she'd be able to walk, feed herself, control her bodily functions, and communicate to some extent."

"Is that all?" Theresa whispered. "What do you mean, to some extent?"

"She may lose some of her command of language, become aphasic. I'd also be concerned that she might develop certain symptoms usually associated with mental illness, particularly visual and auditory hallucinations and behavioral changes."

With a low groan, Theresa sank into the chair beside Damon.

Roger gestured apologetically. "I'm sorry. This is all worst-case conjecture on my part."

"No, we need to hear the possibilities," Damon said.

"Given her age, she has better odds of a full recovery than an adult would. In children, the compensatory abilities of the cortex are much greater. I'd be more optimistic if she were under eight, but her brain tissues should still have a fair amount of plasticity." Seeing their matched frowns, he elaborated. "That's what we call it when parts of the brain can alter their function, picking up the slack."

"Isn't there anything that can be done to fix the damage?" Theresa asked.

He spread his hands noncommittally. "The brain and the nervous system are still very much the final frontier, as our staff computer expert would say. Some scientists have made remarkable progress transplanting new nerve cells into stroke patients, epileptics, and those suffering from certain degenerative diseases. Dr. Lundquist has been working for years with regenerative agents, capable of regrowing or repairing brain cells. The trouble is, most of this is all still very new, and a lot of people aren't willing to consider it as a course of treatment. Even though the benefits greatly outweigh any potential side effects."

Theresa glanced at Lora, then over to Roger. "What sort of side effects?"

He studied her for a moment and decided to be as honest as he could. "We've mapped the brain pretty well, but there are still some areas, some structures, whose function and purpose are unknown. Sometimes, the cerebregens – the regenerative agents – cause the enlargement of tissue in some of those areas."

"Tumors?" Damon asked.

"No, no . . . normal brain tissue. But since we aren't sure what those areas do, or if they do anything at all, it's hard to know if the change is having any effect." He shrugged. "Dr. Lundquist's theory is that those areas were once used to regulate traits or bodily functions we've outgrown as a species."

He broke off and laughed at himself in chagrin. "I'm sorry. Haven't held a university post in ten years, but that still hasn't shaken the professor out of me. I didn't come here to dump a bunch of neurologist-speak on you. Dr. Lundquist just wanted me to come down and go over those test results, so we can figure out when the best time will be to do that MRI."

"You mean you'll do it? Up at Seacliff?" Theresa said.

"Well, we can't do it here; the machine's built into the lab," he replied. "But yes, we'd be happy to help. Trinity Bay has been very good to us, and it's the least we can do in return."

"If . . . if Lora needs longer-term care," Theresa said, "what would it take to have her join the Seacliff program?"

"Dr. Lundquist's okay," Roger said. "But let's not get ahead of ourselves. Let's see what the MRI shows. It's possible, and I hope it is, that Lora will recover perfectly well on her own. I'll talk to you soon, Chief Blake, Theresa. Good night, Lora."

She didn't answer, didn't react in any way, and Roger shook his head in sympathy for the motionless little girl.

"I wish we knew what happened to her," he said as he headed for the door. "It's hard to know what to think without knowing the circumstances."

"She was looking for a friend of hers," Damon said. "Jenny Forrester."

"Yes, the missing girl . . . some of our staff have volunteered with the search parties, but I've heard they haven't found much. Any new developments?"

"No, nothing," Damon said. "We're still investigating a couple of possibilities, waiting on some results. But it's not looking good."

"Scott James found Lora's flashlight down on the beach below Seacliff," Theresa said, her tone telling him what an effort it was to keep her voice steady. "Near a spot where the older kids used to meet for parties. It wasn't broken, so she must have been crossing the rocks, and slipped, or a wave came up . . ."

Damon put an arm around her as her shoulders started to shake. "The current must have pulled her out, and then carried her past the marina. She was lucky . . . it could have thrown her right back onto the rocks."

"But when I think of her . . . in that cold water . . . struggling and trying to swim . . . calling for help and no one hearing . . ." Theresa's chest hitched, and she ripped a handful of tissues from the bedside box to hold them to her face.

Roger, deeply uncomfortable in the raw wound of her grief, murmured something unintelligible but consoling, and went to speak with Elliot Shaw.

*   *   *

2

"That was dumb," Dawn Jessec said to herself.

She was out front of Tom's Market, with a shopping cart loaded to the brim. Stocked up. Stocked up to the eyeballs, on anything and everything she could possibly need. It had been a long time since she'd been able to shop with abandon.

The combination of having a well-padded checking account and empty cupboards needing to be filled had been an indulgence she couldn't deny.

But she'd outsmarted herself. Here she was, with a dozen grocery bags, a gallon of milk, a case of soda, a sack of potatoes, and a potted spider plant . . .

. . . and she'd gotten here on the bus.

Tom's Market was in North Valley, a shopping center to the north and slightly east of Trinity Bay's downtown proper. The bus routes were easy enough to follow, and she'd had the foresight to buy herself a monthly pass yesterday afternoon, but how was she going to get all of this on the bus? Or, for that matter, from the bus stop to her apartment?

She stood there feeling like the world's biggest dummy, and ran through her limited list of options. Cab? Unlikely. Call Dr. McGuire for help? Bad enough she'd made this blunder; she didn't need her benefactress to know about it. Call Francie Howe? Maybe, but Francie had said something about spending the day at the coin-op laundry, and even if Carlotta was clever enough to answer the phone, the pig couldn't drive over and get her.

"Move it," snarled a male voice from behind her.

Dawn flushed, seeing that she was taking up the whole sidewalk. She wheeled her cart out of the way and turned.

The guy, hunched and scrawny, gave her a ferocious look, as if she'd done something much worse than blocking traffic. He was leaning on a pair of crutches, wearing a blindingly bright turquoise smock with embroidered patch on the chest. The patch was in the shape of a bubble-blowing angel-fish, and cursive writing beneath read "Seaquarium Fish and Pets." Beneath that was a plastic nametag, white with 'Lucas' printed in dark blue letters.

"I'm sorry," she said.

"Yeah, right." He hitched on by. He couldn't have been more than mid-twenties, but the thinning pale blond hair, pinched and sour mouth, and scraggly goatee made him look much older.

Dawn watched him enter the café, then returned her attention to her own predicament.

A car pulled into a spot right by the doors, and she glanced at it enviously. Not that there was much to envy. It was a slightly bedraggled powder-blue Toyota Tercel hatchback, the sort of car that looked like it would flip over if the door got slammed too hard.

Pasted to the rear window was a 'Starfleet Academy' sticker, and a variety of sentiments were expressed on the bumper. 'Orc: the other white meat.' 'Picard/Riker 2000.' 'Have Dice, Will Travel.' 'Reality is for those who can't handle Science Fiction.' 'Metaphors Be With You."

She puzzled over that last one for several seconds before she got it. By then, the driver had emerged and was looking at her curiously. He was a skinny twenty-something, brown-haired and not unattractive in a pale, nerdy-looking sort of way. He wore brown cords and a scuffed Indiana Jones jacket, over a T-shirt with cartoon figures and the legend: 'Come over to the Dork Side.'

He started to pass by, but hesitated and seemed to collect his every ounce of nerve and courage. "You're in 2-C, aren't you?" he asked. "Birdwood Lane, apartment 2-C?"

Dawn nodded. "Moved in yesterday." She flashed back to a window domi-nated by a cardboard Xena, and made a logical guess. "You're next door, right?"

"2-B, yeah." He hesitated again, taking in the full cart. "Are you waiting for someone?"

"I'm waiting to grow a brain," Dawn said. "I bought all this stuff forget-ting I got here on the bus, and now I'm stuck."

"I can give you a ride. I'm going home too, soon as I grab a couple of things." He said it as if he expected at best a polite refusal, most likely gales of laughter and scorn.

"Could you? Oh, that'd be so great!"

His eyes widened. "Sure, glad to help! I'm Brian Sorenson."

"Dawn Jessec."

He went to the back of his car and popped the hatch. "You can put your stuff back here. I'll only be a second."

"Okay." She smiled gratefully at him and started loading groceries, setting them on and around a clutter of books, plastic cases, and boxes.

Brian came back in a couple of minutes, with a grocery bag in one hand and a two-liter bottle of Pepsi in the other. As he approached, Dawn saw him stop and look toward the café. She looked too, and saw the guy with the crutches. He was sitting in a window booth, and staring at them with such a fixed glare of hatred that Dawn took an involuntary step back.

"Let's go," Brian said, opening the passenger-side door for her and sweeping a stack of notebooks to the floor. "Uh . . . sorry the car's such a pit."

"No problem." Dawn got in, placing her feet amid a litter of empty soda cans and papers. She buckled up, and Brian did the same. "Do you know that guy? In the window?"

"Lucas Gordon? Yeah, why, do you?"

"I was in his way just now. He must still be mad at me."

"Nah . . . probably he was just thinking that he wants to beat the hell out of me." As he drove back to Birdwood Lane, he told her how he and Lucas had gone to school together, and the fights they'd had.

When they arrived, he insisted on helping her carry up all of her groceries. It took the two of them four trips, and when they were done, Dawn's tiny kitchen was overloaded.

"Thanks so much!" she said. "I don't know what I would have done. Wasn't thinking. It's all so new, being here and everything."

"Well, yeah, and you've been through a lot."

"What do you mean?"

"Jessec . . . you're Richie Jessec's mom. I work at Seacliff."

"You do?" Her dubiousness must have showed, because he hastily assured her.

"Computer systems, security, that kind of thing. I have an office there and I also do some work from home. Online. Dr. Lundquist is great to work for. As long as I put in my forty hours, he doesn't really care where or when. Actually, he likes it, because I usually wind up doing more than forty."

"I haven't met him yet, but Dr. McGuire is wonderful. I just know they'll be able to help Richie."

"I bet they will. Everyone seems to really know their stuff." He looked at the clock set into the stove, double checked it with his watch. "Whoops, got to go . . . there's a chat starting in a couple minutes that I don't want to miss."

"Thanks again . . . oh, hey, Brian?"

He turned back at the door. "What?"

Dawn gestured at the groceries. "I was going to make spaghetti for dinner, but I only know how to make enough for like ten people . . . want to come over?"

A series of very surprised expressions crossed his face, as if it was the first time he'd ever been extended such an invite and wasn't entirely certain he believed his ears. "Uh . . . sure, that'd be terrific!"

*   *   *

3

When the rain began falling in earnest, Toby Edwards wished he'd taken his mother up on the offer to drive him. But he'd seen how involved she was in her latest sewing project, and didn't want to interrupt. So he'd told her not to bother, that he could ride his bike, no sweat.

It had been a half-day at school, all of the kids getting out at noon so the teachers could go to a conference. There were fifteen half-days scheduled this year, and a lot of people thought it was way too many. They were paying for their kids to be in school, after all . . . not turned loose to roam the town like delinquents.

Well, that wasn't Toby's plan. Normally, he would have gone to the library or hung out with Dad at their coffee-shop-slash-bookstore, but when Eric invited him to come out and study with him, Toby jumped at the chance.

In some dim way, he wondered if this would help his popularity. A lot of his classmates and the older kids in the college prep courses he was signed up for as electives still treated him as a hopeless baby dweeb. When they weren't ragging him about only being eleven, they were resenting him for blowing the grade curve, so either way, he wasn't Mr. Popular.

But Eric was arguably one of the cooler kids in school, if an aura of ominous rebel darkness constituted cool. There were several types of cool, and he personally possessed none.

Maybe, thought Toby, *I could pick up some pointers from Eric.*

Vista Beach Road, mudpuddles from hell. Toby pedaled on, splashing up sprays of water, the world tinted nuclear-orange beneath the hood of his raincoat. He heard a vehicle coming, wheezing and blatting horribly as it navigated the ruts and bumps, and dismounted to drag his bike as far to the side of the road as he could.

A pickup truck, yellow and cancerous, slogged around a bend. It stopped when the driver saw Toby, and the window cranked down to let a woman stick her head out. She had a brightly-colored scarf tied over her hair, and smiled cheerily at him.

"You must be Toby! I'm Mrs. Raney. Eric said you were coming over today."

"Yes, ma'am," he replied. "Am I almost there?"

"It's still a ways. Want a lift? Provided, that is, I can turn this thing around without sinking up to the windshield."

Toby eyed the sloppy roadsides. "That's okay, Mrs. Raney, thanks. But I got it covered."

"Well, if you're sure. But if you're still there when I get back from my lunch date, I'll give you a ride home. Okay?"

"Deal!" He saluted, and she laughed as she rolled the window back up.

After the pickup jounced past him, Toby resumed riding. The closer he got to the beach, the heavier the scent of brine grew. Not the fresh and healthy scent he was accustomed to, but a nasty low-tide smell. He presumed that one got used to it after a while, or else living here would be a real bummer.

Looked like it was a real bummer even without the smell . . . he expected the ramshackle house to cave in on itself any minute. Toby thought of his own nice house, and felt bad for Mrs. Raney and Eric. It had never occurred to him before that there could be actual poor people in Trinity Bay, as in bottom-of-the-barrel poor as opposed to living-on-ramen college student poor.

He leaned his bike against a tree. The door opened as he started up the swaybacked stairs, and Eric was there.

"Hey."

"Hey," Toby said. "Saw your mom headed to town."

"Yeah." Eric's lip curled. "She's got a date with the school shrink."

"Mr. McGuire?" That should break some girls' hearts!

"That's the guy." Eric opened the door wider and let Toby in.

Inside, the house was in a lot better shape than it looked. Eric had his books piled on the small table, and the TV was tuned to a static-swept game show with the sound turned off.

"Pop?" Eric asked as Toby took off his backpack and raincoat.

"Sure, thanks."

Eric dug a couple of cans of generic store-brand soda out of the asthmatic refrigerator and plunked them down on the table. He indicated with his elbow an open bag of Doritos. "Chips?"

"Okay." Toby crunched a couple and brushed crumbs from the corner of his mouth. He'd eaten a quick sandwich at home – bologna and Velveeta on Wonder bread, a meal that made his mother protest there wasn't an ounce of real food in it – but growing boys could always find room for a few chips.

"So I'm doing my paper on the scientific validity of ESP," Eric said. "What do you think?"

"Whose class is it for?"

"Mittleschut."

"Better lean real hard on the science angle, then," advised Toby. "I know him. He's Eva's dad. Looks a little like a turtle that lost his shell, but he's tough. And ESP, wow, there's no proof, so how can it be scientifically validated?"

"But there is proof."

"Real proof, or conspiracy theory stuff?"

"What do you mean?"

"You know," Toby said. "Like how the government has file cabinets full of documented cases, secret installations where they train psychics for espionage, that sort of thing. But they keep a lid on it so the public doesn't panic."

Eric's eyes glinted like a pair of new pennies. "Don't you think they would? Panic, I mean? If everyone found out that there were people out there who could do things? Things that no one else could do?"

"Well, sure. Same as if they found out about UFOs and all that. But it's all supermarket-checkout stuff. Tabloid city. Alligator Boy of the Yucatan. It's not real."

"That's what you say."

"That's what I know," countered Toby.

"What if you're wrong?"

"Can you prove it?"

"Maybe I can," Eric said. "Suppose someone discovered that there's an enzyme produced in the human brain that fosters the development of those kinds of powers? Suppose someone figured out a way to increase the production of that enzyme in test subjects?"

"Sounds like a neat idea for a movie, but not reality."

"And suppose that one of the test subjects got the ability to sense psychic potential in others?"

"Eric, come on, this is for a science paper, not a creative writing project," Toby said impatiently. "All your supposings don't make for any proof."

"Yeah, I guess you're right. Hey, let's get some studying done, huh?"

"Good idea."

They bent to their books diligently, sipping on soda and munching on chips. After a couple of hours, Eric stretched and leaned back. His shadow moved with him, and once it was no longer blocking the window, a patch of sunlight shining through the slatted blinds made tiger-stripes on Toby's arms.

"Sun finally came out," Toby observed, and reached for his soda. There should be a swallow or two left – nope, he was on empty. He felt stiff all over, too, and achy. He looked at the clock and saw that he'd really lost track of time.

"I'm ready for a break," Eric said. "Want to go down on the beach? It's not bad after a rain."

"Yeah, okay. Can I get another soda first?" He had a glucky, gluey after-taste in his mouth, a bitter tang that overlaid the nacho flavor of the Doritos.

"In the fridge." Eric donned his jacket and waited while Toby fetched a can of generic cherry cola.

The clouds had thinly parted, letting weak strands of light through. They turned the pendulant drops hanging from the trees into diamonds. The wet mud glistened, and sparkles danced in the long puddles of tire tracks. The effect made the ground look even more churned up, as if other vehicles had been driving there since Eric's mom left.

Toby squinted in the sunlight. His head gave a warning thump, the precursor signal to one of his headaches. "Ow," he said. "I must have been hitting the books harder than I thought." He pinched the bridge of his nose.

"Need some aspirin?" offered Eric.

"Doesn't help. Nothing helps except rest and sometimes fresh air. Come on. We'll try the beach."

Eric knew the best path through the marshy place, and they reached the shoreline without getting their feet hideously messy.

The stretch of coast would never make it into one of the calendars or postcards touting the area's natural beauty. But the breeze was fresh, and the sun dazzle on the water was pretty enough.

Toby found a half-buried fallen log to stand on, and turned his face into the breeze. His headache wasn't immediately relenting, and he still had the impression that tiny gladiators were inside his skull jabbing here and there with spears. His arms hurt, too. Right in the crooks of both elbows. He started to roll up a sleeve.

"Hey, weird," Eric said. "What's that?"

Looking in the direction the older boy was pointing, Toby spotted a large kelp-covered hump wedged against a waterlogged trunk.

His first terrible thought was that it would turn out to be Jenny Forrester's drowned and bloated body, but he knew right away that the shape was too big and all wrong. Hints of white showed through the soggy strands.

"Must've washed up," he said, forgetting all about the pains in his arms. He followed as Eric picked his way down to the water's edge. As they got closer, the shape became more and more distinguishable as the upended hull of a small boat, a dinghy.

Eric peeled some of the kelp off, and they both craned their necks to read the upside-down lettering painted along the side. *"Two-Part?"* Eric said dubiously.

"It's Mr. Harmon's," Toby said. "His boat's the *Harmony,* and this is his dinghy, two–part harmony, get it?"

"I get it." He just didn't *like* it, judging by his disgusted expression.

A scrap of denim, soaked black and clotted with sand, protruded from under the edge. Toby tugged, but it was stuck.

The moment his fingers touched the clammy material, he had the most peculiar sense of doubling in his head. As if his headache had chosen that moment to wallop him a good one, except that there was no pain. A prickle of precognition swept him.

"Lift it up," he ordered Eric, still holding onto the cloth.

"Why? It's just some old rag."

"No, it's Jenny's jacket."

Eric bent and hooked his fingers under the edge, and raised the dinghy enough for Toby to pull the denim jacket out from under.

It was Jenny's, all right. At first look, it gave the impression of having been shredded by a shark, but Toby knew the tatters had been done on purpose by Jenny herself.

"Shit," murmured Eric.

"We got to call the police. She was wearing it on Friday, the last time anybody saw her."

"Should we leave it here? Evidence and everything?"

"Yeah, maybe." But Toby held onto it, not able to bring himself to drop it. He could almost *see* Jenny . . .

Fingers snapped sharply in front of his nose and Toby yelped. His headache bit him with beartrap jaws. He let go of the jacket, which hit the mud with a wet smack, and pressed on his forehead.

"You okay?" Eric was watching him closely. There was something in his eyes, some knowing glint . . . it gave Toby a shiver, having Eric look at him that way.

"Uh-huh . . . just thinking about Jenny," he said.

"That all?"

"Sure, that's all. What else would it be?"

Eric shrugged. "Dunno. You just looked really spacey. Come on. We'll go call."

*   *   *

4

Scott James accepted the cup of coffee that Barb Neeman placed in front of him. She made no move to sit opposite him, but stood at the counter instead, slicing vegetables.

"So he was home?" he said. "Here? All night?"

He had to speak loudly to make himself heard. With all but one of the kids out on business of their own, the Neeman household was as quiet as it was likely to get. Which meant that the washer, dryer, and dishwasher were all going full-tilt. The television in the den was tuned to *Sesame Street* for the benefit of little Chelsea.

"All night," Barb replied. "He got home from his bowling league around nine, had a sandwich, watched a movie, and then went to bed."

"Were you here?"

"Yes, of course!" Barb looked incredulously over her shoulder at him, as if he should know better.

Scott supposed he should have. The only time the poor woman ever left the house was to shop, run errands, and chauffeur. She slid a cutting board full of celery and carrots into a bubbling pot of turkey soup and wiped her hands.

"What about Diane?" Scott asked as she moved on to a stacked lumpy pyramid of peeled potatoes.

"She had a date with the Vanders boy. What's this all about, Officer James?"

"Bear with me, Mrs. Neeman … when Diane came in, did she see your husband?"

"He was sitting right in his recliner, and checked the clock to make sure she wasn't late. He doesn't like it when the girls aren't home when they're told. She said hello, and went off to her room."

"When you say he doesn't like it, what do you mean by that?"

Barb knocked a potato on the floor. "Clumsy, oh, that was clumsy." She scooped it up and ran it under the tap.

Chelsea Neeman came in dragging in a threadbare blankie that had probably been handed down through at least three sisters. "Want a cookie please."

"You can have a banana," Barb said, scrutinizing the potato and then bisecting it with one decisive chop of her knife.

"Mrs. Neeman?"

"Oh, yes, I'm sorry . . . what was the question?"

"Your husband doesn't like it when the girls are home late?"

"We expect our children to mind us. We establish rules, and expect them to be followed. It's for their own good." The blade made a heavy *thunk, thunk* as she chopped. "Parents need to be stricter these days. My goodness, if we need proof of that, we only have to look as far as the Forresters. If Charlie were more firm with Jenny, this never would have happened."

Scott drank more coffee, not sure what to do next. He'd probably soon be joining Kel and a host of others on John Neeman's legendary to-sue list, even though nothing he was doing was beyond the sphere of his duties. Just asking a few simple questions.

Didn't matter. When John found out, he'd work himself into a frothing righteous rage.

"Might as well earn it, then," Scott muttered to himself, then raised his voice. "Mrs. Neeman, has Diane been angry with her father lately, maybe enough to try and get him in trouble?"

Barb turned and stared at Scott as if he'd just made an obscene offer. "The girls *adore* their father!"

"I just thought that if they'd had a disagreement –"

Thunk. Thunk! The knife hacked brutally at the potatoes. What he could see of Barb Neeman's face showed lips pressed tight and absolutely stony eyes.

Scott knew when a conversation was going nowhere. He rose and set down his cup. "Well, I guess that's it. Thanks for your time, and for the coffee, Mrs. Neeman."

"John's not going to be pleased about this, not at all," she told him.

"I'm certainly not trying to upset anyone."

"Maybe he's right about you people."

Damon's habit of taking refuge in a soothing western drawl was starting to make a lot more sense. Instead, Scott settled for apologizing for troubling her, and left as fast as he could.

*   *   *

5

The Trinity Bay Bar and Grill, on one corner of the plaza, tried for a historical motif with furnishings of redwood, the walls hung with memorabilia from the heyday of the logging barons. Giant saw-blades painted with rustic scenes hung on the walls, interspersed with rusted examples of old machinery. The tops of the tables were yellowed copies of newspapers from a hundred years before, protected beneath an inch-thick layer of varnish.

In the back corner booth, Kel McGuire pushed aside the demolished remains of a thick omelet and shook his head.

"No more . . . it's delicious, but no more." To make a liar of him, his fork stole out and speared a chunk of ham that had fallen from between the fluffy layers of whipped egg.

Across from him, Marge Raney laughed. "They never got over feeding people like lumberjacks, did they?"

"Did you see the Lumberjack's Breakfast on the menu?"

She groaned and rolled her eyes theatrically. "Yes, how many huge brawny men was that supposed to feed?"

The amber light falling like rain from an overhead wagonwheel lamp lent gorgeous highlights to Marge Raney's hair, touching the mahogany with a sheen like that of a tiger's-eye agate.

Kel took a moment to admire the intelligent slant of her clear dark eyes, and the flawless peach of her complexion. "There was one man in town who could eat the entire meal and still ask for a side of hash browns."

"Tall tale time," she said. "Paul Bunyan?"

"No, truth. His name was Big Al Haverley." Kel forced his mind away from the tragic events of those few wild weeks in Trinity Bay. He still wondered if there might have been anything he could have done to prevent it, to alter the course of those events. If lives might have been saved. Lives like that of his sister, Megan.

"I'm sorry," Marge said, picking up on his shift in mood.

He smiled. "Not you. How was the French toast?"

Like him, she sighed and pushed her plate away. One and a half slices of thick bread were still sopping up a lake of maple syrup. "Wonderful, but too much of it. I may fall asleep right here."

"That's a shame," he said. "I was hoping to show you around town."

"I've been meaning to do more exploring of the shops, but with the move, and getting settled, and working, I've just never gotten around to it. Where did the summer go? I think I skipped a few months."

"Those overnight shifts are rough," Kel said. "I did an internship at a psychiatric facility after grad school, and it wiped me out. I'm impressed that you can juggle your job and Eric."

"There's not that much to it," she demurred. "Eric takes care of himself. He's independent. *Too* independent, I sometimes think. After the divorce, me working two jobs to make ends meet . . ." She paused, finished her orange juice, and added with a wry look, "Come to think of it, I'm still working two jobs, and the ends still aren't meeting!"

"Someone keeps moving the ends," he said.

"That must be it! I keep thinking I should try and find something better, but so far, the opportunities seem pretty slim."

"Unless you get into something really bizarre." Kel shook his head in bemused recollection. "My receptionist has gotten into quite the lucrative sideline lately."

Delicate mahogany brows arched. "Oh? Or is it not what I'm thinking."

"Close. Members-only website called Midnight Lady. Complete with web cam and a line of mail-order videotapes."

The brows arched higher. "And I thought all those dot-coms were dying like flies. So, if she decides to quit and do it full-time, you'll need a receptionist?"

Kel grinned and saluted her with his fork. It had speared another bit of ham and he ate it before setting the utensil down. "Enough. It looks as if the rain's let up, so we can tour the plaza without getting drenched."

As he finished paying and they turned toward the door, his sister came in. Petite and ethereal as ever, Gwynne's presence made her seem twice her actual size, formidable as an Amazon.

Marge's hand, resting on Kel's forearm, tensed slightly.

Gwynne smiled at him, the cool and sly half-smile that had always annoyed him when they were younger. The smile that said 'I *am* better than you, and our parents *do* like me best, so you may as well get used to it.' He found it still annoyed him now, over twenty years later.

"Well, hello, little brother."

"Hi, sis." Her lips twitched at that; she liked being called 'sis' about as much as he liked that smile, so it made them even. "This is Marge, Marge Raney."

"I don't believe we've met." Gwynne extended a gloved hand smoothly. "Doctor Gwynne McGuire."

"Nice to meet you."

"What brings you to town?" Kel asked. "How's Seacliff?"

"Busy," Gwynne said. "We've just added a new student. I flew up with him and the mother on Monday. Had some things to take care of here in town, and Roger – Dr. Brockman – had an urge for a to-go basket of nasty, greasy onion rings."

"Yes, I imagine Cook couldn't manage onion rings." Kel still had trouble believing that his sister had relocated their parents' entire kitchen staff to Trinity Bay.

Marge glanced sidelong at him, and he could almost hear the thoughts running through her head at the realization that he came from old money. What was his interest in her, was she good enough for him, was this a charity case?

"Quite," Gwynne said, sounding every inch the snooty blueblood Mother had always tried to make her into. She flashed her teeth. "A pleasure meeting you, Ms. Raney. But do excuse me. I should be going. I'll see you, Kel."

"Nice meeting you, too," Marge said.

Gwynne breezed past them to the counter, and Kel escorted Marge outside.

"My sister," he sighed by way of exasperated explanation.

* * *

6

It felt like desertion even though he knew it was his duty.

Damon Blake looked around at his office as if he hadn't seen it in months. Scott and Avery had done a fantastic job of keeping up on things, pulling extra shifts on their days off without a whisper of complaint. But there were things piled up already that needed the chief's attention.

So here he was, back in the saddle as of a Wednesday afternoon, ready to pick up the reins. It seemed so wrong to be here, helping himself to a cup of Georgia's tepid but paint-peelingly strong coffee as he began going over the Jenny Forrester case again. He should have been with Theresa.

His wife was insistent, though, and he couldn't help admitting that he was glad to have something constructive to do.

The results had come back on the plaster cast that Chet Underwood had taken. The shoe had been an athletic shoe, belonging to either a male of average size or a large woman.

Georgia Dansbourne, whose husband Ralph had been Damon's predecessor and whose daughter Nyx would probably succeed him when he retired, came in from the back room with a fresh pot of coffee. She wrinkled her nose when she saw Damon drinking from his overlarge cup.

"Tsk," she scolded. "Let me at least give you some that's fresh."

Before he could say yea or nay, she'd whisked the cup away from him, dumped the dregs down the sink, and refilled it.

"Thanks, ma'am."

"How's the little one?"

"No change." He blew whorls in the steam. "Theresa's gone up to Seacliff to talk to the man in charge, and they'll be moving Lora up there later this week to run some tests. Brain scans and whatnot. Things they can't do down at the TBMC."

"I've been praying for her ever since I heard. Praying for all of you."

"It's appreciated." The coffee had cooled enough for him to drink without blistering his tongue. "Where's Scott?"

"Said he was going out to talk to a few people. Mrs. Neeman, before her husband gets off work." Georgia shook her head and sighed. "That one . . . I imagine that if anyone ever sat him down and showed him on paper how much money he'd wasted on his lawyers and his big plans, he'd have his eyes opened right up. It must be more than anything he'd ever hope to get in a settlement. Oh, but he used to make my Ralph just crazy."

"I know the feeling. Anything yet on the descriptions we put out on Jenny? "

"No, nothing. "

She left him to his paperwork, and he spared a grateful thought in her direction. During the time Ralph Dansbourne had served as chief, she'd made herself the station's unpaid secretary/administrator. Even Ralph's death – eighteen years as a cop and he'd never taken anything worse than a cussing-out; a hunting accident had done him in – Georgia had continued her unofficial duties and Damon doubted they could function without her.

The only change was Damon's insistence on properly putting her on the payroll.

The phone rang, and Georgia picked up. "Trinity Bay P.D." She listened, and as Damon began to rise, motioned him back to his seat with the absent sternness of a schoolteacher. "No, that's right. You won't. Don't touch anything else though. We'll have someone right out."

Dread settled over Damon. "What is it?"

She hung up. "That was the Raney boy, out on Vista Beach Drive. He and Toby Edwards just found Tom Harmon's dinghy."

"Oh, is that –"

Georgia silenced him with one hand held up sharply. "There was a jacket in it. They're pretty sure it's Jenny Forrester's."

Damon pulled into the yard of the Raney house ten minutes later, the formerly clean car splashed with mud to the doorhandles from his rapid trip. Toby Edwards, looking distressed and unwell, rushed ahead to meet him. Eric Raney, hanging back, regarded Damon and the cruiser with suspicion.

"Officer Blake, we found Jenny's jacket. It's hers, I know it is. She was wearing it on Friday, the very same one."

"Easy, son." Damon rested a hand on Toby's shoulder. "Tell me what happened."

Eric joined them, though keeping his distance. The poor kid acted like he'd been hassled plenty by the law before. But Eric chose to dress that way, chose to make that statement, so part of the blame had to be his too. Damon couldn't find it in him to be unduly sympathetic.

Toby told him what had happened, the abridged version. He didn't repeat their entire conversation word-for-word, though Damon knew he could have. Two years ago, Damon had spoken at a school assembly on law enforcement and safety. He'd flashed a slide of a crime scene, telling the kids to study the details, then turned it off and asked them questions. Most of them, giggling at first, soon realized how much harder it was than they'd thought. But Toby raised his hand and accurately recounted everything.

"Let's go have a look," he said when the boy's recounting of events tapered off.

They went to the boat. Damon grimly realized that, overturned that way, it could be concealing something more than a jacket. There could, conceivably, be a body curled up under that wooden shell.

"I'll take it from here, guys." He'd brought one of the department cameras, and just to be on the safe side, shot several pictures of the boat where it lay, with the jacket beside it. "Why don't you go on back to the house?"

Toby's eyes bulged. "You don't think she's under there!"

"Go on back, Toby." His tone left no more room for debate.

The boys retreated, but of course they only went as far as the edge of the trees, straining to see.

Damon lifted the dinghy, his nerves braced to have a wrinkled, waterlogged hand come flopping onto the mud at his feet.

None did. He heaved the boat over onto its bottom, splattering mud in a wide spray.

Nothing. Damon exhaled in relief. No body, but they had some evidence, something to go on, at least.

He always carried a handful of latex gloves in his jacket pocket, and now pulled on a pair to begin carefully examining the jacket. Barely visible against the soaked denim were darker ink-doodles on the left sleeve. Flowers, an interlocked row of triangles, a ghost-legible proclamation of 'Joey Mack Forever.'

"Damon!" Scott hailed, and Damon raised his head to see the other officer headed his way with Toby and Eric trailing after.

Scott had had the presence of mind to bring down some more items from the cruisers, and Damon deposited the jacket into a large sealable plastic bag.

"It's Jenny's, all right, " Scott observed. "Pretty sure now she didn't run away."

"Never really thought she had, " said Damon.

"What's that?" Eric pointed at the ground.

Scott bent over, then quickly pulled on a pair of gloves of his own and pried something out of the mud. "Matchbook."

Damon didn't like it. All at once, his instincts came up raving and skeptical. "Matchbook. Of course. From what bar, or is it a motel?"

"Star Eight Motel, Eureka, California," Scott read. "What? What's wrong?"

"Too trite," Damon said. "Too obvious. Someone left it on purpose hoping we'd go off wild-goose chasing."

"But we still have to check it out," Scott said.

The bang and clatter of an old engine made them all turn back toward the house. Marge Raney's seen-better-days pickup stalled to a smoky halt in her driveway right behind the two police cruisers. The lady herself sprang out the drivers' side door like a jack-in-the-box.

"Eric!" she called toward the house, high and fearful.

"Mom! Down here." Eric waved his arms.

She came racing down the beach with no regard for the mess she was making of her nice skirt-and-sweater combo. A colorful scarf fluttered from her hair and billowed gracefully onto a bush. Moments later, she stumbled to a halt, panting and turning her alarmed gaze from one officer to the other.

"What's wrong, what's happened? Eric, are you all right?"

"Come on, Mom." He shifted on his feet, embarrassed. "I'm fine, okay?"

"Sorry to startle you, ma'am," Damon said. "I guess coming home to two police cars doesn't do much for the peace of mind."

"He's not in trouble, is he?" She put a concerned arm around Eric.

Eric looked dismayed. "Mom, jeez."

"No one's in trouble," Scott assured her. "They've helped us out."

Damon told her what was going on, showed her the jacket and the matchbook. "They did the right thing by calling us."

"Star Eight Motel . . . I know where that is," she said, considerably calmer. "It's in Old Town, a few blocks from the place I work on the weekends."

"Mrs. Raney?" Toby said suddenly. "I know it's not raining anymore, but could you drive me home anyway? My head really hurts."

Damon glanced at him, then took a closer look. Toby's dark brown skin had a pasty-green underhue that he didn't like at all. "If you could, ma'am, I'd appreciate it. The young feller here could use a lie-down."

"Of course, Officer." She shepherded the boys back toward the house, leaving Damon and Scott alone on the beach.

"So someone planted the matchbook?" Scott rubbed his chin. "Who'd think we'd fall for that?"

"Anyone who thinks we're nothing but hick cops." Damon sighed, aggrieved. "Which means it could be about anyone. Speaking of which, how'd your talk with Barb Neeman go?"

"One of them is lying, but damned if I can tell which. Diane swears her dad didn't get back until two, Barb swears he was parked in his recliner all night, king of the remote control. It could be that Diane's lying to try and get her dad in trouble, it could be that Barb's lying to protect him because she's scared. I don't know, boss."

*   *   *

7

Jenny Forrester stopped short, and Inge gave her an ungentle nudge to keep her moving.

There were three of them total being ushered into the makeshift gym. Jenny, Chris, and the smaller boy with the dark, haunted eyes. They clustered in a small, protective group and looked around at the mats on the floor, the jungle gym, the rack of balls in varying sizes, and other stuff.

The gym was subterranean and rectangular, and everything seemed barely-used. A row of tinted glass mirrors made up one wall. One-way glass. People back there.

Judge and Inge, their faces mostly concealed by their visors, took up posts on either side of the door. Guard posts.

"What do we do?" whispered Jenny, not sure if it was going to bring down some sort of harsh punishment. But she had to . . . she'd been days now with no one to talk to except for the one visit from the woman called Anne, and she was halfway out of her head with the lonely-crazies.

"Run around," he replied. "Play. Whatever."

"You mean this is like the prison exercise yard."

"Yeah. And over there –" He indicated another door. "There's a shower for after."

"Shower," she almost sighed. "I'm Jenny. You're Chris, right?"

"Yeah." He fiddled with his wristband. She read it: DT-M0187. "He's Julian."

The small boy offered Jenny such a heartbreakingly sweet, sad smile that she could have cried. He didn't say anything, but went over to a set of kid-sized hamster-tubes like those so frequently found at fast-food restaurants. His wristband read KS-M0191. Jenny couldn't guess what any of the letters and numbers might mean.

"We're allowed to talk?"

"But they listen. They know everything."

Jenny didn't care about that; they'd heard all of her questions already. They came bubbling out in a rush. "Where are we, then? Why are they keeping us? What are we doing here? Who are they? What do they want?"

"They want to *use* us," spat Chris, stalking to the ball rack. He selected a soccer ball and kicked it brutally at Judge.

The man batted it aside, and except for a tightening of his jaw, his expression changed no more than did that of one of those guards they had at Buckingham Palace.

Restless, Jenny found a handball and began bouncing it against the wall and catching it. "For what? Why?"

"Our powers. They made us, so they think they own us."

"What powers?"

"Mind powers. From when your brain got hurt."

"Nothing's wrong with my brain."

"That's how they get us," Chris said, clambering up the jungle gym and hanging upside down. His sweatshirt, one of the drab grey ones provided in their rooms, bunched around his thin chest and exposed his ribs. "They said I was in a car wreck and the car went in the river. And that my dad died, but I didn't. All I know is that they brought me here."

"I don't know how I got here," Jenny said. "I was walking in the woods with Eric, and then I woke up." She paused. "Powers . . . wait a minute, you mean like psychic stuff? *X-Files* stuff?"

Chris flipped down from the bars. "Yeah."

"That woman, Anne. She had those cards that had all the shapes and designs on them. And the ashtray full of paper scraps. And the marble. She was trying to see if I had psychic powers?"

"They can't tell what we can do until we do something," he said. "So they try all their dumb tests instead."

"But that's wacko!" She paused again, and slowly turned to look at him. "I mean . . . you don't, do you?"

Before he could reply, she thought about the man and woman in the lab coat.

He's active again! But we're shielded . . .

You know you can't affect us, so what are you trying to do?

"You do, don't you?" Jenny gasped. "And those headbands, they keep you from using it on them? What can you do?"

Chris riveted her with his gaze. His face contorted into a scowl of concentration. His fists clenched.

Jenny took a step back. "Okay, forget I asked," she said feeling suddenly nervous.

The last place she wanted to be was here with this scary weirdo . . . she wanted to be somewhere else, anywhere else, had to get out of here. Couldn't even look at him anymore. *No Trespassing. Off-Limits. Keep Out! This Means You!*

And then it was gone, the strange coldly forbidding feeling that was like a wave of negative light coming off of him.

She caught her breath, aware that her skin was all goosebumps and her pulse was skittering like a puppy on a waxed floor. Judge and Inge had stirred from their posts, but relaxed back to an alert stance as Jenny recovered.

"That," Chris said with a touch of pride. "They call it telempathic projecting avoidance. I think."

"Wow," she breathed. "And you did it the other night . . . when Lora was coming? You warned her off so she didn't find the place, so they couldn't get her! You saved her!"

"No." Chris threw a glare of pure hate at the tinted windows. "I didn't. They got her anyway."

*   *   *

October,

Interludes

1 – Seacliff

A rare and gorgeous autumn came to Trinity Bay. The sky remained a crisp, clear and stunning blue. The dark green of the redwoods and the changing hues of the deciduous trees became a jeweler's spray of rubies, topaz, and citrine on a bed of dusky rich velvet.

The nights were deep and crystalline black. All the heat of the earth bled off into space during those long hours, leaving rimes of frost on grass and windows.

At Seacliff, progress continued to be made. Doctor Elliot Shaw broke down unashamedly when his son David said 'da-da' for the first time, as he came into the room one brisk and windy afternoon. Overcome, overjoyed, Elliot wept as David looked on, as if he couldn't understand what all the fuss was about.

Benjamin Lundquist, seeing the improvement in so many of his students . . . his *children* . . . began to spend far less time brooding in the dark. His pleasure and pride were infectious, spreading quickly to the rest of the staff.

Aiden Ferguson couldn't quite accept Brian Sorenson's invitation to join a role-playing game. But she listened to him talk about it, and Lundquist chose to take this a good sign.

Brian himself could not recall having ever been so happy with his life. Fantastic job, good salary, access to high-tech gadgets, a new game coming up, and most incredible of all, an actual relationship with a girl.

In his lower moments, he told himself that the only reason Dawn put up with him was for his car, his television, and because she didn't know anyone else in town. But even once she got a job working at the pizza place, and making other friends, she still seemed to enjoy spending time with him. Next step would be introducing her to anime.

Dawn's son Richie was no longer in a coma. He was alert enough to recognize his mother, and his motor functions were hardly impaired. As he was so young, his brain still forming, the treatment team was highly optimistic.

Lora Blake had regained consciousness only four days after being moved from Trinity Bay Medical Center to Seacliff. They fully expected her to be able to go home by Christmas at the latest, and Doctor Brockman was heard to say he'd be surprised if it took that long.

Hers was a recovery which was nothing short of miraculous as far as her family was concerned. She had asked for and been given permission for her dog Ruff to be allowed to visit, even staying overnight in her room on occasion.

The large house high on the bluff rang more often with laughter than with tears as the days shortened toward winter. The mood was one of optimism and relief as years of planning and preparation, decades of theorizing, and a lifetime of hope and dedication were finally beginning to be proven successful.

*   *   *

2 – Missing Person

Damon Blake gritted his teeth, metaphorically cinched his gunbelts across his hips and tilted the brim of his hat, and straight-out asked John Neeman about the night Jenny Forrester had gone missing.

The meeting went about as the Chief of Police had expected, full of ranting accusations and threats. But what he didn't sense, with an instinct honed by years as a detective, was guilt. Neeman might have something to hide, but he had not kidnapped Jenny.

The cast of a footprint suggested a man of average size. John Neeman wore shoes so big that one could have been stuffed with straw and used as a manger in a Christmas nativity scene.

Neeman couldn't swim and feared the water. Damon and Scott had had quite a debate about just what the proper term for that was, Scott insisting it was hydrophobia, Damon saying that hydrophobia was the technical name for rabies. Kel McGuire settled it by looking it up. Thalassaphobia. But what it boiled down to was that Neeman wouldn't have had anything to do with Tom Harmon's stolen boat, either.

Avery Scribner was sent to check out the Star Eight Motel where the matchbook had come from, with the predicted lack of results. Neeman was a self-righteously outspoken non-smoker anyway, but Damon had believed in the invalidity of the matchbook as a clue from the moment he saw it.

In the midst of all of this hassle, which had included several calls from Neeman's lawyer – he *did* have one, and a big-city one at that; the rest of them made do with Fred Vanders right here in town – an astounding piece of news came to light.

Sarah, Rocky and Kaylee Neeman had corroborated what their mother had said about John's activities on the night in question. So Damon had taken it upon himself to talk to Diane, the one who'd made the initial claim. He'd been ready for her to confess to having made the whole thing up. But he *hadn't* been ready for her to start crying and claim that John himself had put her up to it.

"Run that by me one more time, if you don't mind," Damon said, sure that he couldn't have heard her right.

"He told me to say that," Diane sobbed, a huge wad of tissues crumpled in her hand. "It was his idea."

Scott looked at Damon with his mouth agape.

"Why on earth would he do a thing like that?" Damon asked.

"So that you'd question him, make him a suspect."

"Oh, for crying out loud!" Scott said, his face going red to the roots of his blond crewcut. "And then he could try to sue us for wrongful arrest or slander or something? Holy bleeding Je–"

Damon cleared his throat loudly, and Scott caught himself.

"Wellnow," Damon said. "I won't pretend to try and understand the workings inside your father's head, but why'd you go along with it?"

Diane stared down at the tissues. "If he got a bunch of money out of it, and I helped him . . . I thought maybe . . . maybe he'd like me better."

Scott muttered something under his breath. Damon didn't need to hear the words to know that they pretty much mirrored what was going through his own mind.

"All he cares about is Rocky and hitting it big. The rest of us, we're useless. Worse than nothing, because we cost him money. Food and clothes, Leigh and Kaylee's braces, insurance, traffic tickets." Here, she threw Damon an abashed look. "I hoped if I helped him get some money, like he always wants, he'd forgive me. "

That conversation closed the door on John Neeman's possible involvement, and left both Damon and Scott feeling sick and disgusted. Once John realized he had gone and put himself in a spot he usually preferred to keep reserved for everyone else – the potential target of a lawsuit or even obstruction-of-justice charges, for convincing his daughter to lie to the authorities – he shut up straight away.

* * *

Nothing was being resolved so easily for Charlie Forrester. His Sunday visits to Sandy stopped. He started projects in his workshop and then forgot about them. If not for the efforts of Ruth Edwards and Kel McGuire, he would have lived in squalor and both he and Bingo would have starved.

Jerry Forrester, Jenny's brother, was studying drama at HSU and had moved out of the dorm into a big house that he shared with Gary Haverley, Gary's outrageously flamboyant girlfriend, and a few other students. Charlie refused to let him move back home and neglect his studies. It was the only matter on which Charlie took a strong stance.

Jenny's room was kept exactly as she'd left it, tornado-strewn mess and all.

*   *   *

3 – Trinity Bay

Wednesdays were the only days that worked well with Kel McGuire and Marge Raney's conflicting schedules, but by the time the Halloween decorations began going up on peoples' front doors, the lunches had shifted to dinners.

At first, Kel thought Eric was resentful, and threatened by the presence of another male in his mother's life. But after a few weeks, it gradually sank in that Eric was fairly pleased with the situation.

Kel himself was certainly pleased. He knew that his parents, by now jet-setting someplace warm, would hardly approve of him dating a woman who was not only a divorcee and a single mother, but a waitress. No matter how intelligent and well-read Marge was, he could just hear his mother's polite horror.

The relationship had not yet progressed to a physical stage, beyond that of a simple kiss here and there. Neither of them was in any hurry to jump into bed, preferring to enjoy the pleasures of each other's mind first. There would be time enough for their Wednesday evenings to turn into Thursday mornings.

So his only real problem was the way Gwynne, on their infrequent encounters, regarded Marge. It had been with dislike on first sight. They'd barely speak to each other. It didn't matter much to Kel, who wasn't exactly on warm terms with his sister – Gwynne's very nature made that impossible. But he felt badly for Marge, having to suffer Gwynne's chill.

*   *   *

Toby Edwards' parents finally began to wonder if their brilliant son was biting off more than he could chew by tackling material meant for eleventh-graders in his marathon study-sessions with Eric.

At one point, Ruth Edwards hesitantly broached the possibility of drug use to her husband, but Malachi disagreed.

"He's just working too hard, pushing himself," Mal said. "Afraid that if he backs off or slows down, Eric won't want to be around him."

"That's just it," fretted Ruth. "What if Eric uses that to pressure Toby into things? Smoking, drinking —"

"On account of the boy looks and dresses that way," Mal said, "is no reason to judge him. He's new in town, a loner, but according to McGuire, he's basically okay."

Ruth let the matter drop, but was more vigilant than ever over the next couple of weeks. Toby was having his headaches again, the ones he'd gotten as a small child when his body was lagging so far behind his racing mind. Skipping him ahead had taken care of it, but now they were back.

If the headaches don't let up by the end of the month, Ruth told herself, I'll take Toby to see Dr. Shaw. Maybe even get him some sessions with Kel McGuire.

Toby himself was more worried than he dared let on, and might have greeted his mother's concerns with relief.

Something strange was happening to him. He was . . . well, forgetting things. That had never happened before.

Eidetic, it was called. Photographic memory.

It made school a snap, earning him the bitter envy of classmates who had to study and study while Toby could read a book once and forever imprint the words in his mind.

But now his memory was beginning to slip. Beginning to become more . . . *normal.* Or at least, more like what he assumed a normal memory was like for other people. He knew he'd done things, but in a vague and thin sort of recollection rather than the perfectly sharp replay he'd grown used to.

The thought that he might be outgrowing it, that his being eidetic was some passing fluke, terrified Toby.

So he kept it to himself, the anxiety gnawing at him like a rat. He'd lay wakeful staring at the glow-in-the-dark plastic constellations that speckled his ceiling, and try to replay the events of each day as if he could etch them deep in his memory and that would fix whatever was wrong.

No wonder his head was a pounding, stabbing torture.

*　　*　　*

Lucas Gordon was glad for the clear autumn. Not because sunny days and blue skies lifted his spirits, but because every day that held off Trinity Bay's usual rain was a respite from the broken-glass and rusted-metal aches in his twisted joints.

He didn't let his relief at this respite ruin his mood, though. He remained sour and surly, hanging onto his job only because his father owned the pet shop, having no friends and making no effort to cultivate any.

But then, fate dropped an extraordinary thing into Lucas' lap – hope. For the first time in twenty years, hope.

Dr. Shaw had mentioned the advances they were making at Seacliff, and that the doctors up there felt that there might be a chance that one of the new vitamin compounds they'd developed could help him.

"They have primarily been using the cerebregens on brain tissue," Dr. Shaw explained. "But they're also effective on certain kinds of damage to the rest of the central nervous system. I can't promise you anything, Lucas, but even a slight regeneration of the nerves in your spinal cord could give you a marked improvement in mobility."

Lucas had considered it for all of five seconds before asking where he had to sign. Over the years, he had tried everything from naturopathic herbal remedies to acupuncture to a girdle-like contraption fitted with magnets. It wasn't likely he'd wind up any worse.

Nodding in understanding, Dr. Shaw had set up an appointment for him at Seacliff. He underwent a battery of tests that ranged from boring to painful – lumbar punctures were never going to be on his personal Top Ten list.

Following that, he was prescribed a light dose of the cerebregen vitamin formula in addition to the usual truckload of other medicines he had to take. As the month went on, Lucas Gordon told himself he was only psyching himself into thinking it was working.

But he knew himself better than that. Negativism was his thing, not psychosomatic false hope. Which meant that the improvement had to be real. He felt stronger and more agile than ever before.

And more angry . . . every insult and snub was stored up like a cache of hatred, just waiting for him to be able to do something about it . . . just waiting . . .

So Lucas Gordon waited, and dreamed of revenge.

*   *   *

Halloween came, with its attendant ghosts and goblins, and last-minute trips to the market because candy purchased earlier in the month was somehow mysteriously depleted by the big night itself.

A nebulous sense of apprehension hovered over Trinity Bay that sharp, cold night.

Though she had been gone for weeks, and most hope had been given up, Jenny Forrester was an unspoken caution behind the lips of every parent as their little ones donned masks and costumes. More adults than usual joined the flock of witches, clowns, ninjas, devils, superheroes, and children's cartoon characters in the ritual of trick-or-treating.

In the spirit of the season, Theresa Zane dressed up Mark and Travis as fat baby dragons, and took them to visit Lora, who wore a plastic breastplate and helm just for the occasion.

*   *   *

Thursday,

November 13

1

In the caves, it was the down time. What passed for night, whether it was in the outside world or not. Jenny didn't know, didn't care.

Her world had shrunk to the dimensions of her enclosure. She slept as often as she could, because in sleep she was able to escape from the tedium and the terror that were the only remaining things to rule her life.

Helplessness breeds complacency. One of her teachers had said that, and while Jenny couldn't remember who, she did remember not understanding it at the time. Now, though, she did.

She went along with the routine. Ate when they fed her, read the books and magazines that they gave her, did the schoolwork they assigned. She wore the clothes they provided, and stopped worrying that they might be looking when she had to pee. And she slept, as much as possible.

Good girl. Model prisoner. If there was nothing but punishment to be gained by resisting, what was the point?

The only time she rose from her lackluster lethargy was on the visits to the gym room with Chris and Julian.

There was a treadmill, and Jenny ran and ran as if she might by some miracle run fast enough to break the speed of grim reality and find freedom. *Just a hamster on a wheel . . . running endlessly to nowhere.*

After, she was allowed to shower and wash her hair, and that half-hour was the only thing she looked forward to with enthusiasm.

Being with the others was at the same time great and awful. She had never liked being alone, but . . . but there was what they could *do*. The scary, awful things they could do.

Julian hadn't done anything bad, really. All he'd wanted to do was help. *But it's wrong . . . no one should be able to do things like that!*

Chris had been high on the jungle gym the day it had happened. Only yesterday? It seemed longer ago. Chris had slipped and thudded to the mats. He'd cried out, cradling his wrist.

Judge and Inge, their ever-present guards, had started toward him. But even hurt and in tears, Chris had scuttled away from them and lashed out with his mind, trying to drive the guards back. He let Jenny and Julian approach, and they stood over him feeling helpless. Or, at least, Jenny had felt helpless.

Not Julian.

"I help," Julian had said, and he'd grasped Chris' arm in his tiny hands.

First Chris had stopped crying, then his eyes grew round as he stared at his wrist. The puffiness went down, the color faded back to normal. At the exact same time, Julian started to cry, and *his* wrist swelled up, bruised.

"Wow," Chris murmured once Julian had released him. He bent his wrist, evidently without any pain.

Julian, though, had clutched his own arm to his chest. Tears rolled down his chubby cheeks. And then, right before Jenny's astounded eyes, the injury he'd taken from Chris onto himself also went away.

Jenny had been thunderstruck, unable to move. The same was true of Judge and Inge, but two lab-coated scientists rushed in, descending on the boys, examining them and talking rapidly to each other in medical jargon.

Her long-awaited shower had not been as comforting that time. She'd had a case of the chills that no amount of hot water could wash away. She'd been trying so hard not to think about why they were here, what Chris could do, or about the unseen fourth child.

Trying, most of all, not to think about what it might mean to her.

She couldn't not think about it anymore. Curled on her bed pretending to be asleep, she thought. A lot. Hard.

They were different. They could *do* things. Every kid down here could do things that no normal kid should be able to do.

The fourth child had never joined them on their gym days. Chris said her name was Neesha, and that they'd overdone it on her. Whatever evil stuff they were injecting into the kids that were responsible for the freaky powers, they'd gotten carried away. Her brain had grown until they had to cut windows in her skull. Her head was so big that she couldn't hold it up, and the grown-ups were scared of her.

There had been others, too, before Jenny. Others who had died. At least two that Chris knew of.

Kids dying . . . kids with gross bulging heads . . . kids who can do things that no one should be able to do . . .

Jenny shuddered in her bed. It was horrible, unthinkable, but she couldn't ignore it anymore.

I'm one of them.

There, it was out.

She was one of them. Whatever was wrong with Chris, Julian, Neesha, and the others, was also wrong with her. The injections they'd been giving her were supposed to make it stronger. To help her, as the doctor with the cold gaze liked to say, reach her full potential.

Sick at heart, sick in her soul, but already knowing the truth on some deep and basic level, she waited with revulsion to <u>feel</u> it. The horrid inhuman stirring of something inside her.

Some strange hideous power . . . they didn't even know what it might be! But every other day they tested her, the woman called Anne coming in under guard, taking off her protective headgear.

Weird tests.

Concentrate, Jenny . . . what symbol is on the card?

Move the marble, Jenny . . . no, don't touch it . . .

Make this burn, Jenny, can you?

Stupid, stupid tests. Of course she couldn't. Nobody could do things like that.

Except that some people could . . . and she was becoming one of them.

* * *

2

Monty Python and the Holy Grail was on, but Brian Sorenson wasn't watching. He didn't need to. As he tapped and clicked on his keyboard, he was able to automatically recite the lines right along with the actors.

He planned to stop what he was doing and turn his attention to the screen when they got to Castle Anthrax, but in the meantime, he focused on the list that his search engine had just turned up.

As he surfed through archives of newspaper articles and photos that had been taken when computers were not even imagined, he heard footsteps on the walkway and got up to open the door.

The picture he'd just clicked on finished loading, and Brian glanced at it as he was turning away from the computer. His eyes snapped back to the image, and he actually rubbed them and looked again.

Someone kicked the bottom of the door. He backed away from the computer desk and groped for the doorknob without taking his gaze from the screen.

Dawn Jessec, her arms full, came in. "Hi, Bri, pepperoni and mushroom as usual. I – Brian? What's the matter?"

He swept the door shut. "You're going to think I'm totally gonzo."

She shrugged and pushed a rolled-up battlemat, a stack of comics, and a litter of dice out of the way to make room for the pizza and six-pack of cola on the table. "I already do, so what?"

"No, I mean for real. Look at this picture. Look at that guy on the end."

Dawn peered at the grainy old black and white photograph that had come up on the monitor. "He looks kind of familiar, I guess."

"Only kind of? Look harder. Look at his eyes."

"Hey!" she said brightly. "It's Dr. Lundquist!"

Brian sat down hard on the lumpy, ugly couch. Hearing her say it, confirm it, was like a punch in the gut. "Shit."

"What? What's wrong?"

"You know I've been working on the cliffhanger era game."

"Yeah." Dawn grinned. "I'm kind of looking forward to it now that you've explained how it all works. I can't wait to play the gutsy archaeologist's daughter –"

"That picture is from a 1944 Berlin newspaper. If I'm translating the German right, that's a shot of the scientists in charge of Schlossenberg."

"Which is?"

"One of the concentration camps. A small one that hardly anybody knew about, but where the Nazis did some of their worst experiments."

Dawn drew back askance and looked at him quizzically. "What are you saying? That Dr. Lundquist was a Nazi scientist?"

Brian dug his fingers into his hair. "I don't know. But look at him. Same eyes, same everything."

"Okay, you *are* totally gonzo. He's British, isn't he? Benjamin Lundquist is hardly a German name."

"Well, yeah, but of course he would have changed it after the war."

"I think you've been sitting too close to your computer," Dawn said. "The radiation's gotten to your brain."

"You saw it too, you identified him yourself." He scrolled down to read the caption, counting over and matching names to faces from left to right. "This one, Gustav Richter."

"Now, see, *that's* a German name." Dawn spread her hands as if that settled it.

"Lundquist is in his eighties, right? Which would have made him about that age in 1944." He pointed at the stern, intelligent face of the young man on the end.

"Have you been reading those conspiracy books again?"

"I'm serious! I thought it looked like him, you thought it looked like him, what if it *is* him?"

"Dr. Lundquist has dedicated his life to helping people, Brian. Not hurting them."

"So maybe it's atonement."

"Oh, come <u>*on*</u>! You can't really believe this!"

"I'm going to do a search for that name," he said, swiveling and scooting his chair forward. "Maybe we can get some more pictures."

Dawn looked over his shoulder as he went back to the search engine. "Eww," she remarked on reading some of the URLs listed.

"The trick to researching Nazis is in finding the legit historical sites and avoiding the modern-day genocidal lunatic ones," he said.

"So why don't you go to the library and get a book?"

He spared her an aghast look. "Nobody does it *that* way anymore. That'd be like hand-cranking ice cream."

"Your pizza is going to get cold." She tossed a stuffed tribble from the couch into the corner, where it hit the wall and squeaked.

"Uh-huh." He barely heard her, engrossed in the search.

"Brian, it's not him. I've met Dr. Lundquist, and you work for him. I think if he was a Nazi, you'd know. Next thing, you'll be trying to tell me that he's still doing secret experiments."

"What if he is?"

"Oh, God!" Dawn helped herself to a slice of pizza. "Sure, ask him. First he'd laugh in your face, and then he'd fire you, and you'd wind up working at Pizza X-Press with me and Ernie the psychotic delivery boy."

"Here it is. Richter, Gustav. Born in Austria 1n 1918, studied psychiatry and neurology – see? – took a post at a Vienna university, joined the Nazi party and ended up at Schlossenberg, where he developed his theories on the structure and biochemistry of the human brain."

Dawn stopped chewing and slowly lapped a strand of dangling cheese into her mouth, a motion Brian might have otherwise found pretty darn sexy, if not for the dubious shadow that fell over her eyes. "Probably coincidence," she said weakly.

"One hell of a big coincidence. Look at this picture."

It was a close-up of Richter himself, caught looking up from his work with an expression of annoyance at the interruption. His hair would have been blond but showed as white in the old photo, and his eyes were the same piercing, direct eyes, though their vivid green color didn't show up.

"Okay, that's really creepy," Dawn said. "They're identical. But it says right there the place was bombed, and he's dead. Case closed."

"He could have escaped. Could have survived. Skipped the country, laid low for a while, changed his name."

"Quit it, you're freaking me out." She dropped the half-eaten slice back into the box and wiped her fingers on her jeans.

"Aren't you the least bit curious?"

"No, because it can't be true. Think what that would do to him! An old man like that, and you'd ruin his life with these horrible accusations?"

"What if I'm right, Dawn? I know he's been able to do great things for Richie. Hell, everyone loves him and admires him. But what if he's been fooling everyone for the past sixty years?"

She only shook her head and didn't answer. On the computer, the old photograph looked back at Brian . . . and didn't answer either.

* * *

3

Sam Gordon snored in front of the television. It had probably been that aggravating whistle-whine-snort that drove his wife to drink. And, when drink hadn't been enough, to leave him. Lucas could hear the snores even over the cranked volume of the late-night talk shows.

He stood in the kitchen doorway, the light over the stove throwing his shadow onto the rug. Had his father been awake, he might have noticed something different in the pose and the shape of Lucas' silhouette. How Lucas stood unaided, taller and straighter than he ever had in his entire life. His shoulders and arms had always been good, after so many years of propelling himself on crutches, but now even his chest was thickening.

Dear Old Dad wasn't awake, though. Dear Old Dad slept with a quilt over his skinny pigeon chest and one bony arm loosely grasping a bottle of banana-flavored yogurt drink.

He slept as Conan O'Brian, wearing an expression of painful constipation, took insults from a still photo of the president with a superimposed mouth.

He slept as the shadow moved away from the kitchen door with a stealthy ease that would have done credit to a panther.

Lucas stopped beside his father's chair, looking down at him as Sam inhaled another long whistle and then released it in a rattling snore.

His head ached abominably, even down to the teeth. He felt as if his jaw and ears were being pushed forward and outward by a bulging pressure from within.

His back also ached, but it was a different sort of ache than the one he was used to. This was a single throbbing line of pain extending the length of his spine. He could feel the individual press of each vertebra against the skin of his back.

A glass rested beside the other chair. Lucas had left it there himself after *Wheel of Fortune.* The root beer was warm and had a watery layer on top from the melting ice. Nasty as it was, it served to clear the swampy-herb aftertaste from his tongue.

The medicine. The vitamins. A single pill left him with the aftertaste. After two pills, the residue was like a thin film coating his mouth.

Polishing off the entire month's supply at once, well, suffice to say that he could have gotten a more pleasing and breath-freshening effect from gargling with the runoff from a stagnant pool.

But it had worked. A bad taste in his mouth and a touch of a headache were small prices to pay.

Whistle . . . rattle-snore.

Funny, wasn't it, that Dear Old Dad had never looked into such a remedy before? If he loved his sonny-boy so much and was only looking out for sonny-boy's best interest?

Yes, that was funny. That was so darn funny Lucas forgot to laugh. Dear Old Dad, who just about pissed himself with fright every time his young son had fallen down or bumped his head. Dear Old Dad, never letting him go out because he might get hurt.

But sonny-boy doesn't need Dear Old Dad to baby-sit him, now, does he?

Before Mom bailed out on them, she'd been in the habit of making needlepoint pillows and bolsters. She had done the ultimate bail-out seven years ago, strangling on her boozy puke one night in some trailer park near Fresno, but they still had her damn pillows. Lucas picked one up from the back of the couch and looked at it. Kittens frolicking with balls of yarn.

Conan O'Brian introduced his next guest, a washed-up comedian whose sitcom had been bounced around to every possible prime-time slot and kept getting run over in the ratings.

Lucas shoved the pillow over his father's face.

Sam woke at once, with a startled cry so muffled that even Lucas, right on him, could barely hear it. The snores had been much louder. Sam's arms flailed upward in surprise, flinging the yogurt drink in a splattery arc of banana-flavored sludge.

Lucas pushed harder, pinning Dad's head against the back of the chair, which was itself pinned against the wall, so there was nowhere else to go. His father's legs jerked and kicked, and then Sam began to struggle in earnest as he realized what was happening.

"I don't *think* so," said Lucas, and planted a knee dead-center in Dad's chest. He leaned his full weight into it, feeling the tired creak and give of Dad's sternum.

Sam's struggles reached a frenzy, the entire chair shuddering and squealing beneath the two of them. His hands slapped blindly, then found Lucas' iron-hard arms and began to tug in an effort utterly pathetic in its futility.

"I . . . hope," Lucas grunted, though with the pillow folded to engulf Dad's entire head he doubt his words would be heard, "that . . . when you . . . get to Hell . . . Mom's there waiting!"

His father gave one great convulsive heave that was nearly enough to tip Lucas off-balance, but he steadied himself and pushed harder. Sam stiffened, and a stink assaulted Lucas' nose as the cushion underneath was soaked with urine.

Then Dear Old Dad went limp and became Dead Old Dad.

Lucas stayed where he was until the witless comedian had been replaced with that night's musical guest, former Scarlet Angel guitarist Johnny Harlowe. Harlowe was trying to launch a solo career, and if Lucas was any judge, all of the talent in the dismal rock group had died the same night as their lead singer, Nick Diamond.

Harlowe finished his number, and Conan said good-night. Then and only then did Lucas step back and remove the pillow.

His father's face, smeared with spit and snot and blood, gaped silently upward with the countenance of a clubbed fish.

The pillow hit the floor. Lucas, now on legs that were stilted and shaky, tottered backward and sat down hard on the couch. A hitching moan escaped him as he looked on his handiwork, and then the laughter roared up from his newly broadened chest.

*   *   *

4

Most of Seacliff slumbered in the quiet of the wee small hours. The children dreamt what dreams their healing brains created, and the staff and servants, except for those few who worked the overnight shift, slept the sleep of those whose lives were being fulfilled by important work well done.

Benjamin Lundquist, wakeful despite nearly an entire decanter of brandy, roamed the halls in a silence broken only by the muted bump of his cane and shuffle of his slippered feet on the thick carpets.

There would be no rest for him tonight. Some ghosts of his past were stirring, and demanded to make themselves known.

The clock had ticked past midnight and into the date engraved most deeply on his heart.

Benjamin! Benjamin! Help me!

He had never planned to marry, never expected to have a family. His work had always come first, and he'd known that to ask any woman to take second place to it would be a cruelty. He was a man of solitary habits, of secrets best kept well-buried.

But Elizabeth had changed all of that. Despite an age difference of nearly twenty years. Despite diverse academic fields – his was psychiatry and neurology, hers was history. And, given *his* history, that in itself should have been an even greater deterrent than the conflict between his old-fashioned ideals and her chip-on-the-shoulder feminism.

Yet somehow, proving once and for all that the emotion was irrational and illogical, they'd fallen in love. If at times she'd driven him mad with her independent streak, he knew there were just as many times when his stubborn mannerisms had done the same to her.

William had been born two years after Lundquist had finally decided that he must have just been too old to father a child.

Thirty-eight years ago . . .

Benjamin, for God's sake!

Her voice, cutting through his concentration and making him look up in annoyance. How many times had he told her not to bother him when he was in his study? The presentation tomorrow would be one of the most important ones of his career.

And another thing, he was no dog to come when yelled for . . . she could just as easily come and knock on the door like a civilized person . . .

But then he'd recognized the note in her voice for what it was. Frantic fear, not impatience and annoyance as he'd first thought. He'd caught a whiff of an acrid smell, and then had seen the wispy-thin tendrils of smoke seeping over the top of the door.

"Elizabeth!"

Yanking the door open, a thick cloud billowing into the study. Starting to cough. His eyes watering, squinting.

His study had been on the bottom floor of their split-level home, and the closer he'd gotten to the stairs, the worse the smoke became. It had filled the upper story, a grainy brown-black pall that parted in swirls and was underlit by a banked-coal orange glow.

A pounding noise. His heart? No, Elizabeth, somewhere overhead, banging on a wall or door, and screaming for him in a choked, rasping voice.

Up the stairs, into a flat deadly heat, ascending rather than descending into Hell.

He'd gone hunched over, nearly crawling, until he'd seen the bottom of the front door ahead of him. The stairs doubled back and led to the living room, but everything higher than the next three carpeted risers had been lost in the hot blackness.

In groping for the door handle, feeling for the locks and throwing back all the bolts, his thoughts had not been of escape. Not without his family. He'd only wanted to let out the suffocating clouds of smoke. He hadn't considered what would happen next.

The door, swinging open. Fresh air rushing in as the smoke rushed out. Above him, from the direction of the kitchen, yellow-orange light leaping like a living thing. A whooshing roar filling his ears as the influx of oxygen breathed new life into the flames.

He had tried to call for his wife, but a deep burning ache of a cough had dug its claws into both lungs.

Scrambling up the stairs. His heart thundering against his ribs.

A foot before him, Elizabeth's foot in one of those absurd slipper-socks with the puffball on the heel. In carnation pink.

His smoke-addled brain had made him stop and contemplate that silly pink sock for five seconds or more. He wondered why a woman who unfailingly wore slacks to faculty affairs, because she said skirts and pantyhose were male inventions designed to restrict the mobility of women, would be caught dead in such a piece of attire.

Caught dead?

The phrase, slapping through his confusion. Moving. Gathering up Elizabeth's limp body and half-crawling, half-sliding backwards down the stairs to the front door landing.

He'd carried her onto the porch and into the yard. A crowd of neighbors had converged on him, all shouting at once. Arms had lifted Elizabeth from him, and she'd stirred and coughed and gasped their son's name.

"Willy!"

Fear like a cold iron spike, ramming through his heart and down to his stomach. Spinning, and plunging back into the house, although fire was belching from the upstairs kitchen windows in hails of shattered and partly-molten glass.

The familiar layout might as well have been a carnival funhouse maze. Lundquist had slammed into walls, fallen over furniture.

Can't see, can't breathe!

He'd found another door and fell through, cheek hitting uncannily cool porcelain – the edge of the bathtub, and any harder might have knocked him out.

Scrabbling the other way. Hand sinking into something rough and plush, and he thought it was Willy's hair until he picked it up and felt the hard press of plastic button eyes. A teddy bear.

Something whooping, screaming. A hissing noise . . . someone had dropped an open sack of snakes onto the house and now they were slithering, hissing, over the shingles and roof. Falling through in cold scaly ribbons, venom raining from their fangs in streams.

His head had collided with a doorjamb and he'd gone full-length. His face against the carpet, he'd found a scant half-inch of clean air, which he'd gulped greedily.

Hands. Big rough hands on him.

It was them, the ones he'd failed, the ones who had died writhing and insane in the aftermath of his experiments, consumed by the crematorium. They were reborn in this new fire, and hungry for their long-awaited revenge.

Hands, yes. Seizing him, pulling and lifting, and he didn't try to fight. Let them . . . he deserved it.

His intentions had been the best. For the greater good, for the future of the world. All he'd ever wanted to do was give children like Anton and Gerda a chance at a meaningful and productive life, help them live up to their potential. If he had to deal with devils to get the resources he needed, so be it.

There had been no other way.

He had let the hands take him.

He'd come back to his senses some time later to find himself in a hospital bed. Clean crisp sheets in a clean crisp room with clean crisp sunlight spilling through the window. But with the stink of smoke still in his nose and on his skin, as if it had been ground into him and he'd never be free of it.

Moments later, nurses had come in, and then doctors. Minor smoke inhalation, they'd said. A black eye from his encounter with the edge of the tub, and a good-sized knot on his head from running into the doorjamb.

They'd told him that his wife wanted to see him . . .

Now, thirty-eight years later in the halls of Seacliff, Benjamin Lundquist coughed, as if the residue of smoke still lingered in his lungs. His face contorted as he felt the sting of Elizabeth's hatred as if it had only been yesterday. He could remember what she'd said, word for word. He could remember all of it.

Elizabeth, one arm in a sling. She'd wrenched her elbow at some point, couldn't even remember how.

But the fire, oh, the fire still in her, turning her mild brown eyes into twin kilns, baking her feelings for him into a solid lump of clay.

"Your fault!" she'd said, her voice huskier than usual. "You and your damn tea!"

Tea? Oh yes . . . he had remembered making himself a cup of tea to take down to his study after she'd gone to bed.

"How many times have I told you to turn off the burner!"

According to the investigators, the fire had started in the kitchen. The burner had caught one of the quilted kitchen mitts, and from there spread to the cabinets. It had burned merrily while he sat unaware downstairs, the tea he'd made growing cold and forgotten as he lost himself in his work.

"Willy?" he'd asked in a choked, smoky wheeze. "What about Willy, Elizabeth?"

The firemen had found the boy still in his bed, and the only comfort his parents could take was that he had been asleep throughout. He had never known the terror or panic of being trapped in the fire.

The firemen had brought the three-year-old boy out, and one of them had been able to breathe life back into Willy's spent lungs.

They had saved him, but the doctors later told Elizabeth it might have been better if they'd let him go. Willy had suffered irreparable brain damage. He might never regain consciousness, they'd said. Even if he did, it was doubtful if he'd talk, or walk, or think.

That had not been good enough for Benjamin Lundquist. He'd refused to accept it, but had kept his determination to himself, knowing that Elizabeth would never agree with his plan.

He'd done it in secret.

First in the university chemistry lab, bribes to janitors and long sleepless nights spent trying to perfect the enzyme compound that had already been so close to success.

Then, when the test animals had finally shown the desired results, he'd smuggled the cerebregen compound into the hospital and administered it to Willy.

What choice had there been? Leave his beloved son to lead a diminished, empty life? There was so little to lose . . . so very tragically little to lose.

The improvement had been slow but definite, and finally Willy had been able to come home. He had seemed, to all appearances, fully recovered. Lundquist and Elizabeth had barely been on speaking terms, living like strangers in the same house. But with their son's return, a tentative truce had been declared.

And then Benjamin had shattered it . . . a vain and stupid pride had led him to confess what he'd done.

Her outrage could have strafed the planet bare.

"That you would experiment on our own son! That you would do it without telling me! What if Willy had died thanks to your meddling? You could have cost us our boy!"

Lundquist's retort that his meddling had given them *back* their boy had fallen on deaf ears.

When he had come home from classes the next day, he did so to an empty house. She had packed up hers and Willy's things, and was gone. They were never to be heard from again, not even in the form of a divorce notice.

Where were they now?

He thought of their images in the photographs, and tried to imagine them so much older, so changed. Elizabeth would be in her sixties now, and William . . . William would be forty-one.

Lundquist shook his head, finding it impossible to envision. He remembered a boy, not yet fully toilet-trained, whose favorite food was his mommy's "nooner-toodle" casserole.

It was with those thoughts that Lundquist whiled away the long night.

He might never have made the breakthrough that would lead to the perfecting of the cerebregens had he not been driven to try it on William, and so in a strange sort of way, the children he was helping today owed their futures to that one terrible night.

* * *

Friday,

November 14

1

"Good morning, Lora," said Roger Brockman. "Good morning, Ruff."

Lora turned from the window and looked at him for several seconds before her face cleared into a tentative smile. "Good morning."

His heart went out to her, the sweet little girl in a plaid flannel nightgown, her freshly-brushed hair falling in ebony waves around her shoulders. The dog at her feet, a shepherd-mix with eternally quizzical upthrust ears, raised his head and thumped his tail.

"Ruff looks tired," Roger said. "Usually, he'd be jumping up on me to lick my face hello."

Lora didn't immediately answer. Since her near-drowning, her reactions had been delayed, her mind needing a longer interval to process and respond.

"He didn't sleep very well. Someone was up. Walking around all night. It kept him awake. But he didn't bark, because he didn't want to scare anyone."

"Were you awake?"

She slowly shook her head. Her eyes, as clear and green as new springtime leaves, met his. "Ruff told me."

Another effect of her ordeal had been to make her thought processes seem younger than her age. According to her mother, Lora was a highly imaginative and articulate child. The imagination remained, but with it came the simple faith and speech of a six-year-old.

But each day brought progress, far more progress than he had expected after reviewing the results of the initial perception and comprehension tests.

Lundquist's potion was working its magic once again, luckily for Lora.

"Ruff told you, did he?"

She nodded again. "It's pretty outside. Can I go outside today?"

"I'm sure we can arrange that. What will you need to do first?"

"Put my shoes on?"

"What else?"

Her brow furrowed, then cleared after she looked to Ruff for help. "Get dressed and make my bed!"

"Very good. You remembered."

"No, Ruff told me that too."

"Do you remember my name?" He probed gently, knowing that her slight memory impairment, an inability to recognize even the most familiar faces, was a cause of distress to Lora and her family alike.

"Dr. Brockman. You were in that movie with the dinosaurs."

He laughed. "No, we talked about that . . . I just look like that guy."

"Oh, right." She gazed out the window, and said, "*He* liked dinosaurs."

"Who, Lora?"

"That boy in the woods." Lora padded barefoot to her dresser, and took out a toy. Roger recognized it as something that had come with her from the TBMC. "This was his, I think. I found it in the woods where he was, and it smells like him. At least, that's what Ruff says."

"You found it in the woods?"

"Uh-huh. I went back and looked. For . . . for ebbi – *evidence*."

Roger rubbed at his chin and sat down on the end of the bed. "Evidence of what, Lora?"

"That Chris was real," Lora said. "Because sometimes I 'magine things. But this proves it. He was real, and so were the bad people."

"Bad people."

"They came and got him. I . . . I thought maybe . . ." She faltered, mouth turning down in a pensive bow. "I can't remember."

"That's okay, Lora. It'll come."

The dog whined. Lora sat down and crossed her legs, and Ruff scooted forward to rest his head in her lap.

"Ruff is sad I made him stay home," she went on. "I was going to look for Jenny. Do you know Jenny? They say she ran away."

"That's what everyone thinks happened, that or she was . . . kidnapped. Do you know what that means?"

"Bad strangers. Don't take candy. Don't get in the car. Even if they say they lost their puppy."

"That's right."

"I thought maybe the bad people got her too," Lora said, petting Ruff between the ears. "And I wanted to help because she's my friend. So I sneaked out, and I made Ruff stay."

"Into the woods?" he probed gently.

"Yes . . . it was dark. And scary." She hugged Ruff's neck. "There were monsters."

"Monsters. What kind of monsters?"

"Ringwraiths," she replied, and a shudder wracked her slight frame. "All dark with red glowy eyes and cold hands grabbing me. And they took me to a deep dark dungeon where the Wraith Lord was."

"Mmm-hmm," Roger said, not wanting to own up to the chill that her words gave him. Her little face was so earnest, her words hushed.

"The Wraith Lord stabbed Frodo on Weathertop with a knife all made of ice and it broke off in him. Broke off in him and dug in like a worm, wanting to get to his heart and turn him into a Ringwraith too. He could feel it in there, all cold and melting out."

Ruff crowded closer to Lora, no doubt picking up on his mistress' fear. She clung to the dog like it was a furry life preserver.

"Turning him into a Ringwraith," she murmured, rocking back and forth on her behind. "All inside of him and going deeper to his heart."

"Lora . . ." He wasn't sure what to say; years of training and practice of no use at all because her ghostly intonations and the depth of her emotion were making him shiver.

"And then Elrond and Gandalf made the water all come up in a big wave to drown them. But this time he did it wrong and the water washed Frodo away too. Washed me away in the cold dark water, and I never got to Rivendell so the good elves could get the splinter out. It's still in there."

"Who are the good elves?" The question came out unbidden.

She snapped out of her haunted daze long enough to give him a look full of the rich contempt that only children could master. "Elrond and them, didn't you read the books? Or see the movies? Except in the movies, I think it was Arwen that made the river come up. Gosh, I thought everybody saw the movies."

"I . . . I must have forgotten."

"The good elves can't help me now," she said.

"How about some good doctors? Like Dr. Lundquist, Dr. McGuire, and me? Might that work?"

"I guess so."

"We all do want to help you."

"And you let Ruff stay with me. He's like Samwise. But Mark and Travis are too little to be Merry and Pippin. Besides, they weren't the same as in the books. They weren't so silly in the books. He talks to me."

"Ruff does? Does he talk out loud?"

She laughed, and it was like the bright music of a string of tiny golden bells, blowing apart the unsettlingly spooky mood that had fallen around them. "No! Dogs can't talk. I just know what he's thinking. Right now, he's thinking you don't believe me."

"Why wouldn't I?"

"Because you're a grown-up and grown-ups never believe kids unless we tell them we did something bad like break a window, or spill pudding on the couch."

"Well . . . I've never met anyone who could know what a dog was thinking before."

"Neither did I. But I can." She got up from the floor with a child's unconscious grace and went to the window. "I can go outside today?"

"Yes, I should think so," said Roger. He could tell when a conversation was over. While Lora Blake might not have much more to say, she had certainly given him a lot to ponder.

*   *   *

2

The door to Seaquarium Fish and Pets opened, and Eustace Havelock got two steps inside before coming to a puzzled halt. He was a short man with a gnomelike face and twin puffs of pure white hair sticking out from under his cap. A wire shopping basket on wheels trundled behind.

"Your doorbell's busted," he said, cocking a thumb at a box above the door. "Didn't play its little song."

"Yeah, I know. Tragic, isn't it?"

The 'doorbell' in question was an electronic gadget which, when anyone broke the beam by coming in, triggered a recording of dogs and cats loudly barking and meowing the first stanza of "It's a Small World." Lucas had deep-sixed the damn thing five minutes after arriving at work that morning.

Havelock seemed satisfied and came further into the shop. The contents of his shopping basket varied little from week to week. Widower-groceries and a big bag from the pharmacy. To this, he'd add a box of birdseed for his finches and a package of hamster chow to scatter on his back porch for the squirrels.

What a waste. Dried-up, useless old fart. Lucas contemplated vaulting over the counter and snapping Havelock's neck like a chicken bone. *Be doing everyone a favor . . .*

"Where's your dad today?" Havelock asked, moving to the birdseed aisle. "Where's Sam?"

"He had to stay home," Lucas said. "Might be out the rest of the week."

"Not feeling well, eh? What's wrong with him?"

"Cold," Lucas said shortly. Which was certainly true. Dear Old Dad had been room temperature when Lucas wrapped him in a paint-stained plastic tarp, but the earthen dugout shed at the back of the property wasn't heated. It stayed cool and damp even in the summertime, cool and damp, just like Dad.

"Shame," Havelock said. He selected his birdseed and moved down to what Lucas thought of as the rodent aisle, the wheels of his basket squeaking as he went. "Hot tea with honey and lemon."

"This isn't the North Valley café," Lucas said. Below the counter, his fists curled and uncurled. Just jump right over, he could do it, too, with his newfound agility. Jump over and *snap!* Exit one dried-up old prune.

"No, no, for Sam. Make him feel better. But here's a better trick!" Cackling, Havelock dug among his parcels and came up with a fifth of whiskey. "Sure-fire cure for what ails a man."

In his mind's eye, Lucas saw himself with cinematic clarity, a low and wide-angle shot as he snatched the bottle from Havelock's arthritic hand and shattered it across his face. The absolute shock in Havelock's eyes would come even before the spray of blood and the bleat of pain. Havelock flying back, striking and overturning his basket before crashing into the shelves. Cans rolling every which-way. The box of birdseed splitting, spilling gritty confetti.

He gripped the edge of the counter as hard as he could. The intensity of the image both appalled and inflamed him. Reason won out – everyone in the North Valley shopping center knew Havelock's routine. With a titanic effort of will, Lucas wrestled his murderous urge under control and bared his teeth in an approximation of a smile when Havelock came to the register with his items.

Havelock paused and looked him over. "Best be careful you don't come down with Sam's cold, Lucas. You don't look so good."

"Didn't sleep well." That was also true, because he'd woken several times during the night with the conviction that his father was shuffling clumsily down the cellar stairs like an extra from a George Romero movie.

"Look different, too, I've noticed. How's the back?"

"Hey, do you want your damn birdseed or not? Three-fifty-eight."

"Here's four." As he always did, Havelock tapped the donation can for the animal shelter. "Change goes in there. Same thing every time, am I right?"

"Same thing." He bagged the purchase and handed it over, trembling with the exertion it took not to ram it down Havelock's throat.

Havelock put the bag in his cart. "You tell Sam I said hello, and maybe I'll see him next week."

"Maybe even sooner than that," Lucas replied as Havelock made for the door, but his voice was pitched low and Havelock was indifferent at best about using his hearing aid. "Maybe a lot sooner than that, if I catch up with you, you old fart."

* * *

3

Gwynne McGuire finished watching the videotape of Roger Brockman's meeting with Lora Blake, and switched off the television.

She was alone in her private office, a room that she thought adequately reflected her personality. Everything was clean, sharply delineated, and in its place.

The room was done in frost white, obsidian black, glass, and chrome. All angles and lines, everything functional and severe. No homey or personal touches softened the scene, not so much as a potted plant or photo of her family.

Against that stark background, her pale apricot hair was a flame, and her winter-blue eyes bright as sapphires. Even her complexion, normally so fair as to make her appear only a step or two from albinism, appeared rich and vibrant in the glacial setting of her office.

Gwynne read over the transcript of the conversation she'd just watched. She sat back in her chair of tubular chrome and black vinyl, and gathered her thoughts as she raised a tiny tape recorder.

"Subject: Blake, Lora. Designation MC-F1198. She has been in treatment for six weeks, following the deliberate infliction of oxygen deprivation and subsequent immersion. The cerebregen compound was first administered within one week of the damage. She is evidencing definite progress.

"Moving on to the case of ET-M1013. Damage was sustained at birth, and treatment was begun at age seven . . . while regeneration of the tissues has been within normal projected parameters, there is no indication of increased growth in the area of interest after almost twelve weeks of treatment.

"When combined with results from other subjects, this clearly indicates that the enzyme is produced in greater amounts as an immediate response following damage to the pertinent areas of the brain.

"Thus, the more time that elapses between the damage and the introduction of the cerebregens, the less likely we are to obtain the desired results. Recommended that we concentrate our efforts on the most recent subject, SK-M1029, who best meets this criteria.

"That brings me to the problem of the alternate test subjects. KG-F1196 and SF-M1023. Although both do show higher than average concentrations of the enzyme, neither of them have thus far shown any measurable results.

"We had been operating under the assumption that, since these two had sustained no brain damage to begin with, the compound would be able to devote all of its strength into reacting with the enzyme, producing quicker, or more dramatic effects.

"I suggest we continue as planned with them, but that we hold off on introducing any new alternate subjects to the program, and shelve the long-range plan. They simply aren't responding well enough to justify the effort and the expense and risk of trying it on a larger scale.

"It is my strong impression that without the pre-existing condition – and no matter how bad the quality of public school is, it still doesn't constitute brain damage – we're not going to see any sort of significant results.

"Overall, frankly, we're not getting the success rate we anticipated. In eight months, we've had only four show any sort of potential. One of those is dead, another is to all intents and purposes both paralyzed and insane. The two others, however, DT-M0187 and KS-M0191, do prove that we're on the right track.

"What intrigues me the most is how personality and background seem to be indicators in what kind of abilities they develop.

"For example: DT-M0187. He was, according to his records, a sullen child even before his injury, and subsequently gained the ability to tele-project an empathic aversion field.

"KS-M0191, on the other hand, was a minister's son. The entire family was dedicated to 'helping' people. We now have a boy who can literally take the pain of others on himself, and heal it.

"Add to that MC-F1198. Whose mother says she's always had a way with animals . . . and who now appears to be developing some sort of animal-telepathy, and it is certainly something worth considering."

She turned off the recorder, a small cool smile like the remote curve of a crescent moon touching her lips.

* * *

4

Dinner was a corn dog, fries, and lime Jell-O dessert with bits of mandarin orange and miniature marshmallows suspended in it. And milk and juice. Jenny Forrester would have killed for a Pepsi.

Thinking of soda made her think of her friends and school and the rest of her life. If she got out of here, she wouldn't care about anything Rocky said. There were worse things than his mean gossip.

Thinking of school and her friends, though, suddenly reminded her of Eric Raney, and a supernova burst of understanding flared so bright in her head she thought rays of light would shoot from her eyes and ears.

Eric Raney is one, too! Like Chris. Like Julian. A Seacliff kid. Has to be!

She was seized by a shudder as she remembered that night in the woods, and the strange look in his coppery eyes as he leaned toward her.

For a brief but thrilling moment, she'd thought he meant to kiss her, Eric Raney and her first real kiss. But then something terrible had happened . . . that great dark wave crushing her down, down, down . . . until the next thing she was aware of was waking in the cave, strapped to the bed.

That great dark wave . . . Eric had done that to her. His power.

Why me?

He'd known somehow. The lab-coated doctors kept talking about what the differences in her brain. Maybe they'd sent Eric after her for just that reason.

Jenny resolved then and there that if she ever saw Eric Raney again, she was going to kick him right where it counted. Hard. Really hard.

The door to her enclosure opened, and she turned around fast, sure that they knew what she had just been thinking and were going to punish her for it. But instead, Judge came in with the folding table, Inge right behind him. Anne brought up the rear, smoothing her dark hair behind her ears and fingering the red marks left by her headband. Behind them, one of the other doctors watched through the clear wall.

"Time for some more tests," Anne said.

Suddenly deciding that there couldn't be much they could to do her that was worse than keeping her prisoner and screwing with her brain, Jenny glared at her. "I'm not going to do your dumb tests anymore. You people are monsters and you can all go to hell!"

"That's not a very productive attitude," Anne said, unruffled, as she sat down.

Jenny shoved the table as hard as she could. The edge struck the unsuspecting Anne in the stomach, and she went over backwards, taking the chair with her in a loud clatter.

Pain exploded in Jenny, and a white-hot burst of sparks engulfed her vision. When she could take stock of her surroundings again, she was sprawled on the floor beside her bed, feeling like she'd been struck by lightning. The table was crooked, the chair was overturned, and Anne was hunched over but slowly straightening up.

Inge was standing by Jenny, the red of her visor turning her eyes to hard amethysts. She was holding something that looked like a taser.

"You will not act out again," Inge said harshly, looking as if she'd dearly love to beat Jenny cross-eyed. "Sit."

She did so, confused. She couldn't remember what had happened, just that the door had opened and the next thing she knew, she was on the floor. Uncontrollable little twitches jerking her arms and legs. Her hair was staticked to her cheeks and some strands rose in a wavering halo. The doctor outside sighed and shook her head, as if to say, 'see what we have to put up with?'

"Now, let's try this again," Anne said, sitting opposite Jenny. She took out a deck of oversized cards, the ones with the weird symbols on them.

Jenny tried not to cry. "Look, I know what you're trying to do, but I can't. Please. I don't want to be like them. I just want to go home. Please, can't I go home? Let me out of here, let me go back to my dad."

As she spoke, she felt a sensation deep within her mind. It was the mental equivalent of bending a fresh accordion-straw, the pleats unpopping with a sort of *zwoop-zwoop-zwoop* sound. The sheer strangeness of it stopped her tears even before they began.

Anne set down the cards. "You're right, Jenny. You want to go home. So we'll let you go home to your father."

Jenny didn't know who was more astonished, herself or any of the on-lookers. A shocked gasp burst from the doctor.

"Really? You'll let me go?"

"It's what you want, isn't it?" Anne stood up, and scowled at the guards, who had moved between them and the door.

"Suggestion!" said the doctor in the tone of someone who'd just ma-chete-chopped through a thick jungle and discovered the lost city of El Dorado. "Get her out of there, Judge, and get her visor back on."

"Hey, wait, no fair!" Jenny protested. She started forward, but Inge threat-eningly raised her taser, and Jenny cringed back.

They hustled Anne out, the dark-haired woman arguing all the while that they should do what Jenny wanted. When they got her headband back on, a befuddled expression overtook Anne's face.

"What the . . . what was I doing? Dr. McGuire, I –"

"Suggestion," the doctor said again, this time with smug satisfaction. Jenny recognized her at last. The school counselor's sister. "She told you what she wanted, and you were going to do it unquestioningly."

"It never occurred to me not to," Anne said.

"And it does go along with her personality, doesn't it? The bossy little wretch. This will come in so handy . . . far better than trying to rely on . . ." Abruptly, the doctor's mood soured. "It seems I was too hasty in my judge-ment. This has shown some definite results after all. We'll have to continue following up with these new subjects."

"What?" Jenny flung herself against the barrier. "Hey! I want to go home, didn't you hear me? She said I could –"

Dr. McGuire addressed her directly for what Jenny figured was the first time ever. "Of course she did. You made her say that."

Pressed against the cool, transparent wall, Jenny let herself slide down. "No . . . no, I can't do that . . . it wasn't me."

"Whatever she said just made perfect sense to me." Anne was still shak-ing her head, bewildered and amazed.

"We'll have to devise some careful tests for this one," Dr. McGuire said to Judge. She crossed to someplace out of Jenny's line of sight, and returned with a can of Pepsi. "As you've made such excellent progress, Jennifer, I think a reward is in order." She opened the small door that admitted the meals, and placed the can on the shelf inside.

They removed to the far end of the cave, where all of their computers and equipment were. Jenny, from where she remained crouched by the wall, watched them in incomprehension. They examined Anne, drawing some ampoules of blood . . . then she understood. They wanted to see what effect her power might have had on her victim.

My power . . .

She looked at the can. She found she had never wanted a Pepsi less in her entire life. Not that one. Not earned this way. Not as a reward for proving she was a part of their freak show.

Stifling a sob, she whirled and flung herself on the bed, burrowed under the covers, and cried herself into a dark, troubled sleep.

* * *

Saturday,

November 15

1

Toby Edwards faked feeling okay until his parents had kissed him goodbye. They were going down to Ferndale to visit scary old Aunt Bebe, and he had begged off with homework excuses.

Once the car was out of sight, he let the cheery smile fall away and closed the drapes. Retreating to his room, he snuffed the light and stretched out on the bed with his arms crossed over his face.

The headache was back and stronger than ever, stomping through his head like a team of Clydesdales pulling not a jolly Budweiser wagon but a grim black funeral hack loaded with dead bodies.

He shut his eyes, which felt hot and throbbing even through closed lids. He wondered if his head was going to pop like a balloon . . . and would have almost been glad of it just to get rid of the pain.

It had come on starting last Wednesday. He had gotten through two days of school without letting on, but his teachers had remarked on it and he'd done so badly on a math test that he'd earned the first B+ of his academic career.

He couldn't talk to anyone about it. They'd just say the same things his mother felt. That he was pushing himself too hard. Trying too hard. About the only one he might have been able to talk to was Eric . . . but . . .

Toby groaned and rolled his head on the pillow. He'd downed six aspirin already that morning, having bought a bottle out of his allowance and hiding it in his desk rather than risk Mom noticing. Hadn't made a dent in his headache, but now he also had an upset stomach.

Think, he told himself sternly. *Think about it. Last week. Wednesday evening. You rode out there . . . said hi to Mrs. Raney . . . she left for her date with Mr. McGuire . . . you watched game shows . . . and then . . . and then . . .*

Despite the way it made his head rock sickly like a ship on a wave-tossed sea, Toby sat up fast, frowning.

Jeopardy . . . Alex Trebek being smug . . .

Toby replayed it in his mind. He could have written down the first half of the show word-for-word. But he couldn't remember the rest, nothing after the Double Jeopardy round began. Not even the categories.

He logically, cognitively knew they had watched the rest of the show, then turned it off to study.

It didn't seem real. It seemed like his mind was dredging up something he'd been told, but of which he had no specific recollection. The details, the clarity, weren't there.

Hollow. False. Everything else was crystal-sharp as ever.

The box . . . the puzzle box . . .

Toby rolled and pulled the pillow over his head as if he could block out that memory as easily as the others seemed to have been erased.

It didn't go.

The box had been sitting on top of Eric's dresser, compact and mysterious with its design of intricate wood. Eric said it was a puzzle box, and gave it over with a sly grin as if silently betting that Toby couldn't figure out how to open it.

As he'd held it, turning it over in his hands and trying various combinations of sliding the moving sections, Toby became suddenly sure that the box had been given to Eric by his father, after a trip to San Francisco. He could even see Eric's father in his mind, though there weren't any photographs around the house and Toby had no real idea what the man should have looked like.

He had the weirdest idea that the box could, if he held onto it long enough, tell him plenty about Eric. His so-called friend. Oh, yes, the box remembered a lot . . . its memories were impressed into its substance and just waiting to be read, like words on the pages of a book.

Unnerved, Toby had dropped the box. When Eric had reclaimed it, checked it, and put it back on the dresser, good-naturedly scolding Toby all the while, Toby asked where he'd gotten it. Eric looked him square in the eye and told him it had come from a garage sale.

Eric was lying.

The box told the truth.

Toby had no idea why he was so sure of that, but he was. As sure as he'd ever been of anything. But he didn't want to believe. Not that awful dark certainty that Eric was bad, Eric was dangerous, Eric was lying.

The doorbell rang, drilling into his head like a wasp and bringing him back to the here and now. It rang and rang until he had no choice but to go answer it.

He opened the door, and there stood Eric Raney, slouched in black leather with his mother's battered pickup parked behind him at the curb.

"Hey," Eric said, raising his chin in greeting. "Going out to McD's. Wanna come?"

"I . . . I have to work on my book report. For history."

Eric's dark brows drew together over his coppery eyes. "Thought that wasn't due for a couple of weeks."

"I want to be sure I get it done. Plus, I've got a headache."

"Yeah?" Eric's gaze sharpened like that of a hawk. "What else?"

"What do you mean, what else? Who said there was anything else?"

"You can tell me, Tobe."

"I don't know what you're talking about." He'd never been a good liar, and he felt like it showed now more than ever. All over his face.

But Eric pretended to believe him, which was as transparent to Toby as his lie must have been to Eric. "Okay, then. Hop in. Buy you a Big Mac."

"You know something, don't you?"

"Lots."

"I mean about what's happening to me!"

"What is?"

Toby's breath puffed rapidly. "It's you, isn't it? You're doing something to me. Drugging me, maybe. That's why I can't remember, and what's giving me the headaches."

Eric gestured to the pickup. "Get in, Toby. We can talk about it on the drive."

"No way. Not until you tell me."

"Look," he said, and his eyes narrowed until they were copper spear-points nailing Toby to the spot. "I don't want to hurt you, okay? But unless you want a real headache, you'll come with me."

"You've been lying. All this time. You don't want to be my friend."

A look of terrible and genuine sadness crossed Eric's face like a cloud over the sun. "Yeah, I do . . . but it's gotta be this way."

"What does?"

"Besides, we can still be friends. Better than friends. Brothers. We've got to stick together, people like us. Once there's enough of us, no one can tell us what to do anymore. But if we don't, they'll use us, treat us like freaks. I'm tired of being the only one!"

Scared to the core now, Toby tried to back into the house and shut the door. But Eric slipped past him like an eddy of dark wind in the shape of a boy, and shut it himself. In the dimness, his eyes glimmered, glimmered.

"There's more of us now, Toby," he said. "Different from everyone else. Stronger. More powerful. We can do things that they can't do, that they don't know how to handle. I can, and so can you. Am I right?"

"Go away," Toby quavered. "You need to go away or I'll . . . I'll . . . call the police."

"No you won't."

"My folks'll be home —"

"They're gone for the day. Come with me, Toby."

"I'm not going anywhere!"

Whatever Eric's sadness had been, it now hardened into determination. "They'll take you anyway. They'll make it look like an accident, or a kidnapping, or that you ran away. Do it this way, go along with it, and maybe they'll let you come home after. No one will have to know."

"Who? What's going on?" Chills swarmed up and down his back. "Kidnappings . . . you mean like Jenny? You know what happened to her?"

"You don't want it to happen to you, do you? Or to end up on the beach like Lora Blake?"

He could only gape at Eric in the rawest, deepest horror he'd ever known.

"This way's easier," Eric said. "Come on."

Toby followed on numb, stilted legs. They went down the walk to the pickup, and he obediently climbed in on the passenger side as Eric got behind the wheel.

"Who's doing it?" Toby asked as his house disappeared behind them. "Lora . . . Jenny . . . what's going on?"

Eric shook his head.

"Please! Eric, I have to know. It's driving me crazy. Is it brainwashing? Like the government when you see something you're not supposed to?"

"What can you do, Toby?"

"Huh?"

"What can you do? It's started, hasn't it? It's working, it's started. Telepathy, TK, pyro, what?"

"Huh?" he said again, even more bewildered than before.

"Your *power*," Eric said, exasperated.

A picture of the puzzle box sprang up in his mind, and the knowledge that had come from it as clearly as if it had been speaking. And other things . . .

Looking in his mother's purse for a stick of gum and knowing that she'd just gotten back from a checkup and there was a lump in her breast but she didn't want to say anything about it and worry his dad. Setting the table for dinner and being able to tell who had used which utensil the night before, even though the knives and forks had been washed spotless-clean. Borrowing his dad's pen and knowing what the exact checkbook balance was after Dad finished paying the bills.

"I don't understand," he said.

"You're the smartest kid in school. Figure it out."

"There's no such thing as telepathy, or psychic powers. I told you that a few weeks ago . . ." he trailed off, hearing Eric's voice replayed in his head:

Suppose someone discovered that there's an enzyme produced in the human brain that fosters the development of those kinds of powers? Suppose someone figured out a way to increase the production of that enzyme in test subjects? And suppose that one of the test subjects got the ability to sense psychic potential in others?

"You did something to me," he accused Eric, his skepticism flip-flopping to utter belief in a heartbeat.

"I sensed you," Eric said. "Out of all the kids in school, I picked out the two with the most potential so they could bring you into the program."

"Me and who?" The truth rose up and struck him in the nose. "Jenny? It's Jenny, right? What did you do to her?"

"She's okay. They wouldn't hurt her. Wouldn't hurt any of us. We're too valuable."

Toby's mind raced. His hands were pressed flat to the split and peeling vinyl of the seat. "So they give us something to develop these powers they think we have? They took Jenny away to their secret lab, but couldn't risk having too many kids vanish, so after you singled me out they decided to do it to me and cover it up with brainwashing, right?"

"Dead on."

"And they've been using you to find more of us."

"Yeah."

"Why are you helping them?" Toby nearly shrieked, surprised to find himself feeling a surge of real fury at the older boy. "How can you do this to other kids?"

Eric's mouth turned down, and his fists tightened on the steering wheel. "I had to. I didn't have any choice once they found out what I could do."

"You . . . you bastard!"

"Hey!" Eric snapped. "I had to, huh? I didn't want to be alone anymore, the only one, the only freak!"

"You tricked us! We trusted you, we liked you, and you tricked us!"

Eric had to stop at the light at the intersection of Trinity Bay Boulevard and Bay Road. Going straight would take them to Agate Way, and eventually to North Valley where the McDonalds was. A left turn would lead to Vista Drive as it skirted the back of the bluff where Seacliff loomed.

Toby knew even before Eric hit the left blinker that there were no Big Macs and fries in his immediate future, though he'd probably remember it that way because the people Eric was talking about would program him to remember.

They were headed back to Eric's house. Where it had happened before.

He threw open the door and jumped out of the still-slowing truck before he was fully aware that he meant to. By the time the brake lights flashed, Toby was running hell-bent down the street.

*   *   *

2

It wasn't often that Kel McGuire had an entire Saturday to himself.

On the spur of the moment, he decided to indulge his newest hobby, photography.

His only regret as he packed up his Minolta in its padded bag was that Marge couldn't join him. The weekends were roughest on her. By now, she would be enjoying a well-deserved sleep.

He admired her for keeping vampire's hours without complaint, especially for barely more than minimum wage plus tips. She was strong, intelligent, beautiful, dedicated. Admired her? Heck, a man could fall in love.

Kel thought that wherever they were jet-setting, his parents must have looked up at that moment with a shiver of undefined horror.

Luckily for them, they at least had Gwynne to live up to and even exceed their expectations. Cold, condescending, brilliant, severe Gwynne.

He deliberately shook off thoughts of his sister before they could spoil his mood. The day was bright and gorgeous, and if he were lucky, he'd get some great shots today.

The Agate River campground was closed for the season, so Kel had the area to himself. The scatter of leaves crackled underfoot as he tramped along the hiking trails. His passage disturbed some birds and small animals, and he had a perfect photo opportunity when one large squirrel chose to perch on a stump like a preacher in a pulpit, and chatter sternly at the interloper while lashing his bushy tail.

He crossed an old wooden bridge, his footfalls as always making him think of goats and trolls, and glimpsed a pair of otters twisting in a sleek yin-yang of fur as they played by the shore. The beach, a smooth curve of sand dotted with driftwood and the water-tumbled agates that gave the river its name, was deserted except for some stalking seabirds on long jointed legs.

The wind coming in off the bay stirred his hair. It was too cold to sit here for long, once the warmth brought on by the walking dissipated from his limbs.

Kel let his mind float free of his gamut of concerns and duties, and just drank in the day through eyes and viewfinder. When he'd satisfied his photographic urge, he sat on a picnic table to eat an apple and one of the oversized oatmeal-raisin cookies from the bakery in Tom's Market.

He tossed the apple core into a trash barrel and slung the strap of his camera bag around his neck. He'd parked on the far side of the wooded area, and now strode briskly along the path that would lead him to the upper lot.

Under the deep shadows the temperature was several degrees cooler. The trail was paved in wood chips laid over the springy mat of decades' worth of pine needles.

The sound of a sobbing child brought Kel up short.

His first irrational thought was of ghosts, of the girl-specters whose short lives and brutal deaths had so affected Theresa Zane.

His second thought, like a starburst dwarfing the first, was of Jenny Forrester, now missing for nine weeks. Kel quickened his pace, veering off the path toward the source of the crying.

Split-log benches were situated here and there along the hiking trails, and as Kel came around the bole of a massive redwood, he saw one of those benches set in a nook off to the side. On the bench, his head buried in arms crossed on his knees, was a boy. The dark-brown skin, thin frame, and cap of wiry hair identified him for Kel without him needing to see the boy's face.

"Toby?"

Toby looked up with a harsh and ragged gasp. His face was streaked with tears and carved with lines of pain and weariness. His clothes were dirty and torn, and a few scratches laddered his arms.

He tensed for flight, and Kel raised his hands. "Toby, it's okay, it's me. What's the matter?"

"Nuh-nothing," Toby stammered, the lie evident in every aspect of his tone, posture and expression.

Kel approached. "Looks like you fell down."

Toby looked dully at the holes in the knees of his pants, the fresh scrapes visible through the torn denim. "Yeah."

"You're not lost, are you?" Kel sat at the other end of the log bench.

"Huh-uh."

"You seem pretty upset. Want to talk about it?"

He shook his head.

"And you must be cold," Kel added. Toby only had a short-sleeved checkered shirt on over his jeans. He took off his own windbreaker and draped it around the boy. "What are you doing out here?"

Toby seized the edges of the jacket and held it firmly in both hands, his forehead furrowed and his eyes closed. The tension seeped out of his body bit by bit, until he loosed a choppy sigh and looked up. "You're all right. You're not one of them."

"One of who? Toby, what happened?" He drew on what he knew of the boy's occasional troubles at school. Smart and small as he was, Toby had been a not infrequent target of bullies. "Were some kids chasing you?"

"Just one. I ran away. But you won't believe me. It's too crazy. No one will believe me."

"Try me."

"Eric."

"Eric Raney? I thought you guys were friends."

Toby began to cry again, and his words tumbled out in a near-hysterical babble. "I thought so too. But he's helping them, and he's going to let them do things to me. I jumped out of the truck and ran away. Ran all the way across town. Can't go home, because he'll find me there and Mom and Dad won't be back until late."

"Sounds like you think he's pretty mad at you."

"He wants me to be like him, another one like him. He did it to Jenny too." Toby's chest began to hitch. "I . . . I . . . it's already starting, because I can *know* things . . . just by touching something . . . I can't go home, I'm so scared to go home!"

He screamed the last words, startling flocks of birds into sudden whirring flight. Toby fell from the bench and sprawled among the leaves, hyperventilating and wracked with spasmodic convulsions.

"Toby!" Kel dropped beside him, sweeping branches out of the way with both hands as the seizure continued. It lasted less than a minute, and then Toby's eyes rolled up and he fainted.

*   *   *

3

"Finally," Gwynne McGuire said, impatience radiating from her like the frosty glare of a florescent light. She braced her hands on her hips, one foot tapping and her lips pressed together in a thin white line.

The trailer was an old one, its silvery hue pocked and rust-spotted, weeds and undergrowth springing up through the axles. The interior had been a haven for mice and sparrows, and remained a dusty, mildewy mess that grated on Gwynne's nerves every time she was forced to make one of these trips.

A far cry from tidy laboratory conditions, that was for sure. Only her sincere belief and dedication to Seacliff could have gotten her to work in such wretched and unsanitary surroundings.

The western sky was a riot of purples and reds, shading to pure cobalt directly overhead. Gwynne was unmoved by the beauty of the heavens, caring only that she'd been waiting here for hours and had been about to give up when she'd heard the rattle and cough of the pickup's engine.

The sunset's gleam turned the windshield to stained glass, making it impossible for her to see within. Long moments passed and she tapped her foot harder.

"You'd better have a very good explanation," she said as the driver's side door opened and Eric Raney emerged.

Alone.

He gave her a sullen glance and came toward her with his hands stuffed in the pockets of his leather jacket.

"Well?" She packed a wealth of annoyance into that one word.

"I don't have him."

"I beg your pardon?"

"He wouldn't come."

"I need to examine him, to test him," she said icily. "I thought you were aware of that. I thought the importance of that had been well impressed upon you. Instead, you spend the afternoon doing . . . what? Joyriding? While I'm waiting out here for nothing."

"I was looking for him," Eric snarled. "Driving all over this stupid town. He ran off, okay? He's got something, all right, I know he does. He's been having headaches, and he just knew somehow what was going on. Picked it out of my head, maybe. Or maybe you screwed up. Maybe the implanted memories didn't take. How should I know?"

"If he suspected, if he was showing signs of developing his potential, that's all the more reason why I need to examine him. Why did you let him go?"

"What was I supposed to do? He jumped out of the damn truck and ran off!"

"Unacceptable." She turned away from him and fisted her hands behind her back, lifting her face to the blazing sky. "I was against this method from the beginning. If we're to conduct these experiments, they need to be in a controlled environment. We should have taken him to the lab, like the Forrester girl. I did not even like administering the initial injections at your so-called home. Let alone this notion of leaving him with his parents and letting his gift develop naturally! We couldn't be sure that the memory erasure would take."

"Hey, you were the one worried about too many kids going missing," Eric said. "You suggested the mind wipe, the fake memories. It was supposed to work."

"Too many variables. We can't properly monitor him on a once-a-week schedule, even with you keeping an eye on him at school. He should be confined in the lab, like the others."

"It's not my fault, okay? Wasn't my idea. I'm just doing like you guys tell me. You're the ones who got greedy."

"Greedy?" She whirled back to stare him down. "You fail to appreciate the scope of what we're trying to accomplish."

"Oh, I get it all right, I do. You want results. You want to be able to go to someone and say, 'hey, lookie what we can do, we can make kids with psychic powers,' and they'll give you all the money you could ever want."

"I don't like this tone of insolence, Eric."

He ignored her warning and kept on, his words hammering at her. "But it wasn't enough, testing it on the vegetables you've got up at Seacliff, not once you found out I could sense it in some of the healthy ones too. You don't care about them, about the kids! You don't care about anyone. You'd turn this whole town into *The Village of the Damned* if you thought there was funding in it!"

"Do not turn around and attempt to blame your failure on me," Gwynne said. "What it comes down to is that *you* chose Toby Edwards. *You* said that he could be managed. And *you* let him get away. Am I correct?"

"Hey, you know, I don't *work* for you! I'm not one of your lab techs or hired thugs that you can order around."

"But you *are* part of the project. It's not as if you could resign."

"There's other things I could do." His voice dropped to a near-growl.

Gwynne arched her brows, unimpressed. "We're well aware of your dissatisfaction with your circumstances, Eric, but need I remind you, you did agree to the terms. And no matter what you might do, you will always be a part of the project."

"The project made me that way! It's not my fault!"

"It doesn't matter whose fault it is. The point remains, it *is*, you *are*, it cannot be changed." She sighed. "Lundquist is right . . . so much energy wasted in discontent. If everyone could only learn to accept and live within their stations, how much better off they'd be."

"Yeah, yeah, I've heard the pep talk," Eric sneered. "Just mind-control everyone to be good little drones, and they'll all be so much happier. Well, I'm through. I don't know how I got into this shit, but I'm done. I've had enough."

"You had no choice. You still don't."

"Yeah? I can walk out right now. Tell everyone. Shut you down."

"And do what, go where? Who would believe you?" She regarded him with contempt and arrogant pity. "We give you the opportunity to use your gift for the betterment of humanity —"

"By getting other kids to trust me, then turning them over to you so you can make freaks out of them."

"The more of them there are, the less alone you'll be. You've often said how tired you are of being alone."

"I'm tired of betraying my friends, too!" He kicked the side of the trailer hard enough to make rust sift down in reddish flakes.

"You're endangering the entire project," Gwynne said. "And several lives."

"Saving others!"

"Eric, Eric. You're not cut out to be a crusader, boy. You're cut out to be a Judas. Accept it and do your job."

He went for her then, the treacherous little bastard. His eyes narrowed, and she felt the heavy mental pressure of his psychic attack trying to crush her into unconsciousness. Gwynne dipped a hand into her pocket and came out with a tiny cylinder.

She sprayed the contents into his face. Eric gasped in surprise, inhaling the fast-acting drug. He was out cold before he even hit the ground.

*   *   *

4

Dr. Shaw came up to Kel McGuire just as Kel was clipping the phone back onto his belt, and feeling like he'd struck out twice in a row.

"How is Toby?" Kel asked.

"Awake, but shaky and confused. Physically, he's a little scratched up, nothing to worry about. Mentally, though . . . we had to give him a light sedative to calm him down. He kept insisting he had to get out of here, that 'they' would find out he was here and come and get him."

"They who?"

"He can't, or won't, tell me what happened. My best guess right now is that it looks like the seizure was brought on by a hysterical reaction, but I was hoping you could tell me more."

"Did you run any blood tests for drugs?"

"Drugs? Toby? Toby Edwards?" Dr. Shaw looked understandably askance.

"Some of the things he said led me to wonder if . . . if some older kids might have talked him into trying something," Kel said.

He was reluctant to believe it of Eric, after all of Marge's assurances that her son's tough-guy image was just for show. Too, it went contrary to what he himself had learned of Eric's personality. But he couldn't get Toby's words out of his mind.

"I'll order a tox screen," Dr. Shaw said. "Any ideas what I might be looking for?"

"I wish I knew."

"We tried to get in touch with his parents –"

"Not home, I know. I just tried them too. May I talk to Toby?"

"He's in Exam 1."

They walked down the hall together, to a small room where Toby Edwards huddled in the middle of a hospital bed, his eyes large and fearful, and slightly glazed from the sedative.

"Hi, Toby," Kel said. "Can I come in?"

"Okay."

"I need to have one of the nurses draw a little bit of blood," Dr. Shaw said.

"No injections!" Toby thrust his arms under the sheet.

"No injections . . . just drawing some blood," Shaw assured him.

"Well, okay." Toby submitted to the needle, and they both saw that the inner crook of his elbow, under the unforgiving glow of the florescents, was faintly yellowed.

When the doctor asked to see the other one, Toby showed it, and it, too, had a vague discoloration. The darkness of his skin prevented them from being able to tell for sure, but the look Shaw gave Kel told him that they were thinking along the same lines. The yellowed marks could well be the faded residue of bruises. Shaw nodded at Kel as he left the room with the blood samples.

"Have you been using drugs, Toby?" Kel asked, striving to sound gentle and non-accusing. "We're not trying to get you in trouble, but we need to know so the doctor can treat you."

"I guess I must have," Toby said. "But I don't remember."

"Smoking something? Taking pills?"

"I don't know."

"Shooting up?"

"I don't know!"

"With Eric?"

"I guess . . ."

"What kind of drugs?"

"I told you, I don't know. But they must be working, because it's happening, like Eric said. I can do things."

"What sorts of things?"

Toby cast around, looking for something. He reached out for a pen on the bedside table. As he held it, his face took on that same look of intense concentration as when he'd been holding the camera bag. "It's Mr. Daley's . . . he's a nurse . . . he cheats on crossword puzzles."

Kel stared. "Toby . . ." It was all he was able to say. His mind felt as if he'd been through the spin cycle.

"They'll find out I'm here." The boy said it calmly enough, but there was terror lurking behind the drowsy glaze in his eyes. "I got away before they could do it, before they could brainwash me again. So now I remember what Eric told me, what I bet he wasn't supposed to tell me, and they'll be afraid someone will find out."

"Who, Toby?"

"Promise you won't let them do anything to me. Don't let them take me out of here or give me any shots. Promise me, you've got to!"

"I promise," Kel said, crossing his heart. "We're going to get in touch with your parents. No one will take you out of here except them."

"Look out for Eric." The sedative was kicking in strongly now, and Toby had developed a distinct list to the left. "He lies. He helps them and he lies. They did it to Jenny, to Lora. And me. Making us be like him."

"I don't understand."

"Look out for him," Toby stressed in a sleepy whisper. "He's bad."

Kel leaned forward. "Toby . . . who are they? What did they do?"

"Enzymes," he sighed, and closed his eyes.

*   *   *

5

Saturday was on the verge of turning into Sunday when the good-looking redheaded guy walked in.

The Blue Owl was on the north end of McKinleyville, an all-night café boasting twenty different kinds of pie and a round-the-clock breakfast menu. On Fridays after midnight, it was often taken over by the noisy, pesky members of some college gaming club. They made the usual Saturday crowd of truck drivers and millworkers seem placid by comparison.

Hannah Perkins smoothed her unflattering uniform over her too-wide hips and went up to the man, plucking a menu from the holder. He was scanning the room expectantly, and the flush of interest she'd had quickly dimmed. He was here to meet someone.

Half of the tables were filled and the air was redolent with the mingled smells of hamburgers, coffee, bacon, and pancakes. She led him to a booth with a view of a dark parking lot and a drive-thru bank. He ordered decaf, then asked if Marge was around.

"Marge?" Hannah echoed. "Marge who?"

"Marge Raney," he said. "She's on tonight, isn't she?"

"I don't know anybody named Marge. You sure you've got the right place?" He double-checked the back of the menu, where "The Blue Owl" was written over a cartoon owl not only colored blue but looking exaggeratedly depressed. "Yes, this is the right place."

She shook her head. "We had a Maggie once, but never a Marge. You must be mixed up."

The redhead refused to let it go, though she could tell he knew he was getting nowhere. "A tall woman, dark brown hair with chestnut and gold highlights, very striking?"

"She told you she works here?" Hannah laughed, feeling a bit vindictive and unkind. "Maybe she was trying to ditch you. Did you get her number?"

"It's nothing like that –"

"Well, when you're ready to order, Maria will be right over." She flounced off with a sniff that was almost a snort, leaving him to stare unseeingly out the window.

Moments later, a very peculiar look on his face, he rose and left before she had even brought him his coffee.

*   *   *

Sunday,

November 16

1

His headache was gone, totally gone.

Toby Edwards woke Sunday morning feeling more rested and at peace with himself than he had in weeks. It might have been because of the hospital, because of whatever medicine they'd given him. But Toby was sure that he knew the real reason.

He wasn't fighting it any more. That was it.

He had come to terms with what he was becoming.

At some point in the dead of night had realized that he didn't need to resist, that it did make sense. There was a reasonable explanation for it after all.

Things remember, too. They hold memories just like they hold fingerprints. And I can read those memories.

It wasn't that much different from those shows on television, when the crime scene detectives could find the residues of blood spatters even after all outward signs had been scrubbed away. It wasn't that much different from a dog being able to sniff out stuff that a person couldn't detect, or a dolphin navigating by sonar. Just because most humans couldn't do it didn't mean that it was impossible.

The more he thought about it, the more it explained a lot of things. A haunted house wasn't home to ghosts, but to memories so strong that they expressed themselves in ways that people could see or hear. Nothing so supernatural about it.

Perfectly logical. Scientifically reasonable. He hadn't necessarily gained any sort of magic or occult power . . . it was just that his senses had been enhanced. His sense of touch in particular, letting him read the memories of things. Most people couldn't, but then, the naked eye couldn't pick up details all too apparent to a microscope. That was all he was . . . a sort of human microscope.

Pleased and relieved, Toby sprang out of bed. He could hear his folks moving around downstairs, Dad getting ready to go to work, Mom making breakfast. He showered and dressed, and went down for a huge meal of scrambled eggs, sausage, and toast.

"You're sure you're all right?" Ruth asked for the fifth time as Toby dumped his plate and orange juice glass into the sinkful of soapy water.

"Fine, Mom, honest."

They had shown up at the hospital last night just as he was waking from his sedative-induced nap. He'd felt clear and alert, but a little disconnected from himself.

Dr. Shaw explained to his parents that the drug test had come back negative, though his odd manner made Toby wonder if something else had shown up that the doctor wasn't ready to discuss in front of him.

His parents, once assured by Dr. Shaw that there was nothing physically wrong with Toby, had elected to take him home rather than leave him in the hospital overnight.

And now, he felt fine. If he could just convince his folks.

Malachi Edwards folded the morning paper and laid it on the table. "Mr. McGuire seemed to think that you were hiding out from Eric, that he was trying to get you to do something. What was it? Smoking, drinking?"

"I never did much care for that boy," Ruth said. "Something shifty about him."

"Aw, Mom, jeez."

"I'm waiting on that answer," Mal said.

He looked at them, their old and stodgy but loved faces turned toward him in worry and concern. If he told them anything about brainwashing and all that, they'd cart him straight back to the hospital in a jiffy. Or maybe even the special hospital, where Jenny's mom was.

"Well . . . I do think maybe he's into some bad stuff," Toby said, cautiously, feeling his way. "He was really weird yesterday. Talking kind of crazy. It scared me, so I got out of the truck. But he came after me, and I . . . I guess I panicked." He shuffled his feet and looked at them with downcast eyes. "I think maybe he was joking, and I took it too seriously."

"I don't want you spending any more time with him," Ruth declared. "No more studying together. For all we know, he could be in some cult. That music he listens to —"

"Okay, Mom."

"I wonder if I shouldn't talk to the boy's mother?" Ruth asked Malachi. "Or the principal. If he's into God knows what, we can't have him corrupting the other kids."

"Now, Ruthie —"

"Oh, don't you 'now Ruthie' me, Malachi Edwards. I know you were against judging the boy on his appearance, but it's gone a little beyond that. It's gotten dangerous. Look at our son, wound up in the hospital."

"Mom, I'm okay," Toby protested, fidgeting.

"Well, you know best, dear." Mal rose and kissed her on the cheek. "Do what you think's right. I'd better get to work."

"I was going to go over to June Reilly's today, but I'd better call her and cancel. I don't feel right about leaving Toby by himself."

"I could go with Dad to the store," Toby said. "Please, Mom, can I? Please, Dad?"

"That's a fine idea," Mal said. "Get your jacket on."

The day was capped and gowned in a fine silvery haze through which the sun shone like a burnished pewter coin. Wisps of fog curled in cat's tails between the trees.

Toby was edgy on the walk into town, half-expecting Eric to come darting out from behind a hedge or parked car, grab him, and run off into the fog like Jack the Ripper.

The Square wasn't exactly bustling at this hour, but old Dobie was picking up some bottles strewn in the bushes by the statue, and Mrs. Mittleschut was sweeping a drift of leaves into the gutter in front of the Trinity Bay Bar and Grill.

Agate River Books and Coffee was on the corner, on the bottom floor of the closed Bay Towers Hotel. Toby, even with his memory, couldn't recall a life before the warm and well-lit shop, divided into two sections by a raised hall floored in toffee-colored tile.

Malachi went about the business of opening up, with Toby helping. They got the coffee going, wrote the day's specials on the blackboard behind the bar, set out the newspaper, and filled the plastic case with muffins and Danishes. The regular customers began filtering in.

Theresa Zane arrived at nine-thirty, pushing her twins in a double-wide stroller. Mark and Travis were sassy and active, grabbing everything within reach and crowing about their triumphs to each other.

"Theresa!" cried Mal. "The usual?"

"Better make it a little stronger," Theresa said. "These two kept me up half the night, so I need an extra boost of caffeine. Mark's getting a new tooth."

"And how's Lora?" Mal asked as he set to work on Theresa's latte.

"Doing better." She pushed the stroller near the window, where the twins could see out and not get at anything. "Dr. Brockman says she's making better progress than he hoped. She might be able to come home by Thanksgiving."

"I'm glad. That was a terrible thing."

"I know. When I think . . ." She shuddered and shook off the rest.

"We had a little scare ourselves yesterday," Mal confided.

Toby, arranging a new display in the window of the bookshop, knew he wasn't supposed to be overhearing, but sound carried well across the brick hallway. His father outlined what had happened, and Theresa went pale beneath her golden-mocha skin.

"Mal . . . you should have called me!"

"It all worked out. He's fine. Dr. Shaw gave him a clean bill of health. But Ruthie's still pretty worried. So am I, as a matter of fact."

"I would be too! I don't know Eric, but I've met his mother. Kel's dating her. She seems nice, intelligent, friendly . . . to hear her tell it, Eric makes a show of looking tough but he's not a bad kid. But you never know, do you?" She smiled. "Teenagers can get pretty good at fooling their parents. I know I was."

Toby paused as he was putting the last of the puppets back on their spoked wooden tree. Amid the host of impressions he'd gotten from the toys, a flutter of moods and images like the riffling of a deck of cards in his mind, one leaped out strongest of all.

Lora. This puppet, this winged fire-maned critter that vaguely resembled something out of *Where The Wild Things Are,* had been her favorite. She called it 'Balrog.' And, handling it, he thought of her more vividly than he had since hearing of her accident.

Lora . . . long black hair like her mother, big green eyes, and when they were all a few years older, he knew she'd be a knockout. They had been friends but argued a lot, her flights of fancy conflicting regularly with his well-grounded realism.

You want that to happen to you? Or to end up on the beach like Lora Blake?

Eric. Eric had said that. Lora's accident hadn't been an accident . . .

"Dad?" Toby blurted. He held up Balrog. "Can I have this? Buy it, I mean? Out of my allowance? And give it to Lora? This one was always her favorite. I thought it might make her feel better. Can I, Dad?"

"Absolutely," Mal said. "If that's okay with you, Theresa."

"I think it's a wonderful idea. That's very sweet of you, Toby. I'm going to see her after I drop the boys off at home. I can take it with me."

Toby clutched it. "Could I come with you, Ms. Zane? And visit Lora?"

"Mal?"

"Fine by me, if the docs up there don't mind."

"I can't imagine they would. Thank you, Toby, yes. We'll go see Lora. I know she'll be happy to see a friend."

*   *   *

2

"Morning people should be shot," Dani Kensington mumbled from the depths of her pillow.

Scott James pulled on his running shoes and laced them tight. "What about joggers?"

"Them too." She burrowed deeper into the blanket, until only a sheaf of wheat-colored hair was visible. The rest was a shrouded, but still shapely, lump.

"It's almost ten o'clock, you know. Not like it's six."

"If you woke me at six crashing around looking for your shoes, I *would* have to shoot you."

He fondly slapped the curve of her hip. "Be back in an hour. Maybe you'll be conscious by then."

"Smartass. You know I didn't get home until three. Do I give you this kind of grief when it's your turn to pull late duty hours?"

"Yeah," Scott said. "You do."

"It's times like this I'm glad I have my own apartment."

"So how come you never sleep there?" he challenged. "You might as well move in. You're here often enough."

One eye appeared through a tunnel in the covers. "That a proposal?"

He laughed. "If I thought you'd take me up on it."

Dani snorted. "I'm always here because you don't like being at my place."

"I never said that. But my place is nicer."

"Go jog," she said. "Maybe I'll have all my stuff moved in by the time you get back."

"You've got a key." He peeled back the blankets enough to smack a kiss on her forehead. "See you in an hour."

She grunted and went back into hiding. Scott grinned and grabbed a sweatshirt off the back of a chair as he crossed the bedroom.

He had a small house on the corner of 11th Street and River Way, its blue-grey paint nearly fading into the lingering fog of the overcast morning. It was decorated in James Family Attic, and while few of the furnishings matched exactly, they were all of a type and went well together. Much like the members of the family.

It occurred to him as he locked the door and began jogging toward the Square that if he did end up marrying tall blond Dani, she'd blend right in at the holiday get-togethers and summer barbecues. His mother would certainly be all in favor of the idea, even if Dani was four years older than Scott. Mom's hints had been dropping like autumn leaves lately.

The smell of the sea was heavy in the air, and the drip of condensation from the trees underlaid the distant melodious chime of the churchbells. Scott quickly worked up a sweat traversing the hillier streets of Trinity Bay, on a course that would bring him to the Square. Then, having pre-emptively worked off the calories, he'd swing by the donut shop to pick up maple bars and cinnamon twists, and take the shorter and more direct route home.

It went as planned until he noticed Kel McGuire sitting on the low stone wall in front of the Leland Building, which housed his office. Even from across the street, Scott could tell by the man's posture that Kel was troubled. He angled that way.

"Morning," he huffed, coming to a stop.

"Hi, Scott."

"My grandfather would say you've got a face as long as a wet weekend."

"Your grandfather must have a lot of long wet weekends in this part of the country."

"What's on your mind?"

Kel mulled something over, then glanced sideways at Scott. "Here's a hypothetical situation for you. Suppose you had reason to believe that someone's been lying to you. What do you do about it?"

"Depends on who, why, and what about." Scott hiked one leg onto the wall and bent along it, groaning at the stretch of tendons. "And somehow I don't get the idea this is very hypothetical."

"You know I've been seeing Marge Raney."

"Sure."

"And she works nights."

"I know how it gets with those mismatched schedules, believe me."

"But here's the thing . . . I went out to the Blue Owl last night, and she wasn't there."

"Out sick?"

"No, they said she didn't work there at all, and never had. So I drove all the way to the Olde Towne Tavern in Eureka, and they'd never heard of her either."

Scott stretched his other leg. "You mean that both of the places she supposedly works have no idea who she is?"

"Right. What do you think it means?"

"What could she be doing that she wouldn't want you to know about? Well, for starters, there's that topless place out by the county line –"

"No. I can't believe that. Not Marge."

"Got to pay better than waiting tables. Have you considered asking her flat out?"

"And have her think I don't trust her?"

"You could ignore it."

"And have it eat at me until I go bonkers."

"Is that the professional term?"

"I'm serious, Scott. I don't know what to do."

"The only other things I can think of are follow her in secret, or dump her." Kel looked at him, shocked. "Dump her?"

"I didn't say they were good choices."

"What would you do?"

Scott scratched his blond crew cut thoughtfully. "Probably follow her. But you know me. I love playing at being a spy."

"Follow her . . . I can't. I've already got this problem with Eric." Kel briefly told Scott about Toby Edwards and the previous day's events, not as someone reporting an incident to a police officer, but as off-duty friends. "Suspecting her, suspecting Eric . . . how's that going to look?"

"Pretty shitty," Scott said. "What did he say about Jenny again?"

"That Eric wanted to make Toby just like him, and that he – meaning Eric – had done the same thing to Jenny, too."

"Creepy."

"Malachi Edwards told me that Ruth's worried about drugs, or a cult. I've seen Eric lots of times, and he just doesn't seem like a druggie. His taste in music is on the death-metal side, but that could be said for half the kids in town."

"And the other half into the Flirty Boys," Scott said dryly, thinking of his cousin Nonie. "But maybe we should look into it. We've gotten nowhere.

Damon called in the FBI, not that those stone-faced bastards were much help. The only good they did was to throw a scare into John Neeman. Suing small-town kiddy-cops is one thing, but he wasn't about to tangle with Uncle Sam."

"I don't know how seriously we can take anything Toby said yesterday. He was out of it, Scott. Confused and emotionally overwrought."

"But with that memory of his, he's still the most reliable witness in town. There may be something to it."

"A sixteen-year-old kidnapper?" Kel shook his head.

"Younger kids than that have done worse," Scott pointed out. "Maybe not here in Trinity Bay, but open any newspaper. Turn on any television. Crazy stuff, Kel."

"You're right."

"And we don't really know anything about this Raney kid. So he doesn't have a record . . . that could only mean he's never been caught. Where did they live before?"

"San Jose, and Redding."

"For all we know, he could be in a cult, could have dragged Jenny Forrester out in the woods and sacrificed her in the name of some ugly Lovecraftian blob-monster."

Kel stared for a long silent moment, then said, "You're not thinking of accusing him of anything like that!"

"Right now, I'm just running my mouth, trying to say that we simply *don't know*. We're down to grasping at straws, Kel. No, strike that, we don't even have straws. We're down to chaff."

"Let me talk to Eric, and Marge, before you say any of this. Even to Damon or Dani. If rumors like that got out . . ."

"I hate to say it, but can you be objective? I know how you feel about Marge."

"Right now, *I'm* not sure how I feel about Marge, truth be told." He combed his fingers through his hair.

His eyes were haunted, as if seeing in some interior darkness a scene culled from a thousand movies, a smoke-filled club where sweaty-handed men waved crumpled bills at writhing women, Marge Raney center stage. Older than the others, but with a ripe and mature beauty . . .

Scott caught himself envisioning it too – what the hell, he was a young, healthy, straight, red-blooded male and therefore helpless not to – and banished the image with a self-conscious cough. "What are you going to do?"

"I'll go out there this evening," Kel said after a weighted pause. "And be hoping there's good answers for all of my questions."

*   *   *

3

"You had this with you?" Toby asked.

"It's Chris' toy dinosaur. I found it in the woods," Lora said.

They were in the backyard of Seacliff, close to the fence that ringed the edge of the property. They could hear birds twittering in the forest beyond, and Ruff's ears pricked up with interest at the sound of a dog barking.

A nurse sat on the terrace behind the house, reading a book and keeping an eye on them. Lora's mother was inside somewhere, meeting with Dr. Brockman.

It had taken Lora a few minutes to remember his name, and the way she spoke was like a much younger kid. It shocked Toby, and when he thought about what Eric had said, it made him mad. Awful enough that something like this should happen to Lora. Worse that it was on purpose.

He had been planning to talk to her right away, but the security camera in her room had given him pause. Now, though, they were as private as he could reasonably expect.

"Okay . . . can I see it now?"

Lora gave him the toy, a plastic Tyrannosaurus. Toby held it loosely in one hand and then folded the other hand over the top, enclosing the dinosaur so that only its tail stuck out. He closed his eyes.

"Toby?"

"Shh, just a minute."

Memories struck him in a hard series of jolts.

King of the dinosaurs. Mighty T. Rex. Roaring and stomping, steered by a different hand than Toby's over a play-mat showing plains, swamps, a lava-spewing volcano. That hand, a boy's but not Toby's own. Fair-skinned, dusted with pink-brown freckles. Short, chewed nails.

Playing. A herd of brachiosaurs, a row of dimetrodons all lined up by the riverbank. The blue swoop of a pterodactyl.

Playing. Mat spread out on the floor. A big room, jungle gym. Another boy, much smaller, younger, sitting in the corner with his thumb in his mouth. A girl, with carrot-orange hair, angrily scribbling looping streaks of red and black in a coloring book.

Playing. Then a sudden flare of light, a baking wave of heat. And the girl, the girl who had been coloring, screaming as crayons melt to drippy wax in her hands, as the pages of the coloring book char and curl up in a blossom of fire.

Then *she* bursts into flame, her clothes, her hair even oranger now, and she shrieks and dances, dances and shrieks, and they are rushing toward her, yelling at one another, the doctors and the guards, and a fire extinguisher is belching out foam. And now it's her face melting and dripping like colored wax.

Playtime is over. The girl is taken away, and they say she'll be fine but the truth is in their eyes. As they busy themselves at their computers, at their medical equipment, they forget about the other children. They forget about the door.

A chance, taken. Mighty T. Rex in hand. Out the door, tiptoe-quiet but quick, and they don't even look his way. Out and up, up and up, stairs and doors and then out.

Bright spring day, sunshine and green, and someone sees him. Cries out in alarm, comes toward him to grab, to capture.

"No! Go away!"

The man flees, the boy runs. Yard and grass, garden and trees, tall trees and dark shadows underneath, silent carpet of needles.

Running. Running. Finally hiding, gasping and exhausted. Hollow tree. Hiding and hugging the dinosaur. Then barking, a dog, a girl —

"His name's Chris St. John," Toby whispered when he came out of it. "One of them died, one of the kids died, caught on fire and burned up, and the alarms were going and everyone was yelling, and he escaped. Brought this one with him. So he hid. But a girl . . . you, Lora . . . found him."

"Poor Chris," she said.

"Then they came after him. Judge and Inge. He tried to run, dropped the toy. He left it there. A long time. All alone and forgotten. And then you came back, found it. It remembers what happened to him. It remembers what happened to you!"

"When the Ringwraiths got me?" she asked. "And took me to the dungeon where the Wraith Lord was?"

"Not Ringwraiths," Toby said. "I bet it was those same people. You were looking for the cave, almost found it, and then you say you turned around. Why? I don't know why. But they followed, and you couldn't get away. Caught you. Took you back. Down into the cave. Knocked you out so no one would hear, and messed with your memories so you wouldn't know. But *this* remembers. Things remember, Lora, they do."

"And you can hear them," she said.

He scowled. "I know it sounds crazy –"

"I can hear what Ruff is thinking."

Toby felt grey and ill, but didn't disbelieve her for a second. "They injected you, too. But they also . . ." He clutched the dinosaur again, fiercely silent for several seconds. "They drowned you."

Blue lights and chill shadows. Soaring cave-ceiling but hospital stuff, a hospital in a cave, mighty T. Rex in the pocket of her jeans as they bent over her, lifted her, lowered her. Slack and limp. Trailing hair, dangling arms and legs. Into a tub, into a tank. Icy flood of water, engulfing, held under.

"I fell in the ocean," she said.

"Huh-uh. The dinosaur was still in your pocket. It remembers. They put you in a tank, kept you under. Deep cold water, drowning you. Almost killing you. Then they pulled you out and did like on the doctor shows, and took you to the beach to leave you where you'd be found. It wasn't an accident, Lora. You didn't fall. They faked it. They faked the whole thing. They thought nobody would ever know, because they didn't let you remember. But this does."

"Why? Why would anyone do that?" That vague, mild look had finally faded from her eyes, to be replaced by fear.

"They made it look like an accident, and then they arranged to bring you here."

Toby turned toward Seacliff, and for the first time in his life, regarded the huge and majestic house with dread. He'd never paid attention to the ghost stories, because his concise and logical mind insisted there were no such things.

But this, this wasn't the occult, wasn't spectral hands reaching out from beyond the grave. This wasn't even memories of old tragedies and evils held by the inanimate wood and stone. This was real, this was science, this was a more insidious and sinister thing than any haunting could ever be.

"Here, it's all here," he said.

"You mean Chris is here?" Lora asked.

"Under. In the cave. And I bet that's where they took Jenny, too."

"The cave . . . I saw a cave, but something scared me, so I ran away. That's when the Ringwraiths got me . . . but they weren't really Ringwraiths at all, were they?"

"And they gave you the stuff to make you psychic."

"To make me what?"

"Psychic. Like . . ." He cast about for something Lora could relate to, then thought of her love of movies and books. "Like in *X-Men*. They gave you a mutant power."

"I'm a mutant?" she cried.

"Shhh!" hissed Toby, glancing anxiously at the nurse. He had raised his head from his book, and was peering curiously at them.

"Oh. Right." She scootched closer to him. "But *powers?* Really? That's . . ."

"I know."

"So *cool!*"

"What?"

"It's almost as good as being able to do magic, isn't it? And I've always wanted to be able to do magic. Like Harry Potter. What's my power? Can I fly? Can I move things?"

"Hey, hold on! Lora, what's the deal? You're . . . you're happy about this?"

"Why not?" Sudden comprehension, beautiful and alight, dawned in her emerald eyes. "It's Ruff! Understanding Ruff, and know what the birds are thinking, and Mr. Montgomery's guinea pig. That's my power. I can talk to animals!"

"Yeah, but . . . they messed with us. They shot stuff into us that messed with our brains, and turned us into freaks. They kidnapped Jenny."

"Oh." Her smile sagged. "That wasn't very nice. Well, when I tell my mommy –"

"No! We can't tell anyone. They'll think we're crazy and lock us up."

"I don't want that," Lora said, distressed and apparently, to Toby's mind, missing the point that she was already locked up. "But what about Jenny, and Chris? We have to help them. We have to do something."

"Yeah." Toby shredded a blade of grass, thinking hard. "But what can we do?"

Before she could reply, her mother hailed them from across the lawn. Toby realized that the nurse was still watching them, with a measured frown of cold calculation.

He was suddenly sure that they'd heard everything, and would find a way to get him at Seacliff too.

*   *   *

4

Soup and a sandwich were all she had appetite for, and even those went largely untouched as Marge Raney listened to the grim hush of the empty house.

She wondered what had gone wrong. And how much of it was her fault. And how she was going to explain it.

Kel's messages on the machine, and the tension in his voice an hour ago when she'd finally awakened to answer the phone, told her that this wasn't going to be an easy conversation. She'd tried to prepare herself. Brace herself. But here he was, his car already pulling up in the muddy drive, and she knew she wasn't ready.

But as she let him in, something in his expression told her that this wasn't just about Eric, either. He studied her, and she tugged at the hem of her pullover self-consciously.

"Kel, what is it? What's wrong?"

"Where is Eric?"

Her shoulders slumped. "I'm so sorry. I wanted to tell you, but I hoped . . . I hoped things would get better. I was wrong. I had to send him back to his father's."

"Why, Marge? What's going on?"

"He's a good boy, he really is. He just has some . . . some behavioral problems. I thought the move would help, and it did for a while. But things must have just been building up. He . . . he gets irrational, loses his temper."

"So you sent him to stay with your ex-husband?"

"Yes. He left this morning on a bus. Greyhound. To Sacramento."

Kel clasped her hands and drew her to the couch, sitting beside her but angled toward her so that their knees almost touched. "Marge, I'd like to know the truth."

"While he might not have been the best father, William knows his responsibilities." She freed her hands deftly from his, prepared to be angry. "You think I'm lying to you, Kel?"

"I went to the Blue Owl last night. They'd never heard of you. Neither had the Olde Towne Tavern."

The sudden change of topic threw her for a moment, but then she gasped in understanding. He'd been checking up on her. He knew. There was no point denying it, so she went on the offensive. "And I suppose you've gone to the DMV to see if Marge Raney's my real name!" She shot to her feet.

"You couldn't have asked me? You had to go snooping around?"

His look of misery did not soften her in the least. "I haven't snooped, and I'm asking you now."

"I thought you came out here to talk about Eric. Instead . . . how could you?"

"Marge . . ." He rose. "There's nothing you have to hide from me. I care about you. A lot. I'd like to help you, help Eric. But I have to know the truth."

"I care about you, too, Kel," she said, looking down with her hair hanging in her face so that she wouldn't have to see him. "That's why I lied. I didn't want to ruin what we had. I thought it was . . . special. I was afraid that if I told you, it would change how you feel about me."

"Honesty's always better."

"Is it? You don't know how hard this has been for me. On my own with a sixteen-year-old, trying to keep us both fed and clothed and housed . . . I had to do whatever it took to get by."

"I understand that," he said, and she could sense him girding himself for the worst.

"So I've done a lot of things I'm not proud of, telling myself it was all for Eric. Hoping that he'd do better. That he'd go to college, make something of himself. Isn't it enough to know that, without my having to go into all the gruesome details?" She fiercely dashed away an errant tear. "I do everything I can, all for nothing!"

"Marge, I'm so sorry." Kel sounded miserable, absolutely wretched.

Her strength sapped, Marge sat down and snatched a tissue from the box on the end table. "I'm . . . too used to being on my own. I'd never had anyone to turn to before."

"You do now, if you'll trust me." He sat again as well, and she let him reclaim her hands. "Why not have Eric come back here? We can help him together."

"It's too late for that. By sending him, I've shown William that I failed, that I'm unfit to take care of Eric. Even though there's no love lost between them, even though he'll hate having Eric around as much as Eric will hate being there, he wouldn't agree."

"But you're his mother. The courts —"

"It's not that easy anymore and you know it, Kel. If I tried to take it to court, one look at this house and my income compared to William's would settle the case in a snap." She lost the last of the steel in her spine and leaned against Kel's side, resting her head on his shoulder. He put his arm around her, but the embrace felt tense and withholding.

"Still, there's always some option —"

"Can we talk about something else? It's going to be hard enough facing the principal tomorrow morning. I still need to apologize to Toby's parents for Eric frightening him. Now, please, can't we talk about something else?"

He seemed about to argue, but gave in with a sigh.

They discussed other things – the change in the weather and the impending rain, the latest developments on the movie theater that might or might not be built at North Valley. But the conversation was stilted and formal, both of them uncomfortable, and it came as no great surprise to Marge when Kel pleaded an appointment, and took his leave.

Alone again in the small house, Marge stood for a few minutes at the window with her forehead against the pane and her breath fogging the glass. A sense of loss deeper and more poignant than she had expected hollowed her heart, and her steps were heavy and spiritless as she finally went to the telephone.

*   *   *

Monday,

November 17

1

Dr. Brockman's office at the end of the hall had windows in three walls offering fantastic views of the town, the bay, and the woods. He favored lots of polished wood, dark earth tones, and had an egg collection taking up one entire glass-fronted curio cabinet.

There must have been a hundred or more, in every conceivable substance and every possible size. Ceramic, stone, glass, brass, wood, plastic. Candles shaped like eggs. Little sculptures of things hatching out of eggs – birds, dinosaurs, dragons. An egg with chicken feet sticking out the bottom.

"Nice eggs," Brian Sorenson said, knowing it was a lame thing to say the minute the words were out of his mouth, but he was so tense that he wasn't sure what he was saying. Paper crackled in his hands.

"The way these things get started," Roger Brockman said, rolling his eyes. "See that one there? The cedarwood one on the end? I bought that in a gift shop, must've been seventeen years ago. I thought I'd keep it in my sock drawer. My wife decided I must like eggs, and over the next five years until the divorce, that's what she got me. Eggs. Christmas, anniversary, birthday . . . I never had the heart to tell her to stop, and eventually I got to like them." He laughed.

Brian joined in hesitantly. He knew that Brockman could tell he was stressed, and was trying to put him at ease. "Were you hard to shop for, or something?"

"Before the eggs? She always said so. But anyway, what's on your mind, Brian?"

He blew out a slow breath through pursed lips. "Um . . . it's kind of weird. I don't even know if I should be mentioning it. But I had to talk to someone about it."

"Now you've got me worried."

Whenever Dr. Brockman was smiling or laughing, Brian noticed, he didn't look quite so much like Jeff Goldblum. But when he looked concerned and intent, it was eerie.

"It's about Dr. Lundquist."

"What about him?"

"Well . . . there's no good way to say this . . ."

"Just spit it out."

"I think he used to be a Nazi."

"Excuse me?" Now Brockman looked exactly like the actor, in one of those moments when Ian Malcolm had just heard something from the old dinosaur guy played by Richard Attenborough that he thought was at once both nuts but hideously plausible.

Mutely, Brian spread out the papers on the desk blotter. He'd printed them all out, the group photo of the Schlossenberg scientists and the close-up of Richter. The biographical listing.

Dr. Brockman picked them up and studied them one after the other. "Good God . . . you mean that this . . . this is . . . Brian, if this is a joke —"

"No! I'd never . . . who'd pull a joke like that?"

"A mistake, then." He grinned rather sickly. "I know a thing or two about being mistaken for someone else."

"I thought about that, but the way the dates and the . . . the area of study . . . the way it all adds up . . . it can't be coincidence."

"The dates . . . where did you get all of this?"

"On the Internet. I was looking up some stuff, and ran across it totally by accident."

"You found this on the Internet. Lundquist . . . I'm sorry, Brian, but I'm having a hell of a time believing this. The dates do add up . . . it would have to be one whopper of a coincidence . . . but Dr. Lundquist? I've admired his work for years, followed his career since I was an undergrad! How many people have you told about this?"

"No one but you. Well, and Dawn, because she was there when I found it."

"Dawn Jessec, Richie's mother?"

He nodded. "I didn't want to say anything to anyone else yet. I spent all weekend thinking about what I should do. Dawn says that whatever he may have done in the past is over now, and he's making up for it by helping kids like Richie. But . . . do we do something?"

"We can't go to anybody with this yet," Brockman said, staring at the close-up with his fingertips massaging his hairline. "If this got out, it could ruin everything we're trying to do here."

"But . . . and this part's going to sound way out there . . . what if it is true, and he's up to something?"

He regretted his words instantly, because Brockman raised his head and looked at Brian as if Brian was an absolute lunatic.

"Like what? Evil experiments on the students?"

It was almost the exact same thing Dawn had said, but made him feel a lot more stupid when it came from Dr. Brockman.

"Well . . ."

"Brian," Brockman continued, sounding like he was trying to hold onto his patience with both hands, "you're in charge of computers and security, for heaven's sake! If there was something like that going on, don't you think you'd know about it?"

"That's just it . . . I went back over the computer activity archives this morning, and found some anomalies."

"Anomalies." Now he massaged his temples as if trying to rub the fact of this discussion into his brain. "What kind of anomalies?"

Figuring he'd already gotten himself fired for being a nutcase, Brian decided he might as well tell him the whole thing. "I have a program that keeps track of which computers are being used at which times. To figure out when the peak hours are, when the biggest drain is on the system. I went back over it, and the records show times when some of the computers are being used, but nobody's there."

"I'm not following you."

"Each of the computers has an ID number," Brian explained. "Four of the computers show activity at times when nobody's supposed to be using them."

"Someone's sneaking into the offices?"

"That's the really weird part . . . according to their ID numbers, those four computers are the ones in the medical labs. I went back and reviewed the security videos, and during the times when supposedly they're being used, there's no one there. Not a single person. In the middle of the night, mostly."

"The computers are running by themselves?"

"Those ones aren't even on. At first I thought it was just a glitch, but then I remembered something else."

"What?"

"When I was first setting up the network, first programming all of the computers, four of them crashed and I had to redo their entire hard drives. Those are the ones that are showing up on the activity log. You know what I think?"

"I hope it's something that makes sense, because so far I'm not following you."

"I think . . . I think that the computers never crashed," Brian said. "I think they were switched, and I programmed four all-new ones, because the originals had been taken somewhere else. And wherever they are, someone's using them in the middle of the night."

"Where? And for what?"

"I don't know. They're still connected to the network, so they almost have to be in the building someplace, because if they were connected by modem, I'd know the difference. And I can't find out what they're being used for because every time I try to remote access them, I get the ones that are in the medical labs."

Dr. Brockman frowned. "Let me see if I've got this straight. You think that we've got four extra computers hidden somewhere in the building, and someone's using them for God-knows-what."

"Yeah."

"But where? Forgetting for the moment *why*, where are they? We've both been through every room in this building. You've got all the security monitors. Where?"

"I don't know! Maybe someone . . . maybe someone found the secret passage."

"What are you talking about?"

"There's an old story, local history, that Jacob Cliffwood was a smuggler, a pirate. He had a secret passage connecting the house to some sea caves, where he stored his booty. My mom knows all about it. Maybe it's real, and someone found it."

"And what? Built a secret lab down in the caves, and stole four of our computers?"

"I know how crazy it sounds."

"We certainly can't go spreading a story like that around." Brockman lapsed into thoughtfulness, drumming his fingers on the edge of the desk. "Let me handle Dr. Lundquist. I'll go to him privately and ask him about . . . about . . ." he flapped his hand at the photos as if he still couldn't get a grip on the concept. "You compile a list of all these supposed computer usages. But for now, we'd better keep this to ourselves."

*   *   *

2

Dawn Jessec opened her eyes to a looming shadow right over her, a shadow in the shape of . . . of . . . oh. A warrior princess.

She rubbed the disorientation from her eyes and looked around. She was on Brian's couch and had fallen asleep with her head on the arm of it, which explained why she had such a crick in her neck. Turning her head this way and that made the bones clack like someone trying to open a childproof cap without pressing down first.

She groaned and craned her head hard to the side, and a sharp crack from just below her ear made her momentarily sure that she'd just managed to paralyze herself from the neck down.

The room was lit only by the shifting color pattern of the screen saver. Brian was asleep in his chair, tipped back against the wall with his feet up on a filing cabinet. The sky visible through the gap in the curtains was black, and according to the digital readout in the VCR, it was 4:12 in the morning.

"Ugh," Dawn said, swinging her feet off the couch.

She had come over to Brian's after work as usual, meaning to share a pizza and talk for a while before heading back to her apartment. But the poor guy had been so wound up, all stressed over what he'd had to do that morning – ratting out his boss as a possible Nazi war criminal – that she ended up agreeing to watch a PBS marathon of some English show about four guys on a spaceship to help him relax.

Evidently, it had relaxed her right into a four-hour nap. But what the heck; she had the day off. She could sleep until noon if she wanted to, and right now that was all she wanted. A real pillow, and a blanket because she was freezing.

But she couldn't leave Brian in front of the computer like that. If the chair rolled, he'd go down and probably crack his skull open.

She got up, teeth chattering. "Brian. Hey, Bri."

He jerked awake so fast that the chair did roll, and his arms and legs flailed as he caught himself before crashing to the floor. "Huh! What? Oh. Jeez, Dawn. I was dreaming I was back in school and fell asleep in Poly Sci."

"It's after four. I gotta go home."

Brian scrubbed the heels of his hands up the sides of his face. "Yeah. Okay. What time?"

"Four . . . uh . . . seventeen. In the morning."

"Damn. Okay." He stood. "Walk you back."

"You don't have to. It's only next door. Go to bed."

"Mean it?"

"Yeah." She nudged him toward the hall.

He blinked groggily at her and smiled. "See you in the morning."

"It is the morning. See you in the afternoon." She kissed him on the cheek, not missing the startled but delighted look on his face, and put on her jacket.

The inrush of cold air when she opened the door almost made her change her mind, but she hurried out and shut it behind her. The walkway was covered, but still slick with rain. The streets were dark and silent, the whole world sound asleep, and the phrase 'dead of night' had never seemed more appropriate . . . but at the same time, scary.

As she reached her apartment, she thought she saw someone move in the courtyard. Dawn paused, peering down at the playground. It looked like a person crouching under one of the slides . . .

She told herself she was being silly, she had the key already in the lock and was only a turn and a push away from being back inside where it was warm.

* * *

3

Brian's got a girlfriend! Brian's got a girlfriend!

The litany, in singsong schoolyard cadence, ran thought Lucas Gordon's mind. But instead of bringing jeering satisfaction, it made the coal of resentment burn brighter in his heart. Maybe because he knew that the taunt wouldn't have the desired effect. If it had been in the schoolyard, ten years ago, Brian would have been all red face and vehement denials. But now, if Brian could hear it, he'd grin and remark that yeah, he did, wasn't it great, wasn't she pretty?

The worst of it was, she *was*. Even in a bulky coat, even in the unflattering black polyester pants and red uniform shirt of the pizza place, he could tell that she was a trim little babe with a blond French braid hanging down her back.

When she stopped and looked down into the courtyard, Lucas shrank stealthily into the shadows. Their eyes seemed to lock, hers wide and momentarily apprehensive. Then, evidently deciding it was only her imagination, she proceeded to the next apartment and vanished from Lucas' sight.

Brian's got a girlfriend.

It's so goddamn unfair!

Brian had everything now! And Lucas, what did he have?

Well, he did finally have full use of his limbs, better than ever before . . . and he was free from the tiresome burden of his father . . . but it wasn't enough to make up for a lifetime of injustice. The hour of payback had arrived, and it would be Lucas' distinct pleasure to carry out this particular mission.

He made himself wait until he couldn't stand it any longer, then left the shelter of the slide and crept noiselessly up the stairs despite their creaky wooden tread. It was uncanny, how quickly he'd gotten used to his new fluidity and grace of movement.

On one level, he realized that this was crazy, that he was risking everything for a stupid act of revenge, just when he had finally reached a point of life worth living. But the rest of him knew this had to be done. This was a compulsion that couldn't be denied, and an order that he didn't dare refuse.

Brian's door was locked, but the windows of Birdwood Lane weren't exactly designed for security. A minimum of wiggling and jiggling caused the sliding pane to pop out of its track, and Lucas worked it open far enough to allow him to climb through. He let his eyes acclimate to the gloom, listening intently until he heard the sounds of deep, even breathing from the direction of the hall leading to the bedroom.

Probably sleeping off an acrobatic bout of whoopie with his blond cutie-pie . . .

Hope you enjoyed it, Bri-old-buddy, Lucas thought coldly, *because it was the last whoopie you're ever gonna get!*

Hell! If he'd shown up an hour earlier, he might have found them both in bed, maybe even doing it. Then he could have wrung Brian's neck in front of the girl, and given her the opportunity to bargain for her life with her body.

Then, after, he could have killed her too . . .

Anticipation coursed through his veins and flooded his mouth with saliva. His erection pushed at an awkward angle in the front of his pants, and he had to stop to adjust himself.

Maybe I'll have to pay a visit next door . . .

Absorbed with that pleasant idea, he didn't see the tower of soda cans until it was too late. They'd been piled against the wall in a pyramid shape, but as he kicked the bottom row, they all came tumbling down in a cacophony of shallow aluminum jangle.

"Shit!" Lucas hissed under his breath, springing back.

The hand he threw behind him for balance hit a stack of videocassettes that had been precariously balanced on the edge of a table, and several hours' worth of bootleg R-rated Japanese animation clattered around his feet.

No point in being sneaky now, so Lucas opted for the attack. He sprinted down the short hall and into the bedroom just as Brian Sorenson sat up and slapped at the wall. The overhead light snapped on.

Lucas squinted in the harsh sudden light but kept moving. By the time recognition had flashed in Brian's eyes, Lucas was on him and reaching for his neck.

Brian rolled off the far side of the bed, tearing a poster of Gillian Anderson looking sultry and David Duchovney looking broody in half as he went.

"Lucas! What the hell are you doing in here?"

He answered with a spate of curses as he upended the mattress onto the messy floor. Brian gave up asking dumb questions and bolted for the door. Lucas lashed out and punched him a glancing blow on the side of the head, knocking him down.

Brian swept up a handful of multi-colored dice and flung them in Lucas' face. One, nearly the size and shape of a golf ball and a neon alien green in hue, clacked against his front teeth and chipped two of them.

As Lucas recoiled, Brian shot past him like a rubber band. Lucas whipped around and tackled him. They hit the wall hard enough to bring down an entire shelf of *Star Wars* action figures.

At last, Lucas' hands closed around Brian's neck. Strangle the son of a bitch, choke the air out of him, choke until he turned purple and crapped himself! His coherent mind was swamped in a red fire, burning through his brain and making him scream more obscenities.

Pain, huge cracking pain . . . it felt like the bottom of his skull was splaying outward in response to terrible pressure from within, stretching the ligaments that connected it to his spine. Pain all down his back, too, a searing line of it.

Brian, gagging and tugging at the iron-clamped hands at his throat, looked at Lucas with a burst of new horror. Lucas could see himself reflected in those bulging brown eyes, the curve of their lenses making his head look distorted and misshapen, like a harvest gourd.

Agony and a sound like thick ice groaning underfoot . . . and Lucas felt his skull change shape. Thin but silvery-hot streaks of additional pain were followed by warm trickles as the skin split along the back of his scalp.

His grip loosened and Brian broke free, coughing and retching. He ran for the hall, dodging around and jumping over the piles of clutter with the skill born of habit and memory.

The brutal torture of his rebelling bones eased. Lucas, staggering and feeling as if his head was caught in an industrial vise, nonetheless gave chase. He could hear a muffled pounding and at first mistook it for the thundering heart of his fleeing quarry, then realized it was someone banging on the door. And voices, many voices clamoring in alarm.

Brian went for the door. About to escape. About to survive. Not allowed! Lucas found a new reserve of speed and strength, and brought him down in a flying leap. They slid together across the long table that took up most of the living room, sending gamer crap skittering in all directions.

Their momentum had been so great it carried them clean off the edge in a thrashing tangle. Metal clanged again, not aluminum this time but steel, as they collided with a shelf of assorted medieval weapons. Lucas got his grip on Brian's throat again, his fingers settling into the vivid scarlet weals they'd left the first time. A perfect fit. Like donning a pair of gloves.

He saw Brian grabbing for something, ooh, what was the big stud going to do, hit him with a sword? Fat chance . . . Lucas was on top of him and there wasn't room to get up a good swing, and most of all, no time for Brian to do anything –

The sound was puzzling, a sort of *troing* like the breaking of a violin string.

The pain was immediate and piercing, a stabbing spike ramming through him. Lucas gasped in shock, felt the gasp as a bubbling slurp in his chest, and looked down in astonishment to see a dark, wet hole in the middle of the right breast pocket of his navy-blue flannel shirt.

His breath stuttered out and he saw it in the spit and gurgle of blood coming out of what he understood was what the TV shows called a 'sucking chest wound.'

A furnace-blast of wind seemed to roar through his lungs. There was an unbearable tickling sensation deep down and bronchial. He tried to cough it up, and only sent new paroxysms of pain shooting out from the center like fireworks.

Occupied with all of this, he barely noticed as Brian scrambled out from under him. Barely noticed as the door flew open to admit the landlady, the blonde, and half a dozen neighbors shivering in their pj's.

Now fighting not to cough, Lucas fell onto his back and screamed as whatever was impaling him hit the carpet and pulled to the side. He clutched at nothing but air as he sank into a roiling red-black darkness.

*   *   *

Tuesday,

November 18

1

At five-thirty in the morning, the tiny emergency room of the Trinity Bay Medical Center was usually as lively as a library. A somnolent hush lay over the place, and the staff on duty had reached the becalmed horse latitudes of their shift.

Dr. Elliot Shaw was on the verge of giving up with only three squares left unfilled in the *Gazette's* normally kindergarten-simple crossword when the call came in.

As if a switch had been thrown, the mood changed to one of bustling expectancy tinged with consternation – had the paramedics really said they were bringing in someone who'd been shot with a crossbow? That couldn't be right . . . sure, they saw some strange things from time to time, but a *crossbow?*

Strange, yes, but it turned out to be true. Marty Arnes, one of the paramedics, rattled it all out to Elliot as they transferred the blood-drenched man from gurney to operating table.

"Yes, it's a crossbow all right. Miniature one, bolt's only about *yea* long, but it's still mostly in there. The tip is sticking out between the back ribs, right here."

"A miniature one and it went almost all the way through him?"

"Point blank range. He was right on top of the shooter. On three . . . one, two, *three!*"

They heaved and set the man down, bound to a body board on his side to prevent jostling the bolt in his back. Elliot glanced at his face as the nurses moved in to cut away the shirt.

"It's Lucas Gordon," he said. "But . . . his head . . ."

"I know." Marty Arnes shook his own head. "You tell me, Doc . . . he sure didn't look like that last week when I bought a new pump for my aquarium."

Blood crusted around Lucas' collar and in his lank blond hair. The bottom part of his head and the upper part of his neck were horribly swollen. The pressure had pushed Lucas' jaw forward so that it jutted like a drawer drawn partway out, his mouth not quite able to close. The skin hadn't been able to stretch to accommodate such a sudden change, and had split in small fissures.

"Doctor!" Paula Spencer said. She had just finished scissoring through the flannel of Lucas' shirt, and was gaping at the prominent knobs of his spine. They stood out in sharp relief, tenting the skin of his back.

"What's happened to him – never mind, first things first." Elliot began briskly issuing orders as he determined what needed to be done for the most important injury.

Marty had covered the entry wound with a taped-down pad, but with each inhale and exhale, air bubbled from the ragged slit in Lucas' back. The crossbow bolt, a tiny thing no longer than a pen but tipped with a razor-sharp brass head, had gone through his right lung.

Not much air was escaping; the lung was at least partially collapsed. Elliot inserted a chest tube and began the delicate work of removing the bolt. His hands worked cleverly and well, as they always did, and the orders for lab work and x-rays issued from his lips almost automatically, leaving his mind free to wonder what in God's name had happened to Lucas.

Elliot himself had performed a routine check-up on the young man not a month before. It was at that time that he'd referred Lucas to Seacliff, believing that a variant of the cerebregen vitamin compound could have a beneficial effect on the damaged tissues of Lucas' brain and spinal cord.

They had a follow-up appointment next Thursday, as a matter of fact, and he had, just through seeing Lucas in casual passing, noticed that there had been definite, even amazing, improvement in his motor functions and balance already.

But this? Are the cerebregens responsible for this deformity? Not regeneration but an uncontrolled surge of growth?

Hours later, when Lucas had been transferred upstairs to ICU, Elliot reviewed the series of head films he'd had done. His exhaustion had been dashed apart, and as he looked at the images of Lucas' brain, sleep became the furthest thing from his mind.

Uncontrolled growth, that was indeed it. In the part of brain relating to motor control, and all through his central nervous system. The protuberant bumps of his vertebrae had been caused by the very spinal cord itself expanding, not dramatically enough to crack the sleeves of bone but enough to expand them to the very limits of their endurance.

He went down to the waiting room to see if anyone was lingering who might be able to shed more light on the evening's events. Lucas' father was not present, and when he asked, Elliot was told that the only answer at the Gordon house had been the machine. Damon Blake had arrived, taken a report, confiscated the crossbow bolt, and left.

Brian Sorenson was admitted for overnight observation after being half-throttled and severely banged-up. No one, seeing the clear impression of Lucas' hands on his neck, doubted that the shooting had been a last-ditch effort at self-defense.

Elliot went up to Brian's room. A mostly-untouched breakfast tray sat on the rolling table over the bed, and Brian was gazing out the window at the sun-dappled bay with a floating, dopey expression. The room's other occupant, who had broken his back falling from a ladder, slept soundly in his plaster body cast.

"Brian?"

"Hi, Dr. Shaw," Brian rasped. "Is Lucas okay?"

Dragging a hard curve of plastic chair to the side of the bed, Elliot sat down. "We got the bolt out, but he faces a long recovery. Mind telling me what happened?"

"I'll try, but my throat hurts. I was sleeping, and then I woke up and there he was. In my apartment. In my room." Brian sipped at a carton of milk and sighed as the cool liquid went soothingly down. "He grabbed me, choked me, slammed me against the wall."

"Why?"

He shrugged. "Hates me, always has, but he never tried to kill me before. He was like a berserker. Swearing, yelling. And his head . . ."

"What about his head?" Elliot demanded. "It looked different?"

"Not at first. At first, he looked like normal . . . better than normal. He wasn't limping, didn't move like it hurt him, the way he used to. But while he was pinning me against the wall . . ." Brian's already hoarse voice dropped to a whisper. "His head *bulged*. Like there was a balloon inside. Bulged. I could hear a cracking, like his skull was coming apart. So fast that it ripped his skin. It was gross."

"But he didn't let go?"

"He did for a second, enough for me to get away, then came after me again. We went over the table, and knocked down all the weapons. I saw the crossbow and knew I had to do it or he'd kill me for sure." A bleak and haunted look surfaced through the haze of painkillers. "I didn't have any choice."

"I believe you."

"He would have killed me."

"You saw his head change."

Brian nodded, and goosebumps broke out on his arms. "Like something out of a movie. I thought it was going to explode. And then he went crazier than ever."

"Out of control? Psychotic?"

"Seemed that way to me, that's all I know. I saw him a few weeks ago and he was the same as always, and now . . ."

One of the nurses came in. "Dr. Shaw? Those lab results you asked for are back."

"Thank you, Vivian. Brian, I'll come back and see you later, but for now, it's best that you get some rest."

He took the chart that Vivian offered and went into the hall to read it. Some anomalies, but nothing there that would tell anyone else what was going on unless they knew specifically what to look for. But he knew, dammit, he knew.

Irrational behavior, rages, uncontrollable swearing . . . those can be explained by the incredible growth in the brain tissue. But the growth is supposed to be benign . . .

He'd referred Lucas to Seacliff, setting up the initial appointment himself. A vitamin treatment, was that all they'd given him? That couldn't be all, not when it had an effect like that! He certainly hadn't noticed anything like this in any of the other Seacliff students.

And what they were doing at Seacliff, when you stripped away all the bells and whistles, was still experimental or very close to it.

Elliot went to his private office and reached for the phone, meaning to place a call up there and demand some answers. But as he punched in the first three numbers, his fingers slowed.

Seacliff had an answer for everything . . . good answers. *Too good, maybe? And too readily accepted, even by me?*

He realized in a flash of self-loathing that he would have been much more inquisitive had he not been so overwhelmingly grateful for the help they were giving David.

Maybe it was time he quit letting himself be hobbled by his gratitude, quit turning an indulgently blind eye to some of the things about Seacliff that bothered him.

Starting with finding out just what they'd done to Lucas Gordon.

And what, maybe, they were doing to his son.

*   *   *

260

2

The drawn curtains of the Gordon house gave it a secretive look.

In Dawn Jessec's stomach, a thread of disquiet grew into a coiling knot. She was not supposed to be here, not supposed to be doing this . . .

But Brian had asked her, almost begged her, to come. She didn't even know why she was here, what she was looking for. Surely if there was anything that needed to be done, the police would be taking care of it.

Still, here she was, walking up the front walk and noticing a small white rectangle tucked in the corner of the screen door's frame. Getting closer, she was able to read the Trinity Bay P.D. logo. A business card. The police chief's business card. He had already been here, probably right after talking to Brian in the hospital.

Dawn, after a furtive glance over her shoulder, turned the card over and read the scrawled message on the back: *Sam, sorry I missed you, need to talk. Will try you at the store but if I don't reach you, please give me a call. D.*

She wondered if the police chief had had better luck . . . when she had driven out in Brian's car, she'd found Seaquarium Fish and Pets to be closed and dark. Maybe Mr. Gordon had shut up the store and dashed to the hospital . . . maybe she'd missed him in transit. He was probably there now, while she was snooping around his house and risking getting busted for trespassing.

The yard was large and wooded, giving only glimpses of the houses on either side. The Gordons lived at the end of a cul-de-sac and backed onto a spur of hilly, undeveloped forest.

Dawn roamed around to the back yard, and crouched to try and peer through the cellar windows. Again, she wasn't sure what she was looking for – a manifesto written by Lucas announcing his intention to murder Brian? It was to no avail, anyway. The windows had been painted over in solid black.

A low growl issued from behind her.

She yelped and sprang up, visions from a thousand scary movies flashing through her head. This was the part where the idiot girl who snuck off alone to the spooky old house got offed by a psycho with a post-hole digger . . .

It was a dog. A rail-thin, ugly mongrel with matted fur the color of mustard and wrinkled black lips pulled back from its teeth. It had been digging at the edge of a shed built into a hillside at the rear of the yard, and was hunkered down fearfully yet defiant by its hole.

Dawn held still, now thinking about rabies and dog bites instead of murderers with garden implements. She glanced around for a weapon, but nothing presented itself.

Standoff. Snippets and tidbits of animal-confrontation lore flickered past her consciousness . . . play dead was for a bear, but for most animals, the trick was in showing no fear and not making eye contact because they took that as a challenge.

The dog barked a warning, but skittered back a step.

"Go on!" Dawn shouted. "Get out of here." She waved her arms without meeting its gaze, and made her voice as forceful as she could.

It gave her a hate-filled look over its shoulder as it slunk away. Dawn spotted a softball-sized rock in the grass and picked it up. She advanced on the dog.

"Go! Git!" She hurled it, missing by several feet but startling the mutt. It bolted to the fence and squirmed through a gap left by a missing board.

Dawn stopped, breathing fast and adrenaline pumping, telling herself it had only been a dog, more afraid of her than she was of it. She convinced her pulse into slowing to a more normal level, and was about to go back to the car when her nose wrinkled.

Something stank. A gassy spoiling stench of decay.

That was what the dog had been after . . . some animal must have crawled into the Gordons' shed and died there. Yuck-o-rama, as her high school friends back in Joshua Flats might have said.

She turned back to the house, and saw that the back door was open.

A nasty spurt of fright shot through Dawn. *Now* the psycho would come roaring out, having armed himself from the kitchen drawers while she was busy with the damn dog . . . he'd rip the screen off its hinges as he barreled through with a cleaver or knife or cheese grater or potato peeler, and slice her to julienne fries.

No psycho charged out. The door was just ajar, that was all.

Hey-hey . . .

No.

She was *not* thinking about going in there and snooping around.

So what if that's what Brian would have done? He was a *gamer,* trained since his pre-teen years to check for traps and then barge on in for monsters and treasure. Kill 'em and take their stuff. In real life, there were things like breaking and entering, or unlawful entry, to think about.

But she didn't feel right about leaving the door standing open. The next person to happen by might not be so law-abiding.

Dawn warily mounted the steps, keenly aware that it was a bad idea. Good-neighborly impulses only stretched so far. She knew she was just daring someone to be waiting in there, ready to thrust out a huge hand and seize her wrist as soon as she touched the doorknob.

"Mr. Gordon?" she called.

No reply. Through the gap, she saw a messy kitchen and a wedge of living room visible through the doorway.

Something dark was crumpled beside an easy chair.

"Omigod," breathed Dawn, suddenly sure that it was Lucas' dad, that Lucas had come for Brian as the main course only after whetting his appetite for violence on his own father.

She burst into the house before her common sense could catch up with her. Her thoughts were a mixed jumble of the CPR and first aid courses she'd taken a year ago when Richie was born.

It was only a quilt, bunched on the floor.

The smell reached her then, a reek of stale urine and sweat mixed with a sour tang issuing from a bottle of yogurt drink left unattended for several days. A pillow lay askew on the stained seat of the chair . . . a pillow streaked with dark smears of what on first glance looked like chocolate.

On second glance . . .

Dawn took that second glance and then a third, and convinced her reluctant mind that yes, indeed, it was dried blood.

Her breath snagged in her throat on a fishhook of fear. When she tried to call for Mr. Gordon again, only a squeak came out.

Say! spoke up a vividly cheery voice in her mind. *Remember that other smell? Here's a story for you, Dawn . . .*

She didn't want to hear that story, and brutally cut off the voice that sounded too much like a commercial announcer telling her that she could get not one but two bottles of E-Z-Go stain remover for only $19.95. But wait, there was more, if she called within the next five minutes . . .

The phone was in the living room, not far from the easy chair. The digital display on the answering machine read '3', and before she could think about what she was doing, Dawn pushed the 'Play Messages' button.

The first was from the hospital, the second was a long pause of dead air followed by a click, and the third was a familiar voice that made Dawn jerk in surprise.

"Hello, Lucas. It is seven-thirty Saturday, and I haven't yet heard back from you about that matter we discussed. Contact me."

What was *he* doing calling Lucas Gordon?

Brian would make much of this. Brian would totally paranoidly make way too much out of this.

Acting on an impulse she couldn't explain, Dawn erased the third message. Now she was bound to be guilty of some crime or another . . . if interfering with the postal service was illegal, tampering with people's answering machines probably was too.

Weirder and weirder . . . and since she'd gone this far, she figured there was little harm in taking a quick look around.

Dawn hurried through the house. Here was Sam Gordon's bedroom, the bed neatly made. Not slept in? The hospital had called him before daybreak, yet he'd never arrived. Bathroom, tidy and untouched.

According to Brian, Lucas lived in the cellar like some evil goblin, lurking in the bowels of the house. At the bottom of the stairs, a pair of crutches hung on wall pegs with an air of abandonment. The room was dark and cramped, cluttered and strewn with dirty laundry and dirtier magazines. A fitting goblin's lair.

In the small bathroom opening off of the downstairs room, she found an empty container in the sink.

Dawn picked it up and read the label, and her skin prickled with a chill. She knew some of those long words, had seen them on Richie's chart and on the releases she'd signed, authorizing them with permission to give him the medicine.

She remembered Brian telling her that Lucas' limp was a result of an injury to his head and back when he was a baby. But this . . . the label said it was a month's supply . . . dated only six days before.

His head . . . omigod, his head . . .

Taking the empty bottle with her, she went back upstairs. In the kitchen again, she looked at the litter of dishes, cans, and crumbs.

Say, Dawn! chirped the merry voice again. *How about this? Lucas snaps and kills his dad. Not just beats him up, but all-the-way deadsville. A few days ago, see? So that his dad's not around to clean up, and Lucas just leaves his mess. But get this, Dawn, here's the real nifty bit . . . get this . . . he stows his dad's body out there in the shed! Hey yeah! How about that? Explains everything, doesn't it?*

"No," Dawn said, unaware that she spoke out loud.

And it was the pills that made him do it. Like when someone gets a brain tumor and goes crazy. How about that, Dawn?

"No, that's not what it was, there's another explanation. His dad went out of town for a few days, that's all. That explains it too."

Sure . . . except for the blood on the pillow, and the smell in the backyard.

"Went away for a few days," she repeated, but heard her own lack of conviction.

You know what the next step is, said the voice that reminded her so sourly of her own mother, the voice that loved telling her things she had no desire to hear.

Clutching the pill bottle, the plastic feeling nastily organic against her palm, Dawn reluctantly went to the back door and looked out at the shed. Was it imagination, or did an aura of evil cling to it?

But it was the only way to silence the nagging mother-voice, so against her will Dawn crossed the yard.

"No lock," she murmured. "If he really had done that, he would have locked it."

Mother's voice had no answer, only a smug see-for-yourself silence that Dawn considered highly irritating. To prove it, she pushed open the door.

The vile atmosphere hit her like a humid slap. A second later, as her eyes adjusted to the dimness, the sight of the tarp-wrapped shape on the workbench slapped her again.

A single bare foot stuck out of the end. A man's foot with yellowed but square-clipped toenails. A man's foot with bugs on it, a smattering of flies and one roach that seemed the size of a sports car. As she watched, rooted to the spot by galvanic horror, the roach scuttled up the corpse's leg and vanished under the edge of the tarp.

* * *

3

Bored with being confined to bed, feeling pretty much okay and figuring he was only down a couple of hit points by now, Brian Sorenson went for a stroll around the ward.

His throat still hurt like hell, but it wasn't that much worse than the numerous times he'd had strep and tonsillitis as a kid. He felt quite a bit better off than most of the other people taking an afternoon constitutional down the hallway. Most of them were older, and a lot of them were sick.

Even so, by the time he reached the skylit atrium overlooking the front lobby, Brian was as tired as if he'd just run a marathon. Not that he'd know just what running a marathon was like. Physical fitness had never been much of his thing. But he could imagine.

His parents had stopped by that morning, while the painkillers were still in full force. His father, Henry, was a foreman at the mill and greeted Brian with a gruff mix of pride and chagrin that was woefully familiar. Shoulda seen the other guy, yessir, that's my pop.

Joanna, his mother, was holding it together well, but he could tell she was biting back the urge to baby him. She'd focused instead on her first meeting with Dawn, embarrassing everyone. Like with his father, there had been that mix of pride and chagrin. Her son finally had a girlfriend, but she was an unwed mother and probably a tramp as well.

Recalling it now, without the comforting cushion of painkillers, Brian winced.

His mother probably thought that Dawn had been over until four-thirty in the morning taking him through the *Kama Sutra* page by page. Which would have been nice, granted, he wouldn't have turned it down, he wasn't a moron . . . but it hadn't been the case and there'd be no telling Mom otherwise.

The upper gallery of the atrium made an effort to offset the usual greyness of the coastal climate with a lot of potted plants and bright warm hues. Brian lowered himself onto a couch and his bruised body sighed with relief.

Clear-headed and finally feeling more like his usual self, Brian tried to piece together what had happened. Try as he might, he couldn't think of what he might have done to set Lucas off this time.

And his head, that had been freaky! Much as he would have liked to have put it off on the confusion of waking, he couldn't do it. The sight, and worse, the *sound* of Lucas' head bulging like that . . .

Hadn't been much like a game, that was for sure. Good thing for his miniature replica crossbow . . .

Brian winced again as he dimly remembered having an argument earlier that morning with Chief Blake as to whether a *working* miniature replica crossbow still technically counted as a 'replica.' He'd only fired it once before, at the SCA fair at which he'd bought it, and had been impressed by how far that little bolt sank into a bale of hay. Never thought he'd find out how far it would sink into an unarmored human body, especially at point-blank range.

Lucas Gordon. Goddamn. He just couldn't come to terms with it. *A grudge, yeah, but a killing grudge?* He hoped Dawn would be able to talk to Lucas' dad, find out what had been going on with him. Find out why. There had to be a why.

In the meantime, the poor bastard was in Intensive Care. Brian doubted he'd be allowed visitors, except maybe close family, but he decided to meander on up there anyway. At least ask how he was doing, maybe leave a note. He went up to the third floor, where he was politely but firmly told what he'd been expecting to hear. They wouldn't even give him a progress report without Dr. Shaw's permission.

Speak of the devil . . . as he was heading back to the elevator, Brian saw Dr. Shaw and another man pass through the door marked 'Stairs.' The other man was tall and lanky, with a crop of black hair – Dr. Brockman from Seacliff.

Brian started to hail them, thought better of it, and hurried to catch up. He reached the door as it was easing slowly shut on its hydraulic hinge, and paused as he heard low but urgent voices.

"I think you owe me an explanation," Shaw said. "The cerebregens were supposed to be safe. You never mentioned this sort of side effect!"

Brian slipped through the door and let it close the rest of the way. He was on the upper landing, unable to see or be seen by the men below. His instincts told him that something fishy was afoot.

"They are safe . . . as far as we know," Brockman said. "Remember, the compound is still very new. And this is a different case. The initial damage done to Lucas Gordon's nervous system wasn't caused by oxygen deprivation, as in our other subjects. His was a more . . . speculative treatment."

"An experiment," Shaw said flatly.

"As you will, an experiment."

Brockman sounded at once amused and clinically detached, a combination that Brian didn't much like. The way he'd so casually tossed off the word 'subjects,' too . . .

"Damn it, Brockman, what's happened to him? Sudden catastrophic swelling, not only of the brain but of the spinal cord as well, coupled with violent outbursts . . . what have you done to him?"

"The purpose was to attempt to restore mobility and motor function. It appeared to be working quite well." Brockman chuckled coldly. "So well, in fact, that it wouldn't surprise me in the least if Lucas decided to self-medicate himself into an overdose. It's quite common, really. If one pill is good, two must be better, and if two are better, why not six? Before you know it, the bottle's empty."

"Doesn't this concern you?"

"It concerns me greatly. This is of course not the result we were looking for."

"That's not what I meant and you know it. Lucas is going to need surgery. Extensive, drastic surgery to relieve the pressure on his skull before his head splits open like a walnut. He's already on very delicate medical ground thanks to that crossbow bolt, and frankly, I don't know if he'll survive another operation. You've got to stop using the cerebregens."

Brockman sighed. "Elliot, you've seen for yourself how beneficial the compound is when used properly. Sometimes things like this happen. Regrettable, yes. Inconvenient, yes. But hardly worth taking the hope away from the others. Like David."

Ooh, that was a low blow, thought Brian.

"It's David and the others I'm thinking of," Shaw said stiffly.

"I should hope so. They're making progress. Striving toward their potential. Dr. Lundquist's dream, met and exceeded. You of all people should appreciate that."

"At what cost, though? We're talking about people here, about children.

How can you justify taking these risks?"

"You weren't questioning it when you learned we could help give your son a real life, a life worth living."

"So that's how," Shaw said, his disgust plain. "That's how you justify it. That their lives weren't worth living. That if something goes wrong, they're no worse off. Even if they die, they're no worse off."

"Exactly!" Brockman said. It sounded like he was smiling. "And yes, we will have some setbacks, even some failures. But for the rest, they'll be made better than they ever could have been before."

"They are just subjects to you, aren't they? Lab animals. Experiments."

"A certain amount of professional distance is required. Now, are you through with your moral dilly-dallying? Once Lucas is stable enough to be moved, you'll make the arrangements to transfer him to Seacliff –"

"Seacliff?"

"Of course. You're lucky to have the best neurologists and neurosurgeons in the country right here in town. We can monitor his condition, try and reverse the uncontrolled growth. Even if Lucas doesn't survive, think of the information we'll gain."

"My God . . ." Shaw's words were muffled, as if he was burying his face in his hands. "I can't believe this. I can't be a part of this. What you're doing up there is wrong, Roger. Unethical and wrong."

"Elliot, you already are a part of it. We need your help, your cooperation."

"No. No, I can't. No more. Not even for David. I'm taking him out of the program, taking him home."

"To lead his pathetic, diminished life? To love him in that pitiful way that you do, raddled with guilt, flavored with hate and disgust?"

"That is not –"

"Oh, I know how you feel about your son, Elliot. Believe me, I know. I can feel it coming off of you in waves. You can't let David go back to being what he was before. You can't do that to him, and you can't do it to yourself."

A wretched sob floated up the stairwell to Brian Sorenson's stunned ears. He didn't dare move, hardly dared breathe. A hot coal burned in his heart, the awful vindication-without-triumph of finding out that he'd been right about Seacliff, right about Lundquist.

"Right now," continued Brockman in a low tone that Brian had to strain to hear, "you're probably thinking you should blow the whistle on Seacliff, expose the project. That would be a serious mistake."

"If you think I'm worried about what it'll do to my career," Shaw said in a broken voice, "you couldn't be more wrong. It'd be worth it to put an end to this."

"I don't think you're understanding me," Brockman said. "This is the part where I'm telling you that if you know what's good for you, and for David, you'll keep quiet."

"Threatening. You're threatening me."

"If that's how you choose to see it."

"Kill me, I suppose. Kill me, and David too." Shaw's breathing was ragged and audible. "But didn't you say David's life is already not worth living? And mine isn't, without him. So what would we have to lose?"

"I sense you getting ready to do something ill-advised and regrettable," Brockman said. "Kill you? I hardly think it would come to that. Not when we have so many other resources available."

"What do you mean?" asked Shaw apprehensively.

"Think of Lucas Gordon and imagine David in his place, brimming with psychotic fury, a programmable murder machine. Think of the tremendous advances that have been made these last few years in memory repression therapy and mind control. Think of all that we could do."

"Then why don't you do it?" challenged Shaw. "If you're so worried about me exposing Seacliff, why even bother trying to convince me, coerce me, when you could do that instead?"

"We've made advances, yes," Brockman said, "but many are still, like the cerebregens, an imperfect science. Plus, it would be a shame to destroy the mind or life of a man with your education. You know the Seacliff philosophy. We hate to see potential go to waste. But now, Elliot, we both have a lot of work to catch up on. I'll be in touch."

With that, he descended the stairs in a clatter of footsteps, even whistling a jaunty tune. The door on the second-floor landing wheezed and exhaled, and Brian took advantage of the noise to open his own door just enough to slip back into the hall.

* * *

4

His mom had kept him home on Monday 'just to be sure,' even though he'd gotten through the rest of the weekend with no problem. On Tuesday, Toby Edwards walked to school just like usual, but with many a glance over his shoulder.

He spent most of the morning paying only half attention to his teachers. His thoughts were full with wondering what, if anything, he should say to Eric if he saw him at lunch.

But when the bell rang and the students crowded the halls, Toby realized he didn't need to worry about it. Eric wasn't at school. Hadn't been yesterday, either, and some of the kids had seen his mother going into the principal's office.

The gossip flew on both sides of the athletic field separating the elementary from the high school. Nobody's parents had a private meeting with Principal Lemke unless it was seriously bad news.

The rumors were all vicious – Eric shipped off to detox, Eric busted for shoplifting or vandalism or thievery, Eric sent to juvie hall because he beat up his mother.

Toby didn't believe any of them, secretly knowing it was far weirder, far worse, and had something to do with what had happened on Saturday.

Mrs. Raney had called the Edwards house yesterday, but all Mom would tell Toby was that she'd apologized for Eric scaring him, nothing more.

He went through the motions of a regular school day, but a deeply troubled hunch lingered, telling him that Eric was still around. Still close. Maybe hiding out, looking for another chance to get at Toby.

So that he won't be the only one.

But Eric wasn't the only one. There was Toby, and Lora. And others. Like Jenny, wherever she was. And Chris, the boy who had lost his toy dinosaur. Visiting Lora, he was sure that they'd been listening, spying, and would find a way to keep him there. But when Lora's mom was ready to go, no one had said a thing about it. His relief as Theresa Zane drove out through the decorative gates with him belted securely into the passenger seat was beyond description.

Now, though . . . he knew that the only way he was going to find out more was by getting inside Seacliff again. Getting into wherever they were keeping the other kids. Down in the dark. Down in the caves. Where they had taken Lora and done unspeakable things to her.

What will they do to me?

It was a risk he had to take. As things stood now, no one would ever believe his crazy story. Not even if he demonstrated his power for them. But if he could somehow do it, get in and get out again with proof . . . even better, if he could get in and rescue them, rescue Jenny after the whole town had given her up for lost, they'd have to listen then!

*   *   *

5

Kel McGuire felt like a dirty skunk. A sneaky betraying dirty skunk.

"So, let's re-cap," Nancy Ellsworth said, shuffling through the printouts and photocopies they'd spent the day compiling. "What we've got here is a woman who apparently didn't exist before January of this year."

By night, Nancy tended to dress in black vinyl and go by the moniker Midnight Lady, strutting her stuff and whipping her boyfriend in front of a web-cam for the viewing pleasure of slavering kinks who paid well for the privilege. By day, her impressively statuesque proportions were concealed by 'business casual' and she worked as Kel's secretary, receptionist, and all-purpose assistant.

Today, however, hadn't been about business. He'd canceled two appointments and rushed through his other duties, his thoughts consumed with the deepening mystery that was Marge Raney.

"I feel like a skunk," he said. "A louse."

"She *suggested* you to go to the DMV," Nancy retorted. "Might as well take her up on it."

"But the more we find out, the less sense it makes," Kel said, shaking his head. "I don't get it. What's this all about?"

Among her other, less mentionable, accomplishments, Nancy was a computer hacker of some skill. Not in the league of someone like Brian Sorenson, but she could run circles around Kel. She'd spent the day ignoring the filing and paperwork, in favor of gathering data.

"California driver's license issued for Margaret Anne Raney on January

12th of this year," Nancy said. "No driving record, no credit history, no marriage license, zilch."

"She could have gone back to her maiden name after the divorce," Kel said. "But Eric's last name is Raney, so that doesn't seem likely."

"There's no record of a William Raney in California at all," Nancy said. "Google turned up three, but none of them would seem to match what we're looking for."

"What about the house? With no credit history, how did she get a bank loan?"

"She didn't. The house on Vista Beach Drive was purchased outright by Coalition Science and Technologies, Inc. Based in Chicago."

"Did you find out anything about them?"

Nancy nodded. "Sure, they have a very flashy website. Long on spiffy graphics, short on actual content. The gist of it seems to be that they're a small but growing company, and produce a wide range of computer and medical hardware and software."

"Why would an outfit like that buy a run-down house out here?"

"Your guess is as good as mine. Then there's the kid."

"Eric. What about Eric?"

"For starters, the birth certificate he's got on file with the school is phony."

"What?" Kel sat bolt upright.

"Usually, something like this, you give the Hall of Records a call and they tell you, sorry, those records were all destroyed in the big mysterious fire. At least, that's how it is in the movies and trashy novels. But not this time. That hospital doesn't have any record of the kid . . . and I had them fax me an example of the birth certificates they were using sixteen years ago. Doesn't match. Not even close." She gave him the two copies and he didn't need to compare them to see that she was right.

"According to this, Marge's maiden name is Smith."

"Uh-huh. If she's even his mother."

Kel blinked at her. "Excuse me?"

"Everything else is turning out to be a lie, why not that? They look nothing alike."

"Now, Nance, come on!"

"Kel, I know you like the lady, and believe me, nothing would have made me happier than to see you find someone. But this is all too bizarre. You know what it's starting to sound like to me?"

"An episode of *The Twilight Zone?*"

"No . . . the witness protection program or something like that."

"What? Nance, that's insane!"

"Think about it. It could all be fake. An assumed name, a whole new identity."

"As a night-shift waitress in a tiny town in the middle of nowhere," Kel said.

"But she's not. That's just what they want it to look like."

"For the love of God, why?"

"Well . . ." Nancy paced the office, long shapely legs scissoring beneath her skirt. "Okay, here's a wild scenario for you. Let's say we've got a nice little family unit, and Dad works for Coalition S&T. He's in charge of something top-secret, delicate. A competitor wants to get the inside scoop, but Dad won't be bribed, won't talk. They threaten his family. To keep them safe, he has the company send them away under new names. The company buys a little house, arranges a bogus school transfer for the son, and tells Mom to pretend she's a waitress. Meanwhile, though, the company's taking care of their needs."

"That is pretty wild."

"But plausible?"

"Vaguely."

"Well, at least I'm trying to come up with an explanation for you."

"Sorry, Nance. I'm just blown away by all of this. I hoped by looking into it, we'd find some answers. All I have now is more questions. I don't know what to think anymore, what to do next."

"Here's something else to chew on – I talked to the Greyhound station in Eureka. They didn't sell any tickets Sunday morning to Sacramento, and none of them remember a kid of Eric's description getting on a bus for any destination."

"What are you saying? That she lied about that, too? That she didn't send him to his father?"

"What father?" Nancy tapped a piece of paper. "No such person as William Raney, according to this. She didn't send the kid anyplace by bus. Or by plane. I checked the airport, too."

"And I thought I was being a snoop," Kel said. "Then where's Eric?"

"Another question for your list."

He raked his hair, disheveling it. "God. What is all this?"

"Are you going to talk to her again?"

"And say what? Tell her everything we've found out, and demand the truth?"

"Well, yeah. It beats driving yourself insane trying to make sense of this."

He took a long slow breath and released it in a gust that blew papers across the desk. "No, since we've started snooping, I may as well go all the way."

*   *   *

6

She hadn't come back, still hadn't come back, and Brian stood at the foot of the stairs wondering what to do.

Whatever it was going to be, it had better be quick, because he hadn't been discharged from the hospital yet. Any minute now, someone who knew that might come along. Dr. Shaw would be paged, and Brian would have to look him in the eye.

He couldn't do that. He knew that if he did, eye contact would be like a key to unlock him, and everything would spill out. What he'd heard. What he knew. And if Shaw knew that *he* knew, what might the doctor do?

A passing woman with a bouquet of daisies glanced curiously at him. Brian managed an inane, toothy smile, and turned away to study the items on display in the gift shop window as if they were of intense fascination.

Dawn had his car, and while he wasn't such a mouse potato – the computer geek version of a couch potato – as to balk at walking home, the rain was coming down in sheets and buckets. And to make things even better, he was wearing his pajama bottoms and a cheap terrycloth hospital robe. And socks. Not even slippers. Just socks. No shirt, because Lucas Gordon had bled all over it and so an orderly had taken it away in a red biohazard bag. Probably to the hospital incinerator. No wallet, either, and no money.

Under such shoddy circumstances, leaving the hospital seemed like a nutty choice. But the whole day had been rife with nuttiness, and he had a hunch that if he stayed here, he might develop complications. Have an adverse reaction to his painkillers. Wind up dead.

He had practically memorized the contents of the window, and if he lurked here much longer, he'd be sure to attract attention.

Just then, a man in a brown sport coat hurried by, digging in his breast pocket with the impatient gestures of a severe nicotine addict. Inspiration struck, and Brian fell in step behind him as the smoker pushed through a side door that let onto the covered patio.

A few other people were out here, huddled in groups according to type – patients, staff, visitors. The brick tile was muddy and cold, soaking through Brian's socks. Beyond the edge of the shelter, a low slope of sodden woodchips and evergreen shrubs stretched to the sidewalk.

Brian scanned the parking lot without much hope, but there, in the furthest rank from the building, was a familiar powder-blue Tercel. His car.

Was Dawn inside? Or had he missed her on his way out?

The smokers were watching him out of the corners of their eyes, all of them with their shoulders hunched in a sulky, defensive posture that said yes, they knew smoking was bad for them, they knew second-hand smoke was bad for everyone else, it'd probably be outlawed nationwide any minute now . . . but screw you anyway.

Brian hadn't lit up, thereby making himself a person of suspicion. Plus, in the dismal grey light of the day, the bruises on his neck probably stood out like a string of red and blue Christmas lights.

Well, he'd given them something to really be suspicious about . . .

With purpose and as if he knew exactly what he was doing, Brian strode through the squelchy bed of woodchips. The rain pasted his pajama pants to his legs and turned his robe into a thin washcloth. Water ran in rills from his hair, and by the time he reached the sidewalk, he was as soaked as if he'd just climbed out of a full bathtub.

He pressed on, weaving through ranks of parked cars and doing his best to ignore the looks. A quick glance back proved him right; all of the smokers were staring incredulously after him with cigarette butts held forgotten between fingers or lips.

It would be a good joke on him if the car was empty, because of course he didn't have his keys. And while he had played no less than six characters with skills in lockpicking and hotwiring – that had been in a dark-future urban gloom game set in Seattle – Brian himself could no sooner jimmy a lock than he could sprout wings and fly to Mexico.

Which was sounding better and better all the time, the flying to Mexico part. He was freezing! His feet slapped and splashed through puddles, disturbing the rainbows of oilslicks. Sunny, sandy beaches . . . lots of tanned girls in wish-and-a-promise bikinis. Yeah. Basking in the hot sun, smelling coconut suntan lotion . . .

On second thought, he was only making himself more miserable imagining it.

He reached the car, which was idling. Through a rain-spotted ripple of water sluicing down the windshield, made out the shape of someone sitting in the driver's seat. It was Dawn. Her head was tipped back against the headrest, hands curled tight around the steering wheel.

Brian tapped on the fogged window.

Dawn jumped and screamed, the scream so loud even to him that it must have been deafening to her, closed inside as she was. Her elbow whacked into the window, leaving a clear divot in the condensation. Through that divot, he saw her recognize him.

She opened the door so fast that he had to spring back or else be knocked on his ass. Before he knew what was happening, Dawn was in his arms, shaking and crying, not caring or even aware that she was getting drenched.

"Dead, he was dead, the roach, the flies on him, dead and stinking, the dog, the dog was going to eat him, I forgot to close the door, omigod, what if the dog comes back, what if it comes back and eats him?" she babbled, clinging to Brian.

"Dawn! Whoa! Hey! Come on, get in the car, we'll catch pneumonia." He tried to untangle her from him – it would always have to be this way, wouldn't it, a girl all over him for one of the dismayingly rare times in his life, and he was trying to get her to let go. "In the car before we drown, huh?"

He didn't think he would get through to her, especially with his voice still sounding hoarse and sandpapery, but he did. She scrambled across to the passenger seat. Brian got in and shut the door, turning the sound of the rain into a drumming thunder. Warmth snuggled around him like a lover, letting him forget for a minute that he was dripping a lake onto the seat and floorboards.

Dawn had settled down, but her huge maple-syrup brown eyes were fixed on his face. "Brian . . . omigod, what are we going to do?"

"I don't know . . . but you're not going to believe what happened to me a little while ago!"

"It was horrible!"

"It sure was. And I was so dumb to go to him! I should have known better." Brian could have socked himself in the head for his stupidity. "I should have known he'd be in on it with Lundquist. They're probably all in on it, everyone at Seacliff."

"Dr. Brockman is one of them. I recognized his voice on the answering machine," Dawn said. "And I found the vitamins. They're the same kind as Richie's getting."

"So *dumb!* I bet that's what set Lucas off . . . 'programmable murder machine,' yeah, sure, that's just what they did. Sent him after me because I'd found out, and they wanted me dead before I told."

"What are they doing to Richie? What if they're doing the same thing to Richie?"

They were both talking at once, and abruptly fell silent together as some of what each other was saying permeated their consciousness.

"What?" they said at the same time.

"You first," Brian quickly added. He pointed to a can of orange pop in the cup-holder. "But can I have a drink of that?"

Dawn looked at it like she wasn't even sure what it was, then nodded. "I don't even like that kind, but it was all that was left, and I had to wash the taste away. I threw up."

"When?"

"When I found the dead man."

Brian sputtered and coughed, more torture for his abused throat. "The *what?*"

"The dead man." Her skin seemed clear as glass, bright firespots burning in her cheeks like twin votive candles. "I think it must have been Lucas' father."

Haltingly, she told him what she'd seen at the Gordon house, and showed him the empty pill bottle. The font and the style of gummed label were familiar to him from the in-house pharmacy at Seacliff. Not that he needed any such confirmation of her story after the exchange he'd overheard between Shaw and Brockman.

"I threw up," she said again. "In the backyard. And thought about calling the police, but I couldn't. I chickened out. I ran . . . drove away as fast as I could." Shame added more fire to her cheeks. "I dented your car, too. I hit a stump someone had their mailbox on when I was backing out. I'm sorry. I'll pay for fixing it."

"Screw the car. Are you okay?"

Her full lower lip shook like an earthquake in miniature. "What do we do? We've got to tell someone."

"We can't." He told her his story. "I think, I really do think, that he sent Lucas to attack me on purpose, to kill me. If we try to tell anyone, they'll shut us up."

"The police –"

"I thought about that, but look what they did to Dr. Shaw. They've got his son up there, and it gave them a hold on him. He won't dare do anything against *them* because of what they might do to David, or because he feels like he owes them so much for helping him. And Chief Blake might be the same way, because his stepdaughter Lora's up there too."

"So is Richie." Dawn's hands, pale gloves filled with snow, found his and held tight. "What are they going to do to Richie? What have they already done to him?"

"I'm sure he's okay," Brian said. "They . . . I didn't get the idea they wanted to hurt the kids. Something went wrong with Lucas. They didn't mean for it to happen."

"I trusted them, I thought they were helping, but . . . but what do we do? If you're right and they did want to kill you because of what you knew about Dr. Lundquist –"

It hit him with the force of a hammer blow. "I told Dr. Brockman that the only other person who knew was you."

"You mean . . . you mean . . ."

"*Stupid!*" Brian gave in to the urge this time, and did sock himself in the head. "Shit!"

"So we're both on their list." Her near-panic had given way to a flat calm, the eye of the storm before absolute hysteria. "They'll kill us both to keep us from telling anyone."

"Maybe they think that they can control you by threatening Richie –"

"We just need to let it go, Brian. Forget it. We'll . . . we'll do what they want."

"But, Dawn –"

"I can't let them hurt Richie. This is my fault anyway. My mother was right." The squall, the hurricane, blew in on ferocious winds of tears. "First I let him nearly drown and then I turn him over to these people –"

He tried to hold her but she flailed at him and crumpled against the passenger side door, crying in great heaving sobs.

Brian sat there feeling useless, a big uncomfortable lump, wet to the skin with socks full of woodchip splinters. The windows were opaque with fog, so thick that he couldn't determine the color of the car next to them. He drank more cloyingly sweet orange soda and waited her out.

When Dawn had subsided to hiccups and sniffles, he offered her the rest of the can and she drained it.

"It's not going to be like that," he told her. "We're going to get out of this. We're going to get Richie out of Seacliff. If they don't have him, they can't do anything to us."

"How?" She wiped her eyes and looked at him. God, she was beautiful, even after a long day of emergency room visits and finding dead bodies and throwing up and crying her head off, she was beautiful.

"We'll bust him out. Tonight. And then we'll get the hell out of here, and spill the whole thing. Blow it sky-high."

*   *   *

7

When Judge and Inge ushered them out for a trip to the gym, Jenny Forrester noticed that a fifth enclosure was lighted and occupied. She sidled that way for a look just as the person inside came up to the clear wall.

A squeak of a gasp burst from her and she stumbled backward, colliding tush-first with a table. Inge whirled, already raising her taser with a merciless glint in her arctic eyes, but Jenny barely cared.

"Hey," Eric Raney said, lifting his chin in sarcastic greeting.

"Eric!"

"Jenny, come on," Chris said, pulling at her arm. "Don't talk to that guy."

"You jerk! You creep!" Jenny spat. "I know what you did —"

"Leave off," Inge commanded. She all but dragged Jenny away, as Jenny squirmed and tried to glare back at Eric. He only sneered.

"I'll kill you, you creep!" Jenny cried, then hissed in pain as Inge's pinch settled brutally into the juncture of her neck and shoulder. Her defiance fled, and she went obediently along to the gym.

Julian came up to her, his dark gaze solemn. "Jenny okay?"

"Jenny is *pissed*." She looked at Chris. "You know that guy?"

"Yeah." He said it as if the admission tasted bad.

"He's one of us. He used his power on me."

"Yeah. And brought you here. But he's not one of us. Not really. He was born that way. Because his dad was like us."

"His dad?" Jenny goggled. "How long have they been doing this?"

Chris shrugged. "But his dad's part of it too, and I guess they wanted to see if Eric would get even stronger if they gave him the medicine on top of what he was born with. Now they use him to hunt us down."

"Then why's he here? Locked up and everything?"

"He made them mad. I woke up and heard him and the doctors yelling at each other. They said he was endangering the whole project and threw him in a cell until he proved they could trust him again."

"We've got to get out of here," Jenny said. "That's not how I'm going to end up, working for these mad scientists and doing whatever they say."

"That's what they want."

"But it's stupid!" She shook her fists at the mirrored glass, knowing they could hear her. "What are you thinking, anyway, huh? You kidnap us and turn us into freaks, and then we're supposed to *help* you? Work for you? You crazy people?"

"Jenny, quit it!" Chris said.

"Don't you know how dangerous it is, too? If you didn't have those damned old visors on, you'd be toast. And what's going to happen if you get one of us who can do something really major? Like in those old Stephen King books? Huh? What if you get some kid who turns out to be able to start fires or knock down walls just by thinking about it? What then, huh, smart guys? Your stupid visors won't do *shit* against that!"

"They already did."

She broke off her rant. "What? When?"

"One of the kids that died, she burned herself up. Right over there." He pointed to a spot on the floor, and for the first time Jenny became aware of a perfect charred outline, the imprint of a child's hand. "She hadn't ever been able to do anything on their tests, and then one day, *whoosh*, she was on fire."

"What happened to her?"

"They put her out, but it was too late. That was when I ran away." He frowned glumly. "But they caught me."

"You mean they've already had something like that happen, and they keep on doing it? Even though it could happen again?"

"Don't forget Neesha." He spoke in a very low voice, so low that Jenny had to strain to hear him.

"You told me you didn't know what she could do."

"I didn't want to scare you."

"Jeez, thanks, like I haven't already been totally terrified! What does she do?"

"They call it telekinesis. She can move things just by thinking about it. I saw her kill one of them once. It was like he was in an invisible car-smashing machine. That's why they keep her doped up all the time."

"But she's all . . . messed up."

"Yeah. She can't walk, can't talk, can't move. But they keep her alive to study her even though they know she could wreck the whole place."

"We've got to get out of here," Jenny said. "There's gotta be a way."

"I tried once, I already told you. It's no use."

"If they didn't have those damn visors . . . maybe if we could take them by surprise? Pull the visors off? I could talk them into letting us go, then."

"Well now you just told them you were thinking about it," he said in disgust. "Girls. They never shut up."

"We never *give* up either," Jenny said. "What about your power?"

She paused, slightly amazed and amused at herself. How quickly her thinking had changed! From denial to horrified acceptance to this . . . actually viewing their abilities as assets!

"It doesn't work on them with those visors."

"But is that all you can do, that – what did they call it?"

"Telempathic projected aversion," he said. "I can make someone go away."

"Can you do it backwards? Pull someone toward you?"

"I dunno. Why?"

"To bring people down here to rescue us. Why can't it work the other way around too?"

"Would you zip it?" he hissed anxiously.

"You reached Lora that time, so I know the person doesn't have to be real close. Call for someone."

"Jenny, shut up!" He jabbed her in the side.

"What is your prob – oh." She looked up.

Inge stood over them like a Valkyrie Terminator. "Exercise time is over."

*   *   *

8

Just a cozy family evening at home.

That was the picture presented in the spacious wood-paneled sitting room at the end of the second floor west wing. A hearty blaze crackled in the fireplace, offsetting the rainy November wind howling dismally at the windowpanes.

Benjamin Lundquist sat in a comfortable silence, engrossed in a book, with a snifter of brandy within reach. In one corner of the room, a small television was on with the volume turned low, and Aiden Ferguson concentrated on the swift-flying paintbrush of a bushy-haired man as he dotted in 'some happy little trees right over here.'

Very cozy indeed, thought Gwynne McGuire.

At the end of the couch with a book and some brandy of her own, Gwynne studied her mentor over the top of the pages. She knew what he was doing. Playing at being the patriarch, the doting grandfather with his surrogate family. In Aiden's late father Kenneth, he had seen the son he'd lost. Aiden, for all her problems, was the demure and sweet granddaughter he'd never had.

And Gwynne? What was her role in the fantasy? The daughter to follow in his footsteps? To inherit his genius and carry on his work when he was gone? Yes, that was probably it.

He sensed her scrutiny and looked up, hawklike emerald eyes and those chiseled, noble features with their careworn lines. "Yes, my lamb?"

"I was wondering where Roger had gotten to," she said.

"The hospital, last I heard," Benjamin replied, turning a page. "Elliot called him in for a consult. He probably stopped to get a bite to eat."

"I think I'll go downstairs for a while. I have some things I need to catch up on."

"Your dedication is commendable," he said, "but it's also important to take some time for yourself now and again. And we've been having such a nice evening —"

"Oh, but you know me, Benjamin. I can't relax if there's something left undone." She smiled at him, as warm a smile as she ever unlimbered, and left the sitting room.

Seacliff was quiet. In the other wing, the students would be already tucked into bed and the staff settling in for another night. Everything over there was going well, though she knew they would soon be facing the issue of what to do about MC-F1198, otherwise known as Lora Blake.

Roger, in nominal charge of her case, favored discharging her to her home and observing the results at a distance. Gwynne scorned this tag-and-release method — just look at the troubles they were already having with the Edwards boy. Not to mention Eric. To her, it was proof positive that these subjects simply could not be left in their natural habitats. They had to be monitored closely, with diligence and professional standards.

She descended to the first floor on her way to the library when she heard the front doors open. Brian Sorenson and Dawn Jessec came in, moving in such a furtive manner that Gwynne would have believed they were teens sneaking into the house after curfew.

"Working overtime, Mr. Sorenson?" she asked. "And Dawn, I didn't realize we held visiting hours so late."

They stifled yelps as she materialized out of the shadows.

"Dr. McGuire, hi!" Dawn said with overdone brightness. "I know it's late, but it's been such a crazy day that I didn't get a chance to see Richie. If I could just look in on him for a minute, kiss him goodnight, that'd be so great."

"You'll have to check with the attendant on duty, but I'm sure it will be all right this once." Gwynne looked at Brian, noting the ring of bruises on his throat. "I thought they were keeping you for observation, Mr. Sorenson."

"They were, but they said there was nothing really wrong so I could go if I wanted." He coughed. "And I felt bad for calling in sick."

"Under the circumstances, I think it's understandable."

"I just had some stuff I needed to do. Is Dr. Brockman here?"

"Not at the moment, as far as I know."

"Okay. Well, I can leave him a note if I don't see him."

When they had vanished in the direction of Brian's office, Gwynne let herself into the dark, windowless library. The armchairs were unoccupied, the bar in the corner untouched, the books mute upon their shelves. The room held its own deathless hush.

She crossed to the wall of shelves. Here, barely perceptible even to one who knew where to look, was a seam in the paneling and a faint breath of a draft. A leather-bound volume rested ever-so-slightly out of alignment with its fellows.

Gwynne pulled it out, probed with her fingers into the space left by the removed book, and there, set into the back of the shelf, found a recessed and very small button.

She pressed it, and stepped back as the section of shelf swung outward on its silent hinge, revealing a spiral stair descending in a narrow stone throat. She took a flashlight from the rack affixed to the wall and started down.

This discovery, when she'd been scouting for a home for the project three years ago, had been the clincher. It had come when she'd been poring over the blueprints of the house, and noted a discrepancy in the stated dimensions of the room. Further exploration had led her to the passage, as hidden and archaic as anything out of a Sherlock Holmes story.

Quite a bit of hard work later, all conducted in the utmost secrecy, it was clean, scoured to the stone and free of dust, cobwebs, or moss. At the bottom landing, frosted, low-wattage bulbs shed an even but muted light. At the end of a wide and low-ceilinged hallway was a pair of steel panels. Elevator doors. The shaft that connected the wine cellar to the kitchen and upper floors had been extended a level down, but Gwynne rarely used it for fear of raising suspicions among those of the staff who were not in the know.

She walked the tunnels that had once held smuggled goods. Indeed, one such cache had been found during the remodeling, tucked far back in a shadowed nook. The Alaskan jewels, layer after layer of polished amber, hematite, and amethyst, had been quite the find. Gwynne considered it amusing that she was now overseeing a different sort of piracy. The theft of thought and memory. Even the workmen who'd accomplished all this had no recollection of the good job they'd done.

At the end of the hall was a doorway of arched stone, the door itself iron-bound oak, just the sort of thing one might see in a castle dungeon. It was the last holdover of Cliffwood's original design, because the room beyond was modern and very much to Gwynne's own tastes. It had gleaming black-tiled floor and an acoustic tile suspended ceiling. The walls were white-gloss enamel, except for the one that was all tinted glass, looking down into the small gymnasium beyond. A workstation with two computers stretched under the length of the window. Another wall was taken up by a row of lockers, and a small door led to a hall with living facilities for the staff who lived down here, under conditions not dissimilar to those served by submariners.

Gwynne took a lab coat from her locker and put on a visored headband, in all its clunky, heavy discomfort.

The only other door out of here was as unlike the iron-bound oak one as humanly possible. This one was of brushed steel, and an observer wouldn't have been surprised if it slid open at her approach like something out of a science fiction movie. Instead, she had to resort to a press-bar like anyone else.

Beyond was a corridor that had been hewn from the stone, enlarging and squaring off the narrow passageway that had once connected the larger caves together. When she'd first seen it, the walls had been stained with antique soot from torches or lanterns, and there were two or three places where she'd had to squeeze through sideways. Now cleaned and widened, it sloped down at a gentle angle, the floor covered in ribbed rubber for traction.

Cables, pipes, and metal vents ran along the ceiling. The air was pressurized and heated to keep dust and damp at bay, handled by a ventilation system so quiet that it blended easily with the distant muffled pounding of the surf.

At the bottom of the slope, the hall emptied into a cavern. The cavern, the cave, where Seacliff's real work was done.

*   *   *

9

Kel McGuire still felt like a louse. A skunk. A rotten no-good sneak.

He liked to think of himself as basically an honest, forthright kind of guy. His actions over the past couple of days, however, left him feeling coated with slime. There was no thrill, only a sort of sick resolve that kept him going.

The honest, forthright kind of guy was parked on a muddy patch of road, listening to the rain beat tattoos on the roof of his car, squinting through the streaming darkness.

He was cold and cross, not even having the engine running enough to provide heat and the radio, making himself suffer outwardly as much as he was inwardly for doing what he was doing.

Skunk. Louse. Rat. Weasel.

He was a veritable chimera of loathsome vermin.

Light appeared, a wavering, feeble yellow glow on the trees. It resolved itself into two headlights, one flickering like a candle about to gutter out in a breeze.

Marge Raney's truck passed Kel's hiding place, one taillight out and the other a cyclopean red eye. He couldn't see well enough to know if it was Marge behind the wheel.

Rotten no-good sneak.

There was still time to call it off . . . still time to go home and salvage a modicum of his self-respect, and not be reduced to spying on the woman he loved. Who did he think he was? One of Scott's dime-store detectives?

Kel doubted he could handle it if the worst was true. Suppose he did follow her, and that she did go to the topless bar. He couldn't stand the thought of seeing Marge like that. Of learning her stage name – 'Marge' was all wrong for that kind of job; it would have to be something like Lacy Spanks or Cheri Pye.

When the single taillight had vanished, Kel started the car. It wasn't even his car, which told a clear tale of his premeditated lousiness . . . he'd borrowed Nancy's for the occasion. And he picked his way along without benefit of the headlights, which might have given away the pursuit.

Rat. Skunk. Scumbucket.

He followed, trying to gird his mind for what awaited.

He'd barely had time to even begin girding when the pickup turned left onto the old access road that looped up the back of the bluff to Seacliff, then down past the Zane and Forrester houses to the marina.

Either she was taking the scenic route, or she knew he was onto her. And it wasn't a good night for the scenic route.

Kel turned left anyway. The sick resolve ruled him, and he knew he was doomed to see this night through to its inevitable conclusion, no matter how much worse the truth might make him feel.

He saw the brighter flare of the single taillight, and braked. His entire face felt twisted into a mask of confusion.

The pickup was stopped in front of the security gate that let onto the back driveway of Seacliff, what the late Brad Thornton had always and with unfailing smugness referred to as the servant's entrance. The fence had been improved considerably since the mansion re-opened, and the gate was now hooked up to a remote control.

It opened. Marge drove through. It closed again.

Kel was beyond dumbfounded.

If she works there, even in some lowly janitorial capacity, why not just say so? Why the waitress story?

The pickup had disappeared from his sight.

What now? March straight up to the front doors and ask to speak to her?

He let Nancy's car roll closer to the gate.

Climbable? He was in pretty good shape –

What in the hell was he thinking? He was not about to go courting broken bones trying to shinny over a fence in the middle of the night!

It's only nine-thirty . . .

That didn't matter. At best, he'd be let off with a stern talking-to by Lundquist and slink away with Gwynne's scornful laughter ringing in his ears. At worst, they'd call the cops on him, and Damon or Scott would show up to haul him away.

Nonetheless, he stopped the car and got out, hiking his jacket up over his head in a largely unsuccessful effort to keep the rain off. He splashed closer, through shallow puddles and one modest lake that immersed him to the shin.

He told himself that this little foray was purely hypothetical, in the interests of determining if the fence was electrified or anything of that nature. As if he'd be able to tell by looking. He had no intention of really going in. If nothing else, suppose that Marge *did* work here in some legitimate capacity, and his snooping cost her her job.

There were no warning signs on the fence. None reading 'Beware of Dog.' Not even a 'Trespassers Will Be Prosecuted.' But that didn't change the fact that it was still private property, and he'd still be in deep trouble if he tried anything cute.

"Don't try anything cute," advised a voice over his right shoulder.

Tricked for a moment into thinking he'd heard his own thoughts aloud, Kel didn't immediately react to the danger. He caught on a second later, when he was grabbed and flung to the ground.

"You should have let it go," said the man standing over him.

Kel stared blankly, first at the gun, and then at the stranger behind it.

The man was six-foot-something, hard to be sure when Kel was sprawled on the ground at his feet. His build was tough and rangy, not overly muscular but he carried himself like someone who could take on a wolf barehanded and walk away unscathed. He wore jeans and a black rainslicker, and what little of his face could be seen through a translucent red visor didn't promote hope on Kel's part.

It was a weathered and lined face, one side drawn into a grimace of perpetual hostile suspicion by a scar that joined the corner of his eye to the corner of his mouth. A few days' growth of beard stubbled his chin. He would have looked intimidating and dangerous enough even without the gun.

The gun.

Kel's attention was drawn helplessly back to it. He was a peaceable man who only refrained from labeling himself a pacifist because he'd never been put in a situation to test his capacity for violence. And now hardly seemed the time to sail those uncharted waters. The scarred stranger would have been more than his match unarmed.

Because of that peaceful nature, Kel knew hardly anything about firearms. All he knew now was that it didn't matter what kind of gun it was. The bad end was pointed at his head, and that made it look as big as a cannon.

"I think we've started off on a misunderstanding," Kel said, putting every ounce of his calming counselor's tone into his voice.

"Get up."

He rose, trying his best to appear nonthreatening – it wasn't hard to do, and he had the feeling that even if he'd uncoiled from the ground like a martial artist and suddenly sprouted weapons from every extremity, the man with the gun would have yawned and then turned him into liversausage.

"I was looking for someone, that's all."

"Yeah." The man nodded. "That was your first mistake. You should have let it go. That's not your car. Whose is it?"

"Not my . . . what? It . . . you know who I am."

"Kelwyn Douglas McGuire Jr., and that's about the only thing keeping you alive right now. Whose car? Your stacked blonde receptionist's, I bet." A repugnant leer spread across his face like oil oozing from the ruptured hull of a tanker. "I watch her some nights on the computer. She's hot."

"Who are you?" Kel demanded.

"Momma named me Judson, but most just call me Judge. In the car."

He very briefly entertained the idea of trying to run for it, but knew that would only earn him a bullet in the back. Or in the leg, if Judge were serious about keeping him alive. He complied, opening the passenger-side door.

"One more thing," said Judge.

Kel started to turn and look at him, and that was when the butt of the gun swooped down and crashed into his skull, plunging him into a star-swirled darkness.

*   *   *

10

Toby Edwards imagined that this must be how a lighthouse-keeper must feel. He probably even looked like one, in his yellow vinyl slicker with hooded head bowed against the windblown slant of the rain, here on the rocky bluff with the sea leaping and churning against its bed of stones below.

His newfound power had led him to the top of the path that Lora had discovered, but upon reaching it, a new thought had occurred to Toby.

They had known she was coming. They had seen her somehow.

Cameras. Security cameras.

The vision/memory given to him by the plastic dinosaur showed him the cave, with its banks of monitors. Approaching this way, Lora must have been seen. And if he did the same thing, he'd be seen too.

But the only other way in was through the house, and he was sure that if anything, it was even more carefully watched. Mrs. Sorenson's son Brian had gone to work for Seacliff in charge of their computers.

Toby had a more-than-passing acquaintance with Brian. A child of the Information Age, Toby's parents had wanted to make sure he was raised on the high-tech gadgetry so much a part of everyday life. When his level of computer savvy had outstripped theirs — when he was five — they'd asked Brian to take over as a sort of tutor and mentor.

Brian Sorenson wasn't cool like Eric Raney, but had a definite King of the Geeks thing going for him that Toby could respect. If Brian had set up Seacliff's security systems, they'd be beyond Toby's ability to circumvent.

Did that mean Brian was part of it? Toby couldn't believe that . . . surely no one from town could be involved with something so horrible. The rest of them were from away — all the doctors, the nurses, even the janitors and the people who worked in the kitchen.

Toby remembered the undercurrent of grumbling in town when word of that had gone around. He'd heard most of it in bits and pieces at his father's coffee shop. Jobs were hard enough to come by in Trinity Bay, but what had they done? Brought in a bunch of people from the outside to work in the new school.

Even if Brian wasn't a part of it, he still wasn't going to let Toby wander on in against the rules. He'd tell someone, they'd check it out, and Toby would be caught for sure.

If there had been one grownup in town he might possibly have gone to, it would have been Brian. Not that Brian really counted as a grownup in Toby's eyes, or the eyes of most of the other kids. Sure, he was over twenty, but he could still be seen down at Galaxy West, plugging tokens into the video games. He bought *Star Wars* toys and comic books. He wore tee shirts with the Wolverine or the guys from *The Matrix* on them. He'd spent sixteen hours camping outside of the movie theater to get tickets for *The Return of the King*. Basically, he was a tall kid who could drive.

But he worked at Seacliff. He was there right this minute, because as Toby had been trudging up the road past Jenny's and Lora's houses, he'd faded back into the woods to let a car go by. It had been Brian's, the one with all the bumper stickers. By the time Toby reached the field surrounding the mansion, Brian's car had been parked in the front driveway.

If he worked at Seacliff, it meant he almost certainly had to be in on the bad stuff.

Between that depressing realization and the ceaseless downpour, Toby was getting ready to give up and go home. What could one kid do against a conspiracy that big, that well-equipped?

*   *   *

11

Stan Montgomery had his nose in a magazine and his mouth full of fast-food burrito when Dawn emerged from the elevator. He tucked the last bite in, brushed shreds of cheese from his chin, and smiled at her. It was a hard and contemptuous smile, the sort that told her exactly what he thought of teenage whores who got themselves knocked up and then had their boyfriends run out on them.

She steeled her spine and returned a smile of her own. "Hello, Mr. Montgomery. Dr. McGuire said I could see Richie for a little while."

"He's already sleeping." He checked his watch, though the clock on the wall was large and unmistakable. "And visiting hours are over."

"Dr. McGuire said I could," Dawn repeated. "I'll be quiet."

"Too bad . . . I like 'em loud."

His meaning was not at all lost on her, and given all of the other crazy-terrible things she'd learned about Seacliff lately, she wouldn't have been surprised if he vaulted over the counter of the nursing station and raped her right there in the hallway. Nazi doctors, mad scientists, inhuman experiments, why not the rest of the gamut of human scumminess?

She tried not to show her sudden spurt of fear, but could tell by the smirking gleam in his eyes that she was laughably unsuccessful. And that he liked it. Savored it.

"I'm going to go see Richie now," she said, silently promising herself that if he tried to come after her, she was going to kick his nuts up to his ears.

"Go right ahead." He swiveled his chair to make sure she noticed the monitors, which showed each of the bedrooms on this floor as well as views from elsewhere in the building.

Dawn's hopes sank like lead weights. He meant to watch her, the bastard, not because he thought she was up to something but just because he was a slimeball and a pervert and because he knew it would bug her to know he was watching. The moment she tried to do what she'd come here to do, he'd be on her in a flash.

A small light lit up on his console, and a soft 'ping!' sounded. A scowl of irritation wiping away his smirk, Stan leaned over and pushed the intercom. He made himself sound polite and concerned as he said, "Yes, Lora?"

"Hi, Mr. Montgomery, Ruff needs to go outside."

"It's too late for that, Lora. You're supposed to be sleeping."

"I was. He woke me up. He has to pee."

"I thought Aiden took him out after dinner."

"He has to go again. He says he can't wait."

Stan sighed in aggravation. "All right. I'll be there in a minute."

Wild hope flared in Dawn and she struggled not to show it.

"Damn dog," he said as he got up. "Why they let her have that damn dog here, I don't know. I'm not paid to stand outside in the rain while that mutt looks for a place to take a piss."

Dawn said nothing, and followed him down the hall. He stopped at one of the rooms. As the door opened Dawn glimpsed a fall of nightsilk hair and eyes as green as deep still waters.

Lora caught her gaze and held it, and there was something in those eyes that made Dawn pause, brought a tingle of wonder to the back of her neck. As if Lora could look right inside her and know her thoughts and intentions.

The moment of meaningful connection passed as a dog squeezed eagerly through the gap and snuffled at Stan, tail battering the wall and door. Dawn kept going, past rooms where other children slept, until she came to Richie's door.

Glancing back, she saw Stan leading the dog to the elevator. Adrenaline raced and pounded in her veins. Her hands shook as she reached for the knob, then the light switch.

Richie slept curled on his side around a floppy stuffed lion nearly as big as he was. In fuzzy green footie pajamas, with finespun blond hair several shades lighter than her own, he looked angelic.

Thanks to Seacliff . . . if not for this place, he'd still be in the hospital, or in a grimy grey institution somewhere . . .

The guilt rushed up on her like a tidal wave. When Brian had told her about the conversation he'd overheard between Dr. Shaw and Dr. Brockman, she had instantly understood Shaw's dilemma.

Whatever else, these people and this place helped her son, gave him back to her, gave him hope and life.

Dawn wanted to believe that Dr. McGuire, at least, wasn't in on it. But it didn't seem possible that Dr. McGuire could be so involved with every other aspect of Seacliff and still be ignorant of what her colleagues were up to . . . so Dawn had been forced to conclude that she couldn't trust her.

That poked a sharp pang of shame into her heart. Everything she had now – home, job, friends, hope for the future – she owed to Dr. McGuire. Was this how she repaid those kindnesses?

"Miss Richie's Mom?"

Dawn uttered a squeak of panic and spun. The little girl, Lora, was standing in the doorway with her hands clasped before her like she was about to sing in the Sunday School choir.

She had pulled on a pair of sweatpants under her nightgown, buckled what looked like a plastic suit of armor over it, and wore a coat and galoshes. A plastic helm perched on her head, and a fake sword was stuck through the belt of her coat.

"You better hurry," Lora said. "Ruff didn't really have to pee. And he said something's going to happen. Something bad."

"Huh-how do you know?"

"He told me. Animals can know the future sometimes."

Those eyes . . . strange wisdom reflected in emerald green. Dawn almost imagined she could hear the child's voice in her head, whispering, whispering so faintly that she couldn't make out any words, but with a sense of urgency and premonition.

"Okay," Dawn said, unnerved. She gathered up her sleeping son as gently as she could, praying he didn't wake and start to cry and alert others in the house. To soothe him just in case, she also picked up the toy lion.

Lora padded past her and stuffed a pillow under the blanket, creating the impression of a small body in Richie's bed.

"What are you doing?"

"We have to go. The animals know. Something bad's going to happen. They can feel it. Can't you feel it?"

With her nerves jangling like discordant guitar strings, Dawn wasn't sure what she felt. She pushed all her other worries out of her mind and decided to concentrate on nothing but Richie. Richie and getting him out of here.

Lora followed her, and at the elevator Dawn stopped to look at her. "Lora . . . you can't come with me. I'm breaking the rules already by taking Richie out of here. You need to stay."

The girl only pushed the button, and when the doors slid open, she stepped inside.

"Lora, you're going to get in trouble."

"I don't care. It's like Cirith Ungol."

"What?" Dawn asked, totally blank.

"The tower where the Orcs took Frodo. But Samwise came and got him out, and they escaped. Except I don't have *mithril* armor, just this plastic stuff." With that, the enigmatic child fell silent.

Dawn just knew that Stan Montgomery was going to be waiting for them right outside the doors, and Dr. McGuire would be with him, and even before the lecturing and the anger would come the scathingly cold look of disappointment. *Then* the lecturing. Then, maybe, legal machinations to wrest custody of Richie away from her on the grounds that she cared so little for his welfare that she'd endanger him by sneaking him out of Seacliff against medical advice.

Ding.

The doors opened.

∗   ∗   ∗

12

Brian Sorenson wanted to bang his head on the desk.

The answer was here somewhere. It had to be, but kept eluding him. Like Old Granther, the legendary and likely mythical wily old otter of Agate River, whose prowess at stealing fish right off the hook and escaping every trap known to the fishermen of Trinity Bay.

He wished Dawn hadn't insisted on going alone to fetch Richie. For all they knew, Dr. Brockman could have already given the order to have them killed on sight. But if that was the case, surely Dr. McGuire would have done something.

Maybe Brockman wasn't back yet. He didn't show up on any of the security cameras, all of which Brian could access from his computer terminal. He could still be out, at the hospital. Fitting Lucas with cybernetics, maybe. Lacing his skeleton with adamantium. And extendable claws. Yeah. So that next time, he'd be better equipped to handle the job of erasing the equation that was Brian Sorenson from the big chalkboard of life.

Even without Brockman, there was still Dr. Lundquist to consider. Brian knew for a fact that he was here. Lundquist had even stopped by to say hello upon seeing the light under Brian's office door.

Damn, Lundquist was a good actor . . . he'd expressed sympathy and concern for Brian's injuries, told him not to worry about his work but to take as much time off as he needed to recover. Not a breath of a threat came through. Not so much as a flicker in those clear green eyes.

Lundquist gave a flawless impression of having no idea whatsoever that

Brian knew his dirty little sixty-year-old secret. He carried on just as if the ruse was still perfectly sound, and no one at all had figured out he was really Gustav Richter, evil mind control expert of Schlossenberg.

Brian was tempted, horribly tempted, to say something. Just to see what would happen. If he could get a reaction out of Lundquist. But he knew that he'd only be asking for it if he did. Best to play along too, for now . . . until he could find what he needed and get the hell out of here.

After Lundquist had continued on his way, Brian went back to his computer. He knew the hidden lab had to be somewhere on the premises, and it had to be supplied with power at the very least. Probably plumbing as well. But where, dammit, *where?*

He called up the floorplan of the house, but it told him nothing that he didn't already know. In the course of setting up the security systems, he had been all over Seacliff from the attic to the wine cellar.

Brian spun his chair in a tight circle, the casters squeaking on the plastic floormat. When he came to rest, he was looking at a framed snapshot of himself with his parents and sister, five years ago at the town 4th of July celebration.

Rare historical document, that . . . the only photo in history that showed all four of the Sorensons looking pleased to be where and with whom they were. They actually appeared to be enjoying each other's company, and that was a memory worth treasuring.

It came to him in a gigantic burst of understanding, the sort of mental explosion that made him want to jump up and shout "Eureka!" except that in this part of the state, Eureka was a place and not a motto.

His mother! Fourth-grade teacher and dabbler in local folklore. No, not a dabbler . . . Joanna Sorenson had gotten so well-versed in the history of the area that she was frequently invited to guest-lecture at the university. And her favorite subject was Seacliff. Seacliff and its long, troubled past.

The sea cave! Jacob Cliffwood's old smuggler's hideout!

According to his mother's compiled sources, the entrance to the cave from the bay had been destroyed shortly after Cliffwood's death, though no one could agree if it had been by earthquake or not. Humboldt County was known not for the prospect of one apocalyptic Big One, but was on a fragmented section of tectonic plate and thus subjected to frequent, smaller temblors. So it was possible that an earthquake was to blame, but the collapse of the cave mouth might also have been caused by an explosion of dynamite or gunpowder, accidental or deliberate.

The cave had never been found. But what if there was another entrance? What if, even, there was an entrance that came up right under the house?

Brian's honed gamer mind seized onto that idea. Secret doors, dungeons.

Spinning back to the floor plan, he also brought up a file of remodeling invoices and began comparing dimensions of the rooms.

Less than a minute later, he'd found the discrepancy, and knew where the secret door was. And of course, as was only right and proper, it was in the library. The only more fitting place would have been from the throne room, and Seacliff didn't have one of those.

He tried to tell himself to get serious, that this wasn't a game. But the rest of his clamoring emotions insisted on treating it like one, and he set about preparing himself for a little after-hours delving.

Brockman's threat hadn't been lost on Brian, so he wasn't about to walk in unarmed. Nor was he enough of a dork to think that a sword, even Aragorn's . . . or even a miniature replica crossbow or Klingon *bat'leth* . . . would do the trick this time.

Before coming to Seacliff, he and Dawn had driven out to Uncle Gus' auto shop, in search of a more fitting weapon. Gus had been delighted to see his nephew taking an interest in more manly pursuits like girls and guns. He would have loaded Brian to the gills with macho toys, but Brian drew the line at a single handgun, a .38.

He was just hoping, as he stuffed some granola bars in his pocket to pretend they were iron rations, that he got his +2 I.Q. bonus to his handgun proficiency . . .

*　*　*

13

Gwynne, deep in paperwork, didn't even flinch. But Anne, seated across from her and engrossed in filling out her weekly chart reports, jumped when Judge walked up and slung a man's body on the table.

The bedraggled tangle of auburn hair identified him even before Gwynne saw his face.

She looked at her brother for a moment, lips pursed. Then, as she saw the water and mud spreading from Kel's soaked clothing, she shot a cold glare at Judge.

"These are important papers," she said, collecting them.

"Kel!" Anne cried, clearly stricken. She reached to touch him, stopped, and flushed beneath her visor. "What . . . why?"

"You let yourself be followed," Judge told her, face twisting in a sneer. "Lover-boy was playing detective to see what his precious Marge was up to."

"Oh, my God . . ."

When all of her papers were moved to safety, Gwynne turned back to Kel. He was alive, though unconscious. An ugly, crusted and swollen knot had risen above his ear.

"He's usually more trusting," she said. "Your speech on the woes of single motherhood should have at least shamed him into letting the matter drop for a while."

Anne downcast her eyes. "He's your *brother*. Maybe things have gotten too dirty when we're reduced to hurting our own loved ones."

"The fact that we share genetic material and an upbringing is no reason to burden myself with sisterly affection. Even loved ones shouldn't be nosing about where it doesn't concern them. Your role was only to *pretend* an interest in him, Anne. Don't start overacting."

"No, of course not," she said, staring at the floor.

"So what do we do with him?" Judge asked.

"Another death or disappearance would arouse too much suspicion," Gwynne said. "We can't afford close scrutiny right now."

She glanced across the cave at the row of enclosures. Five of them were occupied, and if she had her way, that number would jump to seven before much longer. Two of the children were watching her, Jenny with horror and Eric with simmering anger.

Eric's eyes met Gwynne's briefly, and even with her headpiece securely in place, she suppressed a qualm at the memory of what it had been like to be exposed to the boy's hurtful power.

Even though she'd been expecting just such a move, even though she'd been prepared, there was something deadly but weirdly exciting about facing him down unshielded as she'd done. Had she been a heartbeat slower on the draw, the neurospray wouldn't have had a chance to take him down before he snuffed out her consciousness.

Or even killed her . . . they had never tested the boy to quite that extreme, but it stood to reason that if he continued his attack long enough, the victim's brain wouldn't be able to withstand that awful psychic force.

"You're going to brainwash him?" Anne asked.

"It doesn't seem like we have much choice," Gwynne said, bringing her attention back to the business at hand.

"You're the one who wasn't careful enough," Judge added.

"He didn't have any suspicions about Seacliff. It was all me, all trying to find out about me, that led him to this."

"Spilled milk," said Gwynne. "The trouble is, what do we program him to believe?"

"And who's he told, and what." Judge shook his head and exhaled in a snarl. "Swapped cars for the occasion, who knows what else he might have said. Have to weave that in."

Gwynne moved decisively to the pharmaceutical array and began putting together a stronger dose of the cocktail she had used on Toby Edwards. She was a firm believer in mind control, because she was also a firm believer in the overpowering stupidity of humanity as a whole. People would be so much better off if they would let themselves be programmed for their own good, by their intellectual superiors.

In a way, her view mirrored that of Lundquist's desire to rid humanity of their winters of discontent, but instead of reaching that goal by raising them to their potentials and teaching them to be satisfied by excelling at their particular and individual strengths, she would just as soon order them to quit whining and be good little societal drones.

Kel groaned. Judge raised a questioning eyebrow and Gwynne shook her head. The guard refrained from smashing Kel into senselessness again and settled for manhandling him into the restraint chair before Kel had fully revived.

The restraint chair was a throwback to mental hospitals of days gone by, a solid monster of a thing mounted on a thick metal base. Once a patient was securely fastened in, the chair was too heavy to move or tip over even in the throes of the most violent outbursts or convulsions. This particular chair had not only the usual six-point restraints – ankles, wrists, chest, and head – but additional straps binding across the thighs and upper arms.

By the time Kel regained consciousness, he was so well bound into place that he resembled a mummy in the process of being wrapped. Except, of course, that mummies had been encased in cloth, and these straps were of a Kevlar variant . . . they would have been leather or canvas in the old days, but the metal-woven mesh was even more impossible to bite through.

"Marge?" mumbled Kel. He tried to raise a hand to rub his injured head, and could not.

Gwynne didn't consider herself a sadist, to take joy in the pain of others, but she could certainly be amused by it. "You may as well chat, Anne, while you have the time."

Kel heard her voice but couldn't move his head. "Gwynne? What? Where am I?"

"I'm so sorry, Kel," Anne said. "Why didn't you let it drop? Why'd you follow me?"

About the only parts of him that did still have a normal range of motion were his eyes, and they slowly panned to take in what they could see of the cave, the lab, and the enclosures. They widened as they reached the children standing by the doors, watching.

"Jenny? Eric? What is . . ." He trailed off. "My God. Marge . . . Gwynne . . . what are you doing to them?"

"Go ahead, tell him," Gwynne said. She could see that Judge was enjoying himself as he leaned against the wall and watched.

Anne sat down in front of Kel. He tried to draw away from her as much as the prison of his chair would allow. "I am not who you think I am, Kel," she said. "My real name's Anne, Dr. Anne Margaret Raines. I'm a parapsychologist."

He couldn't have reacted more incredulously if she'd said she was the Pope. "You're a doctor?"

Gwynne laughed. "There's the McGuire blood coming through . . . and he always said we were such snobs for that elitist attitude."

* * *

14

Footsteps squished. Light expanded around Dawn, Richie, and Lora as Stan Montgomery opened the door connecting the hall to the back exit.

He got three steps in, shaking water from his hair and muttering. "Damn dog! Run away from me, willya? When I see you, I'll –"

He saw them, jaw dropping.

The original plan had been for Dawn to rejoin Brian in his office and then leave from there, but that was no longer feasible. She clutched Richie to her chest and dashed through Seacliff. The baby was jolted awake and began to wail, but in a droning, groggy way that told of his nightly dose of sleeping pills. Lora fled ahead, the hem of her nightgown fluttering beneath her coat.

"Hey! Hey! What do you think you're doing?" Stan raced after them.

"This way!" Lora veered left, away from the front doors and toward the atrium, where the pool glimmered like an oasis in turquoise.

"Lora, no!" Dawn called, loud as she dared and loud as she could manage with her breath coming in stitches.

Brian appeared from the west wing hallway, gaping at them as Lora sped past him without slowing. He put himself between Stan and Dawn, and waved the gun with bravado but no real conviction. "Hold it!"

Stan skidded to a halt, raising his hands to shoulder level. "Oh, hey, come on . . . don't!"

"Go, go!" Brian urged Dawn when she slowed.

"But –"

"I can handle him!"

Hugging Richie tight, she backed up, then turned and ran after Lora. The little girl yanked and kicked at the leaded-glass doors to the atrium, but they wouldn't yield.

Shifting Richie to one arm, Dawn shoved a hand in the pocket of her jeans and found the key card Brian had made for her on the sly. He'd only been showing off back then, and neither of them thought there'd ever be a need, let alone a need like this.

She swept it through the electronic lock, and the doors clicked obligingly. Lora was through in a flash, circling the pool with her galoshes slapping on marble. The French doors leading onto the terrace were unlocked, and in seconds they were out in Seacliff's garden in the pouring-down rain. Dawn slowed to a rapid walk, the wet stones slick and treacherous.

Ruff, barking and streaming water, streaked out of the darkness and into the glow of the decorative floodlights.

"Good dog, Ruff!" Lora cried. "This way, Miss Richie's Mom!" She hopped over a low stand of bushes, losing one of her galoshes.

Dawn followed, trying to shelter Richie from the rain and comfort him as she stomped through flowerbeds and into the wide expanse of the lawn. "We can't get out this way!"

"Yes, we can, we'll just get muddy!"

Lora made a beeline toward the fence at the back, wooded part of the grounds. As they got closer, Dawn saw a small figure there waiting for them, jumping up and down. It was a boy, an African-American boy who would have been invisible against the night but for a vividly yellow raincoat.

"Lora! Lora!"

"Here we are, Toby. Ruff told us you were here."

"You've got to be kidding me," Dawn said when she saw the hole. A section of ground had crumbled away, facilitated by the rains, and left a muddy trench. The exposed bottoms of four wrought-iron fenceposts poked down like the gate of a castle. A wiry and determined child might be able to wiggle through, but . . .

"You can do it!" the boy, Toby, said.

Ruff threw himself at the hole, mud flying between his hind legs as he scrabbled at the wet earth. Then the dog flattened himself and wiggled through on his belly. Lora followed suit.

Dawn looked back toward the house, but there was no sign of Brian. Fear for him rose up in her throat, filling her mouth with the sour taste of old pennies. But, knowing there was nothing she could do for him, knowing that she couldn't leave Richie, she turned to the fence.

With some effort and coordination, she was able to pass Richie through the hole to the two kids on the other side. He wailed louder as he lost his grip on the lion, so she pushed the toy through as well even though it was a sorry, rain-drenched sight indeed.

Now it was just Dawn, alone on the wrong side of the fence. She eyed the small opening again, shrugged, and dropped to the sodden earth with a blatting, flatulent noise that made Lora and Toby laugh.

Grabbing two of the fencepost bottoms, she pulled herself down, trying to scoop more mud out of the way as she went. She wormed under, tearing her jacket and blouse and sustaining a long painful scrape on her back. When she got to her butt, she lodged tight and couldn't get any leverage to pull herself through. Her feet scrabbled at the grass, squeaking on the wet, waxy blades.

"I gotcha," Toby said, seizing her wrists.

Skinny as he was, she didn't think it would be much help, but he put all of his scant weight into it and Dawn kicked-struggled and came out the other side breathing hard and caked with mud from head to toe.

"But what now? Brian's car is around front."

"My house," Lora cried. "Ruff will lead the way. We're busting out of Mordor, Ruff!"

*   *   *

15

Returning to Seacliff, Roger Brockman attempted to call Gwynne on his cell phone and discovered that the battery was dead. He tossed the useless thing into the passenger seat and sighed, hoping that he hadn't missed any important calls.

The dead battery was only a minor annoyance, but it was the latest in a long string of them. His only consolation was that his discussion with Elliot Shaw had been successful. The good doctor's hands were tied. His helplessness and frustration had radiated from him like a palpable aura.

But Roger's efforts to track down Brian Sorenson had thus far been to no avail, after finding that the computer nut had apparently skipped out of the hospital. Brian wasn't at home, wasn't with his parents. He had to have his little girlfriend with him, because a highly caustic, foul-mouthed jerk at Pizza X-Press said Dawn hadn't shown up and left him doing all her work as well as his own.

Roger didn't like the thought of them out there doing who-knows-what. The information they held was too dangerous to the project if it was revealed now.

If they go public with Lundquist's past . . .

At least they didn't know that Lucas' attack on Brian had been no accident. Thinking of Lucas, Roger's mouth pursed. *Damn you, Lucas! If you had to do it, you could have at least succeeded.*

He hadn't been able to contact Lucas' father, either, and could almost believe that these people were deliberately avoiding him and making his life difficult, if he hadn't learned long ago never to credit to malice what could be accounted for by stupidity.

A swift flicker of movement at the fringes of his headlights made him slow down, scanning the treeline. For a moment, it had looked like someone was flitting through the rainswept night.

Dismissing it as a deer, or a trick of the wind and shadows, Roger drove on. Seacliff came into view before him. This late, only a few lights were on, and the house seemed at rest.

He pulled into the half of the stable that had been converted to a garage, and parked beside Gwynne's maroon Saturn. He collected his briefcase and got out, into the warm and fragrant room that still smelled faintly of hay and horse and manure as well as the stronger automotive scents of oil and metal.

A covered and glassed-in umbilicus of a hall connected the garage to the east wing. As Roger headed for it, he was brought up short by the sight of a car, the shabbiest of all of the staff vehicles, Brian Sorenson's Toyota hatchback.

Back and forth all over town, and where should he find the well-meaning but troublesome young sleuth? Here under this very roof, which made things ever-so-much more convenient.

He entered the house proper, whistling as he went and noting that all seemed to be quiet and in order.

All seemed to be, yes . . . but Roger paused. There was a strangeness to the silence. A feeling, nagging at him.

And someone seemed to have left the door to the atrium standing open.

Careless and sloppy . . . the attendants monitored the children throughout the night, so none of them could go wandering, but even so, it was best to keep the pool locked. They didn't need any drownings . . . well, unless a drowning was necessary.

He took a quick peek, saw nothing, and closed and locked the atrium door before continuing on. His mind was still troubled, and he had the distinct feeling now that something was wrong. That he'd overlooked something important. A wrongness hovered at the edges of his consciousness.

The east wing was dark and quiet, most of the live-in staff nestled all snug in their beds like the children they served. He walked slowly past each door, listening, extending all of his senses, and detecting only peaceful slumber.

Roger let himself into Brian Sorenson's office without knocking, but it was empty. The lights were off, as was the computer. A half-can of soda rested by the mouse pad. It was still cold and beaded with condensation, proof that Brian had, in fact, recently been in the office, and therefore had to still be in the house.

*   *   *

16

Stan Montgomery was four inches taller than Brian and fifty pounds heavier, and in the slack deadweight of unconsciousness, seemed to weight ten times that much.

Brian gritted his teeth and tried not to grunt as he dragged Stan. His heart slammed faster than even his great exertion could account for, pulse spiking with fear at his close brush with discovery.

The gun was jammed down the back of his pants, the rationale being that he'd rather blow off a portion of his scrawny rear than anything around the other side. Not that the other side got all that much use; everything down there was still pretty much under warranty.

For all the good the gun had done him, he might have been better off with his Laser Tag pistol.

He reddened with chagrin, adding to the scarlet brought on by the effort of moving Stan from the front hall all the way to the atrium. But the important thing was, he had won the fight, even if it hadn't gone exactly as envisioned.

Instead of using the gun to threaten Stan into submitting to being bound and gagged, instead of actually shooting him if the occasion demanded, all Brian had managed to do was let his guard lapse. Stan took advantage of that and grappled the weapon away from Brian, and he'd been sure that he was going to get shot himself.

But their tussle had resulted in the gun spinning across the tile floor and clacking into the bottom of the staircase. They had both flinched, expecting it to go off on its own, and Brian had recovered first.

The closest thing at hand had been a brass sculpture of leaping dolphins, and he'd brought it down on Stan's head with a sound that was part gong, part watermelon dropped from an overpass. Stan went down like a felled tree, but Brian, caught up in the frantic moment, had bashed the man a second time before getting hold of himself.

Hastily, knowing that at any minute someone could discover the kids missing, or see Dawn running across the yard, Brian had hauled Stan all the way to the atrium, thankful every step of the way for tile and hardwood rather than carpet.

He'd scrambled back to straighten out all the throw rugs, when he heard someone coming. Heard whistling, the very same jaunty tune that he'd heard earlier that day in a hospital stairwell.

Panic sprang straight up in him like a jack-in-the-box and he froze, then recovered his wits and moved Stan deeper into the atrium, stowing him behind a row of lounge chairs. Only then did he realize the whistling had stopped and that he'd left the atrium door open.

He'd crouched behind a potted plant the barest instant before a shape had appeared in the doorway, and watched with every nerve taut and every muscle quivering as Roger Brockman stepped inside and looked around. Brian just knew that he'd left Stan's feet sticking out, or that Brockman's dark eyes would fix on him in his hiding place, and it'd all be over.

But, after sweeping the surface of the pool with his gaze and seeing that no one was floating facedown or bobbing waterlogged near the bottom, Brockman went out and shut the door behind him.

Brian's breath escaped in a series of rattly gasps. He had nearly pissed himself in his fright, and wanted nothing more than to pack it in and go home. Order up a pizza. Watch back-to-back episodes of *Fawlty Towers* and *The Black Adder* on BBCAmerica.

Yeah. That'll be good.

Good, but not an option just yet. He picked up Stan's legs by the heels and dragged him around to the changing rooms. There wasn't any rope handy, and he had to settle for wrapping Stan from chin to toes in an aquatic volley-ball net, then fastening it together with the chintzy padlocks from the lockers.

He didn't want to gag the guy and have him smother, but figured that Stan would be out of it for a long time after that crack on the head.

The atrium door was locked, but Brian had his keys. He'd also had the presence of mind to grab Stan's, just in case.

As he reached the library, he heard Brockman returning. No longer whistling, and with a quick, purposeful stride.

Looking for me, Brian thought.

Brian slipped into the library and closed the door, and was plunged into velvet-dark silence broken only by his own breathing. Seconds passed, ticking into a full minute as he waited with his back pressed against a shelf of leather-bound books.

Another minute.

A third.

Brian loosed a slow gust of breath.

A light came on, bathing the library in a warm, melted-amber glow. On the upper gallery, which circled the interior of the room but left the center open to the vaulted ceiling-moldings, Benjamin Lundquist stood with one hand resting on the polished oak railing and the other braced on the silver head of his cane.

Slow horror spread through Brian as he remembered the floorplan, remembered that Lundquist's private inner sanctum of an office had a one-way window that looked into the atrium and a secret passage connecting it to the library.

"My dear Mr. Sorenson," said Lundquist evenly, "I do hope you have an explanation for your actions."

*   *   *

17

Kel could only stare at her, at this woman he'd known as Marge, numbed by the magnitude of her deception. Numbed by the evil in which she and his sister were taking part.

"You have to understand," she pleaded. "I'd spent years trying to find valid evidence of psychic powers. Years of investigating poltergeist phenomena and debunking bogus mediums. But all I found were fakes, until I got involved with the Coalition. They approached these abilities not as supernatural claptrap, but as a natural function of the brain. We assembled a group of subjects who showed high natural abilities in ESP, precognition, and telekinesis. We were looking for ways to help them develop their gifts."

"Experimenting on children. On your own son . . . or is he really yours?" Kel asked.

"No." She sighed. "One of the researchers on our team had a . . . I can't even properly call it an affair . . . a liaison with one of the telepathic test subjects. Eric was the result. His mother died when he was still a baby. We soon found out that he was gifted, strongly gifted. His father decided that it was best if he was raised in the lab, so that we could closely monitor him."

"What . . . what can he do?" Kel asked.

Gwynne took over, using her smooth lecturing tone, the one so reminiscent of their father. "To begin with, Eric demonstrated significant clairvoyance and clairaudience. His scores with the Zener cards were off the top of the chart. He had hunches, precognitive flashes. But what interested us the most was his apparent ability to detect latent psychic powers in others. To be blunt, he's a sniffer."

Kel looked steadily at Anne, or Marge, or whatever she wanted to be called. "So you turned him loose on Trinity Bay, hoping he'd sniff out other test subjects for you?"

She flinched. Her face was pale, her mouth turned down in a quivering grimace of shame and despair. "Essentially, yes."

"How long has this been going on?" Kel asked.

"Years," Gwynne said. "But it is only recently that we've begun to see our most dramatic improvements. Only within these past few months, really. Here, at Seacliff, we've finally fully realized our project goals. Even Eric has benefitted. We took him, a subject already possessing potent natural powers, and injected him with a compound designed to enhance those areas of the brain."

As she spoke, she filled a syringe from a vial. She approached Kel with it.

He wrenched from side to side, but the restraint chair held him well despite the extra strength granted him by the sudden terror that the sight of the needle inspired. "What's that for?"

"It is a combination of psychotropic drugs that will make your memory malleable, your psyche open to suggestion," Gwynne said, as coolly as if he were a stranger, as if it didn't trouble her in the least that she was facing her own brother. "It's imperfect, of course, so there may be some side effects. Headaches are most common, strokes much rarer."

"No! Gwynne, you can't do this."

"This part of the job will become much simpler once Jenny has perfected her own power. It's fascinating, Kel. Any suggestion from that girl is impossible to resist, everything she says just seems to make perfect sense. But for the time being, we're still stuck with doing things the old-fashioned way."

"I'm sorry, Kel," Anne said. "I didn't want this."

"You know too much. Not that you'll remember it," Gwynne added. "Judge, hold his arm steady. I wouldn't want to bruise him."

Judge's big, callused hands augmented the restraint straps, pinning Kel's arm into immobility. Gwynne lowered the needle toward the vulnerable crook of his elbow. Kel was struck by the sudden recollection of Toby Edwards, those faded yellow smudges that could have been bruises. Now he understood.

"You can't do this," he said, straining against his bonds as if he could break them by sheer force of will.

"Because you're my baby brother?" Gwynne said with a mocking lilt. "If you weren't my brother, you might already be dead, despite the nuisance it would be to cover it up."

She meant it, he saw, and the last of any familial connection he felt toward her drained out of him as the tip of the needle entered his vein.

* * *

18

His pace speeding to a trot, Roger Brockman returned to the east wing and took the service elevator to the second floor.

The nursing station was empty and smelled like Mexican food. Roger folded up the section of the counter to let himself in. A magazine open to an article on personal VTOL aircraft was open on the desk, and a crumpled bag from a taco place poked out of the top of the trash. Stan Montgomery was nowhere to be seen.

Roger checked the duty log and found the scrawled beginnings of an entry – 9:30 P.M., twenty minutes before, and then an illegible scratch. The pen rested beside the logbook, giving the impression of having been dropped.

Emergency situation? None of the monitors showed anything amiss, just views of dimly-lit rooms and the bumps of children curled up sound asleep beneath blankets.

He looked again at the trash can, then down the hall toward the bathroom. Aha, mystery solved. But leaving the desk unattended for twenty minutes was something that would have to be addressed.

Roger sat down to wait, already anticipating Stan's reaction upon coming back from the can to find him there.

*   *   *

19

Brian fumbled the gun from the back of his belt and pointed it at Lundquist and, stupidly, heard a line from one of his favorite old movies fall from his lips. "Don't move, pal, don't even breathe!"

A sublime expression of shock and bafflement claimed Lundquist's face. "Brian —"

"I mean it!" He steadied his hands because they were shaking so much that if he'd fired the clip empty, he probably would have outlined Lundquist with bullet holes like something out of a Warner Brothers cartoon. "I'll shoot. I will!"

"After witnessing what befell poor Mr. Montgomery, I don't doubt that you would. But why? In God's name, why?"

"God's name?" He was close to raving hysteria and tried to rein it in. "In God's name, why? . . . is that what they asked you at Schlossenberg?"

Lundquist stiffened as if a long blade had just been punched into his belly.

"What did you tell them then, huh?" Brian demanded. "Same thing you tell the kids here, and their parents? Just trying to help?"

"You know about Schlossenberg." He said it flatly, devoid of anger. "How?"

"The Internet's a wonderful thing." He was sounding tougher now, more in control of himself. "But didn't Brockman tell you?"

"*Roger* knows?"

"Oh, come on, I know he tried to have me killed. On your orders."

"Kill you? Brian . . . dear boy . . . I swear to you . . ."

"Just shut up. And come here. Nice and slow. We're going down there and I'm finding out what you people are really doing."

The dapper, dashing, elderly gentleman façade that Lundquist usually wore had shattered, leaving a grey-complexioned old man in its place. "I don't know what you're talking about, Brian. What do you mean, what we're really doing?"

"You're good, very slick, very convincing, but I'm not dumb. Get down here now, and if you try and brain me with that cane, I'll feed it to you."

"Why are you threatening me? At gunpoint in my own home?"

He sounded earnestly mystified, looked sincere, but Brian wasn't about to be fooled. He kept the gun aimed at Lundquist as the old man gingerly made his way down the spiral stair. Part of him felt wretched and ashamed for bullying a guy in his eighties, but the rest of him rose up clamoring that even an ancient tomcat still had claws.

When Lundquist reached the bottom, Brian took his cane and clumsily patted him down. Lundquist made indignant noises of protest. All Brian came up with was a nail clipper.

"Okay," Brian said. "Open it. The secret passage."

"I have no idea what —"

"Don't mess with me, *Herr Doktor!* Open it!"

"Brian, I swear to you on my mother's name, on the souls of my brother and sister, I do not know what you are talking about!"

"Fine, I'll do it myself. Sit down. Right there. Don't budge."

Lundquist sank into the designated chair as Brian went to the bookshelves. "Tell me what's troubling you," he said, as if having just reached the conclusion that Brian had lost his mind — early twenties, right age for a first schizophrenic break. "We can work through this together, Brian. No one is here to hurt you. We are your friends, and wish only to help."

"It's not going to fly, Richter."

The name hit Lundquist like a blow. He sagged in the chair, hands over his face.

"Yes, that part is true," he admitted, voice muffled. "I was Gustav Richter, I did do terrible things in the name of my science. I had little choice."

"That's what they all say."

"I was driven. Determined. My passion for my work consumed me, but I required funding, materials, equipment, that were difficult to obtain. Only the Reich offered the resources I needed, and so I allied myself with the Devil. But that ended after the war. I left Germany and have never gone back, never, not once."

"Didn't need to, when you could continue somewhere else under a new name." He groped along the shelves, twiddling and fiddling.

"My time at Schlossenberg is the greatest shame of my life. I hated what I saw, what I was forced to tolerate. It was madness. It was evil. I was not there to torture. I was looking for ways to heal."

"Uh-huh."

"But what is all this? You cannot think that I am recreating the camp here at Seacliff!"

"Here it is!" Brian crowed, and pushed the recessed button he'd found behind a book.

The section of shelving swung out, revealing the narrow passage and stair beyond.

*   *   *

20

Breaking ahead of Toby and Richie's mom, Lora rushed for the house. Then she remembered that in the books, when Frodo and his friends had gotten back to Hobbiton, they found it changed and terrible. Taken over by bad guys. Fantasy and reality had gotten shuffled in her mind, and she hesitated for fear that she'd walk in her own house and there would be Saruman.

The others caught up with her. By now, thanks to their rough and rapid overland trip and the unending curtains of rain, Richie was squalling at the top of his lungs.

The door flew open and a tall man with long grey hair stood there. Not Saruman; that was Lora's grandfather.

"Grandpa!" she shrieked, and threw herself at him.

Several hectic and confusing minutes passed as they all went in the house and got crowded around and fussed over by Lora's mom and stepdad and grandpa. When Damon made to go for the phone and call Seacliff, Lora and Toby and Richie's mom – her name was Dawn, Lora found out – all shouted in unison, "No!"

Theresa took charge, telling Damon to wait until they got everyone warmed up. She sent Lora upstairs to dry off and change clothes, put Grandpa Travis in charge of getting Toby cleaned up, loaned Dawn some sweats, took care of Richie, threw all their wet and muddy things into the washer, and toweled Ruff.

Only then, when they were all sitting around the fire with good hot cups of cocoa, did she demand to know what was going on.

"We have to tell them everything, Toby. Everything," Lora said. "They won't think you're crazy. Will you, Mom?"

"Lora, honey, I don't know what to think. What are you doing here?"

"It's my fault," Dawn said. "I had to get Richie out of there, and Lora helped us."

"Ruff, too," Lora pointed out. "Ruff helped too."

"Get Richie out? Why?" Damon asked.

"They're doing something horrible at Seacliff," Dawn said, pale. "Brian found out that Dr. Lundquist used to be a Nazi scientist, and when he told Dr. Brockman, Dr. Brockman sent Lucas to try and kill him. They're doing something to the kids, experimenting on them somehow. Dr. Brockman told Dr. Shaw that if he didn't shut up and play along, it could be bad for him, and for David. And since they know that Brian told me about Dr. Lundquist, we thought they might try and get rid of me, too, or tell me that if I said anything, they'd hurt Richie."

Lora was dizzied just listening to her, but her stepdad seemed to follow what Dawn was saying. Follow, maybe, but he clearly looked like he didn't believe it.

Toby, though, nodded. It was his turn next, and he told them all about Eric, his memory troubles, and the things Eric had said about Jenny and Lora. "And I know it's true . . . Eric's right . . . I can do things now. That normal people can't. I can touch something, and know all about it."

"Toby, honey," Theresa began in a voice Lora knew very well, the voice her mother used when she thought Lora was getting too carried away with her imagination.

"Test me," Toby said. "I'll prove it."

"Go ahead, Mommy," Lora urged. "And then it can be my turn."

That made her whole family look at her very carefully.

"Test me," Toby repeated. "Give me something."

"Well . . ." Travis glanced at Theresa and Damon, then went to the mantle and got a stone sculpture of a coyote, head tipped back against a rising full moon. He gave it to Toby.

Toby did like he did with Chris' dinosaur, folding it in his hands and shutting his eyes. After a while, he looked up.

"It's Theresa's. You bought it at a souvenir shop in Portland when you and your first husband went on a driving vacation to visit your mom. You were pregnant with Lora then, only a few weeks. It's made from Mount St. Helen's ash."

Shocked silence answered this.

"Yes, that's right," Theresa finally said.

"How'd you know that, son?" Damon asked.

"Things remember, just like we do. And I can know what they remember when I touch them. I think it's because I've always had such a good memory myself."

"And you say Eric Raney did this to you?" Travis said.

"Not him . . . but someone. He helped, he was in on it."

"What does this have to do with Lora?"

"They took Jenny, Mommy. And I almost found her, but they caught me. They caught me, and made it look like I drownded so you'd send me there, and whatever they did to Toby, they did to me, too."

"You can do stuff like that?" Dawn gasped.

"Not just like that." Lora beamed, full of pride. "I can talk to animals, and know what they're saying to me. Even what they're thinking and feeling."

Her mom's voice trembled. "Lora, that's impossible –"

Damon put his arm around Theresa. "So are some of the other things we've seen in our lives. Give her a chance to explain."

"That's all there is, though," she said. "I talk to Ruff all the time, and I can hear what the birds are saying, and things."

"Show them," Toby suggested. "What's Ruff saying right now?"

She glanced at the dog, who was sniffing at his sheepskin-lined doggie bed by the fire. "He's glad to be home, even if Jack's been sleeping in his bed again and getting it all full of cat hair."

"Can you tell him to do something and have him obey?" asked Travis.

"If he wants to. It's easier with dogs than cats, because cats don't do tricks to please anyone but themselves. But Ruff's a good dog." She thought: *Ruff, hey boy, bring me a stick from the wood box, okay?*

Ruff snorted and went to the wood box, clamping a stick in his jaws and bringing it to place in Lora's lap.

Now they all looked at her very carefully again, except for Toby, who smiled and seemed relieved.

"I told him to do that," she said. Something occurred to her, and she got serious again in a hurry. "But animals, they can sense things. Like when there's going to be a storm or an earthquake? And tonight, when I was trying to go to sleep, all I could hear were the animals. They're upset. Something is going to happen at Seacliff, something bad."

"No," Dawn said. Richie. on her lap, cooed. He held his stuffed lion in the crook of his arm but his curious gaze was on several of Mark and Travis' toys. "No, it can't be, is that what they're doing to the kids? Richie's not weird . . . he's fine, he's just fine!"

"We're not *weird*," Toby said, sounding hurt. "We're still us. We can just do things."

"Not Richie. Not my Richie."

She turned to look at her son, and at that very moment as if to make a liar of her, a soft quilted ball with the letters of the alphabet stitched all over it rolled across the living room floor of its own accord. It stopped at the base of the couch below Richie, quivered, and floated up into the air so that he could grab it. He gurgled in delight.

A hush fell, and in it Lora saw that the grownups had been trying really hard to think of ways coincidence could have explained what Toby and Lora had done. But this, clear and undeniable visible proof, suddenly tipped their inner scales to belief.

A wrenching twist of fear and denial crossed Dawn's face, and for a moment Lora was sure she wanted nothing more than to dump Richie off her lap and run as far as she could.

No one said anything. Finally, with a shuddering sigh, Dawn said, "Okay. It's true, okay."

"We're all in it together," Theresa said. "Whatever happens, at least there's that."

"I think I better give Mal and Ruth a call," Damon said, rising. "They'll be wanting to know where their boy is. And then I think I'll round up a couple of deputies and mosey on up to Seacliff."

*   *   *

21

Jenny Forrester slammed her fists against the thick clear wall. "Stop it! Leave him alone! Just leave him alone!"

But they didn't listen to her, didn't react. Ignored her, though she was pouring on her power as hard as she could, until her brain felt like it would blow a fuse.

Those damn old visors of theirs . . . from hearing their technical conversations, she'd figured out that the circuits in the headbands had something to do with wavelengths, something to do with generating an electrical field that shielded their minds from the influence of any outside effects. Such as hers.

Mr. McGuire went rigid as the drug worked its way into his bloodstream. His eyes, which had been flashing back and forth in hateful accusation between his sister and Anne, glassed over like grey-blue marbles.

The activity had drawn Inge from elsewhere in the cave. The other kids, except for the sedated and bedridden Neesha, lined up along the front walls of their enclosures with the same frustration as Jenny. Help had finally come, someone from the outside finally knew they were here, but all hope was being lost even as they watched.

Inspiration!

"Mr. McGuire!" Jenny yelled. "You don't want to listen to them. You don't want to listen to anything they say."

She felt like she had her shoulder to the back of a car and was trying to push it over a crest. Pushing and pushing, straining with the effort . . . then glorious relief and release as gravity took over and the car started rolling down the far side of a hill. Dizzied by the exertion, Jenny braced herself so she didn't fall over.

"No!" barked Dr. McGuire, composure rent asunder as she realized what was happening.

"They can't mess with your memory unless you let them, and you're not going to let them," Jenny said.

"Judge! Shut her up."

Jenny stuck out her tongue at Dr. McGuire. "It's too late. You can't get him now. It won't work."

Judge loomed before her, and Jenny scrabbled backward. In the next cell down, Chris shouted and struck at the wall with a chair. She could hear Julian sobbing in fright and concern, and Eric's sardonic laughter.

Dr. McGuire ripped the needle out of her brother's arm, leaving a bloody trail. She flung the syringe against the wall and it smashed, dripping crushed glass and medicine.

"You little idiot," she said, stalking to Judge's side as the tall man waited with one hand on the controls that could flood Jenny's room with sleep-gas.

"Do you realize what you've just done?"

"Stopped you from brainwashing him!"

"Stopped me from giving him a new set of memories, which was the only way we could afford to leave him alive."

Jenny went cold. "Oh . . . no . . . I didn't mean —"

"Congratulations, Jennifer. You've just signed my brother's death warrant."

"No, please! I didn't mean it."

"There is only one way to undo this mess you've made. Judge, bring her out."

"Stay away from her!" Chris' face twisted with fury.

Jenny suffered a sudden wave of aversion, a compulsion, to get away, stay away, not go near Jenny . . . not go near herself. She wanted to hide, but where could she go? She coiuldn't wrench herself out of her own skin.

"Chris, stop it," Jenny said. "They're protected. It won't help."

Judge opened the door and beckoned her out. A mean, hard light in his eyes turned them blood-maroon through the visor. He'd gotten an appetizer of violence with Mr. McGuire, and Jenny knew he'd just love it if she gave him an excuse to make her the main course.

She came out and stood in front of Dr. McGuire, bowed in anguish and defeat.

"It's up to you now," Dr. McGuire said, having reverted to her normal cool and collected self. "You can save Kel's life the same way you endangered it. Talk to him. Tell him what I want him to believe. If it works, we can let him go free."

Jenny gulped. "But then he won't remember anything about us. He won't get us out of here."

"And the project will continue unhampered."

"Gwynne?"

Everyone whirled, and here came the tall, spare form of Benjamin Lundquist, ushered into the room at gunpoint by a wild-looking Brian Sorenson.

"Gwynne, my lamb, what in the world . . .?" Lundquist trailed off, taking in the surroundings with astonishment and growing horror.

Jenny screamed as Judge grabbed her, making a hostage and human shield in one quick motion. He set something to Jenny's temple. "Drop the gun, kid, or I'll fry her."

It was her old buddy the taser. She could feel the tiny metal prongs indenting her skin. Brian had instinctively brought the gun to bear on Judge, but she saw him falter. She knew what would happen next. He'd surrender. And then there'd be more midnight executions, or another quick brain-scrub.

"Shoot this creep!" Jenny cried, at the same moment jerking her head and body as far from Judge as possible. "Do it!"

Brian responded without hesitation. The gunshot was an evil whipcrack, not the deafening boom Jenny would have expected. She felt a jerk of impact transmitted from Judge to her, and a hot spray of blood erupted from his right shoulder.

Then the taser went off, and Jenny Forrester was swallowed up by a bright blue-white sizzle.

*   *   *

22

When several minutes had gone by and Stan still hadn't returned, Roger Brockman got up and walked to the bathroom. The lights were off. When he flipped them on, he could clearly see that the stalls were empty.

Brushed by suspicions, Roger began a systematic check of the floor. When he got to Richie Jessec's room and found a pillow in the bed, he understood at once.

"Damn it," he muttered, hurrying to the nurse's station and punching in the extension for the lab, tapping his foot in irritation and impatience.

It rang . . . rang . . . and then cut off in a jangle and clatter, as if the phone had been knocked from its perch.

He ran for the elevator.

*   *   *

23

Brian saw the blonde woman out of the corner of his eye, a fraction too late to evade or fire. Strong and quick as a lioness, she got him with a flying tackle into a table.

His funny bone hit a ringing telephone and sent it skidding off the edge, but the nerve-numbing jolt up his arm was the least of Brian's concerns. The woman drove her knee into the small of his back, which in turn squashed his groin against the solid surface. As he was still trying to draw breath to express that agony, she flipped him onto his back and punched him in the stomach.

He slithered from the table and sprawled like a limp noodle on the floor, able only to groan and retch. He didn't resist, couldn't resist, as she yanked him up, heaved him into a chair, and stood over him with his own gun pressed to the back of his head.

His available brain power was divvied up on a bunch of tasks. Part of him was busy trying to get a handle on the pain – all of this new stuff added to what he'd been dished up by a berserk Lucas Gordon less than twenty-four hours before left him in sorry shape indeed.

Another part was busy being offended and indignant, trying to come to terms with what had happened and fit it into game-rules contexts that he could grasp. It wasn't helping much to think that he couldn't have lost that many hit points, or that she shouldn't have been able to launch so many brutally efficient attacks in so few combat rounds.

He also observed with wry triumph that here they were, the four computers, just like he'd suspected. And ascertained that the clunky space-age headbands with red visors that the rest of them were wearing were computerized somehow. High-tech toys. He didn't know their purpose, but that only made him itch to get a better look.

One last miniscule part of him was left over to wonder what in the hell he'd been thinking, shooting that man. He couldn't believe he did it. But when Jenny Forrester had told him to, why, it just made the most perfect sense in the world. So he'd done it.

Now the man, who Gwynne McGuire called Judge, had stripped to the waist to let an unfamiliar brunette woman clean and treat his gunshot wound. He glared hateful arrows at Brian, apparently more pissed off than hurt.

"I demand an explanation!" Benjamin Lundquist said. His voice resonated with authority, but beneath it was unfeigned shock that made Brian reconsider. "Now, Gwynne."

"It's your work, Benjamin," she said with magnificent calm under the chaotic circumstances. "Taken to the next level."

"This is no work of mine. My God! What have you done to these children?"

"Helped them. Helped them to strive for their full potential."

He looked at Jenny Forrester, whose limbs still tremored with convulsions from the taser shot she'd taken. "No . . . no, Gwynne, my lamb. This is a mistake, all a terrible mistake!"

"Mistakes have been made, yes," she agreed. "Bringing in these additional subjects, for one. We should have limited our research to the subjects already present at Seacliff."

"That is the girl, the missing girl . . . do you mean to tell me that *you* are behind her disappearance? Why, Gwynne?"

"That wasn't my idea," she said icily.

"No," said Roger Brockman, adjusting his lab coat as he came in. "It was mine." Unlike the others, he didn't have one of the visored helm-things, but the lack didn't make him look any less ominous.

Brian's throat and stomach lurched. He was dead, so dead, they were all dead . . .

"One of many decisions to which I objected," Gwynne said.

"I listened to your arguments, but in the end, we decided to proceed my way."

"Enough!" Lundquist struck the tip of his cane sharply on the stone floor. "Roger, you are a part of this as well?"

"*Et tu, Brute?*" chuckled Roger.

"What have you done?" Lundquist's anger was thunder and lightning, his knuckles white on the head of his cane.

"We've expanded upon your discovery." He grinned, a sharklike grin devoid of humor. "You knew that the cerebregens interacted with the enzyme produced by oxygen-starved brain cells to encourage repair and regrowth of the damaged tissue. But it went a little beyond that. In certain subjects, the ones given the cerebregens closely following the oxygen deprivation, it triggered development in another section of the brain as well."

"A section," Gwynne said, "devoted to those dormant abilities generally referred to as 'psychic.' Telepathy, telekinesis, psychometry, clairvoyance, that sort of thing."

"Good Lord." Lundquist looked again at the enclosures. "And that is what you are doing here? Trying to . . . to . . . instill these abilities in the children?"

"Succeeding," corrected Roger. "And isn't that what you've always wanted? To raise them up? Make them not only whole again, but better than before?"

Gwynne McGuire touched Lundquist's arm, but he pulled away from her with a look of disgust. She had the gall to look hurt, as if she still sought his approval despite her heinous deeds. "Benjamin . . . try to understand. Look at what it's done for them . . ."

"I recognize those two," he said, indicating a boy of about ten and another even younger. "But they were discharged, sent home!"

"We had to follow their cases," Gwynne said.

"Keep them to study, you mean!"

"And why not?" Roger cut in. "If not for us, they'd still be drooling and wetting their beds, unable to feed themselves, dress themselves. All that they are, they owe to us."

"That's how we began, initially," Gwynne said. "But within the past few weeks, a decision was made to extend the benefits of the program to others. Some children – we've not found it occurring in any adults yet – already showed natural development in those areas of the brain. Not quite full-blown powers, but . . . well, the potential."

"You took them to study as well?" Lundquist asked, in a tone that said it couldn't possibly be true, he couldn't possibly believe such a thing.

"Two of our subjects remained at their homes," Roger said.

Gwynne huffed. "I still need to take it up with you about the Gordon boy. What were you thinking, Roger? He didn't fit any of the criteria, the damage to his brain and nervous system was different, and he had none of the indicators we look for. What were you *thinking?*"

"Every mad scientist needs a creature," Roger said with a one-sided shrug.

"You already had your son!" She flapped her hand at a teenage boy glaring at them from the far cell.

*   *   *

24

Waiting for his officers, Damon Blake called the hospital and was informed that Dr. Shaw was off-duty. He tried the doctor's home number, but had gotten no further than three exchanges into the conversation before Elliot Shaw closed up like a clam.

Damon could see right through Shaw's excuses, could feel the man's nervousness in every word, but couldn't get him to admit to or deny anything. Shaw wouldn't discuss Seacliff or Lucas Gordon, and when Damon paraphrased what Dawn had told him, Shaw fell silent for a long uncomfortable span and then made an excuse to hang up.

Malachi and Ruth Edwards showed up just as Damon was getting off the phone. They were drowsy-eyed, hastily dressed. Ruth was all set to scold the bejesus out of her wayward son for sneaking, but held off as Theresa took her into the kitchen, brewed up a pot of coffee, and told her what Dawn and the children had said.

Avery Scribner and Rodney Peterson arrived next. Damon would have preferred to have Scott James; the only better man to have at his side and watching his back would have been his own twin, Derrek. But even Scott deserved the occasional night off.

Rod Peterson was the very image of the bad-cop-on-the-take from a hundred action movies, beetle-browed over shifty dark eyes. In contrast to his appearance, he was one of the jolliest men Damon had ever met, and gentle as a kitten. Avery Scribner was tall and gawky and looked like a rookie – he'd been on the force for two years already, but Damon suspected that

Ave would still look like a rookie the day he retired.

Upon hearing that Damon meant to go up to Seacliff for a look-see, Malachi Edwards insisted on accompanying them. He was twice again as old as any of the officers, and his arthritis pained him on cold humid nights, which meant nearly all of them in this part of the state. But he was determined, and would not be denied.

Travis Zane's house was within sight of Seacliff, a former guest cottage. But with the weather and the darkness, Damon elected instead to pile the four of them into his brown patrol car and swing around on the road rather than trudge across the soaked and muddy meadow.

The drive took just long enough for their breath to fog up all the windows, and then he pulled up out front.

*　　*　　*

25

Kel McGuire, who had been fighting to follow the conversation despite whatever they'd doped him with, finally managed to speak. "Eric is *his* son?"

Anne had finished with bandaging Judge's shoulder and came to Kel's side. He could hardly bear to look at her, knowing what she was and what she was a part of.

"Dr. Brockman was one of the research team," she said. "The one I told you about. He had an affair with –"

"I'd hardly call it an affair. Another experiment," Roger interrupted. "I wanted to see if a combination of abilities would be passed on to the next generation. Eric, I think, was a rousing success, long before this spring, when we treated him with the compound to boost his natural gifts. That was when he discovered he could project a psychic attack, mind-to-mind. Really quite amazing."

Lundquist looked at Roger as if he had wriggled from underneath a damp rock. "Your own son? You did this to your own son?"

Roger looked back, steadily, evenly. His smile was a slow curve as warm and comforting as the blade of a headsman's axe. "Why not? You did."

"You know about that as well?" A spasm of pain clenched Lundquist's face. "You know about William? How?"

That executioner's blade of a smile widened. "My mother told me everything."

The only sound in the room was the hum of the computers and the rhythmic echo of the waves as Roger's words sank in.

"William?" Lundquist was ashen, his voice robbed of its majesty and reduced to a choked whisper. "You are William? You are my son?"

"Mom remarried after she left you," Roger said, like a man enjoying a meal for which he'd waited his entire life. "Her new husband wasn't very happy about giving me his name, but Mom could be very willful and persistent."

"Yes . . . Elizabeth . . ." Lundquist searched Roger's features, nodding to himself as if he spotted resemblances to the boy he'd once known. "She was that, yes."

"Before she died, she told me all of it. Your past life as Gustav Richter, the fire, what you did to me."

"Died . . . my poor Elizabeth! How? When?"

"Breast cancer. I was Eric's age. And don't sound so grief-stricken. She went to her grave hating you."

Lundquist hung his head.

"She knew that you were responsible for changing me," Roger said. "Making me different. You and your experiemnts, your compound, your drugs. I was eight before I realized that no one else could feel the emotions of those around them, feel them as real as if they were my own. I can feel yours now. The guilt, the shame, the pitiful doomed love. You see what you made me, and it disgusts you."

"Then why? If you so despise what you've become, why inflict it on others?"

"I don't despise what I am. I never did. It's a gift, a left-handed gift and the last one I ever got from my father. Yes, being an empath set me apart from everyone, but it gave me an edge. It gave me a purpose."

"And this is your great work? To torment others, change them as you were changed?"

"To raise them up," Roger said. "Look at them . . . they are the start of a new world. A new breed of humanity. Gifted and powerful, each in their own special, unique, creative way. That's the most beautiful part of it . . . each of us gains an ability that matches our personality. Gwynne here was the first to suspect that, and it seems to be proven true."

"How can you say that?" Lundquist's words lashed out. "You claim to be able to feel the emotions of others, and yet you are this cruel, this . . . mad?"

"You think being an empath means I have to care? Be soft and gentle? No . . . I knew from an early age that the only way to be stronger than others was to know their weaknesses. To be able to tell when they were lying, to know what they really felt, and use it against them. For me, empathy has always been the greatest weapon in my arsenal."

The attention of everyone else in the room was focused on the three of them. Even the kids in their cells were watching intently, especially Eric.

The rest might have missed it, but Kel hadn't . . . Roger's announcement that he was Lundquist's son had rocked Eric almost as much as it had the old man. And the tone in which Roger had so casually dismissed Eric and his mother hadn't gone over all that well either.

Something else that nobody was noticing but Kel – Jenny Forrester was coming around. She turned her head slowly, resting her cheek on the stone and only moving her eyes as she took in the tense scene. He could tell she was struggling to put it all together, her short-term memory probably scrambled by the taser.

"But it's falling apart," Anne said, her voice low. Kel heard her genuine unhappiness, and his heart tried to warm to the woman he'd thought he loved. "It's all falling apart, and it's gotten too extreme. Talking about killing people . . . we can't do that! This slope is too slippery. We've got to dig in our heels and stop this before it's too late!"

"When we're on the verge of such great discoveries?" Gwynne said in her loftiest manner. "While I may disagree with some of Roger's methods, I cannot deny that the results are proving most gratifying. We just need to tie up some of these loose ends to bring the project back under clear control."

Lundquist didn't appear to hear either of them. He was concentrating solely on Roger, and the revelations he'd made. The enormity of them, the sheer horrendousness of them, had pierced the old man like javelins.

"You used me, used my work, to further these goals," he said.

"Oh, yes," Roger said. "And it's not over yet."

"It most assuredly is!" A bit of strength returned to Lundquist's voice and he drew himself up, though still supporting himself on his cane. "It ends now, this instant. I will not have you doing this. Not under my roof, not anywhere."

"Or what? You'll expose the project?" Roger flashed the shark's smile again. "What do you think would happen then . . . *Gustav?* Who do you think they'd believe? The dedicated young doctors –" he gestured grandly to Gwynne and himself, "– or the war criminal?"

"That was your plan," Lundquist said in stunned realization. "To, should you be found out, put the blame on me."

"I just didn't count," Roger said, with a sour glance at Brian, "on having the truth come to light quite this early." He turned his attention back to Lundquist. "And all of the good you've done these past fifty years will be for nothing. They'll pick it apart. Every paper you ever published, every post you ever held, every lecture you ever gave. They'll scrutinize everything, and find things to point at as proof. You'll be discredited, reviled. They'll say that Schlossenberg never stopped."

* * *

26

Aiden Ferguson took a long skeptical look at her painting. Bob Ross made it seem so easy, dab-dab-dab and there you were. Seeing her fascination, Dr. Lundquist had gotten her the entire series on video.

Her happy little trees looked like blobs of green cotton candy on the ends of toilet paper rolls. Her sky was diseased. And the reflections in her lake were reminiscent of an oil spill.

Bob Ross also made it so quick . . . a completed piece in under half an hour. It had taken Aiden that long just to get her mountains done.

Plus, she'd found out the hard way that his recommended method of cleaning the brush – dip it, shake it, and then "beat the devil out of it" on the leg of the easel, sprayed fine misty droplets of paint all over everything. She left her painting to sit while she cleaned up, thinking that maybe when she went back after allowing time to give a bit of perspective, it wouldn't be as bad as she thought.

Dr. Lundquist had gone to bed an hour ago. Or so he'd said; when last she'd seen him, he had been headed in the direction of his study. She hoped he wasn't in there brooding in the dark again, but knew it wasn't her place to say something about it. Even if it was her place, she couldn't imagine being so presumptuous.

A distant melody of chimes sounded from deep in the center of the house. A bulb mounted beside the family room door blinked green. The doorbell.

Aiden glanced at the clock and realized she was probably the only one still up, except for the night-shift attendants in the other wing. And they wouldn't be leaving their posts to answer the door.

A tight constriction of fear wrapped itself around her throat. Doorbell meant strangers, and strangers could mean anything. Opening the door was tantamount to inviting fate to take another swing at her.

But she knew she couldn't spend her life hiding within the same set of walls. Couldn't find a nice hole to crawl into and pull shut after her, as tempting as such an idea might be. She had to learn to face the world, and the people in it. They weren't going to hurt her.

Most of them. Not all. How could she know which ones were which?

The doorbell chimed again. If she didn't scurry down there post haste, it might disturb Dr. Lundquist. He wouldn't be able to hear it in his sound-proofed study, but the green signalling bulbs were located throughout the house.

Steeling herself to face the unknown, Aiden hurried down the west wing hall and the sweeping flight of stairs. She almost always used the stairs, loving their graceful curve and gleam of wood. Like something from a fairy tale.

The front door had windows to either side and a peephole in the middle. Aiden made use of all three, peering out from every possible angle. She recognized the police chief at once.

*　*　*

27

". . . that Schlossenberg never stopped," Roger Brockman said, satisfied.

Brian felt like a fool. There was no way he could have known, but he still couldn't help thinking that he *should* have. And he'd been right here at Seacliff this whole time! Right here in the same building, while they were gathering their subjects and conducting their experiments under his very nose.

An empath, Roger might be, but a precog he wasn't. None of them saw it coming until Lundquist swept his cane through the air.

It struck Roger a vicious blow to the head, and set off a ruinous series of events.

Inge leaped forward. Brian thrust out his feet, hitting her square in the shins. She reflexively squeezed off a shot as she fell, which plowed into the computer consoles. Smoke and sparks leapt from the shattered circuitry. A shrill electronic squeal vibrated the room.

Roger stumbled into Gwynne, both hands clapped to his bleeding head. He knocked the petite woman over. Anne cried out in alarm.

Jenny sprang up, behind Judge, and snatched the headgear off of him. The tight strap abraded his jaw as it went, then she gave it back to him by bashing the visor into the bridge of his nose.

Inge started to get up and Brian, though it was unchivalrous as hell, kicked her again as hard as he could. The gun flipped from her grasp and dropped into a wastebasket as neatly as if he'd aimed.

Judge grabbed for Jenny but she dodged and ran for the row of enclosures. She smacked her palms along the controls as she went, and the doors slid open.

"Chris, Julian, come on!"

"Not that one!" Gwynne, on hands and knees, flung out one arm as Jenny reached the next cell.

Lundquist stood with the tip of his cane once more planted firmly between his feet, his back straight but his face a rictus of anguish. Roger produced a small but mean-looking pistol of his own from the pocket of his lab coat and aimed it at his father.

"Judge, stop the girl!" Gwynne ordered.

Judge lunged toward Jenny, but the older of the two little boys darted into his path, brow wrinkled in concentration. The fire in the kid's eyes brought Judge to a halt.

Jenny kept moving. When she reached the fifth cell, she hesitated, staring at Eric Raney on the other side of the clear barrier.

Brian rolled his chair at Inge as she tried to get up again. It crashed into her, and down she went on her face for a third time. She snarled something that he guessed was German and also guessed was obscene.

Anne, tears streaming down her face, tugged at one buckle after another, trying to free Kel McGuire from the restraint chair.

"Hey. Jenny. Let me out. Don't leave me in here."

Jenny met Eric's eyes for a long moment, then she spun away from the enclosures and left him locked in.

A heavy, weird, invisible effect spread outward from the skinny kid in the *Jurassic Park* tee shirt. Brian found he could barely even look that way, didn't want to be anywhere in the vicinity.

Judge got the brunt of it, because he backpedaled, then spun to flee. As he did so, he slammed straight into Inge – downing her for the fourth time – and stepped on her right hand as he went over her. Bones snapped. She howled.

Lundquist stood his ground, impervious to the confusion raging all around him. Roger was likewise motionless, the pistol leveled, ignoring the blood that coursed from his split scalp down his neck and into his collar.

Flames burst through the seams of the computer console. The squeal worsened until Brian thought his skull might shudder itself apart in sympathy. Rising with that inhuman noise came a very human but still strange one, a banshee cry of unutterable agony. It was coming from the fourth cell, the one Gwynne had tried to stop Jenny from opening.

"I never meant to hurt you, William," Lundquist said quietly. "I always loved you, and only wanted the best for you."

The truth of it was apparent in the sincerity of his voice, and must have come through loud and clear to Roger's empathic power. His mouth worked, dull color flooded his face, and when he was unable to otherwise express a lifetime of ingrained hatred, he fired.

The report was flat and dull amid the din, but Lundquist crumpled with dark crimson blossoming on his shirt.

"No!" Eric yelled, hammering on the wall. He recoiled as the door slid open, and looked down to see that the smallest boy had stretched up on tiptoe to reach the controls and set him free.

Judge was cornered at the end of a cul-de-sac in the cavern wall, his face to it and fingers splayed as he desperately clawed for a way through, a way out. The kid in the *Jurassic Park* shirt advanced one slow step at a time, and the closer he got, the more frantic Judge's efforts to escape became, until the man was a panicked animal in a trap, unable to think, battering himself against the rough stone walls.

Gwynne ran for the fourth cell, her eyes wide and frightened in a way that they hadn't been even when the gunplay started. Her terror was so great that she barely seemed to notice when her mentor hit the floor with an awful, final thud.

"You lied to me!" Eric seized Roger by the collar and whirled him around. "You told me my grandfather was dead!"

"He is now," replied Roger.

Pure hatred, wrath distilled, boiled from Eric like a great black wave. Brian and everyone else in the cavernous chamber only felt part of it, enough to make even their desperate individual struggles pause.

But it swamped and overwhelmed Roger Brockman, probably magnified by Roger's own power. The mental attack ripped ruthlessly through his defenses, stripped away coherent thought, and reduced Roger to an instant catatonic state.

Brian, stricken with horror at having dragged Lundquist into this and then having the old man turn out to be innocent after all, scrambled to his side.

Lundquist looked up at him, those piercing emerald eyes fully aware and more full of pain and sorrow than anything Brian had ever seen. One of Lundquist's trembling, clawlike hands rose from his lap.

Brian knelt and clasped it. "Dr. Lundquist . . . just hold on . . . Jeez, I'm so sorry . . . hold on, we'll get help . . ."

"Too late," Lundquist said, his voice a ghost of its former commanding self. "Help the children. It's all I ever wanted. Tell them that. This . . . I did not know about this. Would never have . . ."

Those last words rode out on a dank breath, and Lundquist went limp.

Brian choked. He dropped Lundquist's hand, repelled at having felt it go slack and dead in his very grasp. He stood, tottering on numb legs, and stepped back from the body.

Someone shoved a sharp, searing poker through the back of his thigh and right out the front. He went down gasping, clutching his leg and feeling the hot liquid jet of arterial blood.

*   *   *

28

Damon Blake was all set to be tough, gruff, and suspicious, but he couldn't bring himself to do it. He thought that if he did, the girl who'd let them in might just burst into tears.

She was a slight little thing, didn't look a day over sixteen. With her beige hair and soft grey eyes, it was easy to overlook her, dismiss her. But looking closer, he saw she had a delicately appealing elfin quality to her features, and an aura of innocence that made it hard to believe she could be embroiled in a plot the likes of which Dawn and Toby had described.

The house seemed peaceful, too. No signs of any trouble.

To try and put the girl at ease, Damon adopted his most winning smile and charming cowboy drawl. "Pardon me, miss . . . I was hoping you could help us out. I'm Damon Blake." He introduced the others, and waited.

"Aiden Ferguson," she said, hushed and averting her gaze, as if just saying her name was an admission of some terrible transgression.

"Is Brian Sorenson here?"

"No . . . he's in the hospital. He didn't come to work today."

Damon could tell that she believed what she was saying to him. "You haven't seen him tonight?"

"Not since yesterday."

"How about his girlfriend, Dawn? Do you know her?"

Aiden nodded. "She called this morning and told us what had happened. So awful . . . poor Brian!"

"Is Dr. Brockman here?" Damon asked.

"I don't know. I haven't seen him. If he is, he's probably sleeping."

"Do you mind if I come in and have a look around?"

"I guess it's all right. I should check with Dr. Lundquist, but he's in his office and I don't like to bother him."

She stepped back, quivering with tension as the four of them filed past her. Not like she was hiding something, Damon realized, but more like she expected any or all of them to fall on her like the Big Bad Wolf and gobble her up. He thought that if he grabbed her on the shoulder or just shouted *boo!*, she'd go straight up to heaven without passing Go or collecting her two hundred dollars.

"Can you get hold of whoever's on duty?" Damon asked.

"Sure." She went to the fancy intercom. "Mr. Montgomery's the night shift attendant tonight."

"Thanks," Damon said.

He'd met Stan Montgomery on several occasions, coming to visit Lora. The man had not made a very favorable impression. In fact, he struck Damon as more of a thug than a healer. According to both Lora and Dawn, he was the one who had chased them out of the house.

"Uh . . ." Aiden said, after several fruitless seconds had passed. "He's not answering . . . he might be away from the desk."

"Let's go up and see." He didn't make it a request, starting for the east wing. The others followed.

Aiden didn't try to stop them, but trailed along nervously behind as if she didn't know what else to do.

On the second floor, they found everything just like Lora and Dawn had said. Aiden's eyes got bigger and bigger as Damon examined the pillows in Richie's and Lora's beds. He saw nothing in her reactions to make him think she was pretending, and decided that whatever was going on here, this girl wasn't at all in the know.

"Where's Mr. Montgomery? Where are the children?" she asked, with evident distress.

Rod and Avery checked the other rooms, finding the rest of Seacliff's students still sleeping peacefully and nothing out of the ordinary. With Damon's okay, Aiden buzzed and woke Helen Carlyle. The head nurse was just as mystified.

"I've never known Stan to abandon his post," she said when she joined them a few minutes later. "It looks like he was starting to write something in the log, but never finished. I'll have to report this to one of the doctors . . ."

"I think we'd better talk to Dr. Lundquist now," Damon said. "Aiden, can you show me to his office?"

"Something definitely fishy going on here," Malachi Edwards said. "I want to know what they've been doing. What they've done to my boy, and your Lora."

"We're going to find out, Mal," Damon promised.

Aiden led them to Lundquist's private office and rapped, but got no response. "I shouldn't go in without his permission," she said, her key card hovering uncertainly over the lock. "But . . . but what if . . . he's so old . . ." Damon kept quiet and let her talk herself into opening the door. All her worries proved groundless – the study was empty.

"What the blue hell!" swore Rod, peering through the window into the atrium.

Joining him, Damon saw what his startled perceptions first took to be a fat snake or a slug the size of a man, writhing amid the lounge chairs. The tricky, shifting blue-green radiance coming from the lights mounted beneath the surface of the pool contributed to the illusion. Then he saw that it was a man, tied up or wrapped up, hunching and rolling in an effort to get to the door.

They raced back to the stairs, down, and to the atrium. Aiden unlocked the door and they reached the struggling man.

Stan Montgomery was swaddled in a padlocked volleyball net like he was Houdini about to throw himself in the pool and perform a miraculous escape. He'd been struck twice in the head by something heavy, and Damon thought to himself that the man must have one thick skull to have regained consciousness anytime before the biggest shopping day of the year.

"That geeky little bastard!" Stan mumbled thickly. "Dirty-fighting piece of shit!"

"Who's that, Stan?" Damon asked, studying the padlocks and recognizing them for what they were. He dispatched Avery to look for the cheap keys that went along with them.

"Brian. When I catch up with him –" Stan clamped his mouth shut before finishing his threat.

"Brian Sorenson did this to you?" Damon was unable to keep the skepticism from his voice, and frankly didn't try all that hard.

Stan flushed. "He held a gun on me."

Here was some more astonishing news . . . while both Brian's dad and uncle were men of the macho hunting-and-beer stripe, Brian's interests tended toward entirely different eras. Damon had a tagged medieval crossbow sitting in his evidence locker to testify to that fact.

"Why?"

"They were kidnapping the kids," Stan said as Avery came back with the keys. "The Jessec tramp high-tailed it with her son and your stepdaughter. I was trying to stop her when Brian pulls a gun on me, and they got away."

"What happened to your head?"

"Bastard hit me with a dolphin."

Avery Scribner snorted in disbelief, but Damon remembered the brass sculpture in the lobby. "He didn't shoot you?"

"I wrestled the gun away from him," Stan boasted. "So he hit me. And hit me again when I was down, the chickenshit! That's all I remember."

"Where's Brian now?"

"Hell if I know."

*   *   *

29

Kel, with Anne's help, had just managed to free himself from the last of the straps when the blonde woman made it to her feet, holding her mangled right hand gingerly out to one side. With her other arm, she tipped over the wastebasket and retrieved Brian's gun. By the awkward way she held it, she was obviously not left-handed.

She shot Brian from behind. Brian's leg buckled and spilled him to the floor, spouting a bright fountain.

Death and mayhem were all around him, but Kel, still groggy and disconnected thanks to the injection Gwynne had given him, couldn't believe that any of it was real. This couldn't be happening, it was too crazy, none of it could possibly be real.

If it was dream or hallucination, therefore, Kel didn't see any harm in acting irrationally. He seized up the first thing at hand – a metal-frame folding chair much smaller and lighter than the one to which he'd been bound – and whipped it at the woman.

It flew on a better trajectory than he would have had any right to expect in the real world, air whistling at its passage, and hit the woman's arm as she aimed in frowning concentration.

The bullet that would have gone into Brian's head hit the stone floor with a *scree* that set Kel's teeth on edge.

Anne, pale beneath her visor and shaking, snatched up the gun that Roger Brockman had dropped. "Inge, stop!"

Inge spun, her hair coming loose from her ponytail and flying in witchy locks from beneath her headpiece. Her lips were curled in a feral, deadly sneer. Despite her modern garb, Kel had no trouble seeing her as a Norse goddess, not merely a chooser of the slain but one ready to hurry them along, thundering on her mystic horse over a battlefield screaming in bloodlust.

She fired at Anne but missed, blowing a hole in a monitor and turning it into a smoking socket.

"Inge, put down the gun," Anne begged.

"Don't just stand there, shoot her!" Jenny Forrester cried.

Abhorrent as violence was to Kel, under the circumstances he thought Jenny made perfect sense. Anne, though, faltered and let the barrel of the gun dip.

"I can't."

"Hah!" spat Inge in a mocking laugh, and fired again.

Kel dove for Anne, meaning to push her out of the way, push her to safety, no matter what she had done, part of him still insisted that he loved her, couldn't stand there and watch her be shot.

But he was only a counselor and social worker, and that didn't make him Superman, didn't make him faster than the proverbial speeding bullet. As he reached Anne she was brutally pitched backward, a hole in her stomach and a red geyser jetting from her back. She hit the bank of monitors and slid bonelessly down, leaving a gruesome trail.

Inge screeched a victory cry and tore off her visor, looking around for her next target. Those merciless arctic eyes found Kel as he reached Anne's side. Like a cat with a mouse, she took a moment to savor the impending kill.

Kel felt something hard press against his hand. He glanced down. The gun . . . Anne was still holding the gun, swallowing convulsively as she tried to speak.

He grabbed it, swung it around as if he'd been doing this all his life, and squeezed the trigger even as Inge fired at him.

Unprepared and unfamiliar with guns as he was, the recoil slammed up his arm and drove his shoulder into the table so roughly he thought it was dislocated.

The bullet grazed Inge's neck with a searing line of heat. Only an inch or two to the left, and it would have opened her throat, killed her. Kel saw that awareness in her face even as he felt it in his own.

A sudden understanding leapt between them as if they possessed the same sort of powers as the children. Kel knew without being able to say how that she had never actually been shot at before, never come so close to being killed, and it slashed through her gung-ho bloodlust like a razor.

Only then did Kel realize that he wasn't shot. That her gun had not gone off. Empty, or jammed, or he didn't know what.

She might still have been able to take him; he was half-doped and slow. But with her good hand held out like a bundle of broken twigs at her side, and with him having a loaded gun, she didn't dare chance it. Everything seemed too real now, to both of them.

Inge threw down Brian's useless gun and ran for it, vanishing down one of the tunnels that opened off of the cave like rat warrens. The last Kel saw of her was the blond blur of her hair.

Time, which had been racing, jerked back to a normal rate. Kel dropped the gun, hating the lethal weight, the feel and oily-black stink of it. He looked down at Anne, lying in a spreading lake of her own blood.

She was trying to smile, but it was a ghastly grimace.

"Marge . . ."

Footfalls . . . Kel looked up, tense.

The children approached in a loose semicircle. Brian was with them, the leg of his pants soaked almost black but walking, limping but *walking*.

That was impossible, that couldn't be, Kel had seen his femoral artery let go.

A tiny, dark-haired boy of about four held Brian's hand. Tears welled in his eyes at the sight of so much blood.

Jenny moaned and covered her mouth when she saw Anne. The other boy had the shellshocked stare of combat fatigue and exhaustion.

"We won!" Eric said in hot, savage joy. "Kicked their *asses!*"

"Shut up, Eric." Jenny was on the verge of tears. "Just shut up."

He did, his mouth snapping shut with a click, but his eyes still blazed.

"I help?" the little boy ventured.

"Yeah! Julian can help her. Anne was always the nicest one to us." Jenny brought the boy forward, kissed his cheek. "Help her, Julian. Save her."

"Oh, I can't believe this," Eric snarled at Jenny. "She's one of them. Let her die."

"She was practically your mother!"

"So what? He really *was* my father? So what?"

Jenny took a step toward him, fists clenched. "You're such a creep, Eric. Why don't you just drop dead?"

He glared at her, but only for a split-second before his glare switched to a gape of dread. He staggered back, bumping into tables and sending a cacophony of beakers and tubes cascading to shatter on the floor. He went to his knees.

Jenny voiced a choked scream of denial.

Eric raised his head, focusing on her through the sheaves of black hair that fell down over his forehead. With his last bit of strength, he lashed out at her, mind-to-mind in a vicious mental blast.

Jenny shrieked, but then the attack was snuffed out as Eric collapsed facedown. He made a sighing moan, then was still.

"I didn't mean it, I didn't mean to kill him." Jenny leaned down, gingerly, as if she expected him to come up raving like something from a monster movie. She touched him, poked him. "Eric? Eric?"

When he didn't move, Jenny backed up and the color drained from her face. She swayed, and toppled. Brian caught her before she fell, but she had fainted.

Kel turned sickly away from the sight of Eric's body, back to the even worse sight of Anne. She had passed out on her side, but was still breathing shallowly, the lake around her still widening. He gasped when he saw the little boy, Julian, right there beside her.

"No, kiddo . . . you shouldn't be seeing this." He tried to gently move the boy away, but Julian resisted with uncommon strength.

"Let him, it's okay," the kid in the dinosaur shirt said.

Julian put one hand on Anne's stomach and the other on her back, reaching over her with his little arms. Seconds ticked past in heavy silence, and Kel was about to ask what he was doing when the miracle happened. The flow of blood became a trickle, then stopped as the mangled flesh drew together.

At the same moment, a spot of red stained the back of Julian's shirt. It grew, and ran in rivulets. A smaller spot appeared on the front.

Kel could barely draw breath into his frozen lungs. He tore his gaze away long enough to look at the others, but they seemed to be expecting just this, and there was awed recognition in Brian's eyes. Kel's gaze dropped to Brian's leg, then to Julian's, and his suspicions were confirmed when he saw a line of red on the boy's pajama pants.

He understood what he was seeing, but could scarcely believe it. Julian whimpered once, just once, as he took the grievous wound upon himself and then made it fade like time-lapse photography in reverse.

Anne was breathing evenly, and when Kel sought her pulse, it was steady and strong. Little Julian crumpled, worn out from the incredible thing he'd just done.

"Me, too," Brian said in wonder. "He healed me, too." He brushed his fingers against his throat, which was unmarked. "Even what Lucas did to me, and everything."

Kel slowly stood up and surveyed the cave.

Of Judge, all that remained was a huddled and broken mass . . . cornered, he had been reduced to a subhuman state of terror and battered himself to death against the walls trying vainly to escape.

Roger Brockman and his son were in nearly identical postures, both unmarked by any external injury. And Lundquist was dead as well, three generations snuffed out within minutes . . .

Kel bowed his head for a moment, then rose with grim purpose. "Where is my sister? Where's Gwynne?"

*   *   *

30

On the ground floor of Seacliff, a crowd of the live-in staff milled about in annoyance and bathrobes. At Damon's urging, Helen Carlyle had woken Laverne Willis, the chief administrator, and she had assembled the rest.

But of the three doctors and the computer programmer, no sign was found, and no one seemed to have any ideas as to where they could be. Except possibly for Stan Montgomery, who was steadfastly sticking to his right to remain silent.

"None of the cars are missing," Avery Scribner reported. "Even Brian's is out there. Can't miss it with all those bumper stickers."

"So where are they?" Damon said. "Where'd they all go?"

"I don't know, but we should get out of here," the gangly officer said. "This place gives me the willies."

Damon was about to say that it gave him the willies too and for a lot better reason, when he realized that the flesh on the back of his neck was prickling as the tiny hairs there drew themselves on end. A shiver started in the vicinity of his breastbone and fanned outward, bringing goosebumps when it reached his skin.

"We should go. Right now," Aiden Ferguson said, wrapping her slender arms around herself.

A murmur of agreement rolled through the room. On every face, in every eye, Damon saw the same thing – a peculiar and unformed, but growing, sense of dread.

His thoughts spun back three years to another night here in Seacliff, when the house had been deserted and he and Theresa had faced something of terrible and inhuman. This chill was different, this sense of heaviness like the air before a storm was not rife with unearthly demonic evil, but it was still a chill, a heaviness.

Something is going to happen at Seacliff, something bad. Those had been Lora's words, and that hunch, that surety, was abruptly transmitted to Damon.

"The children," Helen Carlyle said, dashing for the elevator. "We can't leave without the children."

"What do you mean, leave?" Rod Peterson said. "Just because everybody's got a case of the —"

"There's something not right here, can't you feel it?" Aiden cried shrilly, and by the looks they gave her, it was the first time she'd raised her voice to that level in living memory.

"We certainly can't abandon the place," Mrs. Willis said in a brisk and businesslike manner that reminded Damon of his own mother. "Not without Dr. Lundquist's say-so, and not without Dr. Lundquist."

"To hell with that," said one of the other attendants. "I'm getting out of here while I still can."

"You take one step and you'll lose your job," Mrs. Willis warned. But her gorgeous cocoa skin — also like that of Damon's mom — had gone ashen.

The feeling — hunch, premonition, warning, whatever it was — kept intensifying. Damon could *feel* it like a hoard of tiny spiders creeping over him, crawling and skittering, brushing and crawling, and he knew they had to get out of here, couldn't stay, had to get *out*, get out *now*.

"Holy smokes, what's going on?" moaned Avery Scribner.

Damon's initial thought was that this uncanny fear had gotten so bad he was actually shaking, but the sway of light and shadow drew his gaze up to a chandelier, jittering on the end of its chain. Even as he looked at it, the crystals began to clitter and jingle in high, brittle tones.

"Earthquake!" screamed one of the housekeeping staff, a proper New England fellow never before treated to California's tectonic hijinks.

He was the first to bolt, pell-mell for the door. As if it was the spark to a roomful of gas, the fear exploded through the others and they stampeded after him.

The fear, the intense compulsion to flee, burst on Damon in overpowering new strength. He held his ground only by sheerest force of will, while everyone around him threw duty to the wind. They were bottlenecked at the front door, herding against it in a blind seeking frenzy.

Got to get *out*, get *away*, go *now!*

The floor rolled gently beneath his feet as if a wave had passed under it.

A chorus of screams from the packed doorway preceded the crash of glass, and then they were shoving themselves through the windows that flanked the door, heedless of shards that slashed at their pajama-clad forms.

The house shuddered. Damon saw that he wasn't the last one, that the girl Aiden was rooted to the spot. He knew by one look at her face that the only reason she hadn't fled was because she was rooted to the spot by conflicting terrors: the pressing demand to run, and her agoraphobia.

Out, out, out! Away from this place, get away, get away . . . it was almost as if he could *hear* that command ringing in his head.

He gritted his teeth against it, but a jolt more violent than before hit the house. It was the frantic lunge of a bucking bronco, and he even thought he could hear the earth itself, the stones of which the bluff was formed, scraping and cracking.

In the wake of that tremor, the compulsion to get away shot to unbearable heights. Damon held out long enough to sweep the paralyzed Aiden over his shoulder in a fireman's carry, and didn't even bother trying to force his way into the maddened throng at the door. They had ceased to be people, ceased to be police and caregivers and dedicated professionals. This was raw panic, their minds reduced to only one concern – escape and survival.

He ran instead for the east wing hall, hearing the din and ruckus of dishes breaking and pans clanging as he passed the kitchen. At the end of the hall was a door connecting to the garage breezeway, and he plunged through into the sirening whoop of car alarms triggered by the troubled earth.

*   *   *

31

It's all Roger's fault. Him and his ideas, him and his plans.

Now the entire project was falling apart, and the only consolation was that Roger had paid for it dearly.

That Lundquist had paid as well was a surprisingly sharp thorn in the conscience that Gwynne McGuire hadn't even known she had. In her way, she truly had admired him, his genius and his accomplishments. Had even, as much as someone like her could, loved the pompous old lizard.

But now he was dead . . . everything was a shambles . . . all thanks to Roger's insistence on trying something new. If he'd listened to her, if he'd kept everything contained under laboratory conditions, none of this would have happened!

Had he done that? No! From the very moment, months ago, when he'd come up with the idea of using Lundquist's compound on Eric and putting him out in the community, everything had gone wrong.

He should have known that Anne's cover wouldn't hold. Should have known that trying to treat Toby Edwards on an outpatient basis was ludicrous! But rather than listen to her, the megalomaniacal idiot had made it *her* challenge, put *her* in charge of monitoring those two while he contented himself with the tidy, controlled cases of Jenny, of Lora.

At the same time, he'd gone and done whatever it was he'd done to this Lucas Gordon person, without even informing her until after the fact!

Every scientist needs a creature . . . of all the nerve!

These thoughts, this venomous outpouring, issued from her in hisses and snarls as she tried to ignore the sounds of gunfire and screaming from outside of the fourth enclosure. She had a far worse situation on her hands. Gwynne spared a few mental curses for Jenny Forrester, who'd gone wantonly punching at controls with no clue of what she might be unleashing.

Her hands flew over the panel of instruments. The fourth enclosure wasn't like the others. There was little in the way of furniture in here. Little in the way of anything except for a hospital bed with a lid that resembled a cryogenic sleep tube out of a sci-fi story.

In effect, that was what it was, except that it was also fitted with circuitry similar to that found in the headsets. Shielding circuitry, to essentially create a field of electromagnetic energy through which the waves produced by the psychic area of the brain could not penetrate.

In the case of the headsets, the purpose was only to keep the minds of the project team safe from the manipulations of their subjects. In the case of OW-F0177, it was to contain her power.

But thanks to Jenny, the shielding device had been opened, and the subject was awake. And the contingency back-up system, which was supposed to dump an immediate dose of sedative into OW-F0177's bloodstream, had failed to kick in.

Gwynne worked fast, knowing that she only had a few seconds before OW-F0177 would become fully alert.

Already, the brain waves on the monitor were taking on the pattern of concentration, which was similar to those found in artists and writers when inspiration had them in its grasp, similar to those found in the other subjects when they utilized their powers. Was it any wonder that the psychic area of the brain was directly linked to the creative center?

But with this one, they couldn't afford to take chances. They'd already seen far too well what would happen if this one was allowed to use the gift they'd instilled in her.

"Gwynne!"

"Not now, little brother."

"Yes, now." Kel came into the enclosure and froze as he took in the sight.

Hoping that his stunned revulsion would buy her those few seconds, Gwynne kept working. Kel moved slowly to the edge of the bed, staring in at the pitiful figure.

Her birth name had been Neesha, and an older step-brother strung out on drugs had done his damndest to smother her by tying a plastic bag over her head. The family had been broke and desperate, in even worse straits than Dawn Jessec, and had relinquished their little girl without a qualm, even signing over all custodial rights in exchange for having all of the hospital bills paid.

Now she was just OW-F0177, and little recognizable remained of the impish girl she had been. Her hair was no longer worn in cornrows and clipped with colorful barrettes, because she had lost all of her hair. Her limbs were wasted sticks covered with dry, leathery skin.

And her head . . . the swelling of the brain tissues had been so sudden and extreme that they'd been forced to operate, forced to open windows in her skull. She had lost all motor control, all ability to manage her bodily functions, all coherent thought and speech.

But in exchange, what she could do was so intriguing that they hadn't destroyed her even though it was plain she'd never lead a functional life. Even though it was plain that she was a mindless *thing*. It was her potential, as always the potential, that captivated Gwynne and Roger.

She was attempting to convey this to Kel, as he looked down at OW-F0177 with expressions of pity, disgust, and horror flickering across his face like fast-moving clouds over the sun.

"No, Gwynne."

"I'm afraid it's true."

"No, what I mean is, I'm not going to let you do this! I'm not going to let you torture this little girl any more! I'm taking her out of here, getting her some help."

Gwynne shook her head, not turning from her work. "Impossible, Kel. If she's not properly contained, she will lash out at everything and everyone around her."

"No wonder! You've treated her like a beast, like . . . what did he say? Every scientist needs a creature? Is she yours? No more, Gwynne. She needs help, she needs to be out of here, she needs her freedom and her family."

"As always, I applaud your devotion, but in this instance it is misplaced. You cannot get through to OW-F0177 by sympathy and gentle counseling."

When he had the temerity to grab her by the shoulders and spin her to face him, Gwynne was so astounded that she could barely speak.

"Don't you understand? Don't you get it, Gwynne? It's over! Lundquist is dead, Brockman is dead, Eric is dead, one of your hired goons is dead and the other deserted you . . . it's over. The project ends here and now. I'm taking the children out of here. All of them. Even this one."

"Kel, don't be a fool. She's too dangerous. Her power —"

"She's a little girl. Only a little girl."

"These children can kill. Haven't you realized that yet?"

"Yes," he said grimly. "I have."

"Then you have to understand —"

Shrill beeps of an alarm made her throw aside what she'd been going to say. Her attempt to bring the back-up system back online had failed, and OW-F0177 was conscious.

"I'll have to sedate her manually," she said, forgetting for the moment that Kel wasn't part of her team, that he wasn't going to make himself useful and hand her a syringe.

He wouldn't let go of her shoulders. "I'm taking her out of here."

Gwynne slapped his hands away. "I don't have time for this, Kel."

A cabinet bolted to the floor in the corner held an emergency supply. She hurried to it, swept her key card through the lock, opened it. There within were neat ranks of capped needles and vials.

She reached in, and the drawer slammed shut with savage force. Gwynne shrieked, more in shock than in pain at first. But the pain came next, roaring up her arm like a living thing. The steel edge of the drawer was pinning her wrist, biting into it, a bear trap of blunted edges.

OW-F0177 cried out, the bestial glottal wail that was the only semblance of language she had left. For all it was wordless, it encompassed more misery and suffering than any number of words could.

A tremendous surge of invisible might flattened Kel against the wall. Even in the midst of her own agony, Gwynne was glad, glad to see him gasp, glad to see the fear spring up in him.

"Look what you've done," she called.

The drawer was pushed further shut, her wrist still caught in it. Around her uselessly spasming fingers, vials burst. The cabinet itself began to bend, the bolts holding it to the stone floor squalling and groaning.

Medical equipment slid across the room, shoved by unseen hands. The air was suddenly full of flying objects, dials and buttons and pieces of paneling wrenched from the surface of the instrument panel. The shielding lid smashed upward, breaking into puzzle-pieces of circuitry.

In the bed, unable to move but with bulging brown eyes glaring malevolently from her misshapen face, OW-F0177 directed the destruction.

Gwynne felt herself seized and thrown straight up, the drawer not relinquishing its grip. She shrieked again, bones grinding in her wrist, skin scraped from the back of her hand. A small opal ring on her third finger snagged under the rim of the drawer with an incredible lance of new pain. She was flung like a doll back into the main lab, landing hard amid the tables.

Scrambling to her feet, Gwynne caught a brief glimpse of Kel running, apparently unharmed. At last, her well-meaning but inane brother had seen sense . . . there was nothing social work could do for this particular child.

Everything in the lab came alive, sliding and veering around, expensive bumper cars of medical equipment with Gwynne corralled in their midst. So, OW-F0177's intention was to crush her to death by the furnishings of her own lab?

"I always did loathe children," Gwynne said.

Not even bothering to look at the ruin that was her right hand, paying no attention to the showers of gravel beginning to rain down from the cave ceiling, she wedged herself into a niche in the natural stone wall.

As strong as OW-F0177's telekinesis was, she couldn't maintain it at that pace for long. Gwynne knew all she had to do was wait her out . . .

Everything stopped, and vindication thrilled through Gwynne. In the end, science always came through for –

It was her final thought before her skull imploded under the incredible pressure of OW-F0177's dying effort, and Gwynne McGuire was dead before the first large falling chunks of ceiling heralded the cave's collapse.

* * *

32

Inge Runolf made it out of the cave on the seaward side, and was cautiously making her way up the dark and rain-slick path that Lora Blake and once tried to traverse when the first tremor shook the bluff.

Her neck still stung, the wound cauterized by the bullet as it skimmed her flesh. But even the crushed and splintered bones in her right hand hurt far less than her shame. The bitter pill of defeat didn't go down well. Her pride demanded that she go back, and either beat her enemies or die in the attempt.

Another deep earth tremor, this one stronger, decided her. She knew, like a bolt of ice-lightning to her heart, knew that the danger wasn't over yet.

She broke into a run, not caring any more that one misstep would send her into the rocky sea. The top of the bluff, a darker blot against the sky, was tantalizingly close.

That was when the stone wall exploded out on top of her.

* * *

33

Jeez, thought Brian Sorenson. *Just like in all the tacky fantasy movies! Just like in 'The Mummy,' and 'Krull' . . .*

He ran up the quaking stairs with Julian in his arms and the beam of the flashlight sketching crazy bright lines in which motes of dust whirled and danced.

It wasn't so bad here, the quaking, but he could hear a horrific rumbling and crashing from behind them, the sound reverberating through the subterranean halls like the cheated furious growls and teeth-gnashings of a dragon.

Just like in those movies. Kill the bad guy, get the treasure, save the girl, and then kerblooie! The whole place comes falling in!

The 'treasure' pounded up the stairs behind him, Jenny Forrester and the boy called Chris, crowding him and urging him to go faster, faster. He didn't even need to hear their voices, because Chris was broadcasting his insistent demand that everyone get out, get out *now*, get away, so strongly that Brian bet they could feel it in McKinleyville.

Bringing up the rear, the protesting Anne was being hustled along by Kel McGuire.

"But your sister! She's still back there!" Anne cried.

"I know." His tone was agony and self-recrimination, and Brian marveled that after everything Gwynne had apparently done, Kel still felt bad about leaving her to die. "There's nothing we can do."

Never make a gamer of him, Brian thought.

"The last child," Kel added, panting. "Who is she? *What* is she?"

The stairs hadn't seemed so long on the way down, not even as he had been descending them in a cold nervous sweat with the gun trained on Lundquist's back. The memory made him wince, but how was he supposed to have known?

If Anne replied to Kel, it was swallowed up in a great cracking bellow of stone. Brian reached the back of the secret door and threw it open, shoving through with the other two kids on his heels, just as a gust of gritty wind pummeled them from behind.

They burst into Seacliff's library and out into the hall, where the stragglers of a panicked exodus headed into the front yard. It was mass chaos, and expecting the entire building to crumble inward and be sucked down into the cellar, Brian plunged headlong into their midst. Car alarms were blaring like crazy, people were screaming and shouting, the entire bluff was wracked with convulsions.

"Get away from the house!" Brian yelled. "I don't know how far is safe."

Chris seconded him silently but even more powerfully, and the crowd parted before them, fleeing away, a flock of disrupted pajama-clad quail scattering across the lawn. He recognized many of them – Stan Montgomery with his hands cuffed behind him, but thankfully Stan didn't see Brian . . . Helen Carlyle and Dr. Shaw's little boy . . . Malachi Edwards, of all people.

Then he spotted a familiar shape, at the edge of the woods, silhouetted by the porch light of the Zane house. Dawn, holding Richie. And Theresa Zane and her father beside her. And Ruth Edwards, with Toby and Lora and Lora's dog. All of them squinting through the blowing rain, calling out needless warnings because everyone already knew there was an intense but strictly localized earthquake going on.

A new clamor of terrified screams split the night. Brian saw people pointing, and turned to look because he was helpless not to turn to look . . . Seacliff was going down like the House of Usher, he knew it, he just knew it –

The cliff, the westernmost edge of the bluff, bulged out. Like Lucas Gordon's skull had done. Bulged . . . and then the cliff wall ruptured outward in a storm of rock and earth.

It was so loud that it seemed to nullify all sound. Brian knew that people around him were screaming, throwing themselves to the ground and screaming, covering their heads, and suspected he might be screaming himself but could hear nothing. Only a flat grey nothing, the auditory equivalent of staring at a blank movie screen.

The nothing lasted the better part of a minute, and Brian had time to think that this was what it must have been like, this only bigger, to be observing a nuclear detonation. It was the sudden awful silence of sheer and unimaginable destruction . . . the almost slow-motion majesty of the rising pillar of smoke – dust and stone-grit, in this case, and not a tidy mushroom cloud but a huge belching spew. The sea, reacting to tons of mass dumped into it, upsurged in a violent, violated torrent.

Finally, sounds began to seep back in. The grinding and crunching of rock, the lumberjack woodsnap of trees going over, and the unbelieving gasping and sobbing of the witnesses percolated through the grey nothing. A bass counterpoint to it all was the slow sliding thunder as the new crevasse settled, boulders and chunks of stone along its edges giving in to the ultimatum of gravity.

Brian realized that Dawn was with him, that they were clinging to each other with Richie between them.

Seacliff was still standing.

*   *   *

Thursday,

November 27

Epilogue

The turkey was cooking, the football game was on, and from upstairs came the thump and laughter of kids at play.

Travis Zane's house was really too small for such a large get-together. Card tables were lined up end-to-end, covered with tablecloths and surrounded by scrounged and mismatched chairs. A centerpiece of festive fall leaves spilled from a cornucopia-shaped basket and tall candles whimsically shaped to look like politically incorrect — especially in the home of a man whose mother had been full-blooded Native American — Pilgrims and Indians gave off a spicy scent.

It was nothing like the Thanksgiving dinners Kel McGuire had known as a kid. Those had been held in Greybridge's cavernous dining room, everything perfectly arranged by the servants, china and crystal and impeccable order. The dinner guests had often been colleagues and social acquaintances of his parents, and the conversations had revolved around politics, business, society functions. The McGuire children, until reaching the magical age of sixteen and being allowed to join the adults, had been fed early in the dayroom and dismissed with orders to be neither seen nor heard.

After leaving home, he'd never paid much attention to the holiday. If he celebrated it at all, it was by participating in the dinners or parties held at the group homes or hospitals where he worked. Last year, for instance, he'd been at Silver Grove, and spent the day listening to the elders reminisce about the good old days. Those meals were well-seasoned with loneliness and sorrow.

This year, this special occasion, marked the first time he'd had a home-cooked Thanksgiving meal in years. Or, really, since the cooks had done it all at Greybridge, the first home-cooked Thanksgiving meal of his life.

He reflected amusedly how this particular holiday, of all the ones on the calendar, brought back old traditional gender roles. The women of this newly-extended family, Theresa Zane and Ruth Edwards and Dawn Jessec, were in the kitchen fussing over cranberry sauce and candied yams.

The men – Travis, Damon Blake, Malachi Edwards, Brian Sorenson, Charlie Forrester, and Kel himself – were cozily ensconced in the living room, watching football and noshing on chips and dip so that the delicious aromas drifting from the kitchen didn't drive them wild with hunger.

And the kids were upstairs, except for Richie and the Blake twins, who were napping on the floor despite the hearty ruckus.

They were all a family now, joined by ties stronger than blood. Joined by the special, awe-inspiring, and scary events of the past few months. None of them would ever be able to forget what had happened at Seacliff, not when its legacy lived on in their children.

In the week and a half since that disastrous rainy night, much had happened. Decisions had been made, action had been taken, and in many cases, lies had been told.

Brian Sorenson had been the first to point out the danger. If the truth got out of what had happened in the cave, none of them would ever be able to go back to a normal life. Least of all the children.

They'd be taken away. Either by the organization that had been secretly funding Gwynne and Roger's clandestine enterprise, or possibly by the government. Taken away and studied, or locked up as a threat to national security.

Those who knew about it would be silenced, either by coercion or something more permanent.

And most damning of all, if it was found out what the children could do, what the children had done, their lives would become a daily hell. Always feared, never trusted, treated as pariahs, shunned, or sought by those hoping to use their gifts to some agenda.

It troubled Kel whenever he thought of it. They were only kids, and hadn't asked for what had been done to them. It wasn't their fault, hadn't been done with their knowledge or consent. But when all was said and done, they were different now. Two of them, at least, had powers that could kill.

He didn't blame Jenny and Chris for what they'd done. In Jenny's case, it had been an accident, and she'd been purely horrified by the results. He was anticipating long hours of therapy with her, trying to help her come to terms with the death of Eric Raney.

Chris, having been held captive and tortured by those people for so many months, had been lashing out in what could easily be seen as justifiable self-defense. Kel was trying to work with him, too, but it was slow going.

An even thornier question involved little Julian. He had the power to heal, to save lives. That was an amazing gift that shouldn't be withheld, shouldn't be hidden away. But who was to say when or how he was to use it? Who was to decide?

For now, Kel had taken the boy into his own home as a foster child. Nancy and Brian had been able to go through and decipher Seacliff's encoded records, and found out that Julian's parents were dead, and that he had no other close family.

Chris' father had died in the same accident that had almost killed Chris, but his mother was still alive. Alive and in a women's correctional facility for drug abuse. And so, without even needing much persuading from Jenny, Charlie Forrester had taken him in.

As it had turned out, most of the staff of Seacliff had been totally unaware of Roger and Gwynne's main project. Stan Montgomery had known of the existence of the cave, but not exactly what they were doing down there. He would be tried as an accessory to kidnapping.

Most of the other children had likewise not been involved in that aspect of the project. They had been transferred to other hospitals and facilities.

David Shaw had gone home to his father's house, though that was a situation that left Kel highly worried. Elliot Shaw was hardly fit to care for himself, much less a child with such special needs. He had resigned from his hospital post and closed his practice. Kel suspected, too, that Elliot had started drinking. Shaw blamed himself for not taking action sooner, blamed himself for being unable to save Lucas Gordon.

Lucas had died three days after the collapse of the bluff, of a cerebral hemorrhage. He'd never regained consciousness.

Damon Blake had not announced any intention that there be a cover-up. It just worked out that way, with the rest of them going along with it unquestioning.

Yes, there had been a secret cave below Seacliff. Yes, some of the doctors were involved in illegal experiments. Yes, Lucas had been one of them, proof that whatever they were doing was dangerous, unethical, and monstrous. Yes, they had kidnapped Jenny Forrester, but she had escaped unharmed.

All of those things were true. That, though, was where the official story parted ways from the true one. They blamed the destruction of the cave and its contents on an earthquake, though the seismologists were still puzzling over how it could have been so intense yet so localized.

The disaster had roused the entire town, and despite the steady rain and the earliness of the hour, they came. In droves in the pre-dawn murky light. To gawk or to help, or more truthfully both, they came.

Half the homes in Trinity Bay had a view of Seacliff, and now everyone could see that the bluff was split and sheared away, the shape that had bulked so permanently in the town's consciousness forever changed.

The small curve of rocky sand, where the high-school kids had gone for beach parties before Angela Cliffwood's suicide, was buried beneath a jumble of stones and splintered redwoods. The stand of trees that had served as a windbreak was gone, along with half of the meadowed lawn on the west side of the house. An ugly gouge where the land had caved in reached to within thirty yards of the end of the west wing.

It was all closed up now, closed up and taped off with warning signs posted all over the place. A team of experts crawled over and through the wreckage, but had realized at once that there was virtually no way to excavate down to the cave. The collapse had been too complete.

Seacliff itself was in decent condition, aside from some broken glass and upended furniture. It had been in Lundquist's name, and Brian and Anne both testified that Lundquist had been unaware of the extracurricular activities going on beneath his school. He was posthumously found not responsible, and his identity as Gustav Richter was never revealed.

Lundquist's will left the bulk of his estate to various children's hospitals and programs. He left his ward, Aiden, handsomely provided for, but his death was such a shock to her that she'd lapsed into a frighteningly withdrawn state.

The last loose end had been Anne. Neither fully a villain in this, nor fully innocent, her actions at the end had gone a far way toward redeeming her. Jenny, Chris, and Julian all insisted that she had been as nice to them as the circumstances had allowed. She had to confess her involvement, but if she confessed too much, about the nature and results of the project, for instance . . .

Her solution had been one of which Gwynne might have approved, a sacrifice that Kel himself doubted he could have made. Anne devised a story that put her as an attendant and counselor rather than parapsychologist, in charge of seeing to the children's needs but not in the know about the rest of the project.

And then, to make sure that she didn't falter in her responses to questioning, she had Jenny suggest it to her. She'd given up the sanctity of her own mind and memories to keep the truth hidden.

Kel wasn't sure what to feel. He'd thought he was in love with her as Marge, bitterly hated her in those moments of revelation in the cave, and come to care for her again as she abandoned her duties and helped them escape. In the moment when she'd been dying in his arms, before Julian worked his miracle, Kel had wanted to love her again. After she'd given herself up, given up part of her self, he was sure.

But now she was gone, arrested and taken away for her part in this terrible crime against children. It was the only thing missing from the day's celebration . . . Anne should have been out there in the kitchen with Theresa, Ruth, and Dawn. She should have been in the next chair over when they all sat down for dinner.

The children came thundering downstairs, interrupting his sad and musing thoughts.

"Isn't it dinner time *yet?*" Lora said with the attitude of someone who'd been living on gruel and pencil shavings for a week.

Kel looked at them, these new children, these gifted ones. They were just happy, excited, ordinary kids. Not freaks, not monsters.

"Yes, it is," Theresa said, coming in from the kitchen with a covered dish in either hand. "Everyone wash up and sit down, because that turkey's ready to carve."

The kids stampeded into the bathroom under the stairs. Kel felt a small hand slip into his own, and looked down into Julian's dark and trusting eyes.

They all sat down at the table together, a new family with many precious reasons to be thankful.

*   *   *

About the Author

Christine Morgan lives in the Pacific Northwest with her husband, daughter, and trio of cats. She is a graduate of California's Humboldt State University, with a B.A. in Psychology. Her overnight-shift job as a residential counselor in a psychiatric facility allows her ample time to write as well as the occasional flash of inspiration.

She divides her writing time among a variety of genres – horror, fantasy, childrens' fiction, and erotica among them. Her previous books include the *MageLore* and *ElfLore* fantasy trilogies, the Silver Doorway series of children's books, and *Black Roses*, the first of the Trinity Bay horror novels. She was nominated for an Origins Award for her zombie short story "Dawn of the Living-Impaired," and various others of her works have appeared in anthologies, magazines, and several online forums. She and her husband Tim co-edit an online 'zine, *Sabledrake Magazine*.

A longtime gamer, Christine can often be found at regional conventions, running games as well as promoting books. She has a fond relationship with the folks at Steve Jackson Games and other names in the gaming industry, all of whom have been incredibly supportive and helpful. In 2003, Christine and Tim released their first role-playing game supplement, the controversial *Naughty and Dice: An Adult Gamer's Guide to Sexual Situations*.

Christine's other interests span a wide gamut – robotic combat, British comedy, documentaries, and reality game shows make up the majority of her television viewing habits; horror, mysteries, and thrillers dominate her bookshelves; and she enjoys cooking and crafts.

Christine welcomes and appreciates feedback from readers. She can be reached by e-mail at christine@sabledrake.com and invites visitors to her website, www.sabledrake.com.

Dork Tower cartoon strip © John Kovalic. All Rights Reserved. Used with permission. http://dorktower.com

If you enjoyed this tale,
look for these other books by *Christine Morgan*.

Black Roses
   Trinity Bay Book #1

He is the man of their dreams – literally. He feeds on the sleeping minds of the women of Trinity Bay, making them believe their most forbidden fantasies are coming true. Now he has chosen the one woman he intends to be his, no matter how many people must die. Theresa Zane, newly returned to her childhood home, is drawn into a century-old mystery of sex, death, and the ominous haunting of the power behind the black roses.
$14.95   •   0-9702189-5-8   •   300   pages

**Black Roses is also available as an Audio Book in
Cassette and CD formats!**

Changeling Moon
   Trinity Bay Book #3

They have lived among us for millennia, an ancient race of shapeshifters whose powers gave rise to our oldest legends. Some see mankind as a race to be ignored or protected. To others, humans are their prey. Now they have come to Trinity Bay, and one troubled young woman is caught in a deadly clash between them.
Coming Summer, 2005

Curse of the Shadow Beasts
MageLore Book I

They come from beyond the walls of nightmare, hideous creatures bent on seeking and slaughtering, leaving only death and misery in their wake.

Arien Mirida knows them only too well. He has faced them before and witnessed their evil, and fears that their hunger can never be stopped.

Cat Sabledrake is about to meet the horror, when deadly dream becomes deadlier reality.

$11.95   •   1-56315-188-X   •   182   pages

Dark of the Elvenwood
MageLore Book II

They are the Morvalan, elves in the service of a god of destruction. To further their war against humanity, they have joined forces with the minotaur wizard Solarrin. Together, they have hatched a plot to bring about the downfall of the Northlands.

Four reunited companions are all that stand between the Morvalan and success. But as Cat, Arien, Greyquin and Alphonse brave the dangers of the woodlands, a worse peril threatens the very home that they left to save.

$11.95   •   0-9702189-0-7   •   272   pages

Archmage of the Universe
MageLore Book III

He is Solarrin. Once his body was as twisted as his mind. Now inhabiting the form of a minotaur, his physical and   magical prowesses are without equal.

The young Highlord is his pawn. The city of Thanis is under his control. His next move will plunge the Northlands into war.

The only ones who will stand a chance against him fled on a foolish quest – to bring his predecessor back from the dead.

$11.95   •   0-9702189-1-5   •   292   pages

Silversilk
ElfLore Book I

Ariana Mirida, sorceress and swordswoman, answers the call to adventure when she travels to her ancestral homeland seeking to clear her father's name. Little does she know how her quest will affect an entire kingdom . . .

$16.95   •   1-930928-66-1   •   340   pages

Knight of the Basilisk
ElfLore Book II

She was not always a warrior-priestess of the dark elven god. Once, she was only Tilanne, granted an unexpected destiny by a dying knight. To attain it, she had to defy convention and give up her dreams. This is her story.

$15.95   •   1-930928-47-5   •   276   pages

Truegold
ElfLore Book III

The future of the elves and the fate of all humanity hangs in the balance. It is a desperate race as the Emerin's rightful king tries to prevent a renegade knight from trading a sacred elven artifact for a poison that is bane to humankind. As they rush toward their final deadly confrontation, the wizards and counts of the Emerin carry on with their own schemes to fill the vacant throne.

$16.95   •   1-930928-92-0   •   276   pages